Nina Milne has always dreamed of writing for Mills & Boon—ever since she played libraries with her mother's stacks of Mills & Boon romances as a child. On her way to this dream Nina acquired an English degree, a hero of her own, three gorgeous children and—somehow!—an accountancy qualification. She lives in Brighton and has filled her house with stacks of books—her very own *real* library.

Rachael Stewart adores conjuring up stories, from heartwarmingly romantic to wildly erotic. She's been writing since she could put pen to paper—as the reams of scrawled-on pages i[...] lass at heart, she now l[...] very own hero and thre[...] not tapping out a story [...] enjoying the great outd[...] Twitter @rach_b52, or at rachaelstewartauthor.com

Also by Nina Milne

Baby on the Tycoon's Doorstep

The Casseveti Inheritance miniseries

Italian Escape with the CEO
Whisked Away by the Italian Tycoon

Also by Rachael Stewart

Our Little Secret
Reawakened
Tempted by the Tycoon's Proposal
Surprise Reunion with His Cinderella

Discover more at millsandboon.co.uk.

THE SECRET CASSEVETI BABY

NINA MILNE

BEAUTY AND THE RECLUSIVE MILLIONAIRE

RACHAEL STEWART

MILLS & BOON

First Published in Great Britain 2021
by Mills & Boon, an imprint of HarperCollins*Publishers* Ltd,
1 London Bridge Street, London, SE1 9GF

www.harpercollins.co.uk

HarperCollins*Publishers*
1st Floor, Watermarque Building,
Ringsend Road, Dublin 4, Ireland

The Secret Casseveti Baby © 2021 Nina Milne

Beauty and the Reclusive Millionaire © 2021 Rachael Stewart

ISBN: 978-0-263-30005-5

12/21

MIX
Paper from
responsible sources
FSC® C007454

This book is produced from independently certified FSC™ paper
to ensure responsible forest management.
For more information visit www.harpercollins.co.uk/green.

Printed and Bound in Spain using 100% Renewable Electricity
at CPI Black Print, Barcelona

THE SECRET CASSEVETI BABY

NINA MILNE

MILLS & BOON

To my mum—
for being a lovely mum and an amazing grandma.

We all love you very much. xxxx

CHAPTER ONE

JODI PETROVELLI STARED out of the hostel window at the surrounding gardens, fragrant and vibrant with frangipani and palm trees in abundance. The squawk and shriek of birds interspersed with the noise from the busy Indian streets—the cries of street vendors selling the *dosai* and *idlis* and other spiced dishes she had grown to love in her weeks on Jalpura.

For a moment she contemplated the twist and turn of fate that had brought her to this lush Indian island, ruled by a mix of royalty and government. To start with it had been a whim. Her brother, Luca, had told her how beautiful the island was—Luca owned a renowned chocolate company and he had recently discovered a type of cocoa bean grown on Jalpura. So whilst on her travels Jodi had decided Jalpura was worth a visit.

As if on cue the ping of her phone distracted her and she glanced down to see a message from Luca.

Just checking in. Hope all is good and the new job is going well. Luca.

Now guilt pinged as loudly as her phone had. Because she'd run away and left her brother to face the shitshow that had come about after their father's death. Not that she considered James Casseveti to be her father in any mean-ingful way—he had left when Luca was five, before Jodi had even been born.

The old familiar desolation surfaced, a different type of guilt bred in her bone. The fear that it had been Jodi who had driven him away, that perhaps if Therese hadn't been pregnant with Jodi, James would have stayed with the wife and son he loved instead of disappearing over the horizon, that she was the catalyst that caused him to abandon his family.

Never to return. Literally. Not for a single visit, so Jodi had never seen her father, never heard his voice speak her name, never held his hand or ridden on his shoulders. James had never so much as acknowledged her existence.

His loss, she told herself, time and again. Even as she'd known it wasn't. After all, James had gone on to a glittering life of success, had married the woman he'd left them for, rich, aristocratic Lady Karen Hale. Then, using her money and connections, he'd set up a globally successful dessert business, Dolci, and led a fulfilling, happy, pros-perous life. With his new family. His new wife, Karen, and his daughter. Ava. Ava Casseveti.

The name enough to conjure up a familiar sense of anger, to twist the spiral of envy in her chest. *Stop.* Jodi knew how stupid, how destructive it was to compare her-self to the half-sister she'd never met. Knew too that it wasn't Ava's fault that she was the apple of her father's eye. His true daughter.

But no amount of knowledge eased the pain.

A pain compounded by the image of Ava that now per-vaded her brain—the epitome of beauty, tall with endless legs, corn-blonde hair that rippled allure and classic fea-tures made arresting by a pair of amber eyes. Looks that had catapulted Ava to supermodel fame.

Whilst genetics had programmed Jodi to be short with impossible-to-tame black curls with a dollop of frizz, and no model attributes whatsoever. Her nose was retroussé; her dark eyes resembled mud rather than a semi-precious jewel.

Not only had Ava been endowed with beauty, she had also been gifted with brains, business acumen, drive and ambition. She'd cut her modelling career short to enter the family business, to take her place as the heiress to Dolci. Jodi contemplated her own less than illustrious career. She'd drifted from one job to the next: waitress, PA, retail assistant, dog walker. James Casseveti had definitely pulled the long straw, picked the right daughter to acknowledge and love.

Jodi closed her eyes and dug her nails into her palms, exactly as she did whenever Ava entered her head, the gesture a throwback to a childhood where her half-sister had permeated her dreams, her adolescence where Ava had seemed to mock her, to exist solely to demonstrate Jodi's inadequacies.

Block her out. The Cassevetis meant nothing to her. Her only wish to paint them out of her life.

Only now she no longer could.

Because in death James Casseveti had surprised them all. He'd left a third of Dolci to *each* of his children: Luca, Jodi and Ava. The news had impacted Jodi with such a hit of emotion she was still reeling months later. Anger that James Casseveti thought she could be bought off, fury that he hadn't even left her a letter, a note, anything personal. Panic that this made it impossible for Jodi to pretend Ava didn't exist. More anger that James Casseveti had intruded on her life. And so many emotions because now he was no longer here, there could never be a chance of her seeing him, hearing his voice.

In the end Jodi had taken the best option available: she'd run away. Of course, she'd spoken to Luca first, got his blessing. Her big brother understood, told her it was fine, that he'd deal with it. And so she'd fled…to Thailand, to India…had let the wonders of travel absorb and deflect her attention. She knew Luca to be more than capable of facing the flak and the publicity—he was tough and in truth preferred to face things alone without his little sister to worry about.

Without her there Luca could focus on what he did best. Make tough business decisions. Because Luca was like Ava. Driven, ambitious, successful.

The poisonous thought began its spread—the tendril of fear that Luca and Ava would be drawn to each other, bond over their similarities… For heaven's sake. *Enough*. Luca loved her and she loved Luca. Nothing could break their bond; they'd grown up together. Luca would do anything for her. And anyway, soon enough Jodi would return; she knew that she couldn't run for ever. Just a few more weeks.

But now it was time to go to work. Jodi glanced at the mirror as she did every day before work to remind herself that here on Jalpura she was known as Jemma Lewes, not Jodi Petrovelli. A ruse to ensure no reporter would track her down as interest grew in the Dolci inheritance and its tales of usurpers, skeletons in closets, abandoned families and Ava Casseveti, beautiful heiress.

Jodi closed her eyes. Soon enough she'd go home. Face it all. Soon…but not yet. For now she would enjoy being Jemma Lewes, temporary assistant to Princess Alisha of the Jalpuran royal court, helping to organise the royal film festival. Jodi turned from her reflection, grabbed her shoulder bag and headed for the door of the hostel, situated a few minutes' walk from the royal palace of Jalpura.

* * *

Prince Carlos of Talonos surveyed the royal palace of Jalpura; disbelief still crowded his brain that he was here, on his first royal assignment in a decade. Because ten years ago he'd walked away from his royal status. Such as it had been. The status of an eldest son who could never be heir.

Talonos royal law had decreed that any child born out of wedlock and over the age of six months when the parents married could not be heir. His father had married his mother, Catalina Drakos, a commoner who worked in the palace kitchens, when Carlos was six months and three days old.

It was only many years later that Carlos understood why.

All he'd known as a child was his father's coldness and distance was mitigated by his mother's love for him, a love he'd never doubted even though he'd sensed the misery that underlay it, masked by mood swings where her exuberance would almost scare him.

'Don't worry, baby, Papa is just a bit mad at Mama. He'll come round. Because we love each other.'

'Don't worry, Carlos. Papa will make it right. You will be King. Because Papa loves me. Loves me. Loves me. And I love you.'

And then when he was six, his mother had died.

Remembered horror shivered through Carlos. The dark hazy recall of finding her body blocked out the bright rays of the Jalpuran sun and he was transported back in time.

To his six-year-old self. Running into his mother's bedroom—he'd painted a picture and he wanted to show her. The still wet paper clutched in his hand, daubed with bright stick figures. His excitement slowly morphed to confusion when she didn't respond, didn't sit up, take his hands, twirl him in a dance round the room as she told him what a clever boy he was, how one day he'd grow up to be a talented artist and amazing king.

But that day there was no praise, no dance, nothing, and his feet had frozen to the ground at the realisation that something was wrong. There was an eerie immobility about his mother, even her long blonde hair seemed completely still. Then his nurse, his mother's close friend, Daria, had swept into the room and swept him away, told him his mamma was not feeling well.

After that his memories were fuzzy; Daria had gone and his dreaded father had summoned him, told him that his mother was dead, had died after a 'tragic short illness', a verdict he didn't understand.

Nothing had made sense to the devastated little boy he'd been; all his six-year-old mind could compute was that the one person who loved him was gone and was never ever coming back. And without her he was truly alone in the world. At the mercy of a father who could barely stand to look at him, and then a year later under the care of a stepmother who saw him as a threat and an affront to the royal blood. And soon enough it became clear that he was not going to be a king; instead he was destined to be an invisible prince, the one with 'tainted blood'. The one sent away to a series of boarding schools, encouraged to spend holidays there, allowed 'home' on rare occasions. And when he was at home, he was kept apart, in a suite of rooms far away from his 'family', shunned by his half-brother, Juan, who was brought up to remain aloof, though in public the King and Queen were careful to present the illusion of a united 'happy family'.

But through the years he held the warmth of his mother's love, her memory, close to him like a blanket of comfort. If only she had lived it would all be different.

Until his world had imploded. When Carlos was thirteen Daria had sought him out in secret, asked to meet him. He'd snuck out late one summer evening, met her in a secluded part of public park and there in the night-time breeze he'd learnt the truth.

He'd known it wasn't good news, had seen the grief and pain on Daria's face and for a moment he'd wanted to cover his ears as he had as a child, close his eyes and refuse to read the letter she held out. The envelope scrawled with his name, written in his mother's hand. The jolt of recognition had moved him backwards, the wooden slat of the bench hard against his back.

But in the end he'd read the letter, seen the words he didn't want to believe and his world had crumbled.

Dearest Carlos,
I am so sorry for leaving you, but I can't see any other way out. I have failed you, my dearest, and I cannot live with that.

Ever since you were born all I have wanted for you was your birthright. I believed your father loved me, that he was going to marry me. When he said he couldn't marry me, that his family would never allow it, I took matters into my own hands.

I thought I was doing the right thing. I tricked your father into marriage; I claimed I was dying, that I wanted my son to be legitimate. I understood that if he married me when you were over six months, technically you couldn't be heir, but I thought your father would be able to change that law when he came to the throne.

So I announced our secret wedding to the world and your father had no choice. To reject me, us, would have caused public outcry. He had to accept the marriage—but I thought it would make him happy.

It didn't—he was furious. And still I didn't get it. I thought he was afraid of his family, was toeing the royal line. That he loved me, loved us.

I kept trying to believe that. Through all these years I told myself that love would win. Today I re-alised it wouldn't...that love is worth nothing. It is now two years since your father ascended the throne and he still has not changed.

Today I confronted him and he told me that he will never change the law. That I killed any love he could have felt for me or you when I tricked him. That he will divorce me and marry a true princess and wor-thy queen who will bear him children. Children who do not have tainted blood.

So now I have to face the truth. He will never love me and, worse, you will never be King and the fault is mine.

I am so sorry, Carlos—I cannot watch this hap-pen. I cannot go on any more. I do not have the strength or the will. I crave peace and silence.

Please know I love you with all my heart, however worthless that love is.

Keep this ring to remember me by. It is from my family.

I hope you are happy, my son.
All my love,
Mama

The words danced before his eyes as his world tilted on its axis. His mother had taken her own life. Anger burned inside him, against his father who had driven his wife to her death. No matter that he had been tricked, it did not excuse or mitigate his cruelty.

But under the veneer of anger was the burn of guilt. Because everything Catalina had done, she'd done for him; the steps she'd taken on the path to tragedy had been done in Carlos's name, to win him a throne. And in the end she could not face a life where that did not happen. In the end Carlos hadn't been enough, *his* love for *her* worthless, not enough to make life worth living. The love he'd always believed in, trusted in, was now tarnished, no longer a weighted blanket of comfort to hold to him in a loveless world.

Of course, he had confronted his father. King Antonio had looked at him with shadowed eyes.

'Yes. Your mother spoke truth. I did not wish you to know but now you do. I will not discuss this. And if you try to create difficulties I will deny it and I will make sure your old nurse suffers for telling you this information. What is done is done, Carlos. Get on with your life.'

Once he was eighteen he'd done just that. Left Talonos, determined to dismiss his father, his heritage, his tainted royalty from his mind. He had rebranded himself as Carl Williamson and built a life for himself, a very successful life. And after that he had visited home on increasingly rare occasions, simply to help sustain the spin that he was a welcome family member.

Then a few days ago he'd been summoned home. His father, white with rage, had evinced no joy at seeing his eldest son.

'Some fool has dug up an ancient statute, one that declares that although you were over six months old when I married your mother you are in fact the heir to the throne of Talonos.'

Carlos had stood and gaped at him, pushed down the hysterical guffaw of laughter that threatened.

'It is nonsense, of course.'

Only it couldn't be, otherwise his father would never have recalled him.

'But whilst I sort it out, it would be good to show Talonos and the world that the case is being given a fair hearing. Revolt is brewing and how this is handled could shake the very foundations of the throne. We will need to renew the illusion of family unity. However, we would prefer you do not stay here, so you will go to Jalpura.'

The Indian island that had long since been an ally to the Mediterranean isle of Talonos, an alliance forged centuries ago, when a Prince of Talonos married a Jalpuran princess and secured a lucrative trade deal in exotic spices.

'The Queen understands the situation and you can take your brother's place as ambassador to the royal film festival.'

The annual festival organised by Talonos and Jalpura to showcase European and Indian films.

So here he was. Perhaps he should have refused, agreed to give up his claim and returned to his normal life. But how could he? Lord knew he had never expected to rule Talonos, but he loved his land. The deep scent of its soil that provided the luscious olives and plump grapes, the abundancy of nature's offerings. He loved the people, the hardy farmers, many of them from families that had worked the earth for generations, nurtured the olive groves that resulted in olive oils known the world over, the cosmopolitan townspeople, the workers who produced the intricate lace and fabrics Talonos was famous for. His country. This was a chance to return, to one day rule, fulfil his mother's dream for him. To vindicate her death.

As if. He knew his father—King Antonio would move heaven and earth to make sure Carlos did not succeed him. The idea grated raw and he plunged his hands into his pockets, grimaced as he recalled he wasn't wearing his usual suit trousers or jeans. Instead he'd had to rapidly adapt his wardrobe, had packed quickly and the lightweight chinos he wore had shallow pockets that caught at the size of his clenched hands.

He gazed at the palace, felt his scowl deepen. Enough of royalty. He did not need to report to the palace until Monday—he would spend the weekend exploring Jalpura before he made an attempt at ambassadorial duties.

Distracted by his thoughts, he realised he had wandered closer to the palace. Time to back away; he had no wish to be recognised by some palace official.

As he turned, his gaze snagged on a woman who exited the palace and headed down the steps. He wasn't sure exactly what had caught his attention—she looked to be about his age, mid to late twenties, and although pretty there was nothing special about her that he could identify. Unless it was perhaps her look of intent thought, as if she was wrestling with an internal dilemma. Short dark curls swung and danced round a heart-shaped face. She was petite, and simply dressed in a floral sundress, sunglasses pushed up and perched on top of her head.

As if aware of his scrutiny, she paused and looked around, and he saw her expression morph to one of suspicion. Instantly he swivelled away, started walking, embarrassed at the idea of being caught staring, unsure why he even had been. Not his style to have his head turned by a pretty woman and certainly not his style to gawp or make any woman uncomfortable. Ridiculous that he still had to fight the urge to turn and watch her walk away.

Yet when he heard the sound of footsteps and then a female voice behind him say, 'Excuse me,' he somehow knew that it was the same woman.

He turned and saw his instinct was correct; the dark-haired woman stood there, pushed a quick impatient hand at an errant curl. Possibilities jostled in his head: perhaps she wished to confront him; worse, perhaps she'd recognised him, was some sort of palace official sent out to drag him inside.

'You dropped this.'

'Oh.' He looked at the silver ring she held out: his mother's ring. The one he'd worn every day since he left Talonos. It must have somehow dislodged when he plunged his hands into the new chino pockets. Relief flooded through him that this woman had picked it up, had been honest enough, bothered enough to come after him. The idea of losing this precious talisman, his link to his tragic mother, the one thing she had left him, unthinkable. He wore it constantly, the chance of it slipping off remote, and for an instant he wondered if it were some sort of sign. Told himself he was a fool.

Yet as he reached to take the ring from her, his fingers inadvertently grazed her upturned palm and an inexplicable frisson ran through him. He stilled as her brown eyes widened, her gaze flickered upwards to meet his and held, and in that moment with the ring between them Carlos felt a shimmer of a connection, a sparkle that he could almost see. Ridiculous. He was not a fanciful man and he forced his vocal cords into action. 'Thank you.'

'It's no trouble.' Her voice breathless.

'Yes, it was. Or at the very least it was a kindness. I would like to repay that.'

'No. Really. There is no need.'

'Yes. There is. I want to. This ring means a lot to me and I want to do something to say thank you.' As they spoke the words seemed almost surreal in their normality, because he felt anything but normal. Her eyes were still on his and almost without his realising it they had moved closer, so close he could see the dusting of freckles on the bridge of her nose, smell the elusive scent of jasmine soap. See the depth of brown of her wide eyes, a brown that held a glimmer of amber and surprise, as if she too were pole-axed. And that sense of connection grew and deepened.

He heard her small gulp, and then, 'OK. Perhaps you could make a donation to your favourite charity.'

'Done.' Carlos knew this was when he should walk away, but he didn't want to. Every instinct urged him to keep talking, told him he'd regret it if he didn't. Even though he knew it didn't make any sort of sense. 'But I'd like to do something else. Something for you. Could I buy you a coffee or a cake or dinner?'

She hesitated and now her eyes searched his and he saw wariness haze them. 'I don't even know your name.'

'That's easily remedied.' Now it was he who hesitated, though only for a fraction of a second. 'I'm Carl. Carl Williamson.' There was no need to mention his royal status—he didn't want to explain, or see her expression change, or be judged. For the past ten years he had been Carl Williamson; that was the man he wanted this woman to know. If she agreed to a coffee, he wanted it to be with Carl. 'And you? What is your name?'

Her gaze flicked away and back, and then she held out her hand. 'Jemma. Jemma Lewes.'

'Good to meet you, Jemma. So, what do you think? Coffee? Dinner? A drink? How can I say thank you?'

Telling himself her answer didn't matter, Prince Carlos of Talonos held his breath as he awaited it.

CHAPTER TWO

JODI TRIED TO think with a brain that was befuzzed and befuddled with a hormonal surge of sheer unbridled magnitude. There was little point even trying to pretend to herself that this stranger hadn't utterly bowled her over. The combination of spiky blond hair, ice-blue eyes that warmed up when they rested on her. An aquiline nose that displayed a confidence backed up by a clean-shaven square jaw that spoke of determination. As for his body, Carl Williamson exuded a quiet, unobtrusive strength. There was a sturdiness about him that made her feel he could weather any storm.

She had to think; looking down she saw that her hand was still clasped in his in what was perhaps the longest handshake in history. But for some reason the feel of his hand around hers was warm and wonderful and sent a thrill of awareness shooting through her body. Made her focus on the shape of his fingers, their breadth and strength, the sturdiness of his wrist, the swell of lithe muscle of his forearm.

What to do, what to do?

Think, Jodi.

This didn't make sense. Mutual, immediate attraction across a crowded room, or in this case a crowded street, was rubbish. This man had stood outside the palace staring at the building for ages, long before he'd spotted her. So what had he been doing? Then he'd studied Jodi as she walked down the path. Why?

Her initial suspicions returned—could this man be a reporter? She'd swear he'd hesitated before he said his name. Was it as fake as her own? If he was a reporter, did he know her true identity—was he here to dig some Petrovelli dirt? Or perhaps he was after a royal scoop? The voice of the royal representative Pradesh Patankar resounded in her head. He was the man who stood between the royal court and the real world, a man who had strongly opposed her employment.

'I will be honest with you, Ms Lewes. I do not approve of the Princess simply choosing someone herself to be her assistant. However, this is what she has done and as she is insistent on proceeding there is little I can do. Please be aware that in your position people will try to get to the royal family through you, will distort your words and try to use you. Please know if you speak to the press this will incur the Queen's displeasure. And mine.'

She had little doubt Pradesh Patankar would tell her to walk away from this man.

Problem was she didn't want to, which also didn't make any sense—she knew better than to listen to her hormones. Knew exactly how painful it was to be used and exploited by a man. An image of Tim invaded her mind and she pushed it away.

Enough.

She was no longer that naïve young girl; why shouldn't she have a drink with this man? And if he were a reporter… well, she would play him at his own game and in the end she would give him short, sharp shrift and enjoy doing so.

So, 'A coffee would be lovely.' And in the time it took

to drink it she would be able to suss out if Carl William-son was on the level or not.

'Great. I'm in your hands.' There was a pause and they both looked down at their still clasped hands and heat touched Jodi's cheeks. Yet it was still hard to let go and instead she focused on the feel of the ring between them, a ring she'd looked at when she'd picked it up. Silver, a simple band engraved with a flower. An odd choice for a man and she wondered what significance it had. A woman perhaps—and the thought caused her to quickly remove her hand.

She ran it through her hair, wished the curls were long enough to shield her face. 'I know the perfect place,' she said brightly, and watched as he slipped the ring back onto his right ring finger.

'Lead the way,' he said. As they walked she was way too aware of his presence, tried to avoid even an acciden-tal brush against him, relieved when he spoke. 'So have you been on Jalpura long?'

'No. I'm taking some time out to travel—I was in India and I decided to come and see Jalpura. I love it so I ex-tended my stay.'

'I can see why. I only got here today and I can already see how beautiful it is.'

Jodi looked around; she knew she'd never get tired of the sheer vibrancy of this island. Women in colourful saris, the rich bright green of the palm trees and shrubs, the rust red of the dust that swirled up from the roads. The noise that had at first overwhelmed her now had become normal: the squawk of plumed birds and the caw of crows, the shrill shouts of the street vendors and the intermittent horns of the cars weaving their way through the busy roads. The smells an olfactory mix of pungent spices, the miasmic scent of flowers from the vivid blooms on sale mixed with

the traffic fumes and the more rural smell from the cows
that sometimes seemed to wander at will.

'This is just a small part of the island. If you go further
out there are tea plantations and mountains and forests
and they are all stunning. Everything is incredibly lush;
it makes the rest of the world seem…diluted.'

'So where do you hail from originally?'

Was it a trick question? Jodi decided the best thing to do
now was engage in some harmless white lies. 'England.'

After all, she had been born in the UK and spent part of
her childhood there until her mum had relocated to Italy,
changed their name from Casseveti to Petrovelli and started
a new life. So in fact it wasn't even a fib. 'What about you?'

'I switch my time between London and New York.'

Jodi paused. 'Here we are.'

They entered the café she'd chosen as one of the most
characterful local venues and she smiled as he looked
around. 'Excellent choice.'

She wondered if he meant it. 'I know it's nothing like
the cafés or bars in cities like London. Or New York, I
guess. Jalpura does have some more cosmopolitan, posher
places but…'

'You prefer the real thing.'

'Yes. Don't get me wrong—tourists come here but so
do locals. I like that.' She glanced round the simple décor.
Beige walls decorated with framed posters of bikers and
bikes, the tables plain wooden and square surrounded by
a mix of benches and a mishmash of chairs. Fans whirred
from the ceilings and the clientele played pool and chatted.

Lai-Lai, the owner and a local character, came to their
table.

'I'll have a masala chai.'

'Make that two, please,' Carl said and waited until Lai-
Lai had walked away.

Jodi studied him; tried to figure out what it was about him that exerted such a pull. Even now she was sitting opposite him, the urge to reach out and cover his arm, to simply stare at the swell of biceps, the jut of his jaw and the firm contour of his mouth mesmerised her. And, dammit, she was sure it was a two-way thing; a shiver ran through her as his gaze snagged on her lips.

'Do you know what's in it?' she asked, hoping words, however inane, would break the spell.

'No idea,' he said with a sudden smile. 'I'm in the mood for surprises.' There was a glint in his blue eyes but there was caution as well and she wondered what other surprises life had thrown at him.

'Then I won't tell you,' she said and returned the smile. There it was again, a sense of a pull between them. An invisible cord twisted with the tug of attraction and a shimmer of connection.

He rose to his feet and gestured to the bar. 'I'll grab our drinks.'

She watched as he walked away, couldn't help but let her gaze linger on the feral grace with which he moved. No swagger, just an assurance, a silent strength that mesmerised her. *Enough. Whoa. Stop. This was a cup of chai and goodbye, remember.* Plus she was supposed to be figuring out who this man was and if he was an undercover reporter. Hope bubbled inside her that he wasn't because then…then what, Jodi? They'd gallop into the sunset to a happy ending?

No freakin' way. Unwanted memories seeped through the barriers she'd erected to keep them buried.

Tim had seemed like such a nice, normal guy. Popular, good-looking and genuine. Yes, he'd turned up as Palazzo di Cioccolato was becoming more and more successful, and although Jodi knew that was Luca's success, not hers, some of the glow did reflect on her.

And Tim had been so sweet, so understanding she hadn't even noticed his expensive tastes, the fact he worshipped at the altar of money. She hadn't minded paying for nearly everything. Believed him when he'd explained he was a struggling student, that it made sense for her to pay because after all she had 'family money'—an allowance from her brother. An allowance that Tim had persuaded her to accept.

But then she'd told him she was planning on giving up the allowance as she wanted to stand on her own two feet and then she'd made the biggest mistake possible—she'd told him that she was Ava Casseveti's half-sister.

Something she never told anyone. When they'd moved to Italy from England a family pact was made that the name of Casseveti no longer mattered, no one needed to know they had been discarded and cast aside by the man who had now climbed to fame and fortune.

But Jodi had been in love, had trusted Tim and he had been so understanding, had promised to keep the secret. Only he hadn't. Two nights later she'd woken up to find Tim, camera in hand, taking photos of her. Naked.

When she'd asked him what he was doing he'd tried to lie but in the end he'd admitted he was going to take them to the papers, sell them for money.

'They'll pay for naked pictures of Ava Casseveti's secret sister. And my story. I can tell them how I was thinking of Ava whilst making love to you.'

Words that made Jodi crumble inside. She'd begged, pleaded, offered him anything and he'd simply laughed at her, before throwing her off him and leaving. In the end she'd done the only thing she could think of—she'd called Luca. Called her big brother.

He'd simply said, 'Leave it to me.'

An hour later he'd banged on her door. 'It's over. You won't see Tim again and the photos have been deleted. It's over.'

'Luca I…' Her voice, her body and soul still trembled with humiliation, a burn no amount of hot showers could get rid of.

'It's over, Jodi. We don't need to talk or think about it again.'

The former an absolute, the latter an impossibility. She knew she could never erase what had happened, knew too she would learn from it. Even if nothing could be the same again—Tim had violated something, changed something inside her. And the sear of pain, the regret, the mortification still burned when memory reared its bleak and ugly head.

'Jemma?' It took a moment for his voice to penetrate the fog of the past, another for her to remember that *she* was Jemma. Blinking, Jodi ran a quick hand through her hair and dredged up a smile as Carl placed a tray down on the table. 'You OK?'

'Fine. Sorry. Just lost in thought.'

'Not good ones.' He sat down and pushed the tray across. 'Hopefully this will make you feel better. Lai-Lai said these are your favourites.'

Jodi looked down at the plate of *pazham pori*, long slices of ripe juicy plantain deep-fried in a batter of flour and spices.

'Thank you.' The appetising aroma, the hint of turmeric and cardamom, rose and dispelled at least some of the lingering memory, and the first bite did a lot to counter the bitter taste. 'These are so good. Try.'

He picked one up and bit into it and she couldn't help but smile at his expression of appreciation. 'These are really good. Do you think Lai-Lai will part with the recipe?'

'In your dreams. She says she makes the best *pazham pori* on Jalpura and I'd say she may have a point. And, trust me, I've sampled a lot.'

'So how long have you been here? You've clearly made friends and fitted right in.'

'I've been here a couple of months.'

'And you work at the palace?'

Jodi froze halfway through picking up her next plantain slice and forced herself to continue the movement. There had definitely been a little more than idle curiosity in his tone—she was nearly sure of it.

'Yes.'

His eyebrows rose in silent question. 'What do you do?'

Her decision was made in a blink—she would not say anything about the Princess, nothing at all. If she made it clear she had no story to tell, and Carl Williamson made his excuses and disappeared, she'd know he was a reporter.

'I work in the palace kitchens,' she said.

A look she couldn't interpret crossed his face. Disbelief and almost shock were the closest she could come up with and whatever it was it disappeared as quickly as it arrived. 'That explains your interest in food.'

'I've certainly learnt a lot about Jalpuran food.' This at least was a claim she could back up—she had visited the palace kitchen on numerous occasions; part of her role in helping organise the film festival was to help arrange catering for some of the royal guests.

'And do you have any contact with the Jalpuran royals?'

Here it came. She met his gaze full on. 'Nope.' This time to her complete surprise she'd swear relief flashed in his eyes, that those broad shoulders relaxed a fraction. Perhaps she should give up on trying to figure this man out.

'So is this a holiday job or is catering what you do in your normal life?'

Jodi sighed. 'It's a holiday job. I don't really have a proper job. I'm more of a drifter.' The familiar realisation of her own shortcomings crowded in on her. Those flaws made all the worse by her family's strengths and brilliance. Luca had successfully launched a global business, driven by his burning need to make his company one to rival Dolci, to stand head to head, toe to toe with his father, and so he had built up Palazzo di Cioccolato from nothing. His whole life he had known what he wanted to do. And he'd done it.

Her mother too was an extraordinary person. Deserted, penniless, pregnant, and with a five-year-old, she'd taken heartbreak and converted it into sheer dogged determination. Had brought up Luca and Jodi with no financial, practical or emotional help from her ex and was an amazing mother to boot. And like Luca she was also a go-getter— Therese had trained as a lawyer and now was a partner in a firm specialising in international law and human rights.

As for Jodi—she quite simply couldn't compete. Not that it was a competition. It was more that she simply couldn't compare. Jodi was *ordinary* and she hated it, hated that she didn't measure up.

'So what have you tried so far?'

What hadn't she tried? She'd desperately tried to be a chocolatier, hoping to be able to work on a par with her brother, to be good enough to be a real partner in his company. She'd made an attempt to study law, until her eyes had crossed. Had then moved on to a business degree, hoping that maybe she'd find a yen for commerce, marketing, finance—something where she could at least play a valued part in Palazzo di Cioccolato, help Luca, be a part of the family business as Ava was part of Dolci… But although she'd stuck the degree out, she knew in her heart of hearts it wasn't her forte, that at best she'd be able to hold down a starter to mid-level role, no more. However hard she tried…she always fell short of excellent. Was depressingly mediocre.

In the end she'd given up, had simply focused on getting any job so at least she could earn her own living.

'Retail, admin, dog walking, floristry, waitressing, catering…the list goes on.'

'Maybe you should just enjoy the variety.'

The words were easy to say—but she couldn't. Not when she yearned to make her mother and brother proud of her, to try to make up for causing James Casseveti to leave. Not that her mum blamed her, at all. If anything her mum went out of her way to reassure Jodi it was nothing to do with her, that the fault lay solely at James's door, and Jodi appreciated her mother's love and support. But she didn't believe her. Anyway, enough about her—the subject of her career was not one she wished to dwell on.

'What about you? What do you do?'

'I'm a land developer. An environmental one,' he added hurriedly.

'Sorry. I didn't mean to look disapproving.' Yet her frown deepened. 'Though is it possible to be an environmentally friendly land developer?'

'Yes.' He leant forward. 'It's not always easy, and of course it cuts profit margins, but it is possible and I think it's incredibly important. And there are so many relatively simple common-sense ways to do it. Obviously, insulation plays a huge part—if you build a house to conserve heat in the winter, or with solar panels, you're already a step ahead of the game. Then think about your construction materials—use as local as possible, use as recycled as possible. Even things like planning which way houses should face can make a difference.'

She watched him, noting the passion with which he

spoke; he wasn't loud, didn't gesture with his hands as she did, but there was a quiet fervency to his words, a sincerity it was impossible to doubt. There was no way this man was a reporter—not unless she was to let paranoia reign. So maybe he was on the level. The possibility thrilled through her that he might be an on-the-level drop-dead-gorgeous man who liked her. Or at least liked Jemma Lewes, kitchen assistant.

'So do you work for yourself?'

'Yes. I run my own company. I have done for the past seven years.'

Jodi suppressed a sigh—another go-getting entrepreneur had entered her life. But only for as long as the chai and snacks lasted.

'So what are you doing on Jalpura?' she asked.

CHAPTER THREE

CARLOS PICKED UP his cup in an attempt to buy time as he considered his answer. His brain raced through facts. Jemma Lewes worked in the palace but had no contact with the royal family. However, come Monday, she along with most of Jalpura would learn his royal identity. So equally obviously he should tell her the truth now.

But herein lay the problem. He didn't want to, didn't want to spoil or change whatever was going on here. Between Jemma and Carl, two ordinary people. He'd tell her later, he decided. If necessary. After all, the likelihood was they would finish their drinks and go their separate ways, and she'd just be a bit puzzled come Monday.

'I've been asked here in a consultancy capacity. By the royal family.'

'Oh.' An expression flitted across her face, as if the information was unwelcome, and he wondered why. Then she nodded. 'That makes sense. There's been a lot of talk about traffic control and developing better infrastructure, maybe developing land. Especially given the island hosts the film festival every two years. There is a huge influx of guests and they all need accommodation and—' She broke off. 'Obviously you know all this. I'm guessing you've done your research.'

'I know a bit but that doesn't mean I'm not willing to

learn more.' That too was the truth. The more he could find out about Jalpura before facing the royal family, the better he'd feel. He was all too aware that they were used to his fun-loving brother, who usually had the job of Film Ambassador and fronted the royal film festival. It was the sort of thing Prince Juan revelled in doing, all part of his publicity-loving, devil-may-care playboy prince persona. The parties, the celebrities and stars all grist to Juan's mill.

Though Carlos only knew this from reading the articles that loved to feature Prince Juan, heir to the throne of Talonos. Thanks to his stepmother and father, Carlos had never been given a chance to bond with his half-brother. After his mother's death he'd craved affection, hoped, prayed that his father would vouchsafe even a scrap. In fact his father had barely ever seen him. Then a scant few months after she'd died, King Antonio had remarried. How Carlos had hoped then that his stepmother would show him some compassion—what pathetic fantasies he'd woven of the woman who would take one look at him and want to mother him, would soften his father's heart.

It had never happened. Instead Isabella had taken an instant and deep dislike to him, which worsened had once she had a baby of her own, 'the true heir'.

He would have liked to be friends with his brother, had crept into the nursery, desperate to see the baby, his family. Isabella had marched him to the King, accused him of trying to hurt the baby.

'He is no brother of yours. Your blood is tainted and you aren't worthy to lick his boots.'

Soon after that he had been shipped off to boarding school.

But right now it was he who was here on Jalpura, not Juan, and whilst he was here he would do his best to help make the festival more successful, in his own way. 'When I have my meeting on Monday I'd like to give advice that allows improvements to roads and public transport without losing any of Jalpura's essence. That's what I was planning on doing this weekend—trying to get a feel for Jalpura.'

He wasn't sure where the next words came from, but it was definitely his own voice he heard. 'Maybe you could show me round?'

Just as Jemma said, 'I could give you a tour if you like?'

There was a moment of silence and then they both laughed. 'Are you sure you don't mind?'

'I'm sure.'

'Then I'd like that very much.' A disproportionate happiness spread over him and he had the feeling his smile had taken on an element of uncharacteristic goofiness.

Now their gazes meshed and he wondered if the fans had ceased to function as the air seemed to thicken around them. 'I...um...' Jemma closed her eyes and opened them again. 'Then that's sorted.' She pulled the plate towards her and cut the last *pori* in half, picked up one half and gestured to him to take the other. 'The essence of Jalpura will be hard to do in a weekend but I think I know the perfect place to start. Do you want to meet me a little later or are you good to start right now?'

'Right now.'

'Then let's go.' Yet neither of them moved and, however irrational, it felt to him as though this was the start of something momentous. He wondered if she felt the same.

They both rose to their feet and with a wave towards Lai-Lai they exited the café into the now dusky streets of Jalpura. The scents on the air had changed, the spice and tang of food stronger now, as stalls selling street food set up their wares. The flower market was closing down, buyers hopeful of a bargain bartering and crowding round the seller. Shops were shuttered and a mix of locals and tourists thronged the streets.

'So where are we going?'

'There's a Friday night market on the outskirts of the city. Try to imagine the largest, most diverse outdoor market you've ever been to or read about and that will give you an echo of a glimmer of what this one is all about. It's incredibly vibrant and it epitomises so much about the island.'

As they walked Carlos knew he should be focused on the sights and sounds around him, not distracted by the way her black curls framed her heart-shaped face. He shouldn't watch the grace with which she walked, the swish of her dress around her calves, the sparkle in her brown eyes. *Focus.*

Pulling his attention to his setting, he studied the dwellings that lined the dusty road and frowned slightly, taking in the mishmash of style and structure. Some of them made of stone, some of wood. As they reached the outskirts it became plain that the dwellings belonged to the poorer parts of the community 'Some of these structures don't look as though they are overly safe.'

Worry creased her brow. 'There has been an outcry recently asking for an overhaul of the building laws, but the Queen is reluctant to listen, even though the Princess agrees with the protestors. She says her mother should think of the people, but her mother says she won't give in to protesters and—' She gave an exhalation of annoyance as she broke off, looked up at him aghast, her eyes wide. 'I'm sorry, please forget I said that. I shouldn't repeat palace gossip. I am sure you will make up your own mind.' Jemma's voice was small and he looked down and saw worry in her eyes.

'It's OK.'

'It isn't. I shouldn't have mentioned the Queen or the Princess. Especially to you, when you are meeting with them.'

'I will not betray your confidence.' Perhaps she thought he would report her, that she would lose her job.

'But I shouldn't have said it. All staff are under strict orders not to speak of the royal family and—'

'Hey.' He halted, sensed that she was truly upset. 'It's OK. You said nothing I don't already know. I know that Queen Suhana has ruled for thirty years, from a very young age. I know there are those who say she is auto-cratic and relies too heavily on her royal representative for advice. I know she has three children, Alisha, Rohan and Riya. I know Jalpura is strategically important despite its small size. So please don't stress.'

She looked down and he realised that somehow he'd taken both her hands in his, realised, too, he didn't want to let go.

'Those are all facts,' she said. 'I gave you personal in-formation.'

'Nothing I couldn't have picked up from a gossip col-umn. It's OK. Truly it is. Let's not spoil the evening wor-rying about it. We'll banish royalty from the conversation from now on, OK?'

'OK.' Her hands squeezed his gently and she stepped forward, so close now that he could smell her perfume, a hint of jasmine, could see the amber flecks in her eyes. Her breath caught audibly and now he too stepped forward, the gap between them wafer thin. 'Thank you for being so understanding. I truly am usually way more discreet.'

Then she stood on tiptoe and brushed his cheek with her lips, the light touch electric on his skin, and she stepped back, eyes wide, and he couldn't help himself, though in truth he wasn't sure who moved first, but now his lips brushed hers and sensation rushed through him as he tasted her, the sweetness of the food they'd shared, and as she gasped he was lost. The world receded and there was nothing except Jemma, the soft lushness of her kiss, the fervour of her response, her hands clenched on his shoulders, the thrill of desire as she pressed against him, and he deepened the kiss.

It was the sound of a bicycle bell, the jostle of the crowd, that eventually broke through and they stepped backwards, stared at each other half in consternation, half in shock.

'I…' Jemma gave a half-laugh. 'I don't know what to say.'

Neither did he, but he knew he had to say something. 'Jemma, I'm sorry. I shouldn't have done that.' Not when on Monday he would enter the palace as a prince. Not when he had no idea how she felt about relationships. When this wasn't even a date.

'Why not?' Now hurt crossed her face and he wanted to kick himself, his brain fuzzed by the after-effects of the kiss, every synapse imploding.

'Because there are complications in my life right now.'

'Oh, my God. You're married.' Her eyes zoned in on his ring and narrowed in anger. 'The old switch-hands trick.'

'No! Absolutely not. I swear it. I am not married, not in a relationship. I would never have kissed you if that were the case. I can't explain it, but I am not in a position to commit to a relationship.' Not now. Not ever. He thrived on being alone, had long since banished the notion of love and relationships from his mind. He'd seen where his mother's love for his father had taken her—to deception, misery and tragedy. She'd believed love conquered all and she'd been proved wrong. Even his love for her and her love for him had proved worthless in the end, hadn't been of enough value to hold her to life. In fact, her love for him had set her on the path to her tragic end and left him with a guilt he knew he would bear for ever.

His own foolish foray into love had proved beyond all doubt that love was a meaningless commodity. He'd been in New York for a few years, well on the way to being a successful estate agent when he'd met Lisa. She was beautiful, sweet, kind and she'd liked him. Or so he'd believed and he'd found himself thinking that maybe, away from Talonos, he could find love. Long story short, Lisa had been using him to discover what properties were in his portfolio and then passing them on to a rival estate agent.

The pain he'd felt, the tidal wave of humiliation at his own stupidity, the realisation how easily he'd been duped and used had *hurt*. His love had meant nothing to Lisa, been worthless, its only value a monetary one.

Jemma's stance relaxed. 'So you're worried you gave me the wrong idea? That I want commitment?' Suddenly she smiled. 'There's no need to worry about that. My life abounds with complications and I am definitely not looking for a relationship.'

There was no doubting she meant it and Carlos wondered why she was so adamant, wondered too what difficulties weighed her life.

She gazed up at him. 'So why don't we escape the complications today? Enjoy the weekend. No commitment, no pressure or expectations. Only the next twenty-four hours and whatever they may bring.'

'Deal.' Qualms struck him and he dismissed them. If need be he'd tell Jemma the truth about his identity at the end of the weekend; it wouldn't be a big deal. As long as he kept the attraction under wraps. Kissing a non-prince was one thing; anything more wouldn't be fair. It would cause...*more* complications. And his life had enough of those in it already 'Let's hit this market.'

But despite his best intentions he took one of her hands in his and warmth touched him when she didn't pull free.

As they walked hand in hand a strange happiness fizzed inside Jodi, bubbled and sparkled and expanded. Desire and anticipation whirled in her head, even if she wasn't completely sure what she was anticipating. All she knew was that the kiss had been a humdinger, had sent her pulse rate to the sky and now had her walking on air.

Carl Williamson liked her for herself; he didn't want to pump her for information on the royals, he didn't know or care that she was friends with the Princess, he didn't know she was Jodi Petrovelli. And she loved it.

A vague warning bell pointed out that on Monday he would discover at least one of those things and possibly in the future discover the other. But she didn't care; her behaviour was completely out of character, yet she could almost laugh out loud. Jodi Petrovelli would never have done this. But Jemma Lewes could and would.

'Here we are.' As she looked at the truly immense market, spread over a field twice the size of a football pitch, she stood still, nearly as amazed as the first time she had visited. It was vibrant, atmospheric, immense and full of an eclectic crowd of people—there was something here for everyone. Designer stalls mingled with local offerings and wares ranged from clothes to toys to food and drink. The beat of music from the central stage thrummed through the buzz of bargains being made, laughter and chatter. 'I was completely overwhelmed the first time I came.'

'I've never seen anything like it.'

'Where would you like to start?'

'Let's just wander,' he suggested.

As they threaded their way through the hustle and bustle, she noted how easily he walked through the throng.

Carl gestured to a stall full of mirrored bags and vibrant scarves and dresses. 'The sheer volume and variety are incredible.'

'Yup. The local clothing is stunning; I wish I could carry them off.' She'd long ago accepted that she didn't have a stylish bone in her body, didn't have the poise or confidence or figure to pull off anything remotely different.

The realisation had come courtesy of Ava; her half-sister had been featured in a glossy magazine, stylish and sophisticated in a beret and shawl. And in a stupid moment of emulation Jodi had decided to give it a try, had gone out and bought a cheap version of Ava's style. Had studied herself carefully in the mirror and recoiled in horror—she looked like a distorted version of Ava, a grotesque parody of her beautiful half-sister. Tim had clearly felt the same—had held Jodi in his arms whilst fantasising she was a better supermodel version. Yuck.

She shook her head, wouldn't let Tim intrude on this time. Carl liked her as she was, and he couldn't compare her to Ava because she wouldn't be stupid enough to mention her half-sister. Though what would happen if she did? Jodi pushed the idea away, but it was too late; a tendril of doubt flickered into being as she imagined Carl's surprise, the inevitable comparison and the even more inevitable judgement.

Pulling herself back to the present, she noticed Carl had come to a stop. Was studying the stall and its wares.

'You *could* carry it off,' he stated.

'Nope. I really couldn't.'

Carl tugged her hand. 'Come on. Try something on. I will if you will. I'll choose for you and you choose for me. Yes?'

Somehow, before she knew it they were inside the stall and he was smiling down at her, a smile that impacted her from head to toe, the sort of smile that would induce any-one to do anything. 'OK,' she managed.

'How about this one?'

After gaining a nod from the stall owner, Carl picked up a long vibrant scarf, a fluid mix of bright turquoise and shades of blue and handed it to her. Jodi looked at it with reluctance. 'It really won't work.'

'You don't know that unless you try.' He studied her and then frowned. 'This is really bothering you. Why? You're actually backing away from it.'

'I'm not.' The denial foolish because in fact she was. This was a definite overreaction, brought about by the memory of Ava, the knowledge that her half-sister would look fabulous in any of these dupattas. But more than that, it was the uneasy realisation that Ava was in Carl's league, Jodi wasn't. *No.* She would not let herself think like that. Quickly she threw the dupatta round her neck.

He stood back, head tilted to one size and he shook his head. 'How about if you tie it differently. May I?'

'Um, sure.'

He stepped forward and she held back a small gulp; his nearness caused her head to spin, recalled their kiss and her lips tingled as she looked up at him. Felt a thrill of satisfaction as his eyes darkened, morphed from assess-ment to awareness to unadulterated desire. The pound of her heart crashed her ribcage as with tantalising slowness he reached out for the scarf, tugged it gently up over her head, smoothed it over her hair, and now she focused en-tirely on breathing, trying to keep the rasp of each inha-lation even, but no amount of force could stop the small shiver that rippled through her.

'Or like this,' he said, and the depth of his voice edged over her skin.

Jodi stood stock-still as he rearranged the folds again,

this time wrapping it round her body, each movement deft and efficient and yet, oh, so ridiculously sensual; the silk of the scarf, the merest brush of his fingers on her super-sensitive skin made her catch her lip in desire. They stood, gazes enmeshed, and she could see her own need mirrored on his face.

Then he stood back, ran a hand over his face and essayed a smile. 'Take a look,' he said, and she turned to the mirror and blinked. She looked…different—somehow the dupatta did suit her, as if this attraction had sparked something inside her, a confidence that allowed her to carry it off. Her whole body felt alive, her face flushed, her eyes bright as she turned to look up at him. 'You're right. I like it. Now it's my turn to choose something for you.'

Looking round the stall, her eyes skimmed over items until… 'That's it.' She walked over to a pile of shirts, picked out a light grey one, long and fitted in an Indian style, a simple monogram of leaves on the top left-hand side. 'Try that.'

He nodded and disappeared behind the stall to the fitting area, emerged a few minutes later and she gulped. The shirt changed him; the colour brought out the ice blue of his eyes and the cut subtly emphasised the lithe swell and sculpt of his arms, the breadth of his chest. A natural masculine strength that pushed all her buttons.

'What do you think?'

The man looked gorgeous.

'You look…good,' she managed, hoping he couldn't tell that she wanted to jump towards him and unbutton the small fiddly buttons of the shirt's V-neck that already displayed a tantalising triangle of bare skin. 'It suits you.'

'Shall I take a photo of you both?' the stallholder asked, and Jodi nodded, held out her phone, before she saw the unmistakeable look of reluctance on Carl's face.

But before she could say anything he stepped forward. 'Use mine,' he said, and Jodi sensed he'd rather not have his photo taken, but if he did he wanted possession of it. She just wasn't sure why or whether it even mattered.

The stallholder clicked and then handed the phone back. 'Now we bargain?' he suggested and ten spirited minutes later they left still wearing their purchases and Jodi dismissed the photo from her mind.

CHAPTER FOUR

AS THEY WALKED hand in hand through the busy market Carlos pushed away the last of his doubts—he wasn't sure what was going on with Jemma, but he was caught in the spell and he didn't care. Could no more walk away now than he could stop breathing, the heady sense of intoxication, the sheer sense of lightness impossible to give up. He knew it could go nowhere but that didn't mean he couldn't enjoy these few hours with Jemma, without thought for the future.

And for the next two hours they did exactly that as they walked and talked and laughed, stood and swayed to the music, an eclectic mix of rock followed by a sitar player whose haunting melodies brought a beat of silence followed by raucous applause. They wandered in and out of the stalls, marvelled at designer bargains sandwiched between a stall full of hats that ranged from the absurdities of fashion to bowler hats. And as they tried them on and walked with arms around each other awareness grew and crescendoed as dusk began to morph into nightfall.

'What now?' he asked.

'Now we get some food and we picnic on the beach. Unless you'd rather call it a day?'

'Picnic on the beach sounds perfect. You're the food expert so I'll leave it to you.'

'Expert is pushing it. I think we should get a sample of everything.'

And so half an hour later, laden with food, they approached the beach. Moonlight dappled and shadowed the palm trees that fringed the sand still warm from the day's heat. The sound of the waves drummed and soothed as they spread the newly purchased picnic blanket and unpacked the plethora of dishes.

'You could add tour guide to your list of jobs. You'd be a resounding success. Or you could organise holidays for people, or perhaps you should become a travel writer or blogger or...'

'And make a glittering high-powered career out of it, set up a franchise of travel agencies, write a bestselling book.'

Bitterness underlay the lightness of her tone and he frowned. 'Actually I wasn't going to say any of that.'

She shrugged as she helped herself to a selection of food, a stuffed *puri* bursting at the seams with spiced potatoes, a spoonful of fragrant delicate pilau rice and a dhal made of brown lentils that smelt of cumin and chilli and ginger.

'No. But it's what you would do, what my brother, my mother would do. If you're going to do something, they think you should aspire to be the best.'

'I'd agree with that. But being the best doesn't necessarily mean reaching the top spot. There are teachers who are amazing. There's no reason for them to aspire to be a head teacher—that wouldn't make them better teachers.'

'If my mum or brother were teachers they'd become head teacher and found a global string of schools that benefited children from all walks of life and abilities.' Her tone held both love and affection but Carlos could also hear a sadness.

'But you are not your mum. All any of us can do is our best without comparison to anyone else.'

'I bet you don't work like that though. I bet your company is one of the best.'

'Yes, it is. But that's who I am and there are downsides to that. My life is work; I am focused on one thing. You are travelling, you do a variety of jobs, you learn different skills, your lifestyle can be different, you're not pigeonholed—there are so many good things about that. If that's the person you are you should embrace it. You only live one life and you should live it the way you want to. Not the way anyone else wants you to. You could keep travelling, work your way round the world.'

Now she smiled, a smile so sweet that warmth cascaded over him, and she shifted round the blanket and took his face gently in her hands, her touch cool against his jaw.

'Thank you,' she said and, oh, so gently she leaned forward and brushed her lips against his, so sweet, so sensual he felt his heart twist in his chest.

Then she sat back, still right next to him, her body vital and warm next to his. 'Now let's eat,' she said.

So they did, until the plates were empty. Swiftly he cleared them away and in tacit consent they lay down and stared up at the night sky.

'When I was younger I thought each country had its own set of stars,' he said. 'I believed that for years and years.' He'd watched the stars from his bedroom window and plotted his escape to a land with different stars. 'And I believed each star held a soul.' That had worried him: that when he escaped, he would no longer be able to see his mother's soul from his window.

Perhaps she heard the sadness in his voice because she turned, propped herself up on her elbow and looked down at him. 'Maybe that's true. I like the idea that a loved one is looking down at us from the stars.'

He saw compassion and understanding in the depths of her brown eyes and somehow knew this was the moment the whole evening had been headed towards, knew he had to kiss her again. Here under the stars, with the sound of the sea lapping against the sand. And it was the most natural thing in the world to gently tug her down into the crook of his arm.

And then he was kissing her, with a glorious abandon that she matched, her hands in his hair, her body pressed against his, and then all there was was Jemma.

Until she pulled away, her eyes wide, her breathing ragged. 'I think we need to leave,' she said, giving a small shaky laugh. 'Before we attract any attention.'

'Yes. Where shall we go?'

'I was thinking one of the hotels around here. If that's what you want.'

'It's what I want. But…' He strove to think clearly, think beyond the desire that burned inside him.

She reached out and gently laid a finger on his lips. 'There are no buts. And no expectations or pressure. We said we'd see where this weekend took us and here we are. This is what I want. You are what I want. I'm not asking or offering more than this night.'

One last vestige of doubt tried to make itself heard and he blocked it out, rose to his feet and held out a hand to pull her up. 'Then let's go.'

Jodi opened her eyes, a luxurious feeling of happiness spreading over her limbs as she gazed up at the white-washed ceiling, wondered if she had dreamt the night before, knew she hadn't. Then she realised that there was no one next to her and panic clutched her gut. Surely Carl wouldn't have left without at least saying goodbye.

'Hey, sleepyhead.' His voice calmed the panic and she smiled a languorous smile.

'Hey.' She shifted up the bed and frowned slightly, felt a sudden awkwardness, to say nothing of being at a disadvantage. He was up, had clearly showered, his blond hair damp and a little spiky, and he looked more remote than the man from the night before. A look of trouble in his eyes.

Play it cool, Jodi.

'You leaving?' She tried to keep hurt or accusation from her voice. One night, that was what she'd offered and requested.

'Yes. I was going to get us some breakfast, actually, see if I can sort out room service. Then we need to talk.'

'Cool.' She didn't know what else to say, had no idea if talking was good or bad, yet foreboding touched her as she watched him exit. She lay back on the pillows and allowed herself to recall the previous night. Stratospheric was the only word she could come up with. But from great heights came great falls.

A knock on the door interrupted her and she swung her legs out of bed and quickly tugged her dress over her head. She pulled the door open and stepped back in surprise.

'Mr Patankar.' She looked at the royal representative of Jalpura, the man who acted as a liaison between the royals and the rest of the world. A man devoted to the cause of the royal family. Why was he here? 'Is everything OK?'

'No, Ms Lewes. It is far from OK. What do you think you are doing with the Prince?'

'Excuse me?' She had hardly any contact with Prince Rohan of Jalpura. 'Prince Rohan isn't here.'

'Do not play the fool. I am not talking about Prince Rohan, but Prince Carlos. Of Talonos.'

Dread began to unfurl inside her. 'I... I don't know what you're talking about.'

Pradesh Patankar sighed. Pulled out a photograph with a flourish. 'Do you know this man?'

Jodi stared down at the picture and realised the supreme irony of the situation. Whilst she had been masquerading as Jemma Lewes, it turned out Carl had been impersonating on a far, far larger scale.

'How could you betray the Princess like this?'

'I don't understand.' Right now she was having trouble understanding anything, her head awhirl as she tried to process the information.

'I don't expect you to.' The man's voice dripped contempt and Jodi realised just how much he disliked her. 'The Prince is here as an ambassador from Talonos, to represent his island at the film festival. If things work out the way the Queen and I believe they will, he is also here as a projected groom for Princess Alisha.'

It took all her pride to keep her standing as she saw the prurient look in the man's eyes, his look of distaste as he glanced around the room, his eyes resting on the dishevelled sheets.

Think.

How could she have got it so wrong? Again.

'It is the usual way of princes. About to enter an arranged marriage, they want a weekend of fun, a last taste of freedom.'

Finally her brain clanged into gear. 'But Princess Alisha never mentioned this.' Sure, Jodi had known that Prince Carlos of Talonos was coming to Jalpura instead of his brother, but nothing more. How she wished she'd asked more questions, done some research, seen a picture. To think she'd been worried Carl had been a reporter. How could she have been such a fool? Again.

'Why would she tell *you*? The negotiations are private and personal. No commoner would be told. Carlos is here so he and Princess Alisha can meet properly. I am only telling you because of the need to make amends for this mess.'

Could he be right? Jodi had thought Princess Alisha was her friend, but what did she know of royalty? And she had only known the Princess a few weeks, after all. And did it matter? The point was Carl was Carlos—a prince. A prince who was here to meet a potential bride. And now it all made sense. His reluctance to be photographed, the complications that meant he couldn't commit to a relationship, the technical truth that he was neither married nor in a relationship.

'I suggest that you leave Jalpura. And keep this a secret.'

'I can't do that. Princess Alisha has a right to know.'

'No. Do not meddle in things you do not understand, Ms Lewes. The ways of royalty are different. The Princess must and will do her duty—do her the favour of at least giving this marriage a chance.'

'But...'

'There are no buts. I have always had my suspicions about you, Ms Lewes. Would you like me to start delving into your circumstances?'

The nightmare, against all odds, had just got worse, threatening an additional dose of mortification. If this man discovered who she really was, exposed her to the press as an imposter... If any of this came out...it would be manna to the press. And she would be exposed to Luca, to her mother, to Ava.

'Truly, Ms Lewes, I think it is better for all concerned,

especially the Princess, if you simply disappear. What the Princess will definitely not want is publicity.'

Jodi knew it was perhaps the coward's way out, but it was true she knew nothing of royalty and how it worked. Perhaps Alisha would not care, would rather not know. Whereas Jodi could not risk exposure, and Pradesh Patankar was right. Publicity would be a disaster for everyone, so better if Jodi faded away from the scene.

At least this time there would be no need for Luca to bail her out. In fact, there was no need for Luca to even know about this. Full stop. No one needed to know ever. She would leave Jalpura, go somewhere for a few weeks to lick her wounds and then she'd go home.

In a fugue of misery and mortification, Jodi trailed back to her hostel, her skin clammy with humiliation. Once there she stood under the shower, wished for the first time it were hotter, stronger, enough to somehow rid her body of the memory of his touch.

She would not let this hurt her—it had been a one-night stand, nothing more. She would put it behind her—she'd leave Jalpura and she'd head…to England. Yes, that was the answer. Somewhere completely different from here, where the skies were a little less blue, the sun more forgiving, the streets less chaotic, where she could eat fish and chips saturated in vinegar…visit museums, find work in a café. And once there she'd look to the future and Carl would seem like some sort of dream. A few weeks and then she'd go home, go back and work out what to do about Dolci and Ava.

Six weeks later

Jodi sat on the single bed of the cheap London motel and stared blankly down at the lines on the test. Panic streamed through her as she wrapped her arms around her stomach protectively and contemplated the seemingly impossible truth. After all, this was test number three. She was pregnant.

CHAPTER FIVE

Three months later

PRINCE CARLOS, NEWLY and precariously acknowledged heir to the throne of Talonos, stared across the polished mahogany desk at Stefan Pedros, his hopefully loyal chief royal advisor.

'Your Highness…' Stefan began, and Carlos's lips thinned as he wondered exactly when he would get his head round his newly found status. The past three months had been a roller coaster that dipped and spun and coasted through levels of the unexpected.

The court case had gained a momentum that proved unstoppable, even by the weighted pendulum of King Antonio and Queen Isabella's reach and royal influence.

So it had been decreed by the highest court of the land that Carlos was the true heir to Talonos. That the statute that had disallowed him because of his age when his parents married was in fact not legal, due to a precedent set over a century ago, when a direct ancestor of King Antonio had been born out of wedlock—the matter only rectified after the six-month statute. And so a conundrum was created—the King could not seek to overthrow the decree without giving up his own right to rule, and was forced to accept the court's verdict.

So now one day Carlos would be King, as his mother had wanted. The belief, the desire, the principle by which she had lived and died had been granted and Carlos knew he had no choice but to take up his new position in honour of her memory. He could only hope that somehow Catalina was looking down from her star and could see the destiny she'd craved come to fruition.

So here he was. His father had had no alternative but to allocate him a palace and a retinue. There had been a stilted acceptance of the decree, along with a statement that said the royal family would work together to adjust to the new laws of succession, that some time was needed but there would be an inauguration ceremony in a month.

He had met with his father and stepmother just the once, the meeting fraught, his stepmother's face taut with bitter disbelief, his father's cold, pale demeanour as he spoke.

'The best way forward would be for you to gracefully step aside. It is Juan who has been brought up for this.'

'It is his birthright,' Isabella had intervened. *'More than that, it is his blood right. You cannot taint the line by taking the throne.'*

Anger had seethed through him.

'It turns out that it is in fact my birthright, and perhaps it is time for Talonos to benefit from new blood.'

He'd known in that moment that he would accept the throne, that to refuse it would be a tacit admission that his blood was tainted, that he was not good enough. It would be a betrayal of his mother's memory and a vindication of his father's behaviour, his stepmother's attitudes.

'I will not abdicate my right, but I would like to see my brother.'

To at least acknowledge that he understood the unfairness of the situation, to try to talk to him.

'You are still not fit to be near him and he does not want

to see you. My son will never cease to look for a way to overturn this ruling.'

Sadness that his brother would be an enemy for life had exacerbated the churn of emotions as he'd turned to leave. And over the past weeks, his doubts had added to the mix as he'd grappled with all the information, met with various officials and tried to learn what Juan had been taught from the cradle—laws and statutes and history. Could he do this? Was it the right thing for Talonos? He had to make the answers to both those questions a yes.

'Go ahead,' he said now to Stefan.

'I wish to speak to you about the possibility of a royal marriage. To Princess Alisha.'

Carlos allowed himself the smallest of smiles. 'I assure you that the Princess Alisha would not willingly marry me.' He had got to know the Princess a little during his stay on Jalpura and he had liked her. But, 'And neither would I marry her.' Alisha wanted romance and love and had told him she would never submit to an arranged loveless marriage.

'I would rather die a spinster, live my own life, do things I want to do. Even if I am royal.'

'It is too early for me to marry anyone,' he said. His role was too new, too precarious. He knew his father would not rest until he had at least tried to unseat his elder son. 'I would prefer instead to discuss the tour of Talonos.' He planned to reacquaint himself with his country, visit different provinces, see how it had changed in his absence.

Before Stefan could respond, there was a perfunctory tap at the door, before it opened and a woman entered. One startled glance and she turned away abruptly. Carlos frowned. An impression of a face, dark hair pulled back in a ponytail, the now familiar dark blue of the staff uniform, then a muffled voice uttering an apology and the door closed.

Carlos frowned, tried to shake the absurd sense of familiarity. Just because the woman had dark hair did not mean she was Jemma—the idea was ludicrous. He had to stop seeing her in every dark-haired woman. Yet her image dogged his dreams, as if he did expect to see her around every corner. Or if not her, then her byline on an exposé.

The events of months ago ran through his mind.

His return to the hotel; the initial shock that she was gone. Nothing left except a single strand of curly hair on the pillow. No note. No message. He'd realised then that he had no idea where she was staying, knew next to nothing about her. Had told himself that it was her prerogative to leave; their agreement had been one night. Perhaps it was even for the best. Yet he'd found himself lurking round the palace to see if she reported to work.

Then on the Monday he'd learnt the bitter truth, from the Jalpuran royal advisor.

'Please excuse Princess Alisha if she is a little distracted. Her assistant, Jemma Lewes, has disappeared. I have started enquiries and there is no record of a Jemma Lewes arriving on Jalpura. We believe it is possible that Jemma Lewes is an alias and the young woman was a reporter.'

It took all his iron control to keep his face politely neutral, even as shock and the red heat of anger flooded his synapses. Followed by the burn of humiliation—how could he have been so stupid? To be duped so easily. Again.

The idea of the type of story Jemma could write, the thought of his family's reaction, had sent horror through his veins. A horror that resurfaced tenfold now—after the past days, weeks, months, Carlos had hoped that perhaps

Jemma wasn't a reporter. Though he knew the likelihood was she was biding her time for maximum impact.

Which would be around about now, when he was the acknowledged Crown Prince, but it was not yet official. Not until the inauguration ceremony in a month. In which case perhaps that woman had been Jemma, looking for the final wording of her scoop.

'Excuse me.' He strode to the door, stepped into the corridor, looked right and left but there was no sign of the woman. But he'd swear there was a linger of jasmine in the air. Returning, he saw that Stefan was looking at him strangely.

'Is everything OK?'

'Absolutely. But can we pick this up a bit later?'

As soon as the other man left the room Carlos picked up the phone and jabbed in the number of the palace house-keeper, the woman who somehow magically ensured the smooth running of the palace.

'Greta. I was wondering if you could help. Have you taken on any staff recently?'

'A few, Your Highness. Two extra kitchen staff, and two additional maintenance workers.'

'Were any of them called Jemma?' Though she wouldn't be fool enough to use the same name, surely.

'There is a Molly, a Matthew, a Robin and a Jodi.'

'Does one of them have curly dark hair?'

'Yes. That would be Jodi. Jodi Peters. I interviewed her myself. She had excellent references, in a variety of jobs but she was honest about that; said she is travelling so can't guarantee how long she will stay. Is there a problem?'

'I don't believe so. It is just that Jodi looked very famil-iar for some reason and I'd like to double-check her cre-dentials, but without upsetting her in any way. Could you send her along to meet Stefan, when she comes off shift? Maybe say it's a staff review? Stefan can use my study.'

'Of course. I'll do it straight away. She should be there in about half an hour.'

Jodi took a deep breath and paused as she approached the study door. Stopped to glance at her reflection in one of the gilded mirrors that adorned the gold-wallpapered walls of the imposing corridor.

Her eyes scanned her figure with care; she'd spent hours, no, days researching how to hide a pregnancy and she was pretty sure no one would detect the swell of her baby bump. Layers. Tick. Busy patterned long tunic top. Tick. Eye-catching necklace to deflect attention. Tick. 'Sorry, little one,' she murmured. 'I wish I could shout from the rooftops.' Come to that, she wished she could even whisper it into someone's ear, but she couldn't. Had not told a soul about this precious little being.

When she'd first discovered she was pregnant, through the mixture of emotions had shone a thread of joy alongside a determination to give this baby the happiest life it lay in her power to do. The instant fierceness of her love had almost overwhelmed her. And that had not altered in the ensuing months, even as questions had jostled and jolted her brain.

The biggest one being: should she tell Carlos or not? A prince on the cusp of a royal wedding would hardly welcome the news and she couldn't put her baby in the path of certain rejection. Not when she knew what it felt like to live with a father's rejection in the womb. So surely it was better not to tell him—why would he ever need to know. But then what would she tell her child? How could she keep his father's identity a secret? Plus, once she went back to Italy there would undoubtedly be publicity and once it was known she was pregnant there would be questions. More than that, it was possible Carlos would see the publicity and work out that the baby was his. Maybe that was the answer—leave it to fate? But if she did that and Carlos had already married Alisha, was that fair to Alisha? And so the questions had gone on.

In the end Jodi had done nothing. Decided to wait until her first scan, make sure the baby was OK. Also to wait until she saw which way the verdict of Carlos's court case would go; she had followed every twist and turn avidly, researched the history of the royal family in as much depth as possible. Then three weeks ago Carlos had won the right to be Crown Prince and Jodi knew she had to do something.

She also knew she couldn't go home until she'd made a decision—she would not ask Luca to bail her out of this mess. This time she had to stand on her own two feet, for her baby's sake and her own. Somehow it felt important to show herself that she could do this alone—work out what was best for her baby.

So she'd decided to travel to Talonos, to get a job and observe Carlos—she wasn't sure exactly what she hoped to achieve, but she'd figured at least she'd be doing something. She knew from working in Jalpura that news travelled fast between royal staff—she'd get the lowdown on what Carlos was really like and how far marriage plans had gone.

And she'd see him again.

That had been the tiny whisper of a voice at the back of her mind; one she'd quelled. Carlos had lied to her and used her and she would not forget that.

Anyway, in the here and now she needed to get through this staff review with the royal advisor. Jodi stepped forward and knocked at the door.

'Come in.'

Jodi was pushing the door on automatic when the first alarm bell sounded in her brain. Even as she told herself you couldn't tell anything from two syllables, her eyes sent a signal to her brain. The man who rose from the enormous antique desk was not Stefan Pedros.

Panic swirled through her and she half turned, then turned back as the panic started to morph to sheer molten anger.

'Hello, Jodi. Or should I say Jemma?'

The cold sarcasm of his voice caught her on the raw, added flames to her fury. Was he for real?

'You can call me whatever you like. More to the point, what should I call you? Carl? Or Carlos? Or shall we stick to protocol and go for Your Royal Highness? Perhaps you'd like me to curtsey?'

'Drop the act. You knew exactly who I was the whole time on Jalpura.'

'Excuse me?'

'Now here you are again, infiltrating yet *another* palace. Just out of interest, do you work for a specific paper or are you freelancing?' His blue eyes were cold and full of disdain.

Her mouth opened and then closed again as she stared at him. 'You think I'm a reporter?' How could he think that? Worse, if he thought that, then, 'You think our time together in Jalpura was a stunt to get information.'

'Got it in one. Fact: you approached me. Fact: you lied to me. Fact: you did a runner.'

She glanced at his hand. 'No doubt I magicked that ring off your finger.' Now her voice dripped sarcasm and she hoped each drop stung.

He shrugged. 'That was a bit of luck. You'd have come up with another reason. Bumped into me accidentally or something.'

'So then what? Do you think I slept with you to…get material for a story?' Her voice cracked with outrage; the very thought she would do what Tim had done made her skin tighten in revulsion.

'Yes. That is what I believe. Which is why I am going to call security. Right now.'

No. She didn't want to be manhandled out of here. Nor would she leave until she'd extracted an apology, set the story straight. 'Without even hearing my side of the story? If that is what royal status has done to you, then I think I prefer Carl.'

Heat flushed his cheeks and he rubbed the back of his neck before gesturing. 'You're right. Please, go ahead. With your side.'

'Fine. Try this for size. Fact: just after you left the hotel room, Pradesh Patankar turned up. Fact: he told me you are a prince, that you were in Jalpura to meet Princess Alisha as a prospective bride and I was a sordid last fling before you settled down. Fact: the newspapers are rife with rumours that you plan to marry Alisha.'

'Pradesh did what?' Carlos rose to his feet and she could see the shock on his face, knew it wasn't counterfeit and a tiny tendril of hope sprouted. Perhaps there was another side to *his* story.

'You heard me.'

'And you believed him? Why didn't you wait to talk to me?'

'Why wouldn't I believe him? You didn't tell me that you were a prince. It seemed to stack up. You said you couldn't enter a relationship but you weren't in one. You didn't want me to have a photograph of us together. So, yes, I believed him.' Her eyes narrowed. 'And nothing I've seen recently disproves it. There have been numerous news stories about your probable marriage to Princess Alisha.'

She'd read the papers, seen the speculation and the potentially impending marriage had haunted her, tormented her brain for reasons she didn't fully comprehend.

'I am not marrying Alisha. I was never marrying Alisha. That was also a fabrication made up by Pradesh.' Anger flashed in his blue eyes, an anger she knew was directed at the royal representative.

'Then why did you lie to me? Why did you tell me you were Carl Williamson?'

'Because I thought this whole heir-to-the-throne thing was a storm in a teacup and my return to being Prince Carlos was short-lived. I wanted you to know me as Carl Williamson, the man I have been for the past ten years. I didn't want my royal status to make you see me differently. But I didn't intend…' He hesitated. 'I didn't expect the evening to unfold how it did…'

She got that. She'd been there, could almost smell the scent of the sea, the spices, the sound of the waves; she could still recall the sheer magic of his kiss, his taste, his touch. 'But you should have told me.'

He moved closer to her and she braced herself against his proximity.

'You're right. I should have. But I swear to you I was going to tell you that morning. But you weren't there. It then turned out you weren't a member of the kitchen staff, you worked for Princess Alisha and you'd done a runner.' He frowned. 'Actually, *why* didn't you tell me that you worked for the Princess?'

Jodi sighed. 'I lied because I thought you were a reporter looking for a story on the Princess and trying to get on side with me.'

There was a silence and then, 'So, just to be clear,' he said. 'You thought I was a reporter. I thought you were a reporter. And in actual fact…'

'Neither of us is a reporter.'

They stared at each other and then she couldn't help it, perhaps the moment had reached too elevated a pitch of tension, but whatever the reason the fact seemed irrepressibly hilarious. She chuckled, a chuckle that turned into a laugh as he smiled. Then he too was laughing, and suddenly she recalled Jalpura, the laughter they'd shared, the sense of connection, the sheer, uncomplicated magic of the time.

Almost without her realising it her laughter died away and she looked at him, really looked at him for the first time since she had entered the room and events had run off and out of her grasp. His face held evidence that the past months had not been easy, a hint of tiredness in and around the vivid blue eyes, the faint outline of a crease on his forehead.

A sudden urge came to move across and smooth the cares away, to let her fingers smooth down the evening shadow on his jaw and linger on its strength, to run a finger over his lips.

And then…her own lips tingled as if in memory and again she was carried back in time…the feel of his skin under her touch, the sculpt of his muscle, the sweep and strength of his back. His hands on her skin, his lips, inciting, evoking, teasing…

Whoa!

Somehow they'd stepped closer to each other. Carlos's blue eyes were intent, dark, focused as their gazes locked. It would be easy…oh, so easy…to take one final step, close the gap, reach up and…she mustn't.

They mustn't. He didn't know about the baby; he was a crown prince; he didn't even know her name.

And as if he too realised the danger, he broke the eye contact, took a small step back. 'I…' He cleared his throat. 'Where were we?'

'Trying to clear up the myriad misunderstandings,' she said. 'So far we've established Pradesh lied to us both. He told you I was a reporter on the run and he told me you were on Jalpura to meet Princess Alisha.'

He met her gaze. 'He was right about one thing though. You did run. Why? Why didn't you confront me? Or expose me to Alisha?'

'Pradesh threatened to look into my circumstances and I was worried he would discover my true identity.'

He frowned, studied her face again. 'Why don't you sit down and tell me who you really are?'

Jodi complied, sank down, tried to do so gracefully but without revealing her baby bump, sat slightly sideways, inhaled deeply and marshalled her thoughts.

CHAPTER SIX

CARLOS WATCHED HER, wondered what she was about to reveal. Noticed now the smudges of tiredness under the deep brown eyes. Her dark hair was longer than it had been on Jalpura and he wondered what she had been doing in the past months. He frowned—there was something different about her, something he couldn't put a finger on. Unless perhaps his memory of her had fuzzed over the past months. Yet… Instinct nudged him that it was something more; he could see trouble, wariness and an elusive something else in her eyes, in her whole stance. Or perhaps he was just wrong-footed by her sudden reappearance in his life and the resurgent shimmer of attraction. The relief, the sense of happiness that their night together had been real hadn't been an illusion or a trick. Yes, they had both been guilty of a deception, but the magic had still existed. And now he would discover the reason for her deception.

She sighed and her gaze met his. 'My name is Jodi Petrovelli.'

Petrovelli, Petrovelli…it did sound familiar. 'I read an article a few months back. Something to do with a business division, a will and chocolate.'

'That's the one,' she said. 'In a nutshell, my father walked out on my mother, brother and me when my brother was five.' Her voice was flat, devoid of emotion. 'He married a British aristocrat and with the help of her wealth and connections he founded a dessert company called Dolci, which became immensely successful. They had a daughter called Ava. Ava Casseveti.' For the first time her neutrality cracked, her voice a smidge higher. 'We never saw him again.'

A sudden sense of empathy touched him. The Cassevetis were a well-known family, they graced the papers, magazines, social media—it would be impossible to avoid them. And he got how hard it must have been to watch the father who had deserted you thrive and prosper with someone else. Watch a half-sister grow up. After all, he'd lived it, watched it from within. Been in a family that wasn't a family and been made to feel his exclusion.

'Anyway, my father, for want of a better word, died ten months ago and he unexpectedly left a third of Dolci to me, a third to my brother, Luca, and a third to Ava.'

'That must have been a shock.'

'It was. It was also a lovely juicy story and the press jumped on it, especially as Ava is an ex-supermodel and has always been in the public eye. I managed to avoid the publicity by travelling, but a reporter tried to contact me when I arrived on Jalpura and I decided to change my name as an added precaution. That's why I didn't want Pradesh Patankar looking into my circumstances. That's why I ran away.' She sighed and he saw weariness in her gaze. 'It's what I'm good at.'

He shook his head. 'Don't feel bad. Pradesh is not a man many like to cross. I think he was playing a long game; he foresaw that I would end up Crown Prince and he wanted to optimise the chance of a royal alliance.' He paused. 'Tell me something, Jodi. I get why you ran away from Jalpura, but why are you here now?'

There was a silence, one that stretched and twanged the air.

'I needed to see you.' She lifted her arms as if to fold them across her stomach, then dropped them to her sides, the movement awkward. Carlos studied her and foreboding morphed as she stared at him, wide eyed, moistened her lips. 'I...' And now her hand rose and in a fleeting gesture she touched her tummy and he knew. The knowledge a bolt out of the blue, blindsiding him.

'You're pregnant.'

He thought, hoped she'd deny it, that he'd got it wrong, but then she touched her tummy again, the gesture so gentle it touched something inside him.

'Yes, I am. Pregnant.' Each word was clear as she met his gaze. 'It's the first time I've said it out loud.'

Those words seemed to come from a distance, tolled and boomed into reality. A reality he rejected on automatic, the idea too huge to even begin to comprehend. How could he be a father? He wouldn't know how. Terror gripped him, but it was a fear mitigated by an instance of awe, of joy and wonder, before a tsunami of panic washed the moment away and left only the terror in its wake.

'That's not possible. We used protection.'

'I know that.' She looked at him as though he were nuts. 'But it obviously didn't work. I've done a lot of research. Apparently there is a very small percentage of condoms that tear or malfunction or...anyway, does it even matter how it happened? The point is I am one hundred per cent definitely pregnant.'

He eyed her still slender frame. 'Four months?' Doubts swirled. Could this be a fabrication? Could it be someone else's baby? Perhaps that magical night *had* been a trickery and an illusion.

Now her eyes narrowed. 'Yes, four months. You see, the

other extensive research I have done is how to conceal your baby bump. Look carefully at this outfit. Note the busy floral pattern.' Here she hooked quotation marks before gesturing to her midriff. And as he followed her gaze a rush of emotion threatened, an urge to move towards her, place his hand on her belly. An urge so strong he clasped his hands together. 'Note too,' she continued, 'the pregnancy hider's best friend—the draped cardigan, combining cunning ruffles with a layered look. Plus, of course, the chunky beaded necklace worn to draw the eye away from the bump and bring on a conversation about my eclectic taste in jewellery.' Her voice became gentler. 'I know this must be a shock, but I *am* four months pregnant, Carlos, and this baby is yours. That's why I'm here.'

Questions, doubts, terror, a joy continued to swirl and he closed his eyes briefly before forcing his brain into action, putting into play the automatic triggers that closed emotion down. The ability learnt in his childhood to allow him to not feel the pain of the numerous petty humiliations his stepmother had delighted in invoking. Presumably to ensure the minimal time he was allowed on Talonos was as miserable as possible. That enabled him to quell any sense of love for his half-brother as Juan was taught to ignore his presence. Life without emotion was simpler, cleaner, less painful.

So now he needed, not emotion, but clarity and facts. He had to think about, not only himself, not even just the baby, but his country.

'Can you prove it?' She rocked backwards and he hurried on. 'It's a fair question. We had one night together four months ago. You turn up a few weeks after I've become heir to a throne. Why didn't you contact me sooner?'

'Because I wasn't sure if I wanted you to know. I didn't want to tell you during the court case, and I thought you were going to marry Alisha. I couldn't work out what was better for the baby—to tell you or not. So it seemed better to wait. I've spent the past few months in London—I got a job in a café, which kept me busy and paid enough that I could afford rent in a shared house. Then I thought if I came here, worked here, it would give me a chance to work out what to do, get the real lie of the land, not what I could glean from the papers. I still hadn't decided what to do but then you saw me and…well, here we are. Now you know.' She lifted her hands and now there was a slight slump to her shoulders. 'It didn't occur to me you would require proof of paternity. I'm not even sure how that would work, but when I know I'll be in touch.' She rose and headed for the door.

Carlos felt rooted to his chair; he forced his brain to think through the fog. This was right; if he never heard from Jodi again, he would know that the baby wasn't his. No, he wouldn't—he would simply know that she didn't want him to be part of the baby's life. Instinct cleaved through, told him he could not let her go, didn't want to let her go. The baby could be his, in which case…

'Wait!'

She turned. 'For what?'

'Because *if* the baby is mine, then he or she is a potential heir to the throne of Talonos.' The knowledge flashed neon in his mind; the sheer enormity assailed his senses. History on repeat. An heir to the throne and a pregnant woman, a commoner. Unmarried with a child to consider. Thirty years before his father had decreed that such a child was a taint and hadn't so much as contemplated marriage, until tricked into it. Had only married his mother because he'd believed Carlos could never bring his tainted blood to the throne.

'Heir?' Her voice rose an octave.

'Yes.' No way would any child of his be a 'nearly heir', he would not allow history to continue in a tragic loop. No matter what it took. The words tumbled from his mouth. 'So if the baby is mine, you need to marry me.'

The words seemed to grow legs and dance before Jodi's eyes and for a moment all she could do was stare at him. 'Marry you? That is…' *Ludicrous, ridiculous, nuts, certifiable…* In the end she settled for, 'Not happening.'

His lips set and in a second of ridiculous distraction her gaze lingered on their firm outline and the almost hysterical errant thought whispered that if she married him those lips would be accessible at all times. *Seriously, Jodi?*

'Not happening,' she repeated.

'I realise how…outlandish this must sound, but you do have to at least consider the possibility.'

'I don't have to do anything except think about what is best for the baby.'

He looked her straight in the eye. 'Our baby. That's what you are saying, isn't it?'

'Yes, I am. You are the one requiring proof.'

'Yes, I do and, given what is at stake, surely you understand that.' Right now, truth be told, she was having difficulties understanding anything; the twists and turns of the past hour were making her dizzy. 'There can be no question over who this baby's father is if he or she is to be heir.'

'The baby is a boy,' she intervened. 'I had a scan at fourteen weeks and they think it's a boy. They'll be able to tell me for sure at twenty-one weeks. But the point is he isn't going to be heir. Because I am not going to marry you.'

His lips thinned and it occurred to her this man was offering to marry her for the baby's sake, as a matter of honour, and that was a damn sight better than what her own father had done. James Casseveti had disowned his pregnant wife, a woman he'd loved, a woman he'd made vows with. Worse, he'd left them and walked away. Right or wrong aside, Carlos wasn't walking away, wanted to be part of the baby's life, and for that she was deeply grateful. But the idea was still nuts.

'I appreciate that you want to be part of the baby's life and I'll do everything I can to make sure you are. We'll figure out visitation rights, a plan, and with technology nowadays it will be even easier. I also do understand that you want a test done.' Though the idea still stung, that he could believe she would lie. 'But I will do that once I get back to Italy. That would be better for us both. You do not need the publicity surrounding a pregnancy scandal right now.' Not when Talonos was still divided over whether Carlos should be Crown Prince. 'And neither do I. I will not risk this pregnancy hitting the papers, being a new twist in the Casseveti drama.' The thought made her shudder. 'So I promise it will be done, but not on Talonos and not straight away.'

Carlos shook his head. 'I accept why you want to wait, but that is not possible. I accept the likelihood is that the baby is mine; I am taking that seriously. I need you to take the marriage option seriously. It is not enough for this child to just be part of my life.'

'Why not?'

'He could be heir to Talonos, be a ruler. I do not believe it is fair or right to take that away from him.' The words caused her to pause; her hand rose to touch her tummy even as she considered the force behind his words.

'Like it was taken from you?' she asked softly. His story was common knowledge now, raked over incessantly in past months. His parents had married when he was six months and three days old, too old to be heir due to an ancient statute that forbad a child the throne if born out of wedlock and not legitimised before six months. So the position of heir fell to Juan, Carlos's half-brother, or so it was believed until a few months before when a royal historian had discovered that the statute had been overturned generations before in order to legitimise one of King Antonio's own ancestors.

The subsequent outcry claimed that the oversight had been deliberate, that the royal family did not want a commoner's child to ascend to the throne, so it would be little wonder if Carlos felt that his right to the throne had been deliberately withheld.

His reaction to her words was barely noticeable, the only tell the slight tension in his jaw, but that inward flinch was all too familiar. One she experienced every time she saw a news article on the Casseveti Petrovelli inheritance, the lowdown on her own antecedents laid bare for all to see.

'Yes, that is part of the reason. My case has caused confusion and potential unrest through the country. Rifts and divides that could rock the throne itself. That must not happen again.'

'I get you have to think of your country. I need to think about our child. I don't want him to be born into strife.'

'If he is undisputed heir he won't be. And I too am thinking about him and what he will lose if you do not marry me. The chance to be a prince, a king, the ruler of a land I hope he will grow to love.'

The fervency in his voice touched her but also weighed her with a sense of responsibility—her decision would affect the future of an entire country. As well as the well-being of her child.

'With all the responsibility and stress that comes with it.'

'A responsibility for a country you love.'

'Equally he can love Talonos and not rule it.' Couldn't

he? Yet she could feel his sincerity; the edge to his voice lent an assurance of his deep belief that he was right, that he spoke from a knowledge she couldn't understand. Because she didn't have a deep-seated love for a country, didn't know how it must feel to hold that level of love, duty, responsibility.

'Perhaps,' Carlos conceded. 'But think how that would feel for him. He will come to Talonos, stay with me, with my wife, our children and he will know that life could have been his.' His voice curt now. 'If you had allowed it.'

'He will be OK with that.'

'Or he will resent the fact that his destiny was taken away from him.'

'Stop.' The word was wrenched from her and she shook her head to dispel the images he had created. But it was too late. In her head her son was a mirror image of herself, and he was watching his younger brother exactly as she had watched her younger sister. In confusion and doubt, bitterness and envy.

A curse dropped from his lips and he moved towards her. 'I should not have said that.'

'It's OK.' Her voice was flat. 'I will make sure he does not feel that, will ensure he is happy with his own destiny.' Only it didn't work like that. Her mother had always encouraged Luca and Jodi to forge their own lives, had been their mainstay and support. But that hadn't stopped Jodi from all the what ifs and questions. What if Therese had never fallen pregnant with her? Why did James love Ava when he'd rejected Jodi, sight unseen? It hadn't stopped her from following Ava's life with meticulous care and an underlay of bitterness.

'No, it's not OK. I have upset you.' He was in front of her now, close enough that his tantalisingly familiar scent tickled her nostrils. His blue eyes blazed sincerity. 'If you do not marry me, I would do my best to make the child part of my family in a positive way.'

'Like your father did for you.' It was the wrong thing to say. She felt the tension exude from his body, saw shadows in his eyes. How hard had it been growing up with a younger brother destined to be ruler of a country they both loved? Had he left Talonos because it was too hard to stay and watch? How would her son feel watching a brother younger than himself be a prince, destined to rule Talonos? Would he feel his own destiny had been stolen?

The questions pounded her brain, incited a tsunami of panic. 'I cannot decide this now. I don't even know you.'

'That is easily remedied. I understand why you want to wait to have the test; I too have no wish for a scandal right now. So I suggest this. Stay on Talonos for two weeks and we can get to know each other better. Then go to Italy, have the test done and decide after that.'

Jodi hesitated. Marriage or no marriage, Carlos was the father. Getting to know him better was important, for the baby's sake. But, 'I don't think it will be that easy. How will we be able to spend time together without people starting to talk? They probably already will be because of the time we've spent together today.'

'I have an idea.'

Foreboding rippled through her; the idea he'd had so far was hardly stellar, who knew what he'd come up with next?

CHAPTER SEVEN

CARLOS PACED AS he turned the idea over in his mind, whilst all the while emotions wriggled and swirled their way to the surface, burgeoned and swelled. He was going to be a father. *Possibly. Could be.* He must keep a healthy scepticism. His own mother had tricked his father into marriage and it had led to tragedy. No repeat would happen on his watch. This baby deserved better than that whoever his father was.

He returned his gaze to Jodi, saw again the tiredness on her face, saw too that she looked a little paler than she had before. An urge to sit beside her, hold her close as he had that night in Jalpura, swooped out of nowhere. Instead he moved into action of a different kind. 'You're tired. And maybe hungry?' He strode over to his desk and pulled open the middle drawer. 'I have biscuits.' Freshly baked biscuits were left in his study every day. 'Or I can get a meal sent up.'

'Biscuits are fine and maybe a cup of tea? I've completely gone off even the smell of coffee, but I crave tea.'

Five minutes later he sat down opposite her, watched as she ate a biscuit and sipped the tea. 'So what's your idea?' she asked.

'I will employ you as an advisor. We will tell a part of the truth—that we met on Jalpura, where you were my tour guide. I was very impressed, so, as I am interested in growing tourism in Talonos, I have decided to take you on as a consultant.

'I am planning a low-key tour of Talonos to get reacquainted with my country and with the people. I have spent hours poring over manuscripts, statistics, articles, reports on Talonos. On the economy, on olive yields, on education. But they are numbers and, whilst important, they cannot tell the true picture. Only people can do that. I hope to learn what the people feel about taxes, house prices, the state of schools. I propose that you come too.' It would give him a chance to show her the country their child might one day rule. 'In your consultancy role. That works, yes?'

She mulled the idea over, a faint crease on her brow. 'Who else will be on the tour?'

'There will be an element of security, a man from the treasury and a woman from the culture department.'

'Then I don't think it will work. We will be under scrutiny and someone may notice I am pregnant.' She hesitated. 'Even putting that aside, surely people may not tell you the real truth. You're the Prince, the heir to the throne. They may be worried they'll get into trouble if they complain. Or they may not like the monarchy, or they may be ardent royalists. Either way, that will affect what they say. It's a bit like when you're at school and the head teacher asks you your "honest opinion" on something, you're not going to tell her the truth. Because that would mean snitching or getting into trouble.'

It was a valid point. 'So what would have been the best way for the head teacher to find out what you really thought?'

'Infiltrate the group of children. Find a way to observe from a point of view where we didn't know she was observing.'

Carlos snapped his fingers. 'You're a genius.'

'I am?'

'Yup. We'll go undercover.'

'Excuse me?'

'I won't travel with an entourage at all. We'll pose as a couple, on holiday in Talonos where we are thinking about moving to.'

'Say what now?' Her brown eyes were wide and she held a biscuit suspended in mid-air as she stared at him.

'It's the perfect cover. I'll get people's real views on Talonos. We'll get to know each other. It's brilliant.'

'It's nuts,' she said. 'You're a prince and heir to the throne. You won't be allowed; you'll be breaking every security protocol in the book. Plus you'll be recognised.'

'Unlikely. I've kept a really low profile since the verdict, and I was barely on Talonos before that. This could work.'

'It *really* couldn't. And I am one hundred per cent sure your advisors will talk you out of it.'

'But if they can't, you'll do it?'

Ten minutes later Jodi looked up as the door opened to admit Stefan Pedros, Carlos's royal advisor. The man was a complete contrast to Carlos, dark where his prince was fair, and where Carlos had a lithe, cool, contained energy and strength, Stefan radiated energy, his movements deft, his dark eyes intense as his gaze rested on Jodi with curiosity before he turned his attention to Carlos.

'Your Highness…'

Carlos rose and clearly suppressed a sigh. 'Stefan, there is no need to be formal. I have told you I am comfortable with being called Carlos.'

'I understand, Your Highness, but, as I have told you, it is better to maintain some formality, especially at this time when people need to be reminded of your new status.'

'Jodi is aware of my new status.'

'Then perhaps, Your Highness, you need to be reminded of your status.'

'Touché.' Carlos smiled and then gestured towards Jodi. 'This is Jodi Peters; she works in the palace. I want you to meet her as she is part of my new plan for the proposed tour of Talonos.'

Five minutes later and Stefan lifted a hand in the air. 'No. Absolutely not. That is not happening. You cannot travel without security.'

'I won't need security. Because no one will know who I am, or where I am. Except you and Jodi. If anyone does discover the truth, I will know who leaked it. Either you or Jodi.'

Stefan frowned and Carlos raised a hand. 'Apologies, Stefan. But it is you who told me to trust no one.'

'I would rather you not trust me and abandon this plan. You cannot simply disappear.'

'You can tell people I have gone to the States to sort out my business affairs before the inauguration ball. This is happening, Stefan.'

In that moment Jodi glimpsed the arrogance of royalty along with its charm, the words absolute but said with a smile, and Stefan inclined his head. 'Then you give me no choice but to agree. But you must follow any protocols I devise.'

'Agreed.'

The advisor's gaze rested thoughtfully on Jodi. 'It was good to meet you, Ms Peters.'

'You too.' Jodi summoned a smile and sat up straight, very aware that this man would see more than most. Once Stefan had left she turned to Carlos. 'I like him. He is nothing like Pradesh Patankar.'

'Though I hope equally loyal.'

Jodi noted the use of the word hope rather than believe. 'Did you choose Stefan or did your family? I know in Jalpura the Queen or Pradesh approved all the Prince and Princess's royal appointments.'

'He applied for the role and was approved by the judge who determined the ascension case.'

'I see.' She hesitated. 'It must be difficult right now for you and your family.'

'Yes. It is. There are a lot of adjustments to make; however, it is not a subject I am at liberty to discuss.'

His tone was final and Jodi raised her eyebrows. 'You are asking me to consider marrying into the royal family, yet you won't discuss them?'

'At this stage, no, I won't. These two weeks are about us—I understand that there will be other factors, but they can be considered later.'

'After the test?'

'Yes, and after you get to know me.'

Don't you need to get to know me?

She bit back the question as she realised its superfluity. Of course, he didn't. Jodi herself was irrelevant; it was ironic really. Three years ago Tim had only been interested in her for her money and connections. Now Carlos wanted her because she was carrying his baby. Tim had been a scrounger, a man looking for a free meal ticket, for whatever he could get. Carlos would want to marry any woman who was carrying his baby, for the baby's sake, and she admired him for that, could see that whereas Tim had been selfish Carlos was not. But neither man had any interest in her, as an individual. Perhaps she shouldn't be surprised—she wasn't anything special…a diluted version of Ava, a pale version of Luca.

A man like Carlos wouldn't be interested in marrying her. She studied him as he sat in the gathering dusk, the shadows softening the angles of his face, shirtsleeves rolled up to reveal lithe, tanned forearms that made her shiver with a stupid desire.

'So what now?' she asked.

'Now I'll order us some dinner. You and the baby must be hungry by now.'

The simple words brought a sense of warmth. For the first time there was someone who was thinking of the baby, thinking of her. The warmth seemed to reflect in the blue of his eyes, gave the room intimacy.

Careful, Jodi.

Intimacy implied trust and Carlos didn't do trust. 'Then we can come up with a cover story. We'll need a name. Mr and Mrs...?'

Mr and Mrs... Husband and wife... The marriage option. Destiny. This baby could be heir to Talonos.

The words streamed in her brain, triggered a sudden panic and she stood up in preparation for flight.

But she'd got up too soon and the blood rushed to her head. She swayed, tried to balance herself, and then there was Carlos, her hands on the solid wall of his chest, his arms around her to steady her.

'Hey. It's OK.' She looked up at him and the understanding in his eyes undid her. 'I get this is all a bit overwhelming.'

She gave a half-choke of laughter. 'You think?'

'I do.' The words were semi-serious but she knew them to be true. For Carlos life must feel as if it were spinning out of control. He had morphed from Carl Williamson to Prince Carlos, heir to the throne of Talonos, and now here she was telling him he was going to be a father. That would be a shock to any man, let alone one with a kingdom to consider.

'So what are we going to do about it?' Her voice was

breathless. She knew she should back away, out of his embrace. But she didn't even as she saw and exulted in the flare of desire in his eyes that sparked and darkened the blue.

'This,' he said and with an inevitability his lips descended on hers. For a fleeting second she tried to resist, but, heaven help her, she didn't want to—the temptation too sensuous, too blissful, too downright glorious to withstand. Just one kiss, his lips so right; she could taste a hint of the herbal tea, a tang of the lemon biscuit. Her lips parted as he deepened the kiss and she let go into a timeless place, let the sensations wash over her, fill her body with yearning and need.

Without thought she pushed against him, and just like that the magic stopped with a brutal abruptness and she realised he'd pulled away. Kept one hand on her arm to support her but the rejection was absolute. It was in his eyes as well as his actions as she gazed up at him, and she realised what had happened. The swell of her tummy must have triggered the reaction.

The idea filled her with hurt, humiliation, horror, and now she stepped back.

'Jodi, wait.'

But this time she didn't. She couldn't; had to get away—what had she been thinking? They were supposed to be figuring out the best thing for the baby—not indulging in a stupid, ridiculous attraction. The rush of tears threatened and she waited at the door. Knew she had to pull herself together in case someone saw her. A deep breath and she pulled the door open and left.

CHAPTER EIGHT

CARLOS CHECKED THE breakfast table, and then smiled approval at Greta. 'Thank you, Greta. This looks perfect. Also, thank you for being so understanding about me poaching Jodi to a different job.'

'That's fine, Your Highness. I'm glad for her.' The housekeeper hesitated. 'And for you. It must be nice to talk to someone you know.'

'It is.' Or it would be if Jodi actually agreed to speak to him again. Guilt pounded him again at the thought of how much he'd messed up. He should never have kissed her in the first place. But once he had he should never have broken the connection that way. He just hoped she'd turn up to breakfast—he'd messaged her last night.

'If there is anything else I can do, let me know.'

'You've done wonderfully already, Greta.'

As if on cue there was a knock on the door and Jodi entered, smiled and said a few words to Greta at the door before the housekeeper exited. Relief coursed through him and he stepped forward to pull a chair out for her.

'Good morning.'

'Good morning.' Her voice was tight, non-committal and redolent of hurt, the smile gone. Carlos closed his eyes; he was already messing this up big time. Little surprise really—he had no experience in real relationships;

his time with Lisa had been fake, based on a lie. Worse, he hadn't even realised it, had walked into her trap like a credulous fool. The only reason he'd even discovered her perfidy was because a colleague had alerted him, told him that he'd seen Lisa with a rival estate agent. Carlos hadn't wanted to listen, hadn't wanted to hear, but in the end the seed of doubt had been sown and he'd discovered the truth. Since Lisa he'd avoided relationships like the plague; he accepted that love and emotion were mysteries he had no interest in or ability to unravel.

'Jodi. I—'

'This looks delicious,' she broke in in a colourless voice.

'OK.' Clearly she didn't want to talk about it and maybe that was the best way. Pretend the whole thing hadn't happened, block it out. A technique he'd perfected as a child. If you didn't let it touch you then it couldn't hurt you.

'I asked Greta to give of her all,' he said and tried a smile. 'We've got eggs, bacon, sausages, meat or vegetarian options, pastries, toast, jam, honey… I was worried that you didn't eat yesterday.'

Her wince showed him that was the wrong thing to say.

'So help yourself,' he said and watched as she took a small portion of scrambled eggs. A memory of Jalpura, of heaping their plates under the stars, the smell of spices, her smile, the way she closed her eyes in sheer appreciation of the food, assaulted him.

'You need to eat,' he said now.

'I know what I need to do,' and he could hardly blame her for the snap in the words. 'Don't worry. The baby is getting everything he needs.'

'I know. That's not what I meant.' His inability to say anything sensible was both ridiculous and excruciating. 'I think we need to talk. There's no way we'll pull off playing at newly-weds if we can't even manage a conversation.'

'I'm so sorry. Forgive my lack of sparkling conversation this morning.'

That was also not what he meant. Resisting the urge to bang his head on the table's edge, he tried again. 'I meant we need to talk about what happened last night.'

'I don't even want to think about it, let alone discuss it.'

'Once we face it, then we can forget it.'

Anger and hurt sparked in her brown eyes and Carlos tried to work out the logistics of kicking himself round the room, away from the metaphorical spade that he kept digging a deeper and deeper hole with. Deep breath. 'I don't want to forget the kiss.' He couldn't even if he tried; he knew the feel of Jodi's lips was indelibly printed on his own. Her scent, the touch, the gloss of her hair... 'I want to forget how it ended. I want to explain why I let you go like that.' One second he'd been kissing Jodi and it had felt so right, evoked memories of their night together, of remembered shared pleasure. Then he'd felt the soft curve of her pregnancy against him, reality had engulfed him, the impending fatherhood and... 'I panicked. Until I felt the baby I don't think I fully comprehended the truth and all it means. And it suddenly felt...selfish to be kissing you... as though it could hurt the baby somehow. But I shouldn't have let you leave like that, without explaining. I was just overwhelmed with...'

'Fear,' she supplied. 'When I first realised I was pregnant, I was terrified. It is such an enormous responsibility. I'm scared I'll get it wrong.'

'You won't.' It would be he who would get it wrong.

'Thank you for explaining. I thought—' She broke off.

'What did you think?'

'It doesn't matter.'

For a moment he was tempted to let it go; that would be

the easy way out. Yet… 'Actually it does matter. To get to know each other better we need to understand each other.'

There was a pause and then she nodded. 'Fair's fair. You told me how you felt so I'll return the favour.' Her hands clenched and she met his gaze, half defiantly. 'I thought you found kissing me unpleasant.'

Carlos stared at her. 'You are joking? That kiss was awesome, glorious, wonderful. But it was also wrong. This week is about us getting to know each other as people. We already know we have a spark and I do believe that is an important factor, but I don't want our attraction to cloud our judgement. So… I am sorry for kissing you.'

'And I'm sorry for kissing you back.' She pushed her shoulders back and gave him the smallest of smiles. 'Then there's only one thing for it.'

'What's that?'

'I think we should eat.' Reaching out for a spoon, she heaped her plate with the eggs, followed by two thick rashers of bacon and a pile of mushrooms.

'Excellent plan.'

Jodi snaffled one last piece of toast and leant back in the chair. 'That was incredible. I am now ready to come up with a cover story. I think we should keep it simple, call ourselves Carl and Jodi Lewes'

'That works. I can call you JoJo. What about jobs? I'll stick to property, so I'll be an estate agent.'

Curiosity surfaced. 'What made you choose property? It seems like a jump from prince to property developer.'

'I didn't. It was sheer chance that set me on the path. I arrived in New York and I needed a job.'

'Didn't you sort all that out before you left? I mean, I assumed with royal connections it would be easy.'

For a fraction of time he hesitated, and then he rolled

into speech with a smoothness that sounded almost rehearsed. 'I was young, I wanted to prove that I could make it without royal connections. So when I got to New York the first thing I did was legally change my name. Then I applied to any and all jobs and I secured one as a trainee realtor, or estate agent. And property fired me up, the idea of it, the economics of it. The sheer necessity of it—after all, everyone deserves a roof over their heads. So it all went from there. I bought properties in auctions, I did them up, sold them on. Raised capital to start a business, made contacts. But that first job, it was just dumb luck.'

'But it fired you up. None of my jobs have done that really. So maybe this is my chance to make up an amazing career. I could be a ballet dancer extraordinaire or a successful entrepreneur. Or a lawyer.'

'What did you want to be when you were growing up?'

The answer that popped into her head was swallowed down immediately. Ava. That was who she'd always wanted to be. Her sister. And that sucked and she certainly wouldn't admit to anything so pathetic. Yet now her brain kept on rolling. What would have happened if it had been Ava who met Carl on Jalpura? How would it have played out? She could see it now—a royal romance with Ava Casseveti in the starring role. That held a rightness. Except according to the press Ava had already found a man, a man who apparently adored her.

'Jodi?' Carlos's voice broke into her thoughts. 'You OK?'

'I'm fine.' Recalling his question, she thought back—once she'd grasped she couldn't be Ava so wanting to be her was pointless, she had decided the most important thing was to succeed in her own right. 'For a while I wanted to be a lawyer. Like my mum. I saw how hard she worked, but I also saw how happy it made her.' She gave a sudden smile. 'My mum is a pretty amazing woman; somehow she held us all together as a family and trained as a lawyer and now she's a partner in a firm in Turin. It seemed like a pretty cool idea to do what she did, but I couldn't do it, couldn't get my head round the law degree.'

'Out of all the jobs you've done, which made you happiest?'

Jodi considered the question. 'I enjoyed looking after the next-door neighbour's son. I was nineteen and their nanny left at short notice. Leo was on the autistic spectrum but he took a liking to me, I don't know why. But he was such a lovely kid, and it made me mad to see how hard it is for kids with difficulties. Anyway, I offered to help out and it worked really well for a couple of months over the summer. I even got him to advance with his reading. He was so bright, he just saw things differently, and I got that.' Maybe because she'd always felt different herself, as if she didn't fit. 'When he read his first few words, because I figured out a way to teach him, I was happy and that gave me real satisfaction. But the summer came to an end. Leo went to a special school.' After that she'd gone to law college. When that didn't work she'd swapped courses to a business degree. She'd at least stuck to that and graduated.

'Perhaps that was the fire-up job,' he said. 'Perhaps you should think about being a teacher, working with disadvantaged kids?'

'Me?'

'Don't look so surprised. Why not?'

'It was just a summer job, a favour for a neighbour.'

'Either way, the difference you made to one small boy is worth more than any amount of money, or business success.'

His words warmed her, more than they should and, embarrassed, she said hurriedly, 'We've strayed from Carl and JoJo. When did we get married? I think two years ago. Long enough that no one will expect us to be talking about our wedding in detail or have photos.'

'Agreed. Also, we are planning on moving to Talonos because we want a change and we're fed up with life in the big city.'

'Which big city?'

'Maybe one we both know well.'

'How about London? Maybe we met in America, moved to London and now we're looking for a permanent change.'

'Sounds good.' He lifted his coffee cup. 'To Carl and JoJo Lewes.'

'Carl and JoJo,' she echoed.

'Thank you for agreeing to stay on Talonos. Now all I ask is that you promise me a fair trial.'

His voice was deep now, and his gaze held an allure, a magnetic force that she knew would be hard to resist.

'I promise,' she said, and the words rang with solemnity.

CHAPTER NINE

CARLOS WAITED ON the platform, relaxed as none of the other travellers gave him more than a passing glance. Relief and bitterness mixed; he was damned sure if his brother was on the platform he would be mobbed, however incognito he was trying to be.

Not that any of the Talonos royal family would ever travel incognito—ever since the debacle of his father's first marriage the royal court had been deliberately shaped by spin. Every appearance in public carefully orchestrated, every step coordinated by the royal advisors appointed to ensure the horrifying mistake that had resulted in Carlos could not happen again.

His thoughts were distracted by the sight of Jodi walking through the barriers and a qualm struck him. How would she deal with being thrown into the royal spin machine? Determination increased his stride; she would be fine. He would not treat Jodi as his father had treated his mother. Never isolate her, or be cruel. Or let anyone else do so.

As she spotted him and walked towards him with a wave, his heart gave a funny lurch. This was the mother of his child, this pretty, sensual, interesting woman. The idea jolted him anew. A warning note klaxoned in his brain. The *potential*, the *probable* mother of his baby. He must remember that. Would never allow fate to tunnel into him again, never sail along in a fantasy world only for it to go Kaboom. Always question, never trust.

So her prettiness was neither here nor there; there was no point in lingering on how her dark hair shone in the Talonos sunshine, highlighting it with a ripple of a deep rich brown, no need to let his gaze appreciate the slender length of her legs, the grace of her movement. And as she approached there was definitely no need for his eyes to snag on her lips, or for his own lips to upturn in such a wide smile.

'Right on time,' he said.

A few minutes later the train puffed into view. 'All aboard,' he said. 'Let the adventure begin.'

'I've looked up Balos. It's one of the most touristy of the cities.'

'Yes. I figured it's a good place to start—we'll blend in and I'd like to see and compare city and rural life.'

'That sounds cool.' She pulled out a guidebook and opened it, ran a finger down the index in the back. 'I bought a history of Talonos and a tour guide. They'll be good props and help me do the consultancy job.'

He surreptitiously watched her as she read; a faint endearing frown furrowed her brow and occasionally she would mutter something to herself.

'We're going to make a stop en route to have a picnic, and I wanted to show you the royal *nuraghe*. It's an ancient building, or what's left of it anyway.'

They alighted from the train, left their luggage behind the counter at the station and Carlos led the way along a dusty pebbled path that bordered a countryside vista, through a gate and across a field to the tall pile of conical stones, surrounded by another circle.

'So this is all that's left. But centuries ago, back in

about 500 B.C., this would have been a royal palace. There would have been three towers, the largest would have been about twenty-four metres. Most of these edifices are made in cone shapes sometimes stacked in different patterns.'

'That's incredible.' Jodi stood as if entranced. 'I know there are some of these on Sardinia but I've never seen them.'

'There are literally thousands on Talonos. They are almost mythical—they are only found on Talonos and Sardinia and there is very little known about the people who built them except they are an ancient civilisation who left no written records. They are mentioned in myths and legends but obviously really existed. It's quite hard to piece together what the buildings were used for, but we're pretty sure they were royal dwellings, meeting halls and some were possibly built for defence purposes.'

'It gives you goosebumps.' She rubbed her arms and instinctively he moved a little closer to her. 'I mean, they date from hundreds of years B.C.—it seems almost impossible they're still here. Yet all those millennia ago real people toiled to build this, stone by stone. People may have died to build this, the individuals long forgotten but their work remains. If these weren't here, there would be no evidence of a whole civilisation, a whole race of people who lived and died and loved and hated. If I close my eyes I can almost see them. Kids racing around.'

'A king and queen, a retinue of servants, animals in the courtyard, a well. A courtroom, a royal nursery…' he said softly, and a sense of connection shimmered in the air. Jodi did what he had always done—made history come alive. She stood, her hair ruffled in the breeze, her eyes closed. Poignancy tugged inside him as she rested one hand on her stomach as though she were trying to share the images with her baby.

'They would all have stood right here, in this very place where we stand now.' She looked down at the ground then back up at him. 'In some ways things haven't changed and in other ways they've changed more than we can possibly imagine. Yet once this was a palace, with a royal family. Is that why this place is important to you?'

'Yes. It is comforting somehow to think that in some tenuous way I linked back to those people. Oh, I know there is no direct family tree, that this civilisation was no doubt wiped out, invaded and the royal family died out. But there is still a link.' He'd always been sure that there had been someone like him, a son who was not a son, an heir who was not an heir. In those more violent times perhaps such as he would simply have been killed. Or perhaps such sons were treated as allies, as family members who would defend the family name. Seen as true brothers and close family members. He'd hoped for his ancestors that that had been the case.

He turned away, all too aware of Jodi's gaze.

'And maybe back then they had picnics,' he said. 'I asked Greta to put together a picnic basket including some of our more traditional dishes, though we have no record of what this civilisation ate.'

He pulled off his backpack and started to unpack it, spread out a picnic blanket as Jodi crouched down to help. It was only then that he frowned. 'Will you be OK, sitting on the ground? I didn't think. I should have bought chairs or we should have eaten inside or...'

'It's OK.' She smiled at him. 'I am fine sitting on the ground. I'm not big enough yet for it to be a problem. Look.' Without further ado she lowered herself gracefully onto the rug and he followed suit, pulled out the various Tupperware boxes and spread them on the plaid square.

'It's better than OK. It's perfect. Thank you for bringing me here.'

'I wanted you to see it. Because this baby…he is linked to here too. To the history of Talonos and its royalty. No matter what you decide he will have that link. Whether he is a prince or not, he will be a part of my family.'

She sighed as she spread olive tapenade on a cracker. 'I can feel the weight of history bearing down. Because that is what we have to decide, isn't it? If he should be a prince or not.'

'It is what you have to decide. I have decided already.'

'You cannot, you should not make a decision of that magnitude so fast. One thing that is the same now as it probably was back then is that a lot of royal marriages are politically motivated. They are alliances. I am certain Stefan would advise you strongly against marrying me and prefer that you marry someone like Alisha. I am sure your family may well feel the same way.' Her gaze was steady. 'If I weren't pregnant, then you would make a political marriage. You said it yourself.'

'There is no point in what ifs.' His voice was harsh now. He'd decided years ago to stop living in a world of possibilities. If his mother hadn't married his father, if his mother hadn't died, if Isabella had been different, if he could somehow make his father love him…the ifs had abounded until he'd realised there was no point letting them in. 'The best way to success is to deal with what is.'

'What about regrets?'

'I will not regret making a decision I believe to be right.' There was a silence and she looked up from her plate and the breath caught in his throat. She looked beautiful, sitting cross-legged, the tapered trousers showcasing the slender length of her legs, her hair caught up in a messy ponytail so dark tendrils framed her face. Her brown eyes shy, a little wary. 'Our marriage is the right decision.'

'Because of the baby.' Her voice was a little flat, a little sad.

'Yes.'

'Just like a political marriage would have been right in different circumstances.'

'Yes.' But unwanted doubt touched him. If he was sitting here opposite Alisha or her sister or some random princess would he feel so sure, so certain? The answer could only be yes.

'And if you were still Carl Williamson? If there were no baby, no need for an alliance.'

'Then I would never have got married at all. I told you I wouldn't lie to you and I won't. As Carl Williamson I fully intended to live out my days as a confirmed bachelor. But now it is different. Now I am a prince. Now you are pregnant. I won't look back to Carl Williamson. I deal with what is and make the best of it. Make it work. We can make this work.'

'Even if you had no interest in marriage or children?' Her troubled eyes met his.

'Even then.' He had to believe that. Knew too that, even if he couldn't be a good father, Jodi would be a good mother. Would give the baby love, the right love, would know how to deal with emotion. His gaze slipped to her belly and for a minute he pictured the baby, remembered his own instinctive love for his brother and how that had been crushed and poisoned. That would not happen here, but if he could not love, if it were not within him, he would be able to provide security and give his son a kingdom to rule. He would not behave as his father had.

'I don't know how you can be so sure. But I think it's only fair to tell you I am not. Nowhere near.'

'But you have listened and you will give me a fair trial, as you promised. That is all I ask.' Now she looked tired, her earlier sparkle dimmed as she glanced across at the remains of the ancient palace. 'Come on. Enough talk of marriage. Now it's time to get back on the train, go to the city and have some fun.'

'Fun?' Surprise laced the question and he nodded.

'Yes. Fun. That is a good way to get to know each other too.'

Two hours later Jodi looked round the hustle and bustle of the railway station of Balos. 'Wow, this really is a major city.'

He nodded as he showed the train attendant their tickets and they exited. 'Yes. Talonos is made up of a mix of urban and rural. This is one of the major city ports and it's also a tourism hub. But it's also incredibly historic and there is a bit of a push and pull going on. There are a growing number of groups that feel the city has become too industrialised, that there are too many tourists, house prices have rocketed, people from abroad are buying second homes. Other people say that this brings money in and there is nothing wrong with attracting tourists and the wealthy jet set with their yachts.'

'What do you think?'

'To be honest, I am not sure. I understand both sides, but I believe there should be a balance. Perhaps some housing should be price capped and only available to locals. Increase wealth tax on second homes and yachts so at least the rich pay more.'

Jodi nodded. 'I read about some of this.'

Carlos gestured to a building on his right. 'This is the hotel.' He glanced at her. 'So we must remember our roles. This is perhaps where I am most likely to be recognised.'

At least that shouldn't be a problem for her. Jodi had checked the papers, not just for stories on Talonos, but also on the whole Casseveti saga and right now it was centred on Ava's engagement to Liam Rourke. A wistfulness shot through her. Once again Ava had done it right—had been swept away in a romantic deluge. Not the 'let's get married because you are carrying my baby' scenario—her sister had achieved the bona fide fairy-tale happy ending. One Jodi couldn't manage even when the prince had been supplied gratis.

As for Luca, she had little to no idea where he stood in the whole affair. The news that he had attended Ava's engagement party had cut her to the quick—the photos of Luca on the dance floor, a pretty dark-haired woman in his arms and next to them, smiling across at them, had been Ava. And jealousy had twisted inside Jodi, so strong that she'd hurled the magazine across the room. Since then she'd avoided any news with the Casseveti name in it.

But she knew that could not continue. At the end of this week she would have a plan. Then she would go home, but now, now she had a role to play.

'I'm ready.'

'OK, JoJo, let's go go.'

The absurdity made her chuckle, made it easier to put her hand in his as he held it out, easier to walk with a natural step through the revolving door of the hotel. The lobby was small but exuded charm. Vases of flowers dotted the two small tables surrounded by comfortable-looking curved armchairs. The desk, though not sleek or modern, was well polished and the woman behind it had a welcoming smile as she studied them.

Carlos stepped forward. 'Good afternoon. I made a reservation yesterday. In the name of Carl Lewes.'

'Mr Lewes, I remember you. I am Roseanna—you

spoke with me. You are staying for just the one night and you requested a suite.' She beamed. 'Our only suite is the honeymoon suite—I hope that's OK.'

'Of course.' The irony was not lost on Jodi and for a stupid moment she wished they were here on a real honeymoon, not considering a marriage solely based on convenience. She blinked as she realised Roseanna was explaining the honeymoon package, pulled a hasty smile to her face.

'We sure do appreciate it,' Carlos added. 'You have a lovely place here. I think your website said it's been family run for a while.'

'It has. My husband's grandparents established it and it's stayed in the family since. But times move on and business isn't as good as it used to be. People seem to prefer the bigger-brand hotels nowadays.'

'That surprises me,' Carlos said. 'Seems to me that this is exactly what tourists would want. Charming, historic, picturesque.'

'Not any more. Talonos seems to attract a different type of tourist now, the jet-setting wealthy crowd, and they tend to stay on their yachts, or they want the huge glass-fronted, mega-modern hotels.' She smiled. 'Sometimes I think we should give in and sell up—a lot of those big hotels are trying to buy out the competition and then redevelop round here. There's talk about building a seven-star hotel, and a plush designer shopping mall. But that would kill off local businesses. Like my daughter's shop and my son-in-law's taverna.'

Worry etched the dark-haired woman's face and then she shook her head. 'I am sorry. Listen to me. You'll be thinking that I drive my guests away with my moaning.'

'Not at all,' Jodi chipped in. 'We're interested. You see, we're thinking about moving to Talonos. For good. So it's interesting to hear how things work.' She looked round. 'But for me, to change this part of the city doesn't make sense. Surely the local government would object. I mean, what about planning permission and—?'

'It doesn't work like that here,' Roseanna said. 'If you move here, make sure you get everything covered by a reputable local solicitor.' She smiled. 'Now, why don't I show you to your room?'

As they followed her up the stairs Jodi saw the slight crease in Carlos's brow, wondered what he was thinking, even as her own buzzed with the unfairness of it. Why would anyone want to redevelop this amazing city, full of history and beauty?

'Here we are.' Roseanna pushed open the door and gestured them in.

'It's beautiful,' Jodi said. And it truly was. A canopied four-poster bed, carved of old wood and decorated with hearts, was set in the middle of the room. The scent of fresh flowers from the vivid bouquet, a floral explosion of reds and yellows and deep purple, on the dresser caused Jodi to move over and sniff in appreciation.

'From the hotel garden. My husband's pride and joy,' Roseanna said. 'He created it when we first got married, forty years ago. I am a country girl and I missed the fields and green. I wanted to grow vegetables and I still do. But he taught me that flowers have value too even if it is a different kind of value than potatoes. It's a good thing to have in life and marriage. Both green beans and sweet peas.' She gave a sudden chuckle. 'So that's my advice to the two of you.'

'Thank you. We appreciate it.'

'Enjoy your time here. I recommend the nearby taverna for dinner. It's good local food and they have a dance group in tonight. In the interests of fairness I should tell you it's run by my daughter and son-in-law. But they will be able to tell you more about the reality of life in this city.'

'Thank you, Roseanna. And for the suite. It's beautiful.' Jodi waited until the hotel owner had left and then turned to Carlos. 'It is beautiful,' she said. 'But…'

'It is not really a suite,' he completed. He walked over to a doorway that led into a small alcove. 'But there is a sofa over here.'

They both eyed the sofa with is heart-shaped cushions; it was more of a chaise longue, suitable for two people to sit close to each other.

'You can have the bed. I will sleep on the sofa.'

'But…'

'No buts. You are pregnant. You get the bed. There is no discussion.'

'OK. Thank you.' There was a silence as they both surveyed the room. Jodi's eyes seemed to be pulled inexorably to the bed, the rose petals strewn on it, the softness of the sheets, and now she glanced at Carlos and unbidden memories of that magical Jalpuran night started to seep into her consciousness.

Carlos cleared his throat. 'Perhaps we should go now, explore the city a little and then find the taverna for dinner.'

'Sounds good.'

It was hard to say who headed for the door quicker.

They wandered the streets for a couple of hours and Jodi absorbed the beauty of the city. The dusk was illuminated by streetlamps that could have come from a bygone era, street vendors sold hot dogs filled with traditional sausages and globs of hot yellow mustard that sizzled the air. Small glass-fronted shops filled with traditional wares and souvenirs were shuttering up. 'I don't understand why anyone would want to demolish this to build a shopping mall,' Jodi said. 'Is that something you would have developed? Would your company take that on?'

'No.' There was no hesitation. 'I have developed a shopping mall, but it was in a town that desperately needed some urban regeneration. And it replaced a row of graffitied, tired little shops and a playground that I'm pretty sure was only there as a drug dealers' hangout. I made sure that all the shop owners got suitable compensation and the chance to be part of the new mall. I also developed a new play area and supported the local groups who wanted it to be a real playground.' He frowned. 'Later, perhaps, in the taverna we can ask what sort of compensation is in place. And I want to know exactly how planning permission does work. Some of these buildings must be listed.'

'It cannot be right to destroy this.' She looked at him. 'With your new position, perhaps you can stop it. You can talk to your father and—'

'Yes. I will.' Jodi glanced sideways at him, could read nothing from his expression. She wondered what his relationship with his father was like. The newspapers' spin was positive, spoke of the way King Antonio had ensured his oldest son was part of the royal family but respected his decision to leave to forge his own life. Official photos of family gatherings showed smiling faces and handshakes. Yet Carlos's visits to Talonos over the past years had been few and somehow he had managed to keep his two personas strictly separate. She could only assume that as his company had flourished, he had decided to meet his family in private.

His lips pressed together now, and she sensed his thoughts were headed somewhere dark and without even thinking she moved closer, slipped her hand into his and squeezed gently. 'Hey, this is working. You are seeing what life on the ground is like. That's a good thing, right?'

'Right,' he said, and smiled. 'I'm sorry, Jodi. I promised you fun, not gloom and politics.'

'I don't mind. I like Roseanna. I don't want her and her
husband to have to give up a business they love, only to
see it swallowed up by some generic hotel brand. I want
to help stop that from happening.'

He came to a halt and looked down at her. 'You care,'
he said. 'Don't you?'

'Of course, I do. Who wouldn't care?'

'A lot of people,' he said softly. 'A lot of people in your
position would be thinking only of themselves, or would
feel a bit disappointed that spending time with a prince
didn't involve the jet-setting crowd, or designer malls and
a yacht and a seven-star hotel.' He smiled. 'Here's me taking you to a local taverna.'

'Which is fine by me. I think I'm more a local-taverna
type of girl.' The truth of the words rippled panic through
her. How on earth could she even contemplate the role of
Princess? Pushing the question away she told herself to
focus on the here and now. 'Here we are.'

CHAPTER TEN

THEY APPROACHED THE TAVERNA, situated on a large patioed area filled with tables and people. Appetising aromas spilled from inside the restaurant along with the strenuous beat of drums and the sound of laughter. A smiling waiter approached and soon they were sitting at a table, a bowl of spiced olives between them and two menus.

'I want all of it,' Jodi said.

Carlos smiled at her genuine enthusiasm. 'Do you have any specific cravings?' he asked.

'Oddly enough, for Jalpuran food. Especially spiced potatoes and dahl and pilau rice.' She shrugged. 'It sounds silly but I wondered if it's because that's what I ate that night.'

His smile vanished as he considered her words. The night their baby had been conceived. Or was it? Was she telling the truth? There was defiance in her eyes now as if she had read his mind, but also anger and hurt and he couldn't quite hold her gaze. Looked down at his menu instead.

'The olives are spiced,' he said, pushing the bowl towards her. 'Perhaps that will help.'

It was clumsy and he knew it as she pushed the bowl firmly back. 'Do you really not believe me? Do you really think this baby is not yours?' She kept her voice low but he could hear the strum of emotion.

'I…' Discomfort touched him and he shook it away. 'There has to be one hundred per cent certainty that this baby is mine, the true heir.'

'I get that. I get the people of Talonos have the right to certainty. I've agreed to take the test. But that's not what I am asking. I am asking if you believe me. Right here and now.'

'It is not about belief. It is about knowledge. It does not matter what I believe because I may get it wrong.'

'So is this what it would always be like? If we marry and we have another baby, would you need a DNA test then?' Her shoulders slumped.

'Of course not. This is different, Jodi. Right now we don't know each other. It is a sensitive time for my country. Please bear with me.'

'Sure.' But she was still upset and he couldn't blame her. But how could he let himself believe in her? The risk was too great. His mother had tricked his father, Lisa had tricked him. This time he had to be sure there was no trickery.

Silence reigned until the waiter arrived and took their orders.

'I get you're upset. Is there anything I can do to help?'

Her forehead creased in thought and then she met his gaze. 'Trust me with something. Something personal. Anything. However small.'

'I…' His brain raced as he tried to figure out what to say, unable to think of anything. His gaze dropped and caught the glint of light on his ring. His mother's ring, the one if you were fanciful had brought them together. He slipped it off his finger and held it out on the palm of his hand. 'This is personal.'

'May I look at it?'

At his nod she reached out and took the ring; her fingers brushed his palm and he'd swear something happened, a frisson that shimmered in the dusky scented air. He'd shown no one this ring, guarded it close and held its secret from the age of thirteen onwards. Known his father and Isabella would take it from him if they suspected he had it. So he'd worn it round his neck and only placed it on his finger once he had boarded the plane that took him from Talonos.

'It's beautiful,' she said finally. 'The engraving is so delicate.'

'It belonged to my mother. She left it to me.' That was perhaps all he needed to say but, 'It's the only thing I have that was hers.'

Her startled gaze flew to his. 'But why? Surely she had other possessions.'

'Not that were kept. Any jewellery she had was from the royal coffers and went to my stepmother. Other than that... her clothes, her personal possessions were all thrown out.'

'But there must have been photographs, perhaps of you and her.'

'I do not know what happened to them. My father and Isabella believed it was better for me not to dwell or brood on grief. They wanted to move on.' The temptation to tell Jodi more swirled words onto the tip of his tongue and he swallowed them. To tell tales, to lay bare the truth was too risky. Yet the look in her eyes, the sweet wide eyes, seemed to almost pull the words out.

No. There was no point in whinging or whining or complaining. More importantly the façade, the illusion of royal family unity, was more important than ever. His ascension could cause deep rifts and divides in his country, bring riots to the streets. That had to be avoided at all costs. That was why the inauguration ball must be a show of union, acceptance, and solidarity. He knew it would be fake, knew his family would continue to plot against him, but for now they would maintain the façade. Nothing could threaten that; he could not undermine that simply because he wanted a bit of comfort.

'They believed that to be best,' he said now. 'But this ring means a lot to me. I understood that my father would not approve of me having it. My old nurse gave it to me and I wore it on a chain round my neck so no one would get upset. Until I left Talonos.' He looked at her directly. 'No one knows about the ring except you and my old nurse.'

'Thank you. I appreciate you sharing that. For trusting me with that.' She reached out, clasped a hand over his; the feel of her, the warmth of her rushed a sweet sensation through him. 'I mean that. And I am sorry. Sorry you lost your mother so young.'

The waiter arrived with their food and she moved her hand and for a second he felt stupidly bereft. 'Thank you.' Dark memories threatened: seeing his mother lying so still, the dawn of realisation that he would never see her again, the finality of loss. There was no point in these thoughts, they led to pointless wishes and what ifs and so he needed to shut them down. He looked down at his moussaka. 'This looks fantastic.'

'Yes, it does.' After that she steered the conversation towards a general discussion and he felt an appreciation that she hadn't pushed it, understood and accepted his reluctance to discuss it further. By tacit consent they kept conversation to general topics as they ate and once the plates were clear he gestured towards the inside of the taverna. 'How about we eat our dessert inside and watch the dancing?'

'Sounds good.'

They entered the bustle and warmth of the taverna and soon were seated at a table on the edge of the dance floor.

The man who came to take their order smiled. 'You are Mr and Mrs Lewes, yes?' At Carlos's nod, the man's smile widened. 'I am Andreas. You are staying at my parents-in-law's guest house, I believe.'

'Yes, we are. Your mother-in-law is a lovely woman,' Jodi said.

'Thank you. We are very fond of her. Now, before your dessert perhaps you would like to try the local dance. The dancers will teach you the steps if you wish.'

'Not for me.' Jodi shook her head. 'I have two left feet.' Seeing his look of miscomprehension, she explained. 'I am a terrible dancer. But I'd love to watch.'

'They are good teachers. They take it really slow. So if you change your mind just jump in.'

When Andreas had moved away Carlos looked across at her. 'I assume that dancing would be bad for the baby?'

'It's not that. I mean, I shouldn't do anything extreme, but the basic steps would be OK.'

'Then why not give it a try? The Talonese national dances are fun—I haven't done them since I was a child.'

'I truly have no sense of rhythm.' Jodi was beginning to wish she'd pleaded pregnancy as an excuse; the idea of going on stage and making a fool of herself made her cringe inside. Last time she'd had delusions of dancing grandeur it had resulted in humiliation and she wasn't going through that ever again.

'That won't matter. I am pretty sure it's the sort of thing JoJo and Carl would do.'

'It may not matter to you, but it does to me. I'm happy to sit and watch but I think *you* should go and do it.'

He shook his head. 'Carl wouldn't go without his wife. But if *we* join in it would be a good way to get talking to everyone and pick up some more information. Also, you might enjoy it, no one will laugh at you, and it may be fun. When was the last time you had fun?'

On Jalpura. With Carl. That was the answer. And look where that had landed her.

'I'd rather not.' But as she watched a few of the patrons take to the floor, and how they were absorbed into the chat and banter on the stage Jodi realised that Carlos was right. This was a good way to mingle, to do what he wanted, needed, to do to gather information and she sighed.

'OK. I'll try it. For two minutes. Just to get us in with the locals. But then I will "sprain an ankle" and get off stage.'

Carlos rose and held out his hand. 'We're in,' he called.

Jodi glanced down, saw the glint of the ring on his finger and the knowledge that he'd trusted her sent a warmth through her, shimmered a connection in the air as she placed her hand in his. Hand in hand they moved towards the group of people on the dance floor. 'Seeing as we are thinking of relocating to Talonos, we think learning a traditional dance would be a good start.'

Jodi felt an irrational surge of panic as they stepped onto the dance floor, could hear the echo of laughter from down the years. Then Carlos squeezed her hand gently. 'You've got this.'

'I'm Katerina and this is Michael,' a tall, graceful woman, one of the dance troupe, said. 'And we'll take you through the basic steps. We'll go nice and slow. Stand in a line and place your hand on the shoulder of the person next to you. Now simply copy our movements. A step to the right, and another and then to the left.'

Jodi tried to concentrate on what Katerina was saying. But the same looming panic she had felt aged ten started to permeate, fuzzed her ability to understand Katerina's instructions. Somehow left became right and right became left and the music seemed to skip a beat as the fear of failure escalated inside her. And just like then, here came the voice of the teacher. 'Perhaps relax a little more, Jodi. You seem tense. Relax into the moves and they will come more naturally.'

'Sorry. Yes. I'll try.' Though she knew there was no point and she'd end up ruining it for everyone else. But if she quit now she'd look petulant or a bad sport. And she'd mis-stepped again. And she knew exactly how fake a sprained ankle manoeuvre would look at this stage.

'OK, guys, take a breather and we'll get going in five.'

Jodi headed back to their table at speed and sat down. 'I told you I was pants.'

'You're not pants, and you aren't the only one making mistakes. That is part of learning.' He glanced at her. 'Tell me why this is worrying you so much.'

She sighed, figured she might as well tell him. 'When I was a child, I insisted on going to ballet classes.' Another pastime Ava had excelled in. The words of a gushing article were still etched on her soul.

'The talented Casseveti heir shows her moves at the national dance contests. Ava has class, grace and a natural talent.'

Oh, how Jodi had tried and, oh, how spectacularly she'd failed. Always a beat behind or the one with the wrong leg in the air. Turned out that was another talent the gods of genetics had bestowed on her sister but not on her. 'I was very bad. The whole thing came to a head during a performance; I'd been given a role I suspect they thought even I couldn't mess up. Well, I did. Not only that, I ended up doing some sort of a slapstick routine and the entire audience burst into laughter. I was mortified.' Even more so because she'd practised so hard, hoped she could emulate Ava in some small way. The laughter, even though she knew it hadn't been malicious, still echoed mockingly in her ears. 'So I've hung up my dancing shoes. For good.'

'This isn't ballet,' he pointed out. 'You have a natural grace; you need to channel it.'

Jodi stared at him. 'Natural grace? Me? I think you may be delusional.'

'Nope. I'm not.'

He sat opposite her, took her hands in his and turned them over, gently swirled his thumb over the palm of her hand; the sensation triggered a rhythmic pulse of plea-sure. 'When you talk you move your hands and you do so with grace. The way you walk; your body moves with a natural elegance. I saw you sway to music in Jalpura. I walked with you... I held you.' She understood he meant more than that; he was remembering how their bodies had moved together, so attuned to each other, they'd moved as one. 'Your grace is innate; you just need to believe in it.'

'I...' Rising, he came round the table. 'Hey. What are you doing?' she asked as he came to stand behind her.

'Relaxing you.' Then before she could protest his fin-gers started to knead into her shoulders, digging deep, unravelling knots that had accumulated. She let out the smallest of moans, hoped the sound of the musicians drowned it out. 'Now I want you to focus on this feeling whilst we're dancing. On how good this feels and then go with the flow.'

The deep rumble of his voice shivered over her skin, mixed with the pressure of his fingers and morphed into a simmer of awareness of exactly how magical his touch could be. Now all she could focus on was Carlos, the rest of the room mere background noise as her body seemed to melt under his touch.

Until the bliss ceased as Katerina recalled them to the floor.

They started again, the music began its beat and this time she let it wash over her and for the first time in her life the moves came effortlessly; she was moving in time to the music, with everyone else and it felt amazing. Until she was aware the music had quickened a bit too much and she knew it was time to stop.

Seamlessly she stepped out of the line, and Carlos moved across. 'I loved it. Thank you,' she said to Katerina as she walked past her and back to the table, smiling a grateful thanks to Andreas when she saw the jug of iced water on the table.

She watched as the pace picked up; Carlos and a few others were still going, the music now swooping and diving faster and faster, and Jodi was soon stamping her feet, clapping and shouting encouragement along with everyone else. Then Katerina and Michael joined the line along with Andreas and his wife, but her attention was riveted to Carlos.

He danced with an almost feral contained vitality, no energy wasted, each step in perfect time with the music, as he lunged down using the controlled strength of his thigh muscles before he rose into the next move. Eventually he mis-stepped; a mis-step Jodi was one hundred per cent certain was false; it must have occurred to him that people might question this level of talent in an American tourist.

He raised a hand to acknowledge the applause and walked back to the table.

'You were amazing,' she said, all too aware that she meant it on way too many levels. Her adrenalin was already buzzing from her own achievement, from the music and the atmosphere. But now as she looked at Carlos, the slight sheen of sweat on the clean line of sculpted muscle, her lungs constricted as her breath caught in pure desire.

He sat down and now his gaze focused on her and she saw something spark in his eyes; looking up, she caught a glimpse of her own reflection in the circular mosaic mirror on the walls. She barely recognised herself: her face flushed, hair dishevelled, lips parted. As if mesmerised he reached out and, oh, so gently tucked a tendril of hair behind her ear.

'You were pretty good yourself,' he said, his voice low, and she shivered. 'I knew you could do it.'

He cleared his throat and then took a gulp of water and now her gaze fixated on the strong column of his throat, the tilt of his head, and the firm jut of his jaw.

Get a grip.

'Yes, but not in your league. I know you said you learnt the dance when you were young, but you looked like a pro.'

'I got carried away.'

She looked across at him, and now she could see sadness in his eyes.

'It all came back to me when the music started—I haven't danced like that in years. Decades. Not since my mother died. She taught me that dance. She loved to dance. I remember swirling round in a frenzy, getting dizzy and laughing, but she would still be keeping time to the music.'

'That is a lovely memory.' And for a moment she envied him that—she would never have any memories of James. All her knowledge gleaned from Luca and magazines. 'Perhaps she saw you dance, looking down from her star.' Because now she knew who he had been thinking of that night in Jalpura when they'd lain on the beach and looked up at the stars.

'You remember,' he said and there was a note of wonder in his tone.

'Yes, I do.' She remembered everything of that day and night, recalled their closeness, the sense of connection and rightness she'd felt under the stars. Knew in the here and now he was sharing something precious with her, sensed he never spoke of his mother. He'd said his father and stepmother believed he should simply forget her and move on. The idea, however well-meaning, seemed callous, and she reached out and covered his hand with her own. 'What was she like?' She hesitated. 'I'm not asking to pry. I just thought maybe you'd like to talk about her, remember her.'

He glanced away as if looking back into the past. 'I was only six when she died,' he said quietly. 'Sometimes I wonder if my memories are real or made up. I do remember she was beautiful, but somehow fragile as well, almost ethereal. She had long blonde hair; she said she'd never cut it so she was like Rapunzel. She loved chocolate pretzels and she loved Disney films and fairy tales.'

'That makes her real,' she said quietly. 'I think she'd be glad you hold those memories. And she would be proud of you. Not only for your dancing ability but for who you are. I am sorry she died when you were so young; she would have loved the chance to watch you grow up.'

His hand clenched involuntarily under hers and shadows raced across his eyes, a pain so deep she flinched. 'I'm sorry, Carlos.'

'You have nothing to be sorry for. It was good to remember her; everyone deserves that—to be remembered to show that their life mattered. And I hope she is looking down.' The fervour in his voice held an edge of bitterness she didn't fully understand. Then again his feelings, his grief, must be so complex. Now his hand squeezed hers gently. 'Thank you, Jodi.'

Before she could answer, his expression morphed to a smile of welcome and soon she realised why as Andreas approached the table.

'You ready for dessert? You've both earned it.' He

turned to Carlos. 'If you do move here you could pick up some extra money in our dance troupe.' He nodded towards the bar where a group of locals were gathered. 'If the two of you want to join us, we're happy to give you some advice or answer any questions.'

Two hours later they exited the taverna and Carlos looked down at Jodi. 'You must be tired. I am sorry. We should not have stayed so long.'

'I am a little tired, but I enjoyed myself. I like them all very much. But some of the things they said were...'

'Unexpected.' In truth he'd been shocked. Andreas had told them of friends of theirs whose taverna had failed due to a sharp increase in tax on local businesses.

'Rises made to mitigate the tax cuts given to overseas corporations.'

His wife, Annette, had snorted. 'They are friends of the royals—so they are given grace and favour.'

'Perhaps the new one will make a difference.'

'Even if he wants to make a difference the King won't let him. And so it will continue for people like Michaelis.'

Carlos frowned—he had long known that his father saw royalty as a special class of its own, believed that it still was as it used to be. Where kings were all-powerful, ordained by divine right, and the people were subjects whose well-being was of less importance than the King's concerns.

Jodi sighed. 'It sounds so tough, especially because they are worried about their children. If their little boy has special needs it sounds like the schools here, especially in the poorer areas, don't have the funding to help.'

'And if you can't afford to pay a tutor your child suffers.' He increased his pace. 'It is hard to hear this about my country.'

'Hey, slow down.'

'Sorry.'

She slipped her hand into his. 'I know it is hard to hear but I believe you will make a difference. It may take time, but you will.'

Frustration gnawed inside him, because he knew Andreas had been right. His father would never take any advice from him and would do everything he could to make his position a sinecure.

'I hope so. Thank you for today. I know you didn't want to go on the dance floor.'

'But I'm glad I did. I feel pretty good that I did something out of my comfort zone, got over something that had affected me more than I knew. And I'm truly glad we got the opportunity to learn more from Andreas and Annette.'

'So am I.' Even if he wasn't sure what he could do about it.

CHAPTER ELEVEN

JODI OPENED HER EYES, stared up at the lace canopy, watched the gauze ruffle in the sweet-scented breeze and wondered what had woken her. Despite her tiredness sleep hadn't come easy, her senses heightened by the knowledge of Carlos so near and yet so very far.

There was a rap on the door, one that seemed to echo from her half-waking state.

'Breakfast,' a cheerful voice called out.

Hell's bells! It all seeped back into her consciousness: Roseanna the day before mentioning a honeymoon package—had there been something about breakfast in bed, delivered at ten o'clock? A glance at her phone showed her that her memory might be late, but accurate.

Now what?

The curtain that separated the suite from the bed was pushed apart and Carlos stepped out. Jodi nearly swallowed her tongue. Managed a strangled, '*Eep...* Honeymoon. Breakfast. Package.' Then, as his eyes glinted sleepy amusement, she realised that the words could be taken in a very different way. 'At the door,' she said, and pulled her eyes away from the fact that he wore only a pair of jeans.

She could see the flat six-pack, the tantalising curve where the waistband of his jeans dipped low. And raising her gaze didn't help as she caught an eyeful of bare, muscled chest, and her fingers tingled as they remembered that magical night, when they had been free to touch, to roam all over and...

Another rap on the door and she cast an agonised glance at Carlos as he headed to open it. Quickly he threw his phone across to her and she placed it on 'his' bedside cabinet and rumpled up his side of the bed. Pushed one of her pillows across.

And tried to look relaxed as Carlos pulled the door open. 'Sorry. We were in a really deep sleep. Must be the Talonos air. This looks grand. I'll take it from here.'

Carlos rolled the trolley in and looked at the room, before lifting the lids of the platters. 'This is a great idea but I'm not sure where we're supposed to eat it.'

'I think the idea is we eat in bed.' No doubt honeymooners fed each other bits of the heart-shaped pancakes she'd spotted along with heart-shaped poached eggs. Large succulent strawberries rimmed a pot of chocolate sauce and her mouth watered.

'I'll take mine through.'

'No,' Jodi said on instinct. 'That's exactly what may blow our cover—if they clean in here and find crumbs in there or the smell of coffee or something we forget to clear away.'

'So what do you suggest?'

'We eat the breakfast in the bed. I mean, it's not really any different than sitting opposite each other at a table.'

He raised his eyebrows. 'Apart from the fact it's a bed and you are in pyjamas. I like them, by the way.'

She narrowed her eyes. 'There is nothing wrong with pyjamas that have a cartoon character on them. At least I have some pyjamas.'

'I didn't think honeymooners would bother,' he countered, and she couldn't help it, she grinned.

'Touché. Now you've out-bantered me, let's eat.'

To her considerable relief he pulled a T-shirt on before sitting cross-legged at the end of the bed with his plate heaped as full as hers. The sheer intimacy suddenly hit her, and her gaze snagged on him as he sat there, his hair ruffled in the breeze, a cheese pastry in his hand. This could be hers if she wanted—breakfast with this man every day. Surely a no-brainer.

Only in reality royal life would not be like this. The only reason they were acting this way was because it was a pretence. Ironically if they got married there would be no need for them to share breakfast in bed. And she suspected this was not something he would do through choice.

'So, is this the sort of thing Carl Williamson did a lot?'

He looked startled. 'What sort of thing? Have breakfast in bed with a beautiful woman in cartoon pyjamas?'

'No. Well, yes, apart from the pyjamas.'

'You mean do I usually have breakfast in bed with naked beautiful women?'

Again she felt laughter bubbling up, along with a happiness that he'd called her beautiful. Twice. 'No. I meant do you go on holidays like this? With a woman, go dancing, visit historic places and, yes, have breakfast in bed? Naked or clothed.'

He shook his head. 'No, I don't. I haven't ever gone on a proper holiday with a woman before. Maybe a weekend or a night away. But a holiday has always felt too much, like it may send the wrong message.'

'What message?'

'That I want a "serious relationship".'

'So you've never had a serious relationship?'

'Just the one, though I am not sure you could class it as such.'

'Why not?'

'Because it wasn't real. I thought it was—I thought we were in love. I met Lisa at a party and we got on really well. Or so I thought—we had lots in common and we started seeing each other. It turned out that it was all a set-up. She was using me to find out details of properties about to come on the market and was selling the tips to another estate agent so they could get in first. The other estate agent happened to be a rival and her boyfriend. Eventually I figured it out.' But not before he'd fallen for Lisa; she could hear the remembered hurt and humiliation in his voice, recognised it all too well. After all, she knew what it felt like to be used.

'What happened.'

'A friend of mine, a colleague, told me he'd seen Lisa with the other estate agent. At first I wouldn't believe him; it was a classic case of "shoot the messenger" mixed with "bury my head in the sand". But I couldn't forget what he said, and once I knew I could see the truth. In the end I followed her and caught her.' Jodi winced, could imagine the pain—he'd trusted Lisa, defended her, believed in her and she'd betrayed that. 'I ended the "relationship" and confessed all to my employer, who promptly and quite rightly fired me.'

'What did you do?'

'Got myself another job. Five years later I bought out the estate agent where my rival worked.'

'Did you sack him?'

'Absolutely not. I simply made it clear I wouldn't tolerate underhanded practices on a moral basis and because I really didn't think they brought success.'

'And since Lisa you haven't had another serious relationship?'

'Nope.' He shrugged. 'In some ways she did me a favour. I learnt from it. Learnt not to put myself in that position again. Since Lisa I've kept my relationships brief, fun and uncomplicated. I am not interested in love.' He met her gaze directly. 'Is that a problem for you? Do you believe a happy ever after has to involve undying love?'

Jodi shook her head. 'No, I don't. Like you I've been hurt and I won't risk that again.'

'What happened?' he asked as he placed his empty plate down and cradled his mug of coffee, his blue eyes intent.

'He was called Tim. I thought he was wonderful; he was attentive, kind, caring. I thought we loved each other. Turned out what he loved was my money—when I met him Luca's business was really taking off, my mum has a highly paid job. I was doing my business degree at the time and Luca offered to pay me an allowance.' She hadn't wanted to accept but Tim had persuaded her, told her they were family, that she had a right to it, that Palazzo di Cioccolato was a family business, that Luca wanted her to be part of it. At the time she'd hoped her degree was the start to her being able to do just that, had visions of being like Ava and working her way up the family business. So she'd let Tim persuade her. 'I couldn't see it until after we split but looking back it's obvious. And then…then he left me.' The memory she knew she would never forget, never truly get over. Waking up and seeing Tim standing there, looking down at her. The cruelty of his words.

'I was thinking of Ava whilst making love to you.'

And the rest of it.

'I've realised now that you won't ever be rich, so I'm cashing in what I can.'

'Because he realised I wasn't as wealthy as he believed.' She could not, would not, share the details of her humiliation with Carlos.

'I'm sorry,' he said.

Jodi shook her head. 'Don't be. Like you, I learnt from

it. But I decided to avoid dating anyone. Full stop. And I have no wish or belief in love—it's too complicated.'

'It distorts things. You saw Tim through the eyes of love, just as I did Lisa. It's like a filter—it tints things pink and rosy and paints illusions. Makes you see what you want to see, believe what you want to believe.' The grim set of his lips made her wonder whether he spoke of more than his own experience with Lisa.

But he was right—she had done exactly that with Tim. Seen what she'd wanted to see and it had ended in betrayal. As for her parents' love, that too had proved to be an illusion that did not stand up to the responsibility of family life. Could not withstand the temptation of another woman and the lure of riches.

Her gaze fell on the heart-shaped pancakes piled up on the plate and she gave a sudden rueful smile. 'I guess these pancakes are a bit wasted on us, then,' she said.

Now his expression relaxed as he shook his head. 'Not at all. A pancake is a pancake—whatever shape it is. And you and I can see that—we don't need our pancakes to be heart-shaped because we can appreciate them for what they really are. A delicious mixture of milk, sugar, flour and eggs.'

Jodi nodded, knew Carlos was right. Yet a fleeting disquiet niggled, a touch of sadness at the thought of life without heart-shaped pancakes.

Ridiculous.

Especially when there was so much more for her to think about. 'You're right. So I suggest we finish them off before we pack up and move on to our next port of call.'

Carlos watched Jodi as she gazed out of the train window.

'It's beautiful,' she said.

'I think so.' As the stations had passed they had left the

urban landscape behind and now they were in the Talonos countryside, where groves of olive trees wended across the horizon with flashes of silver-grey leaves that caught the morning sunlight. Twisted trunks rose majestically from the glow of the rich rust-red earth that lent an air of grandeur to the vista. As well it should. 'Some of those trees are hundreds and hundreds of years old and for centuries they have provided Talonos with one of its most enduring exports. Our olive oil is renowned for its lush, rich overtones.'

Jodi nodded. 'I read that the different areas produce really different types of oil, a bit like vineyards make different wine.'

'Exactly.'

'Is that where we are going? To visit an olive grove?'

'As part of our tour we will, but today we are going to stay in a small rural village. The whole province is made up of lots of small towns or villages, each of which has its own feel or character or sometimes even dialect. Its own separate identity—which is great in some ways, but it can mean they get forgotten in the needs of the cities, the touristy places, the restaurants and luxury hotels. I don't want rural areas falling behind…the problem is there is so much I don't know, so much to learn.'

'Then this looks like a great place to start.'

They alighted and made their way to the sole taxi outside the station. The young man inside the shiny car smiled at them and Carlos gave the name of the hotel.

'My sister, Angelina, runs the hotel,' the driver said. 'My name is Marco and I help out as much as I can so you will probably see me around the place. Are you planning on staying long?'

'We're thinking about moving here permanently, so this is a research trip.'

'Think carefully. I love this village but it's not easy. You need to speak the language and there aren't many jobs and most of them are agricultural or manual. But it's a wonderful place if you're happy to live a simple life. I left, went to England for a few years, but I ended up coming back to help my sister after her husband died.'

'I'm so sorry.' Jodi shifted forward in her seat. 'That must have been awful for her.' Carlos could hear the sincerity in her voice and the concern.

'It hasn't been easy. She has a son, my nephew, Sammy—so running the hotel and looking after him in some ways has been a godsend, she is so busy, but I worry that she hasn't had time to grieve properly. And I am worried that she is exhausted.'

'She is lucky to have you, but it must be tough for her.' There was something in her voice Carlos couldn't quite identify.

'It is but Angelina has a strength I didn't know she had. I think she has surprised herself. She and Sam loved each other very much. The shock when he died was huge; I thought she may give up on the hotel. They took it on as a project but now she is doing it all herself. Angelina works all the hours and the government takes the taxes. So much so that she can hardly afford to pay for the repairs. Yet further down the coast a rich development company got planning permission to build a swanky resort because they get tax cuts and benefits. It's all about the big companies.' He came to a halt and shook his head. 'Anyway, enough. You do not want to hear all this.'

Actually, he did, Carlos thought. There should be help for people like Angelina, people trying to help themselves in the face of adversity and misfortune.

'She sounds amazing and I bet she is glad to have a brother like you,' Jodi said.

'We look out for each other,' he said simply.

A few minutes later Marco pulled up outside and looked at them with a slight worry in the back of his brown eyes. 'It looks a little run-down. But it is clean and you will be well looked after.'

'This looks beautiful,' Carlos said, injecting reassurance into his voice as Jodi chimed in.

'It's beautiful.'

And it was. Yes, the building did look a little weather-ravaged and he could see that there were repairs needed, but potted plants and flowers bloomed vivid and scented the air. Colourful curtains fluttered at the wooden windows and the steps and path to the door were scrubbed and swept clean.

'I try to do as many repairs as I can, but...' Marco shrugged as he unloaded their luggage. 'Come on through.'

But before they could a young boy came running out of the house. 'Uncle Marco.'

'Sammy.'

Sammy broke into a flood of Talonese and Carlos tensed even as he pretended not to understand.

Marco turned to them. 'Could you wait here, please? I will be right back.'

He scooped his nephew up and strode forward and Jodi turned to Carlos. 'What's happening?'

'It sounded like Angelina was preparing our suite when something collapsed. I am not sure whether she is physically hurt or upset or both. Let's go in and see what's happening.'

They made their way inside and Carlos could see the touches of care. Cheerful pictures dotted the walls; the reception desk was a simple old school one but redolent with flowers and polish. Upstairs, they entered a room that still had a cascade of dust. Carlos stepped forward immediately to where a woman lay on the bed, her face twisted with pain. Marco was sitting beside her, and Sammy stood close by, thumb in his mouth.

'What happened?' Carlos asked.

'Please. It does not matter. I told you to go to them.' The woman struggled to sit up, went even paler and caught her lip between her teeth. 'I am sorry. Your booking. I will have to cancel it.'

'Please don't worry about the booking,' Carlos broke in. 'Are you OK?'

'No, she isn't,' Marco said. 'The ceiling caved whilst Angelina was trying to move a wardrobe. On her own.' It was clear he was torn between exasperation at his sister and concern.

'The woman who normally helps has been called away on an emergency,' Angelina said. 'And I did not know the ceiling would fall. We are sorry. Would you like me to book you into another hotel?'

Jodi glanced at Carlos and then stepped forward. 'No. That won't be necessary. The most important thing now is to make sure you're OK. Why don't you get Angelina to the doctor?'

Angelina bit her lip. 'But you need a room.'

'Please, do not worry about us,' Carlos said.

Marco nodded. 'Come, Angelina. I will take you over to Dr Thesapoulis now.'

CHAPTER TWELVE

TEN MINUTES LATER and Carlos paced the garden. 'This is not right. There should be more help for Angelina. From the government.'

Jodi laid a hand on his arm. 'I have an idea.'

'Go ahead.'

'I want to stay here,' Jodi said. 'I want to help Angelina.' She knew she sounded nuts, but there was something about Angelina, her courage, her grit, her determination, her love for her child that reminded her of how her own mother had been with Luca. The parallels so similar. 'In person. She will need help with Sammy. Maybe we could help make some repairs. Help with the cooking.' She shrugged. 'I don't really know. But if we were really Carl and JoJo, I think that's what we'd do. Help the community we plan to live in.'

He looked at her with an expression she couldn't interpret. 'But it's more than that. You really *want* to do this.'

'Yes, I do.'

'Why?'

'Because…' She hesitated. 'It seems to me there are different ways of changing things. Things need to be changed from the top, of course they do—laws and rules—but right here and now Angelina needs on-the-ground help. Now. I want to give her that.'

Doubt clouded his eyes. 'I do want to help, but it's risky.

The more involved we get, the longer we stay, the more likely I am to be recognised. I spoke with Stefan earlier; he says he tried to plant the idea that I had gone to the States but he isn't sure everyone believed him.'

'I think it's worth the risk. To help them.'

'I get that you want to help, but this feels personal.'

'It is.' If she wanted Carlos to agree, to help, then she owed it to him to explain why she wanted to do this so badly. 'Angelina reminds me of my mum. She was left with a child to bring up just like Angelina. My father—' the word felt awkward, tasted bitter '—left her with nothing. She was truly destitute and even worse she was pregnant with me. I know it's different, Angelina's husband died, she has Marco…but she still needs help. There were hard times when the kindness of strangers made a difference—a local shopkeeper who helped with food, a neighbour who lent her enough for a deposit so she could get us a place to stay. Kind people who advised her on benefits. I want to pass that on.' She broke off and looked up at him; the moment held a sense of significance, of senses heightened. The scent of the flowers seemed to drench the air…the drone of insects buzzed. 'What do you think?'

He looked down at her, then he leant down and so, so softly brushed his lips against her cheek, the silk of his lips a contrast to the slight scrape of his stubble. Then he took her hands in his, as though they were making a pact. 'I think you're right. JoJo and Carl would do this. Let's do it.'

Happiness sizzled through her; Carlos had listened to her, was doing this for her. Not for the baby, not for himself, but for her. 'Thank you.' The urge to stand on tiptoe and kiss him properly almost overwhelmed her and she pushed it down. She had to remember that they weren't Carl and JoJo—they weren't a real couple. He was a prince and he wanted to marry her because she was carrying his baby. Or, to be absolutely truthful, Carlos wanted to marry her *if* she was carrying his baby.

That was the bottom line and she mustn't forget it. But in the meantime she could do something good here, for Angelina and Sammy, and that was what she would focus on.

Jodi smiled across the room at Angelina, who sat on a sofa in her bedroom, her leg propped up. 'How are you feeling?' she asked.

'Much better. That sleep really helped. Thank you for helping with Sam. Thank you for everything. This is so kind of you and Carl.'

'We want to help and we told you—this works for us. We get to stay here and get a real feel for the place. And Sammy is gorgeous. All he wanted me to do was read to him.'

'We are trying to keep his English going. His dad was English and we hope that the language can be a link to him. I know he misses him.'

'I'm sorry for your loss.'

'It has not been easy and sometimes it feels so very unfair. Sam was a good man and he did not deserve to die so young. I just wish Sammy did not blame himself. He thinks it was his fault because he was in the car with his dad.' The dark-haired woman shook her head. 'I am sorry. This is not what you need to hear.'

'It's fine.' Jodi squeezed Angelina's hand, her heart going out to both her and Sammy. 'If you want, I could teach Sam some more English whilst I'm here. If he'd like.'

'He would like that very much.'

'Now you look tired. Will you come down for dinner or shall I bring you some up on a tray?'

'If it is OK with you, I will stay up here. Marco has brought the TV up and I will be near to Sam if he wakes.'

'Of course.'

Though as she left the room Jodi almost wished that Angelina had opted to join them; somehow the idea of having dinner with Carlos in such a domestic setting felt scarily intimate and invoked a thread of shyness mixed with anticipation.

Daft. She should see it as an opportunity to get to know him better. To try to find an answer to the burning question of what to do.

As she entered the kitchen she paused and gulped.

Carlos stood behind the stove, shirt sleeves rolled up to reveal tanned forearms, his blond hair glinting in the last lingering beams of sunlight that gleamed through the open window.

She managed a smile as he looked up. 'Smells good.'

'It's my world-famous spaghetti bolognese, served with green salad.'

'That sounds lovely. Thank you for cooking.' The shyness upped a notch alongside a desire to simply stand and watch him. His movements were deft: a sprinkle of herbs, a quick stir and then a swirl of the spaghetti as he dropped it into the boiling water.

'No problem. Is Angelina OK?'

'Yes. Just exhausted, I think.' Jodi pulled open a drawer in search of cutlery. 'I am glad they agreed to let us help. I wasn't sure if Marco would like the idea; I thought he may feel he could help Angelina himself.' She smiled suddenly. 'He reminds me of Luca: a protective older brother.'

Sadness flashed across his eyes, but it was gone so fast she wasn't sure if she'd imagined it as he heaped their plates with swirls of spaghetti and topped it with the aromatic sauce.

Once he'd taken a plate up for Angelina he returned and

sat opposite her; she tasted the food and gave a murmur of appreciation. 'This is delicious.'

'Good. I'm glad you like it. Tell me about Luca. I only know that he founded and runs Palazzo di Cioccolato.'

'His job is massively important to him—he always knew what he wanted to do. Even as a child, he had a passion for chocolate. He can taste a square of chocolate and tell you exactly how it was made. I tried so hard to be like him but to me...chocolate is just chocolate.'

How she'd wished life could be simple, that she too could share Luca's talent, become part of his company. But she hadn't. Not as a chocolatier or a businesswoman. Yes, she'd got her business degree, but she wasn't a natural at finance or marketing, knew any job Luca gave her would be a sinecure and she hadn't wanted that.

'But to Luca it is a vocation—that's why Palazzo di Cioccolato is so successful. That and his drive and ambition. But there's more to him than that. He was six when I was born and as we got older he looked after me a lot. So Mum could study, and then go to work.' Her face softened. 'But he never made me feel like a chore or that he didn't want to be there. He'd always have my back.'

'You are lucky to have that connection.' He sounded wistful and she wondered what his own relationship with his half-brother was, had a sudden urge to reach out and hug him. 'Yet you haven't told him about the baby?'

'No. He has enough on his plate right now. With Dolci and all the surrounding publicity. I jumped ship and left him to face the whole will, inheritance fiasco on his own.' Guilt reignited inside her along with worry—Luca's messages had been different recently. Her brother seemed more relaxed about Jodi's continued disappearance, which was good but...a part of her worried he'd given up on her, had bonded with Ava. Replaced her. *Enough. Just answer the question.* 'If I tell him, he will go into protective mode. He would want to sort it out for me and this time I wanted to, needed to, sort things out myself.' After all, if she couldn't do that what sort of parent would she be? She looked up at him. 'In the next week or so hopefully I'll have a clearer idea of the best thing to do. For the baby.'

'*We* will have a clearer idea,' he said.

She met his gaze. 'You already have a clear idea—you believe the best thing for the baby is for us to get married. Once you have proof the baby is yours.'

'Yes, I do.' He hesitated. 'I did some research into the DNA test and it is completely non-invasive. There is absolutely no risk to the baby at all. I want you to know that if there had been I would not ask you to do it.'

'I know,' she said, and she meant it. Knew Carlos would never prioritise his need for proof over a baby. But the words served as an additional reminder that they truly were not Carl and JoJo. That Carlos only wanted to marry her if she carried his heir. 'And I will do the test. To give you the proof you need. But that doesn't help me with the decision about marriage.'

'What would help?' he asked. 'Are you worried we won't be happy? I promise you I will do everything in my power to make sure we are.'

In that moment she believed him, was almost carried away by the sheer power of his personality. Almost. 'But you can't guarantee it. No one can. And what happens if we aren't happy? If I want to leave. What will happen to the baby? He'll be a prince, the heir to Talonos. I won't be *able* to leave—I won't be allowed to take the heir to the throne away.' Panic suddenly hit her at the realisation of what he was asking her to do.

'I would never let my child grow up without his mother. If you ever decide you want to leave then we would have joint custody.' His voice was calm. 'You would have to live on Talonos, yes, but I would never take him from you. I grew up without a mother—I would not wish that on anyone.' There was no mistaking the sincerity in his voice. 'We can write that into a prenuptial agreement if you like.'

'But what about money? I'll be dependent on you.'

'No. You won't. You will be paid a salary.'

'You mean an allowance.' Jodi could hear the bitterness in her voice.

'No. I mean a salary. Being a princess is a job. If you want, you can take on a specialised role, take on a portfolio—education, finance, tourism...' The idea made her head spin. 'Or if you prefer you can get a job outside the royal court. I would not stand in your way.'

'You have an answer to everything.'

'That's because there is an answer to everything. Not always a palatable one, but usually there is a solution. Of course, there will be things to think about—security, publicity, practicalities, but I promise I will try to find a way for you to pursue any job you want.'

'Thank you.'

'There is no need for thanks.' His voice was gentle. 'I understand that what I am asking of you will have a massive impact on your life. But I believe we can make it work. For the baby. And I believe we can be happy. We'll have liking, respect, affection.' The deep rumble of his voice sizzled heat over her skin. 'And attraction.'

And that should be enough. More than enough. Shouldn't it? Jodi closed her eyes, suddenly wanted to block out his face, the intensity of his blue eyes, the shape of his jaw, the strength and warmth of his body. Liking, respect, affection. Attraction. They were good things, could be the bedrock of a successful marriage.

Yet for a stupid moment she'd wanted to inspire more than that, which was beyond foolish. She knew better than that. Opening her eyes, she rose to her feet, picked up their empty plates. 'And right now we also have dessert,' she said. 'Angelina said we should help ourselves to her home-made chocolate mousse.'

An hour later, the kitchen clean and gleaming, they headed towards the stairs and Carlos could feel his feet lag with every step. The glow of illumination on the deep red of the carpet, the polished sheen of the bannisters, the blanket of silence somehow heightened the sense of intimacy, the fact they were walking upstairs to go to bed. Just as JoJo and Carl might.

He cleared his throat. 'Angelina said to choose whichever room we wanted, so I put our cases in the largest one,' he said. 'You take the bed and I'll sleep on the floor.'

'Actually.' She took a deep breath and turned to him as they entered. 'I don't think that will work.' She gestured to the bed and a slight heat touched her cheeks. 'It's too risky and we are already taking a big risk that you will be recognised. If Sammy runs in here and finds you sleeping on the floor we'd have a lot of questions to answer. Plus we've got a lot of work ahead of us and you'll be exhausted if you don't get any sleep.'

Now his throat was parched as he looked at the bed, tried to imagine sleeping next to Jodi. An image of months before entered his mind: their two bodies twined together, sated and exhausted, the feel of her head on his chest, the silken tickle of her dark curls. He remembered waking in the small hours of the morning to find they'd shifted and he was spooned against her. He had dropped a kiss on the nape of her neck and she'd turned, opened sleep-filled eyes and smiled at him and…

Carlos paused the thought. 'Um… I'm not sure…'

I'm not sure how much sleep I'd get sharing a bed with you.

'So, we can put some pillows down the middle,' she continued, 'and it will be fine.'

Yup. That would make all the difference.

'What do you think?' Her voice sounded overbright, the words a little too fast and he wondered if her mind was travelling the same road as his. 'After all, we are considering getting married.'

'Yes, but when we share a bed then…we'll be married.' That really would make all the difference. He managed a smile. 'Which will make sharing a bed far less…complicated,' he settled for. Decided it was best to keep on talking. 'Plus we'll have separate suites.' Which was a good thing, the idea of sleeping next to Jodi every night not for him. The invasion of space, the intimacy—too dangerous. 'But, yes, I think you're right. It makes sense to share the bed. But first we have to make it. I'll do that whilst you use the bathroom if you like?'

But as he made the bed, tucked in the sheets, shook out and smoothed the duvet the whole scene still seemed eerily intimate, his senses heightened as the flower-scented breeze ruffled the curtains and moonlight dappled the bed.

She exited the bathroom, and he looked away, out at the night sky, then moved towards the bathroom, his newly acquired pyjamas in hand, and heard her practically dive into the bed.

Ten minutes later he walked across the bedroom, heard her low gurgle of laughter as she spotted the pyjamas. He'd deliberately chosen cartoon characters to match hers.

'They suit you,' she said, and he held his arms out and turned, heard her laughter morph to something else, her brown eyes widened in the moonlight.

Hurriedly he climbed into bed, felt the warmth of the barrier of pillows, tried to force his body to relax.

'Goodnight,' he said.

'Goodnight.'

Yet sleep evaded him; he was too aware of Jodi, so near he could hear the rise and fall of her breath, the too regular breathing that told him she too was awake.

'Jodi?'

'Yes.'

'Are you awake?'

He could feel her smile in the darkness at the sheer redundancy of the question, could picture her lips curving upwards, sparkling her eyes with mischief. 'Yes. Are you?'

'Yes. Just thinking.'

'Me too.'

'What are you thinking about?' It seemed easy to ask the question, in the darkened room, the moonlight coming through the flutter of the curtains, the quiet of the night time.

'I'm scared.' Her voice was small now. 'This is going to sound selfish. I do want to put the baby first. I want to give him everything I didn't have. A father, a family with two parents. But what about me? How will my life work? I've no idea how to be royal—you were born to it. Will I make my own bed in my separate royal suite? What happens if I want a cup of tea and a biscuit in the middle of the night? What if I want to go shopping at the local store in my pyjamas with a coat on top?'

'I think you probably will have to pass on option three. As for the day-to-day life in a palace—it is different, but we can work it out together. I have spent the last decade as Carl Williamson, making my own bed, washing my own clothes, cooking my own food. It will be strange for us both.'

'But you grew up royal, it's bred in you. I won't know what to do, how to act. I won't fit.' Her voice was low with a husk of emotion and he reached out and took her hand; the slenderness of her fingers evoked a fierce sense of protection in him. He wanted to mitigate her worry, make this right for Jodi. Because until now his focus had been on this marriage being best for the baby, best for Talonos. But was it the best thing for Jodi? The unspoken words seemed to shimmer in the darkness and guilt nudged him.

'I get that. I don't fit either—because royalty wasn't bred in me or taught to me. I don't know what I'm doing either.'

He sensed her shift, turn her head towards him, their hands still clasped together on the pillows. 'I don't understand.'

For a moment he hesitated but he knew he had to reassure her, wanted her to understand that they would be in this together, that he truly got it.

'I was technically a prince, but my father and stepmother didn't see it that way. To them I was the one with tainted blood.'

'Tainted by what?' There was outrage in her voice.

'By my mother because she was a commoner, by circumstance because I was born out of wedlock. To Isabella I was a threat—she needed to make everyone, including me, see that I could not be heir.' And she had done so from the get-go; as soon as she'd set foot in the palace she'd regarded him as dirt on her shoe.

'But that's cruel. Surely your father didn't really believe that. How could he? He loved your mother.'

'No, he didn't. The true story isn't the one that the papers spun. It's true that my mother worked in the palace kitchens and met my father when he was Crown Prince. They did have an affair and my mother fell pregnant. My father refused to marry her, refused even to see me after I was born. My mother decided to take matters into her own hands. She believed that he was refusing to marry her because of family pressure. So she tricked him into marriage. She pretended she was dying, told him she wanted her son to be legitimate. So he waited until I was six months, so not eligible to be heir, then he married her, believing he would be widowed soon enough. Instead my mother announced the marriage to the world and there was nothing my father could do. But he never forgave her or me. But my mother believed that love would conquer all, that my father would come round, that when he became King he would change the law. It didn't happen like that and my father never changed towards me.'

'But it wasn't your fault. Any of it.' Now she sat up and he saw the anger etched on her face. Anger on his behalf— and the idea warmed him. 'You were a child caught up in an adult's world of tricks and deceits. A child who had lost his mother, whatever she'd done. They were *wrong*.' She turned so she was looking down at him. 'You know they were wrong, don't you?'

'Yes.' But he could hear the hollowness in his voice and so could she. 'They were but they achieved what they set out to do. I am not royal; I do not know how to be a crown prince. I was sent away to boarding school in England, away from Talonos, encouraged to stay there for some of the holidays. When I was home I was given a suite in a separate part of the palace; I didn't eat with the family and I was kept away from Juan.' A sadness he seldom allowed himself to feel unfurled inside him. 'I think they are scared of me; the few times we were together was for the sake of publicity. Now I know Juan will never forgive me for taking his position from him.'

'You didn't take it. It was given to you,' she said gently.

'The result is the same; he has lost something infinitely precious to him.'

'Through no fault of yours. This is your right and you will be a great ruler one day. You care about your country and about your people. Perhaps one day your brother will see that and make his peace with it—now you are here maybe he will see that for himself. Or perhaps you could talk to him.'

'Perhaps.' How he wished she could be right, but he knew deep down that it was too late. Juan had made it clear he did not wish to speak with him; even as a child when they were forced together for public occasions he had kept his distance, would hide behind his mother, wide-eyed and silent. Juan had been taught to fear and despise him; now they would hate him as a usurper. He pushed the thoughts away. He had told Jodi all this to reassure her, not to discuss his brother. 'But what I wanted to show you is that we *will* be learning together and perhaps we can make some of our own rules.'

Now she smiled at him. 'We could have a special cupboard for midnight tea and biscuits.'

'That sounds good to me.'

'And, Carlos, thank you for trusting me with this, for sharing.' Leaning down, she brushed a kiss against his cheek. Her hair brushed his jaw and he could smell the sweet scent of soap and an essence of vanilla. The sensation was so sweet, so gentle he felt warmth thread his veins alongside the realisation that he had trusted her. It had not so much as occurred to him she would betray that trust and that in itself sent a sudden shock through him.

And as she snuggled back down on her side of the barrier, their hands were still clasped. Perhaps he should disentangle their fingers, but he didn't want to, wanted this bubble of closeness, of intimacy, to last a little while longer whilst they slept.

CHAPTER THIRTEEN

Three days later

JODI LOOKED ROUND the room that Carlos had spent the past days renovating, with Marco's help whenever he could spare the time from the taxi.

They'd fallen into an easy routine: Jodi would get up and get Sammy ready for school, and she and Carlos would get the breakfast ready for the two families who were staying at the hotel. Carlos would take care to stay in the kitchen and Jodi would wait the tables, serve the food and chat to the guests.

Marco would come and pick Sammy up and take him to the village school, though one day when the teacher was ill Jodi had looked after the little boy herself. In the meantime Carlos got on with repairs and renovations, breaking for a packed lunch that he and Jodi would share. Angelina rested her leg and chatted to Jodi, who made sure to visit her regularly.

One evening Marco had come round and the four of them had eaten dinner and sat chatting and playing cards. The other nights Jodi and Carlos had taken turns cooking; by tacit consent they had kept the conversation light and cheerful, more fact-finding than anything else. Who would have guessed his favourite books would be English classics and detective fiction? Another night they curled up in front of the TV and watched a film—who would have thought he would enjoy superhero films?

'Lunch,' Jodi said now. 'I've made ham and cheese and chilli pickle sandwiches.'

'Sounds good.'

She gestured to the walls. 'This looks incredible. It will make a real difference to Angelina, I think.'

'I hope so.' Carlos bit into a sandwich. 'I wish I could do more. Make a difference for other families like them. The problem is anything I suggest my father will do his best to veto. I have no connections yet and I cannot risk open conflict with my father. That could bring protests to the streets and I will not do that.'

Though she suspected his father would.

'I've been thinking about that.' She'd been thinking a lot; anger burned inside her at the way Carlos had been treated, alongside a compassion for the boy who'd grown up believing his blood to be tainted, isolated and kept away from family life and his country. An invisible prince. 'And it's all about the money.' She pulled a notebook out of her pocket, and opened it up.

'Go ahead,' he said.

'So, your father shows favour to the large conglomerates in order to attract jet-setting tourists or rich people looking for a tax haven. And maybe that's OK—if the money he makes from wealthy overseas investment and the tourists outweighs the tax losses. And as long as the normal citizens of Talonos aren't losing out.'

'But right now they are.'

'So we need to change the balance.' She leant forward. 'By encouraging additional tourism so that people are fairly taxed. I mean, I am not an economist, but if places like Angelina's can make more money, then they could be taxed a lesser percentage and the government will take the same amount, probably more. So investing in places like this would make sense—maybe with grants or affordable loans, or tax holidays. Because there are hundreds of thousands of people who are looking for a picturesque, rustic holiday. But there also needs to be a push to encourage tourist companies that organise holiday tours—so wine-tasting tours, or olive-oil-tasting tours.' She broke off as she saw the way he was looking at her. 'What? I've said something stupid, haven't I? I mean, I know I don't have a head for business but—'

'Whoa.' He raised a hand. 'Where did that come from? I was thinking the exact opposite. These ideas are good. And if I present them as positive ideas aimed at growth, rather than negative ideas aimed at taxing the wealthy more...'

'You'll have more chance of getting them through.' She shrugged. 'I would like nothing better than to go in guns blazing and point out how unfair it is, but I think the way to help people like Angelina is to have a different approach.' Now she smiled. 'And as a cherry on the cake your father and stepmother will know exactly what you are doing, and they won't be able to stand in your way without looking petty and gaining bad publicity for themselves. Win-win.'

'Exactly.' His forehead creased in a frown. 'Why do you think you're not good at business?'

'Because I just passed the degree; I didn't get a distinction and I knew that I wouldn't be any good working at Palazzo di Cioccolato.'

'Maybe you didn't want to work at Palazzo di Cioccolato because chocolate isn't your thing.' He hesitated. 'Maybe you haven't found your thing because you've been too focused on following what your mother and brother have done. You care about people, Jodi—that's why you've come up with such amazing ideas for tourism. Because you care about Angelina and Sammy and Marco and Rose-anna and Andreas and all the people we've met in the past week.' Now he moved closer to her. 'Maybe that's your vocation: working for a cause.'

Jodi's eyes widened—could Carlos be right? Had she been so busy trying to emulate others all her life that she hadn't figured out what made her tick? The idea sent a short sharp shock through her system; before she could say anything his phone buzzed and he glanced down.

'It's Stefan,' he said. 'I'd better take it.'

Jodi watched as Carlos spoke in rapid Talonese. It wasn't good news; she could tell that from the tight set to his lips as he listened, the deep crease on his brow and the hard glint in his blue eyes.

'What's wrong?' she asked as he finished the conversation and dropped his phone into his pocket.

'We have a problem,' he said, his voice taut. 'The press have established that I am not and never have been in America. Some enterprising reporter spoke to a "palace source" who said that on the same day I left so did a member of staff. There is no story *yet* about us, but it may only be a matter of time. There will definitely be an imminent piece about "The Disappearing Prince" amidst speculation about whether I am planning to abdicate before the inauguration ceremony.'

'Abdicate?'

'Yes. That's what my father and Isabella want me to do. It's the only way Juan can take back the position of Crown Prince. I refused.'

Jodi could hear the faintest hum of guilt in his voice, a glint of doubt in his eyes. 'But you considered it?'

'Of course, I did. But I can't do it—to do so would be tantamount to admitting I believe I am not royal, that my blood is tainted, that because I was born out of wedlock

I cannot rule despite my legitimacy. I cannot do that because it would also be wrong. The case to bring me to the throne was made by people who wanted justice to be done, and I do believe this is justice. It is a new way and I think it is the right way.'

'But your father and Isabella will jump on this, will use it to put the idea of abdication in people's heads.'

'Yes.'

'Then you have to stop them.'

'The only way to do that is to take the initiative, dictate the story ourselves. But that depends on you.'

'What do you mean?' But the question was rhetorical, only asked to buy a tiny bit of time.

'I am sorry, Jodi. This is not how I wanted it to be.' He looked round the room and grimaced. 'There is nothing I can do to make this a better setting. But I have to ask you now.' He took both her hands in his. 'Jodi Petrovelli, will you marry me?'

Jodi closed her eyes, so aware of him, his warmth, his strength, his scent. All these things had become so much a part of her life these past days and that in itself was a danger. She could not get dependent on this man, must always remember what was on offer. Affection, respect, liking, attraction.

'What about the test?'

'The test will have to wait. To do it now under public scrutiny would cause the very doubts I wish to avoid. So I will have to trust you.'

Will have to. The words were enough to make her pause, enough to remind her that she would be foolish to harbour hopes that Carlos would change. She understood why the man had trust issues—a mother who had tricked his father into marriage, which had resulted in his father's selfish refusal to bond with him, a first love who had also duped him, used him for her own gain. He did not trust and he had no wish for love.

And with her parents' example ahead of her, after Tim, *Jodi* should know better than to hope for something as perilous as love. Did know better. She believed Carlos was a good man who she could make a life with. So now what she needed to think about was her baby.

She opened her eyes, looked direct into his.

'We can make this work, Jodi. Be happy.'

'What about your family?'

'They will not be happy, but they will have to put a brave face on it. No doubt we will hold some sort of fake public viewing so the people can see us show solidarity.'

She touched her stomach gently and qualms struck. Was it right to take this baby into a family who would loathe him, consider him doubly tainted and a usurper to boot?

As if reading her expression, he stepped forward. '*We* will be his family. And I will not let my father or any of them hurt him in any way, by word or deed. I will protect him. He will not have the childhood I had.'

She nodded, believed what he said, reminded herself, 'And he will have my family.'

'Yes. Our marriage will give him a destiny, a purpose, security. Two parents under the same roof, no need for visitation rights, no need to have half-siblings and step-parents.'

Everything he said sounded so right, so logical, so sane. She had always wished for purpose in her life, to have a destiny. Envied Luca his certainty. Hell, hadn't her own father wanted success and a destiny so badly he'd walked out on a family?

She could give her child, not only a destiny, but a proper family life. With a father who wanted to be there. This child could have all the things that Jodi had craved as a child. A father who would carry him around on his shoulders, play with him And Carlos was a good man—she'd seen that over the past days. Who would give her liking, respect, affection, attraction. But not love... There was that errant thought again.

Carlos was offering her a chance for calm happiness, without the highs and lows, the roller coaster and the risk. Most important, he would be there for the baby and there for her. And so, 'Yes, I will marry you.'

His face lit up at that, his smile wide and so genuine Jodi felt a funny little shiver run through her as he squeezed her hands. Yet now there was a sense of awkwardness—should she kiss him, should he kiss her? Should they shake hands?

He gave a sudden rueful laugh.

'I am sorry, Jodi. I have no ring, nothing sparkling... there are no violins in the background.' He took her left hand and slipped off the fake wedding band, left only the sapphire ring they had chosen for JoJo. 'I will get you something different, but this will have to do for now.' He thought, then slipped the silver ring off his finger.

She looked at his hand, saw the band of white under his knuckle, proof of how long he had worn the ring for. 'Have this in the meantime, as a token of my good faith.'

As she took the ring, it glowed warm on her palm and she blinked back sudden tears. This man was such an anomaly. He did not trust her enough to fully believe she carried his baby, yet he would entrust this to her. 'Thank you. I will wear it around my neck.' Reaching up, she unclasped her necklace, took off the large pendant and threaded the silver ring on.

'Let me,' he said, and she turned; her pulse rate upped, her heart beat faster as he looped the chain round. Catching her lip between her teeth, she felt her skin shiver goose-bumps as his fingers brushed the nape of her neck.

'Thank you.' So many emotions fluttered through her and she made a concerted effort to shut them down, to focus on the knowledge that this was the right decision. Made with her head rather than her heart because that made sense. 'So what now?'

'Now we start to spin a story. One that factors in you, your pregnancy, our engagement and where we have been for the past week.'

'Right.' Jodi took a deep breath. 'So are we going for royal romance?'

'Yes.'

'Then why don't we say we met when you were Carl Williamson, that we did meet on Jalpura, but in my true persona of Jodi Petrovelli.' She frowned. 'Our biggest problem will be Pradesh Patankar if we say that. He will recognise me, realise Jemma Lewes and Jodi Petrovelli are one and the same.'

'Doesn't matter.' Carlos shrugged. 'We will say that I always knew who you were, knew you were posing as Jemma Lewes, and that you had taken the alias to avoid publicity. Pradesh knows he was lying to you. You confronted me, I told you he was lying, but we decided the best thing would be for you to "disappear" during the court case.'

'That works. Then I discover I'm pregnant, we don't want publicity, and I lie low during the court case. When it is over I come to the palace as Jodi Peters so we can meet in private. We want some time together before the publicity hits, so we come up with the husband and wife idea as a way to be together and for you to show me Talonos.'

Jodi sat back, her mind going over the story for holes.

'It holds together,' Carlos said. 'We are natural fabrica-tors. I will tell Stefan, and we should tell Marco and Angelina.' He rose to his feet, held out a hand to pull her up. 'Then we will return to Sathis and announce our engagement.' He looked round the room. 'But I will not leave Angelina in the lurch. I will send people to finish the work, and to remain here until she is back on her feet.'

Jodi looked up at him, touched by his thoughtfulness—a reassurance that she was doing the right thing. How *could* marriage with a good man go wrong?

'Before we go, I need to tell my family what is going on.'

CHAPTER FOURTEEN

JODI STARED AT her brother's face on the screen, marvelled at a technology that could make it feel as if he were in the same room, his dark hair spiky, his silver-grey eyes full of shock as he absorbed her news.

'You're engaged to marry Prince Carlos of Talonos?' Luca looked as though he had no idea whether to congratulate her or yell at her. Opted for both. 'Of course, I am pleased for you but why have you not told me of this?'

'I told you, it's complicated. We needed to keep it under wraps whilst the court case was going on.' She inhaled a deep breath. 'Plus... I'm pregnant.'

Again she could see a myriad emotions cross Luca's face. 'How pregnant?'

'Five months. I am sorry I didn't tell you, Luca. I needed to figure this out on my own. With Carlos.'

He ran a hand over his face. 'I am happy for you, Jodi—as long as you are happy?' His eyes searched her face and she suddenly felt tears well up. 'If you aren't, then you do not have to marry him, whether he is a prince or not. If he is forcing you, or pressuring you... I will...'

'Have my back. I know you will. But I am good with this, Luca. I am happy. We are going to announce the engagement in the next day and I would like you to attend Carlos's inauguration ball if you can. It is in a few weeks.'

'Of course, I will be there. But is it possible for me to bring someone? I have news too. I too am engaged.' Now his face was transformed and Jodi blinked at the sheer goofiness of his smile, the hitherto unseen softness in his grey eyes. 'Her name is Emily and I love her, Jodi. She is the most amazing, incredible—' He broke off. 'But you will see what I mean when you meet her.'

'Of course, she can come with you.' Jodi stared at her brother. Luca, who she had believed would never fall in love, had found love. 'I am so happy for you, big bro. How did you meet her? Tell me all about her.'

'She is Ava's best friend. I met her at Ava and Liam's engagement party.'

Of course she was and of course he had. With supreme effort Jodi kept her face joyful, even as jealousy permeated her very being. 'How is Ava?'

Her brother clearly wasn't fooled. 'Jodi, I'm not sure you want to hear this, but she's nice. She's not the monster we made her out to be as children. I don't know her well yet, but I think you would like her.'

'That's good to know,' Jodi said, aware that her words walked on stilts.

'But that's for another time. I am so happy that you too have found love, little sis. Now tell me about Carlos, about Talonos and the baby.'

Half an hour later as the screen faded the door to the bedroom opened and Carlos entered. 'How did it go?'

'Fine. Both Luca and Mum are over the moon about the baby and they'd both like to come to the inauguration ball and said they can't wait to meet you. Mum even said she can't wait to be a grandma.'

Carlos surveyed her with a frown. 'Something's wrong,' he said flatly. 'Something has upset you. Luca?'

'No, I'm really happy for him, in fact. He's engaged too. To Ava's best friend, Emily.'

'Then however happy you are for him, you must also be upset.'

'Nope. Why should I be?' Jodi knew how combative she sounded, knew Carlos was trying to be nice. But she didn't want to discuss it, the green insidious strand of jealousy she could feel creeping inside her. The knowledge that as always Ava would ruin everything. Only it wasn't just Ava—it had felt wrong...disingenuous to pretend to Luca that she and Carlos were in love. When Luca truly was. Felt even worse that *both* Luca and Ava were in love, members of a club Jodi was excluded from for ever. The idea that Emily was Ava's best mate was the cherry on the cake, another means for Ava to be in Luca's orbit.

'Because you haven't met Ava, because you must have mixed feelings about her, and it must feel strange that your brother is now engaged to her best friend.'

'I said I'm fine. Really. And we have better, more urgent things to talk about than Ava.'

There was a silence and then Carlos nodded. 'OK. But if you change your mind I'm here.' He hesitated. 'I do have to ask one more thing though. I just spoke to Stefan—he is working out how to publicise everything and he wondered if you want Ava included in it all. Whether you want to ask her to the ball. I said I thought not but now we know Luca is engaged to Emily...maybe that changes things. I will leave it to you.'

'Fine. Ask her.' Jodi knew it would be what Luca wanted. She inhaled a deep breath. 'Truly, it is fine. Luca told me that he and Ava are presenting a united front in order to help Dolci. The company is struggling with all the negative publicity and uncertainty. So it makes sense and I am sorry I am being so...spiky about it all.'

'There is no need to apologise and only do this if you are sure.'

'I'm sure.' It was time to grow up, time to move on from her feelings about Ava. Start her new life on Talonos, a long way away from Ava. As for Luca, Jodi's bond with him was unbreakable and there was no reason for it to change. So she would quite simply push Ava from her thoughts, paint her out of existence as she had tried to do all her life. The words echoed hollowly in her brain as she pulled a smile to her face. 'One hundred per cent sure. And now I really don't want to talk about Ava any more. Let's go and talk to Angelina and Marco instead.'

Two days later

Carlos paused outside the door that led to Jodi's suite and shifted the pile of papers in his hand so he could knock. Glanced down at magazines and collated printouts of on-line interviews. All about Carlos and Jodi. The world had taken an unexpected interest in this wedding, had splashed the romance angle, loved the pregnancy and had woven it all into both the Dolci saga and the royal saga.

He knocked and entered, his heart giving a funny little pit-pat as he looked at Jodi, at his fiancée, who was sitting at the desk in her suite, a slightly preoccupied frown on her face as she surveyed her laptop screen.

'You need a break. Have you eaten? Stayed hydrated?'

She looked up and gave a now, oh, so familiar gurgle of laughter. 'How could I not? Greta keeps appearing with snacks and drinks and I keep telling her I know my way round the palace kitchens. But she said you asked her to keep an eye on me.'

'Only because I know how immersed you are in the report.' Jodi had volunteered to put her ideas into report form, told him that she genuinely wanted to do the travel consultancy role they had used as a cover story. And he'd agreed on provision that she accept payment for it.

'Anyway, I came to show you the reactions to our engagement.'

She moved away from the desk, came to sit next to him on the huge overstuffed sofa, her brown eyes wide as she saw what he carried. 'Wow. We made a splash.'

'We certainly did.'

She took a couple of the articles from him and as they both read Carlos was aware of how intimate this felt. Cosy. Warm. Hell, he'd missed her the last two days as he'd rushed about attending to royal duties.

Then she tensed next to him, her body suddenly taut, and he glanced down to see what she was reading. Saw the headline, 'What will Ava wear to her sister's ball?' This was followed by Ava modelling three different ball gowns and then some blurb. Carlos skim-read:

'I've already met my handsome prince,' the Casseveti heiress said with an adoring smile, referring to her husband-to-be, Liam Rourke.

Then there was a picture showing a framed photograph of the *'happy couple'*, in which they gazed at each other with *'a depth of love and adoration'*. And behind that was another framed photo, of James Casseveti, his arm around Ava, a smile on both their faces.

Carlos cursed himself; he should have checked through the pile better. Should have removed that one. He'd *known* she wasn't OK about Ava—*known* she'd been upset at the idea of Ava being invited. Yet he'd let her convince him otherwise.

'Jodi? Talk to me. I'm sorry—I should have taken that out of the pile.'

'Don't be silly. It's fine. I'm being silly. It's not as though this is news to me. I've always known.'

Gently he put his arm round her shoulder, took the article from her hand and dropped it to the carpeted floor. 'Known what?'

'How loved Ava is. How much my father loved her. And it has always hurt, but when I see articles like this, photos like those, I understand why he did. Why he never had any need of me. Look at her... She is stunning, long blonde hair, tall, a supermodel. But it's not just that—she has everything: beauty, brains, talents. She won dance awards, walked the catwalk in Milan, she got a first at university... she worked in the family business. She is perfect. No wonder she is "loved and adored".' She gave a small mirthless laugh. 'But you know what's even worse? It now turns out she is nice. Luca *likes* her. I didn't think that was possible. Luca adored our father and James loved him, so Luca has always resented Ava for replacing him. Now she's going to replace me.'

'I'm sorry, Jodi. Truly I am.' Anger clenched his fist at the thought of James Casseveti and the damage he had wreaked as a father. On a par with his own. But at least King Antonio had been honest, direct. Carlos knew where he stood. Luca must have been confused and miserable. As for Jodi, the knowledge of how rejected she must have felt made him pull her closer, wish he could shield her from all the hurt and pain. 'But you told me how close you and Luca are. I don't think anything could break that bond.'

'It could.' Her voice was tiny now. 'If Luca likes Ava, if he stops blaming Ava, then...he'll blame me. Realise it was my fault that our dad left.'

For an instant he didn't understand and then he got it.

Jodi's mum had been pregnant with Jodi when James had left and Jodi blamed herself. Just as he blamed himself for his mother's death. He knew exactly how it felt to live weighted inside by a burden of guilt and it tore him apart that Jodi carried that same load.

'It wasn't your fault,' he said, knew how hollow the words would ring to her. Hadn't his nurse said the same words to him?

'You can't know that,' she said softly. 'No one can. I could have been the last straw, the idea of the responsibility of another child when he wanted to start a business, had his own dreams. If my mum hadn't been pregnant maybe my dad would have decided it was possible to follow his dreams with her. They could have stayed in love, founded Dolci together and—'

'You can't do that. You can't say what if. There are too many different paths life can take to second-guess them all.'

'I don't need to second-guess. On this path, in this life, I cost my mother the love of her life, cost Luca the father he adored. I was the catalyst.'

'But the responsibility was his. It was not your fault.'

'But it *feels* like my fault.' She gave a half-sigh. 'I know you're trying to help. My head knows you're right; my mum has told me so many times that it is not my fault, or Luca's. That my dad was a weak man, a man who was tempted away by the lure of wealth and easy success. But maybe he wouldn't have been without the idea of a second child. Me.'

Carlos held her closer. 'I understand,' he said. 'Truly. And I don't know how to change how you feel, because I know no amount of logic makes a difference.'

There was surprise in her eyes as she turned to him. 'That's it exactly. How do you know?'

A fierce need gripped him, a desire to show Jodi she was not alone, that he did truly understand. 'I told you that my mother died. I was only six. I found her body, but I didn't understand she was dead. I just knew something was wrong.' He could almost feel the paint on his fingers, recall standing rooted to the spot, holding the painting he'd come to show her. The one she would never see. 'Then I was told she died of a short tragic illness. As I got older I decided it must have been a heart attack, or a blood clot...' He took a deep breath, felt her shift closer to him, clasp his hand. 'Then when I was thirteen, my nurse found me and gave me a letter from my mum. I knew, just knew that it wasn't a simple goodbye and it wasn't. Instead it was a letter that told the truth—that she tricked my father into marriage—but also I found out my mother had killed herself. She wrote how sorry she was to leave me but she couldn't go on any longer.' Not even for him and his belief in her love for him; his trust in that love had been shattered.

Jodi emitted a soft gasp and turned to face him, her brown eyes awash with tears. 'I am so sorry. I can't imagine what that must have done to you. Everything you believed in changed and rewritten. And your poor, poor mum.' She stopped and took in a breath. 'But it wasn't your fault.'

'It was. My mother said she couldn't go on because my father told her he would never love her or me, that she killed any love when she tricked him into marriage. He told her I would never be King, that he would never try to change the law. But, you see, the only reason she tricked him into marriage was for me, so that I would rule. She couldn't live with the idea that I wouldn't, that she'd let me down. If it weren't for me, she would never have felt the need to kill herself. Never have forced the marriage in the first place.'

'No. It's not like that.' Jodi shook her head, her hand gripping his arm hard. 'It's tragic but you did nothing wrong. There is every chance that your mum was suffering from severe depression or some sort of mental health issue. It wasn't you; she probably believed it was best for you if she was gone.' She blinked back tears. 'She should have been given help and counselling and so should you. Your father should have made that happen. But you did nothing wrong.'

'I was the catalyst.' The words stopped her in her tracks. 'I know my father's behaviour was abysmal and cruel, I get that and I can never forgive him, but... It's like you said. I *feel* as though it's my fault.'

'I wish I could change that. For you and for me.'

'I don't know how to do that.'

She gave a small sigh and for a few moments they sat in a cocoon of silence and comfort. He felt lighter...better...and a warmth unfurled inside him as she rested her head on his shoulder. Then she sat up slightly. 'We can't change how we feel, we can't change the past, but maybe we can change the future.' She touched her tummy. 'Otherwise the past will keep causing hurt—our baby will have no relationship with his cousins, with his uncle and all the bitterness will just go on.'

'But what can we do about that?'

'Try to build bridges. Not with your father and Isabella, because I'm not sure how that would be possible. But with Juan. He was brought up to hate you—maybe we can change that, so he doesn't bring his children up to hate yours.'

His heart turned in his chest at the way she was taking the darkness of their shared pain and weaving it into something lighter, positive and good, and when she spoke somehow the impossible seemed worth striving for. Not for himself, but for the baby, so he wasn't born into, didn't grow up in, a story of bitterness. 'I'd like to try. But the baby will have an aunt too. What about Ava?'

She flinched and he continued gently. 'Because she isn't perfect, Jodi. It doesn't matter if she was a supermodel or got a first-class degree. All of that is spin. Just like the public display of royal solidarity was spin that made the world believe we were a happy family. You don't know the real Ava.'

'But I've lived in her shadow all my life.' She looked at him. 'But you're saying it's a shadow I made for myself, the shadow of an Ava I created. The Ava I wanted to be all my life.'

'You do not need to live in her shadow, Jodi. Because you are beautiful, exactly as you are. The curl of your hair, the topaz glints in your eyes, the character in your face, the lush beauty of your lips. And inside—you are beautiful as well. You care, genuinely care about people. You are going to make a wonderful mother. You are you and I wouldn't change any bit of you. But the point is *you* shouldn't want to change *yourself*.'

Shock touched her face and she said slowly, 'No, I shouldn't. It will always hurt that my father loved Ava but that isn't Ava's fault. Just as it isn't Juan's fault that he was brought up to believe you were a bad person.'

'And I know it's too little too late, but your father must have been trying to make some sort of amends by leaving you and Luca the control of Dolci.'

'And until now I have been running away from any decision, to take it or to not take it. But perhaps what I should do is meet Ava, talk to her with Luca and decide from there.' She sat up straight. 'I don't know if any of this will work.'

'But we are going to try,' he said. 'Together.'

'And now, tonight, will you stay here?' Her voice was small. 'We can have a barrier of pillows if you want but... I'd like it if you stay.'

'I'd like that too.'

CHAPTER FIFTEEN

CARLOS OPENED HIS eyes to the ping of his phone, became lazily aware of Jodi fast asleep in the crook of his arm, her head resting on his shoulder, the barrier of pillows nowhere to be seen. Instead he'd held her all night, this kind, caring, amazing woman.

She opened her eyes and smiled slightly shyly at him, before moving away and rubbing her eyes sleepily. 'Was that your phone?'

He reached out, looked at the display. A message from Queen Isabella. 'The Queen wants to see me. This morning. On an urgent matter.' His stepmother never wanted to see him.

Jodi sat up. 'I'll come too.'

'No. That's not a good idea.'

'Yes, Carlos, it is. That's what we decided last night. That we were in this together.' She gave a gurgle of laughter and put her hand on her tummy. 'The baby agrees. He just kicked.' She glanced at him shyly. 'Would you like to feel?'

'I…' Did he? Visceral panic touched him and he shook it away; he wanted to do this. Feel his son kick.

Slowly, his heart pounding, he placed his hand on the swell of her belly and she placed hers over his. Then he felt it and his heart turned over, made him feel almost faint with sheer awe.

Their child.

Turning, he dropped the lightest of kisses on her lips, the sense of awe so huge he didn't know what to do with it. 'That is…it's blown me away.'

'Me too. So now let's go and see what your stepmum wants.' She narrowed her eyes. 'Though how I will keep myself from giving her a piece of my mind, I don't know.'

Half an hour later they approached his stepmother's anteroom. He nodded at the guard and took Jodi's hand as they entered.

Queen Isabella came towards them, eyebrows raised, and a small smile played on her lips, a smile Carlos instantly distrusted.

'Good morning, Carlos. And this must be Jodi.'

'Yes, it is.'

He turned to Jodi, and saw that she'd paled, her skin a milky white, her brown eyes full of shock.

It was only then that Carlos saw there was another person in the room. A man with copper hair and dark blue eyes.

'It is probably good that you are here, Ms Petrovelli, though in truth I wished to spare you.'

'Spare Jodi from what?'

Carlos could see the small smile that played on Isabella's lips and sensed the impending doom—knew how much his stepmother would delight in seeing him hurt.

'This is Tim Warrington.'

Tim… Surely that was the name of Jodi's ex. And the foreboding deepened, tightened his chest. 'Tim has come here making a claim that I am sure you can prove to be false,' Isabella continued. Fear touched his heart. 'He claims that he is in fact the father of the baby.'

The words pounded Carlos's brain as his own idiocy dawned on him. He should have insisted on the test; then he could confront this man, prove to him beyond a shadow of a doubt that he was a liar and a charlatan. Because Jodi wouldn't lie. He *knew* that.

'Or rather…' Tim stepped forward now. 'Rather that I could be.'

'I don't need to hear this.' He didn't. Didn't want to listen. Because this whole scenario held echoes of the past, wove together memories of messengers who brought news of betrayal—the friend and colleague who told him of Lisa's betrayal. Daria, his nurse, who brought him the letter that shattered his belief in his own past, in his mother's love.

'Actually, Carlos, I think you do,' Isabella said. 'When you marry Ms Petrovelli, then this baby will become heir to the throne. We must be sure that it is yours. In addition, Mr Warrington has it in his power to create scandal so I believe we should at least listen to what he has to say.'

'Very well.'

Tim cleared his throat, gave a small rueful smile. 'I saw the news a few days ago and it was only then after doing some maths I realised that the baby could be mine.'

'We split years ago, Tim.' They were the first words Jodi had said and Carlos could hear the strain in them, squeezed her hand in his. Too tight, he realised.

'I know that,' Tim said, not looking the least bit put out. 'But I am talking about our one night… reunion. In London. A few months ago.'

London. Jodi had been in London. But anyone could know that, surely.

Had they mentioned it in the press release? They must have. He closed his eyes, fighting off the familiarity of this moment, of history repeating itself. Recalled how hard he'd tried to convince himself that Lisa was innocent, how much he'd wanted to not believe the truth about her, about his mother. Glancing down, he saw that he'd dropped Jodi's hand from his.

Jodi stepped forward. 'I haven't seen you for years, Tim. You know that.'

'You saw me in January. We bumped into each other and we got talking, I told you I wanted to apologise for my past behaviour and you agreed to a drink. We ended up having a few too many drinks, and then we ended up in bed. I was a louse, I know, but I ran out on you before you woke up the next day. You always see the best in people, Jodi; I'm sorry I proved you wrong again. But I am not such a louse that I haven't come forward now.'

Isabella shook her head, waved a hand in the air. 'You are still a louse Mr Warrington. You have only come forward because you smell money in this; you hope we will pay you to go away and not tell this story to the papers.'

'There is no story,' Jodi said, her voice tight. 'I will do a test.'

'Playing the odds, Jodi?' Tim asked. 'I guess there's a fifty-fifty chance. But whether the baby is mine or his, that night with me happened. I may even have a stray picture or two to prove it.'

They all heard the sharp intake of Jodi's breath and when Carlos turned to look at her, it was as though something slammed into his chest. There could be no doubt—there was fear on Jodi's face, fear and guilt and anger. The exact same expression he'd seen on Lisa's face when he'd caught her.

Disbelief spun his head, but he knew…knew what he'd seen. Knew too that Isabella had seen it. He tried to pull his racing thoughts together, even as it all made a horrible, terrible sense. Just as Lisa's perfidy had. Just as his mother's letter had. Both had shown him how easy it was for illusions to be created, how easy it was to live a lie.

From somewhere he dug up some semblance of control. Loathed that this was being played out in front of his stepmother. He strode up to Tim, felt a fierce gladness when the other man took a step backward. 'I will ride out any scandal you throw. *If* you have proof, publish and be damned. I'll ride the storm.'

He turned, kept his eyes averted from Jodi's face and headed for the door. His feet were leaden—his heart even more so—as they re-trod the steps they'd walked just a half-hour before. Only now everything had changed and by tacit consent when they reentered his royal residence they headed to his office.

Jodi twisted her hands together, wondered how she could hurt this much even as the deep dark pain hollowed her insides.

'You believe him, don't you?' she asked. The question was rhetorical, yet a tiny bit of her still held out a sliver of desperate hope he'd deny it.

There was a silence…that stretched and pulled her nerves to screaming edge. Then, 'Yes,' he said eventually. 'Or at least I believe he may be telling the truth.'

Against all odds the hurt intensified, twisted inside her. 'You think I would lie to you about our baby? Think I would have reconnected with Tim?' She wasn't sure which was worse.

'Why wouldn't you have reconnected? Back then you had no commitment to me, believed I was a lying bastard. You wouldn't have known you were pregnant. As for lying about the baby, there are any number of reasons. You want to be a princess, you want your baby to be a prince, so you just crossed your fingers and hoped the baby is mine.'

'I would never ever do that.' Now anger started to surface alongside deep, deep sadness that he could believe this of her. 'Not to my baby, not to you. I would never mess with your head like that. And I did not sleep with Tim. The whole thing was a fabrication from start to finish.'

Carlos shook his head. 'I saw your face, Jodi. When he said he may have a picture, tangible evidence. You looked panicked and guilty.'

The anger escalated and she embraced it, needed its fuel to ward away the pain and hurt. 'And based on that one second, that one reaction, you judged me guilty. Negated the past week.'

'I—'

But she would not let him speak.

'I did react. You're right. But not because Tim was telling the truth. Years ago, when I was with Tim, I confided in him, told him that Ava was my sister. That night I woke up and he was standing there. Taking photos of me. He said he was going to sell them to the papers, said he'd been making love to me but imagining I was Ava, that he'd only got together with me because he thought I was going places with Luca. When he realised I wasn't he decided to cash in differently. I begged him not to, but he wouldn't listen. In the end he shoved me off him and left.'

Shock widened his eyes and she saw his fists clench in instinctive anger. 'What did you do?'

'I called Luca. He said he sorted it out, that Tim wouldn't trouble me again and the photos were destroyed. But today I did panic, just for an instant. I thought maybe somehow he still had one. And that's the truth. If you don't believe me, I don't care.' Only she did, cared so much she could feel pain on every nerve end. But she knew what she had to do. 'Because it doesn't matter any more.'

'Jodi, I do believe you.'

'But you didn't believe me when it counted. If you think I would juggle with my baby's life like that, marry you if there was even a chance he couldn't be the true heir, after everything we've shared, then there is no hope for our marriage. You said our marriage would be based on liking and respect. If you had any respect for me, you would know I could never have behaved the way you believed I had. You would have known there was another explanation.'

The words seemed to shadow the air around her with a dark finality. 'I will take responsibility for this, to *our* son.' She emphasised the word and saw him flinch. 'I will explain to him that it was my decision to take away his birthright. Because I do not believe it would be healthy for him to grow up here, with two parents who have no respect for each other, no trust.'

She wished he'd say something, anything. The colour had leached from his face, his hands gripped the arm of his chair, but he said nothing, his eyes slightly downcast. 'Once the test has been done I will send you the results and we can sort out how this will work. You are the baby's father and I still want you to be part of his life. If that's still what you want.'

He looked up now, met her gaze direct. 'I do want to be part of his life. And I'm sorry it has to be this way. I'm sorry I doubted you and believed Tim. But I did.' The words held a depth of sadness that sent her surge of anger into retreat. 'I panicked—I remembered how I had believed my mother died a natural death and how that illusion was shattered, I remembered how my mother had tricked my father, how Lisa had tricked me. How so many times my sense of reality was distorted. How life is full of illusions. And all the trust I thought I had in you dissolved. Trust requires a leap of faith. I thought I had that in me. Today shows me that I don't.'

And she couldn't blame him for that but, 'I'm sorry,

Carlos. I cannot live without trust; I cannot commit my life and my baby's to a man who does not trust me. I cannot spend my life having to prove myself all the time.'

'I wouldn't expect you to.' The words resonated with sadness and a finality that prickled her eyes with tears. 'I am sorry, so sorry that I hurt you in there, in front of a man who had already hurt you.' His lips turned up in a rictus of a smile. 'I know an apology is too little too late.' His voice broke slightly as if he too recalled that he had used the same phrase to describe James Casseveti's will.

Just the night before, everything had seemed so full of hope, when she'd slept safe in the cradle of his arms. And now she never would again. She would not cry—she would not. Or at least not yet.

'I'll leave today.' All of a sudden it occurred to her that the world believed they were about to get married, believed in the illusion of a royal romance. 'If you like you can say that I am going on a visit home.'

He shook his head. 'No. I think it is time to end the perpetual royal spin. I will explain that we have found we are not suited.' She could see the effort behind the words, each one slow, as if he had to focus to make sense of what he was saying. Maybe his brain too felt fuzzy like cotton wool, as though each word had to be found against a backdrop of misery. 'Later we can work out the best way forward for us and the baby.'

After the test, she thought dully.

'In the meantime I will do all I can to protect you from the publicity.'

She nodded. 'I'll leave today. Go back to Ital…go back home,' she amended. Only stupidly it no longer felt like home. Here felt like home, here with the man she loved. In a country she'd grown to love.

Love.

The word broke through the cotton clouds and she focused on showing nothing on her face.

She had to leave. Now, before she told him, before he guessed. Her hands clumsy, she lifted them to her neck and unclasped the chain that held his ring. Slipping it off, she placed it on the desk.

'Goodbye, Carlos,' she said and rushed for the door.

Three days later

Carlos approached the royal suite, glared at the royal guards when they asked if he had an appointment.

'Do I need an appointment to join my family?' he asked.

'Um… Your Highness, it is usual for all guests to be invited into the royal presence by appointment.'

'Well, today I am doing something unusual.'

With a perfunctory knock Carlos entered the private dining room, where the family always breakfasted together on a Saturday morning.

'Carlos,' his father said and sighed as he waved at the guards to have them leave.

'What are you doing here?' Isabella demanded.

'I have come because I want to talk with you. With all of you.' He turned to Juan and emotion conflicted inside him. This was his brother, tainted blood or not. 'I understand, Juan, why you may not wish to see me but—'

He saw his brother frown before Isabella interceded once more. 'I do not see what there is to talk about.'

'I want to postpone the inauguration.'

There was a silence.

'Why?'

'Because there has been enough falsity and illusion.' He turned to his brother. 'I do not intend to abdicate my position and, Juan, I am truly sorry for that. I can only imagine how unfair this must feel to you. Perhaps how unfair it is. But I cannot stand aside.' Now he turned to his father. 'Because my blood is not tainted and this is my birthright. But I swear to you all that I care about Talonos, truly care, and I will do everything in my power to do right by Talonos and all its people.' He turned back to his brother. 'If you wish it, I would like to find a way forward. To build bridges between us.'

There was a silence then Isabella spoke. 'That can never happen. You are a usurper—you have always hated Juan.'

'That is not true and it never has been.'

'Wait.' It was Juan's voice. 'Mother. You told me Carlos refused to see me.' He turned to Carlos. 'Is that true?'

'No.' Carlos willed his brother to believe him.

Isabella's laugh was scornful. 'You know Carlos cannot be trusted. He has taken your birthright from you.'

'That is not true. I did not seek the court case, but neither will I refuse what was taken from me.' He turned to the King. 'You knew, didn't you? All those years ago you knew it was possible to overturn the statute—you chose not to, however much my mother wished it, because you could not bear that you had been tricked. And you believe my blood to be tainted.' The King was silent, but he did not deny the charge. Carlos turned back to his brother. 'Please try to understand I cannot stand aside, in the memory of my mother. But please believe I did not seek it and I have never borne you any ill will.'

'Even as a child you hated him,' Isabella said. 'You crept into his nursery to hurt him; you had a pillow in hand to suffocate…'

'What?' Carlos heard his own voice crack across the room. 'That is a lie.' An image of Jodi flashed through his mind, how she'd stood still as accusations had been hurled at her. How she must have wished to be believed, just as he did now. 'That did not happen. I did creep into the nursery but there was no pillow. I never would have harmed you. You were, you are, my brother.' Cold, hard anger swelled inside him at yet another illusion, another trickery, another myth. 'I wanted to see you, that's all.' He turned to Isabella. 'I don't know if you believe the lies you tell, the illusions you weave, but I have never been your enemy. I just wanted to be part of the family.'

There was a silence and then Juan said softly, 'I do not know what to say. I want to believe you. I want to believe you bear me no ill will. Most of all I want to believe that you will truly be a good ruler for Talonos one day—and I would like to give you a chance to prove that. It will take time, I think, for me to adjust. But...' And now he smiled. 'I am still only twenty-one; if I do not have to be heir, there are so many other opportunities I can embrace.' He rose and walked towards Carlos, hand outstretched. 'I make no promises, but I am willing to give you a chance.'

A trickle of hope washed over Carlos that maybe bridges could be built. Alongside a surge of shame that he himself had not behaved with the same honour his brother had. That he had judged Jodi without giving her any chance at all. Judged the woman he loved, the woman who deserved so much more.

Loved.

The woman he loved.

The realisation slammed into him, poleaxed him, sent neon lights flashing in his brain. He loved Jodi, loved her. And he'd lost her through foolishness and stupidity and his own inability to see clearly. Whereas his brother, who had been brought up to hate Carlos, who had just lost his position, had his destiny taken away from him, was able to take a leap of faith.

It was time he learnt from his little brother. He shook

Juan's hand. 'Thank you,' he said. 'Thank you for giving me a chance. I hope we can become brothers in the true sense.'

There was a small moan and, turning, he saw Isabella had paled, swayed slightly in her seat, and immediately Juan headed towards his parents. 'It will be OK,' he said. 'Carlos is the true heir. Surely it is best to accept that and work together. For Talonos.'

King Antonio rose to his feet. 'I agree,' he said. For a moment he looked like an old man and as he turned towards his wife Carlos saw a question in his eyes. Then he straightened. 'Do not cancel the inauguration ball as yet. Perhaps it is too late for you and I to build bridges, Carlos, but I will not stand in the way of future generations doing so.' He turned to his wife. 'We too must talk, my dear.'

Carlos nodded, unsure what the future could hold for him and Antonio, but if there was any way to stem the dislike and poison and darkness he would do all he could. For the future generations. An image of Jodi popped into his head, the memory of the baby kicking under his hand, and he knew he had to leave, that however important this was there was something even more important he needed to do.

Two days later

Jodi tried to still the nerves that fluttered inside her, wondered if this was even a good idea. Too late for doubts. She could hardly turn and run from the cocktail bar. Silvio's, the bar where Luca had once worked as a young man.

'Smile, Jodi,' Matteo, the manager, boomed. 'I have made you the best mocktail concocted by any bartender in the world.'

'It is delicious,' Jodi agreed, sipping the orange and passionfruit drink and pulling a smile to her face.

And it was, but even the citrus-tinged sweetness

couldn't spark real happiness inside her. Nerves, she told herself firmly. Nothing to do with missing Carlos, wanting him here by her side, or at home ready to reassure and support her. But he wasn't here and wouldn't be here ever.

And now…now she looked at the entrance and the nerves unleashed a flotilla of butterflies in her tummy. There was Ava, moving gracefully across the threshold, pulling off her dark glasses in an elegant movement.

Her outfit was somehow perfect for the occasion. Floaty and discreet, a long navy-blue sundress with a smattering of daisies, her blonde hair beautifully plaited and a light appliance of make-up.

Jodi swallowed, looked round the room for some way to hide, to magically disappear. She couldn't do this.

'You do not need to live in her shadow, Jodi. Because you are beautiful exactly as you are.' Carlos's voice echoed in her head. *'You are you and I wouldn't change any bit of you. But the point is you shouldn't want to change yourself.'*

Somehow the memory gave her the courage to rise to her feet and lift a hand in the air in greeting, even as her heart pounded against her ribcage. Perhaps she *should* have done this with Luca and Emily to dilute the impact. But that wouldn't have been right; somehow she knew this had to be just Ava and herself.

'Hi,' she said softly as Ava approached. Her sister's face was wary as well, though her glossy lips upturned in a smile, Jodi knew the smile to be rehearsed, practised. Realised Ava was every bit as nervous as she was, only she hid it better.

Carlos was right: Jodi didn't know the real Ava, only the one who posed for the camera.

'Hi.' There was a silence as they studied each other. 'Would you like a drink?'

'I'll have what you're having,' Ava said. 'If that's OK? I mean, if it's a special thing Luca made for you—' She broke off. 'Sorry. I'm normally good at saying the right thing, but today... I...'

Now Jodi smiled and she knew her smile was genuine, not at Ava's discomfort but because suddenly Ava felt human. Real. 'It's fine. Matteo made it up—it's a mocktail version of my favourite cocktail.'

'Then I'll order one of those.'

Matteo approached the table. 'Coming right up,' he said, and Jodi knew he'd been hovering, making sure she was OK.

'Thank you,' Ava said, and they both sat down.

'Before we start, I'd like to say something,' Ava said. 'I want to apologise.'

'For what?'

'For what our father and my mother did. To you and to Luca. It was wrong.'

'That is not your fault.'

'No. But I have been an adult for years. I could have sought you out, reached out, and I didn't. You see, I was brought up to think you were...dangerous. That if I wasn't careful, perfect even, then my father would leave, that you were there in the wings waiting. And...'

'You knew it was possible because, after all, he had left us,' Jodi completed, and sudden tears gathered in her eyes. Not just for Ava, Luca and herself, but also for Carlos and Juan, for all families torn apart by complications.

'Yes. And I did love him. I know what he did was wrong but...'

'But he was your father. It's OK, Ava. He is gone now and I am sorry for your loss. Sorry as well that he didn't leave Dolci just to you.'

'Don't be sorry. I think it must have been his way of saying sorry to all of us.'

Too little too late.

Only suddenly it wasn't—instead perhaps it would have an ending that James Casseveti had wanted. To bring his children together in a way he should have done but hadn't.

She smiled. 'Then perhaps we need to think of the future.'

'I'll drink to that,' Ava said as Matteo appeared with the mocktail.

It was hours later before Jodi got home, and tumbled into bed and to sleep, a sleep she emerged from to hear a knock on her bedroom door. A quick glance at her watch and she realised she'd slept in. Therese had insisted she stay with her to at least help avoid unwanted press intrusion and she'd agreed, and she was glad she had. She and her mum had indulged in some much-needed mother-and-daughter time, spent hours talking and it had helped. She'd told her a bit about Carlos and her mum had listened and then hugged her. But had given no advice, had simply told her, 'I will always be here for you and my grandchild. I believe you would have made a wonderful princess, but I know you will be wonderful at whatever you decide to do in life. You will find your passion, your niche, the thing that makes you happy. I know you will.'

'Come in,' she called, and her mum pushed the door open and entered the room.

'What's wrong?'

Therese looked considerably more flustered than she usually did.

'There's someone here to see you,' she said, and Jodi's heart leapt, in absurd hope. Could it be Carlos? 'Stefan Pedros.'

'Stefan.' Hope dipped a level. She'd sent Carlos the test results a day ago; perhaps Stefan had come to discuss what happened next. 'Could you tell him I'll be out in a minute?'

'Of course.' Her mother hesitated. 'You do want to see him?'

'Yes. Carlos will be in my life one way or the other—I need to get used to it.'

Twenty minutes later, simply dressed in black trousers and a flowing tunic top, Jodi emerged into her mother's lounge. 'Stefan. It is good to see you.'

'And you.' The dark-haired man handed her an envelope. 'Carlos wanted to come himself, but we were worried it would cause unwanted publicity for you. He has asked me to give you this.'

Jodi opened it, aware that her hands were shaking. Inside was a card and a ring. His mother's silver ring on a chain.

Dear Jodi,
I know I do not deserve it, but please would you come with Stefanos so we can talk?
    I send this token to show my good faith.
Carlos

What to do? What to do? What did he want? Did he want to discuss the baby? Something else? Should she go? But how could she not?

Before she could reply her phone buzzed and, looking down on automatic, she saw it was Luca.

'I just need to take this.' Moving out of earshot, she picked up.

'Mum called, said you may need advice and she didn't feel qualified to give it. Do you need advice?'

'Carlos wants to see me. To talk.'

'Only you can make that decision, little sis.' His voice

was serious now. 'All I would say is I made a lot of stupid mistakes with Emily. But she gave me a chance. If she hadn't… I don't know what I would have done.'

The words made her happy for her brother and Emily, even as she reminded herself it might well play out differently here. Carlos might not want a chance to be more than a father. That chance she certainly owed him.

'Good luck, Jodi. I'll always have your back.'

A few hours later she emerged from the plane at the Talonos airport, walked down the steps of the private plane and turned to Stefan. 'What now? Or can't you tell me?'

She smiled to show there was no sting to her words. Stefan had been a charming companion and a diplomat at his best. He had kept the conversation general and interesting and successfully deflected any question as to what Carlos wished to talk about. A direct question had simply elicited, *I am sorry, Jodi, but that is up to Carlos to disclose. In truth, I don't know.*

But she was damned sure the royal advisor would have an idea.

Now he smiled. 'Now you get in the car and Roberto will drive you to your destination. I wish you well, Jodi.'

Was that a farewell? Was that another version of wishing her luck? She didn't know, and the answers were no more apparent as the car glided along first the main roads and then the rural country roads until they wound up a hill and she saw Carlos's familiar figure standing on the verge.

Her heart leapt up and she placed a hand on her tummy, tried to ground herself, but without her consent anticipation swirled inside her. *Enough.* This man had hurt her, believed lies about her and…and apologised for it. *Double enough.* An apology was a word—no more. He had apologised for his inability to trust—perhaps nothing could change that.

He moved towards the car and opened the door.

'Jodi.' There was so much emotion in his voice, the overriding one relief. 'Thank you, Roberto.'

The driver nodded and Jodi climbed out of the car, saw his gaze drop to her baby bump and then back up to her face.

'Come this way,' he said, and she could hear a slight catch in his voice.

She followed him along a dusty path to a large white-washed building and when they reached it she gasped. For a moment her surroundings succeeded in distracting her from the momentum of her heart. She'd stepped into a magical world, a hilltop that overlooked a panorama of sweeping slopes, strewn with gnarl-barked olive trees that caught the sunlight in a shimmer of silver.

'It's beautiful.'

'In some ways the olives groves are the heart of Talonos; we never got to tour one on our road trip, so I thought maybe you'd like to see this view now.'

'Thank you.' She stood, hand on her tummy, hoping that somehow she was translating this view to her baby. After all, this was his country even if he would never rule. 'You said you wanted to talk.'

'Yes. Come this way.'

He led her to a patio and she glanced at him, saw hope, anticipation and a hint of shyness in his expression. The realisation was one of shock—the idea of Carlos showing nerves at the prospect of a conversation with her. She looked at the table. It was made of olive wood, the legs shaped into miniature tree trunks, and the top had whorls and knots that spoke of age and history.

Platters covered with domes were scattered over the

table atop warmers that would keep the contents hot. A spicy appetising aroma swirled in the air. Starched white napkins, cutlery, china plates and a massive candle completed the set-up and her heart started to beat faster.

'This looks incredible, and smells amazing,' she said. Amazing and tantalisingly familiar.

'Thank you for coming. I hoped you would.'

Her heart turned in her chest; he'd prepared all this for her, unsure whether she would even arrive. 'Did Stefan not tell you?'

'I switched my phone off. I elected to wait and hope.'

She stepped forward, then back, tried to remind herself that this was the man who had splintered her heart with his mistrust.

'Whilst I waited, I cooked. But before we eat, I need to say something. I want to apologise, Jodi. I treated you shamefully with dishonour and I am sorry. More sorry than I can ever say. I know I apologised before, but this is different. This time I am asking for your forgiveness and asking you to believe that I can change, that I have changed.' He moved towards her. 'When I judged you, refused to trust you, I behaved in a way I will regret all my life. Because that wasn't real. I know you are a person who always acts with honour. You would not be capable of lying about your baby.' He paused. 'Our baby. I know that.'

'I sent you the test results.'

'I know. They are here.' He gestured to the table where the envelope lay, still sealed closed.

'You haven't opened them.' Confusion touched her.

'I don't need to open them. I wanted to show you that.' He picked the paper up and before she knew what he was about to do he held it to the candle flame. 'I know the baby is mine. I know you would not deceive me or him; there is no need for proof. Now or ever. I believe you.'

Happiness fizzed in her as she watched the paper re-
duce to ash, saw the final proof that he truly trusted her.
'Thank you. That means so much. To me. And to him.'
Her hand rose to touch the swell of her belly.

Now she saw his hands clench and unclench, and he
shifted his feet. 'There is something else I want to say.
To ask.'

He moved forward and she could see nerves and something else in his blue eyes, something that caused a small
tendril of hope to unfurl inside her.

'Jodi Petrovelli, will you marry me? Not for the baby's
sake, not for the sake of Talonos, but because I love you.
With all my heart and soul, and I promise to love you for
the rest of my life, to trust you, believe in you, respect and
honour you.' He inhaled deeply. 'But if you cannot feel the
same way for me, then I swear to you that I will still be the
very best father I know how to be to our son.'

Tears of happiness prickled her eyelids as she moved
forward, took his hands in hers. 'Prince Carlos of Talonos,
I will marry you. Not because you are the father of my
baby, but because of who you are. Because I love you more
than I could ever have imagined loving anyone. I want to
walk by your side, wake up to you every morning for the
rest of my life. You are honourable, caring, generous and
kind. You have dealt with such pain in your life, but you
are not bitter or warped.' She gave a sudden smile. 'And
you're utterly gorgeous as well. I trust you and I trust in
you. I respect you and I like you and I love you.'

His face lit up, illuminated by happiness and the love
she could see shining from his blue eyes as he took a jewel
box from his pocket and took her left hand in his.

As he slid the ring onto her finger she looked down and
her heart twisted with even more love. The ring was silver
and embedded with a scattering of diamonds in a flower

shape, the same design that was on his ring. 'It's beautiful,' she breathed.

'Just like you,' he said. 'You're a beautiful person inside and out. You've shown me how to trust, how to believe in love and how to go forward with forgiveness in my heart. I've spoken with my brother and he and I want to try to forge a new bond.' His hands tightened round hers. 'I do not know what will happen with my father, but I believe there will at least be tolerance and respect and acceptance. I believe he will look at our baby, his grandson, in the same way. I hope the royal family can start to heal.'

'And I hope the same for my family. Because it was you who showed me how to move forward. You have made me a better, stronger person. You've helped me to be me. To step out of the shadow of my sister and my past. To believe in myself. I want to make a difference to Talonos at your side. I want to improve the life of the people, improve education, encourage small businesses like Angelina's and Roseanna's to flourish. But most of all I want us to be a family. You, me, the baby. We are going to be the happiest family in the world.'

'You can count on that,' he said. 'Now let's eat. I've made *puris* stuffed with spiced potatoes, pilau rice and dhal.' The food they had shared that magical first night on Jalpura, the night their baby was conceived. The food she'd craved since. 'And for dessert there are pancakes. Shaped like hearts.'

And as they sat and ate and talked and laughed Jodi's heart swelled with love and happiness as she looked forward to her happy ever after with her very own handsome prince.

EPILOGUE

Nine months later, London

JODI LOOKED AROUND the table and beamed. It was the morning after the glittering celebration organised to mark the merger of Dolci with Palazzo di Cioccolato. The event had been fantastically organised by Ava and there were plenty of publicity shots of the reunited family. Ava, with Liam by her side, Luca with Emily and Jodi and Carlos.

But, wonderful though that had been, this meant so much more. This breakfast gathering held because the family wanted to be together, the photographs all being taken on phones amongst laughter and funny faces.

And this family gathering included Nicolas. Jodi gazed at her son, her adorable gorgeous baby boy, sitting now on his aunt Ava's lap.

'He gets cuter every time I see him,' Ava said.

'Absolutely,' Luca agreed as he covered his eyes with one hand in order to play peekaboo with his nephew.

'Peekaboo!'

And as always Nicolas's face lit up in a beaming smile. And as always Jodi's heart turned over with love for her son and, turning, she saw the same love reflected in Carlos's doting expression. This baby was so lucky that he would grow up with an extended happy family. He already loved his other uncle, Juan—Juan and Carlos were making up for lost time and forging a true brotherly bond, not part of an illusion woven by the royal spin machine.

Isabella still held herself aloof, but King Antonio had at least agreed to talk to Carlos about his ideas for Talonos. It was a start, and Jodi would not give up, knew Carlos would not either, hoped in time father and son might at least achieve a better understanding.

Perhaps she would have with her own father if fate had allowed it. But instead she would be grateful for what James Casseveti had done. By leaving Dolci to all three children he had brought them together.

And now Emily smiled and laid a hand on the massive swell of her tummy. 'And soon Nicolas will have a cousin to play with.'

'Very soon,' Luca agreed and the smile he gave his wife spoke volumes.

Liam cleared his throat. 'On that subject,' he said as he reached for Ava's hand, 'Ava and I have an announcement.'

Ava grinned. 'I'm pregnant too,' she said. 'So soon there will be three little ones to play peekaboo.'

Jodi raised her glass of sparkling water. 'And this time, we'll get it right. To family,' she declared, and felt a strum of contentment as they all raised their glasses and echoed the words.

* * * * *

BEAUTY AND THE RECLUSIVE MILLIONAIRE

RACHAEL STEWART

MILLS & BOON

For my mum and dad,
for sparking my love of Greece—
the food, the people, the stunning islands…
Yamas!
xxx

CHAPTER ONE

'Wow!' CATHERINE WILDE pushed her sunglasses back, sweeping her fringe away as she squinted against the rays of the sun and took in her home for the next month. A Greek island surrounded by crystal blue waters with a golden cliff face that curved before her and seemed to hug and welcome in one. 'It's incredible.'

'The most beautiful island, *nai*?' Marsel grinned as he lugged one of her many bags off his small sailboat that she'd chosen to hitch a lift on. Her PA had thought she was crazy—*'You know I can sort you a nice speedboat, right?'*—but she'd wanted to start this holiday as she meant to go on. Relaxed, laid-back and under no circumstances rushed. So when she'd learned of Marsel's regular trips to the mainland to source supplies she'd jumped at the opportunity to climb aboard.

It had nothing whatsoever to do with delaying her arrival at said island and coming face to face with its owner.

Nothing at all.

She stopped herself from shaking her head emphatically as she threw her focus into the beauty of the island. This trip was about relaxing in authentic Greek hospitality. No security detail, no flash vehicles, no celebrity fuss.

And it was a good plan…if only her bobbing feet and drumming fingertips would get the message.

She'd *tried* to relax on the journey. She'd *tried* to focus on the beauty of Greece, to let the heat of the midday sun warm her, the sea breeze soothe her. She'd tried really hard…and maybe that was the problem. Relaxing didn't come naturally, not to her.

And neither did nerves. She was an award-winning actor after all. It didn't pay to let nerves get the better of her. But this kind of unease was different, uncontainable, and she couldn't deny its source—Alaric de Vere.

Her best friend's older brother. Her friend once too, many moons ago.

And this was his private island, his place of solace, cut off from the world and civilisation, just the way he liked it…

Until now.

Was she truly as welcome as the curving cliff face made out?

Or had his sister, Flo, worked the same persuasive magic over him and left him no choice but to welcome her? A burnt-out celebrity, reeling from a breakup and in desperate need of isolation, if the press were to be believed.

And though they didn't know the half of it, they weren't far wrong…

But she wasn't here just to fix herself, she was here for him. As a favour to Flo and to appease her own worries too. She was here to do everything she could to help Alaric. To remind him of his life beyond the island, of those who missed him and needed him to return.

Her stomach churned it over, her head thinking the worst, her heart…too tender. Was he really as bad as Flo had made out? The media even? Was she going to make it worse coming here when she was hardly a picture of mental health herself?

'Nai?' Marsel's brows nudged skyward, his brown eyes dancing and bright.

She frowned. Nai? Yes. Yes, what?

'The island?' He gestured to it as he leapt back onto the precarious gangplank with another of her bags.

'Nai. Very beautiful.' She gave him an unrestrained smile, thinking only to hide her worries, and immediately regretted it.

His knees seemed to buckle beneath him, his body leaning precariously overboard, and she flung her hand out with a yelp, too far away to reach. She held her breath and was forced to watch as he swiftly regained control and hurried to land, his eyes averted, his tanned cheeks sporting a flush he wouldn't want her to notice.

She wanted to apologise. She knew the affect she had on people, but she'd hoped her and Marsel had moved past that after several hours in one another's company. Her efforts to show him she was just another person, a person capable of carrying her own luggage, capable of laughing over the fact he'd run her suitcase over her foot in his haste to get to it before she could herself, paying off.

But it seemed he was still as star-struck, and after a decade in the film industry, she should be used to it… and she was…

It didn't make it any easier to live with though.

She loved acting. She loved projecting another life on the screen and moving people to tears, to laughter, to joy. To provide the kind of escapism people needed when times were tough or to pass a few pleasant hours of downtime.

But fame came with its pedestal and a lonely one at that.

Not that she was being all woe me. She knew how lucky she was; she just wished at times to be able to blend in, be normal, to have her personal affairs kept just that—

personal. Her hand went to her stomach, her fingers idly stroking as the pain of the recent past threatened to invade.

The future would be different; she was determined to make it so. One step at a time. First, a change in career. She wanted to make a difference on the other side of the screen. She wanted to write her own tales for others to perform. Something this trip was supposed to aid with by giving her the space, the freedom and the time to get her first script finished.

Time to work and time to grieve, Flo had said. Time to help Alaric, and time to help herself.

She lowered her gaze to where her fingers stilled over her flat stomach that showed nothing of the slightest baby bump that had once been and swallowed the bubble of pain that threatened to shake her anew. She thought of the soft smile on Flo's lips as her friend had bade her a teary farewell, her own palm resting over her well-pronounced bump. A sight that had brought both pain and happiness, the reminder of what she'd lost contending with her joy for her friend who deserved every bit of happiness.

She pulled her phone from her bag. She'd promised Flo she'd message when she arrived safe and now was as good a time as any. It would also free Marsel to go about his task without another mishap courtesy of her and her world-renowned smile. And though she'd offered to carry her own baggage off the boat, she was relieved he'd insisted on doing it. She really didn't fancy her chances of making it across, bags in hand, not with the way the flimsy gangplank was shifting with the boat. She had to wedge her body against the rail just to text Flo.

She kept it short and sweet, pocketed the phone before she could drop it in the rolling waters and breathed in her surroundings.

It really was beautiful, beautiful and isolated and…quite

unexpected. With the simplest of wooden jetties forming a safe path over the rocks, its white painted railing distressed and peeling away, it was hardly luxurious and so unlike the family to which it belonged.

Or more specifically the man…but then what did she know of Alaric after all this time?

The boat lurched with the waves and her stomach took another roll. A roll she knew had nothing to do with the waters beneath her and everything to do with him. She grasped the handrail to steady herself, wishing she could steady her stomach and her nerves just as easy.

She'd known Alaric her entire life. They'd played together as children, hung out together as teens, got drunk and disorderly even… He'd been her first real crush too, in an intensely forbidden best friend's older brother kind of… A ridiculous bubble of laughter cut off her mental spiel—*not helping, Catherine.*

But so much had changed since she last saw him. His entire life had been upended, and here she was waltzing right back into it…surely it was too little, too late?

Was she deluded to even try? To believe Flo when she'd insisted Catherine could help, even when his own family hadn't been able to?

Her phone buzzed in her bag and she lifted it out, glanced at the screen as it buzzed again and again with more messages arriving in quick succession.

You're on the island?

You've seen Alaric?

Is he okay?

Her brows drew together as she tapped in a reply.

Yes. No. Don't know. Calm down, Flo. Xx

Her friend's response was just as quick.

Sorry! Where is he? Xx

Her frown deepened. Good question. Where was her host? Surely it was polite to greet a guest at the dock... especially one that you hadn't seen in for ever?

She typed back.

I don't know. We've just moored up. He's probably at the house.

Three dots appeared to show that Flo was typing...and typing...and still typing.

The hairs on Catherine's nape prickled, her anxiety aggravated with every prolonged second...

She glanced up to see Marsel landside with all the bags, his phone to his ear as he spoke in rapid Greek. She looked back to her phone, tapped her foot. *Come on, Flo, spit it out...*

Okay. Keep me updated, yeah? Xx

That was it. That was what had taken several minutes to type?

'Way to go in helping me relax, Flo,' she murmured under her breath as she fired off her reply.

Of course. Xx

She shoved her phone back into her bag and lowered her sunglasses, moving before she changed her mind about the whole affair. She needed this break and Alaric needed to get a life, to use Flo's words. It was a win-win.

Marsel saw her approach and quickly cut his call, hurrying to the end of the gangplank to offer out his hand in aid. Gladly she took it, careful to keep her smile to the ground.

'Kyrios de Vere is aware that we are here,' he said once she was safe on land.

'Great.' Though her stomach didn't feel great.

She reached for one of her cases and as Marsel tried to stop her she waved him down.

'I think it will be quicker if I help. It looks like there's a walk ahead?'

She eyed the worn and dusty pier, the sandy pathway through the cliff face, the small cove that looked like it had no decent exit point…it wasn't as though a car was suddenly going to appear. And there were the food supplies Marsel had brought back from the mainland to carry too.

'Is Alaric—Kyrios de Vere—on his way?'

Marsel didn't eye her as he took her other bags in hand and started off down the jetty. 'He says that we should head on up. The jeep isn't too far away.'

'Oh…' She peered into the picturesque distance and saw nothing remotely vehicle-like. She'd just have to take his word for it.

Brows drawing together, she followed him, her mind pondering Alaric's whereabouts. It was perfectly reasonable, she tried to tell herself, that he wouldn't want to greet her at the dock. She didn't have to think the worst. And besides, she was here for her space too, having rejected her security detail and her PA's pleasant company. This was just another element of getting all the space she desired.

Perfectly reasonable. Perfectly fine.

Only…

No one had seen Alaric in a year. The public hadn't

seen him in nearly three, and she…well, she hadn't seen him for almost ten…and she *knew* he was suffering. She got that. But did that mean he really didn't want her here, in spite of the invite?

Her heart ached for him, even as the urge to run nipped at her heels.

'Wait here, Miss Wilde!' Marsel called back over his shoulder. 'The jeep is just a few yards away, tucked into a cave out of the sun. I'll bring it to you.'

She blew out a relieved breath, releasing her case with a nod and fisting her hands on her hips. Not that she *couldn't* carry on up the steep incline ahead. She trained daily. She had to. She wasn't one of those actors who depended on body doubles, stunt or otherwise. If the character had to do it, then she had to—it was important to her. Though her agent and the extortionate fee for her insurance told her she was foolish to insist on it.

But a jeep was good. It meant she wouldn't arrive face to face with Alaric for the first time in years feeling exposed and in desperate need of a shower. She'd at least have her trusty armour—her make-up, her clothing and her composure—all in place.

Shielding her eyes with one hand, she took in the sandy cove, the dusty path ahead, the sprouts of green and flora jutting out of the golden cliff face, the trees looming over the edge high above…and then she saw it—a figure… someone in between the trees… *Alaric?*

She went to wave, but the silhouette vanished as swiftly as it had appeared.

Had she imagined it? Was it a trick of the light, of the haze caused by the heat of the sun?

She wiped the sweat from the back of her neck, flapped the front of her vest top to let in some air…

Yes, it had to be the heat playing tricks on her, or it wasn't Alaric, because Alaric would have at least waved.

But then the Alaric she remembered would have bounded down the path and swept her up into a bear hug the second she'd hopped off the boat.

The Alaric she remembered would have made sure she felt welcome.

The Alaric she remembered wouldn't leave her feeling like this…

This was a mistake.

Alaric had known it the second his sister had asked.

Had known it even as he'd said yes and instructed Dorothea to make up the spare room. For his use, not Catherine's, because Catherine had to have the best his house could offer and that meant his suite.

He cursed, raked a hand through his sweat-slickened hair. Catherine. *Here.* On his island. This was madness.

He'd tried to run off the apprehension, the unease, had ran and ran in the ridiculous heat with no destination in mind, until he'd found himself at the cliff edge and spied Marsel's boat on the horizon.

And then, as the boat had loomed closer, it had been her hair, captivating as it shone like spun gold in the breeze, her presence like a hit of sunshine straight to his frozen core, its warmth far more powerful than the blazing heat of the day.

It had always been this way with Catherine…or was it Kitty now?

Kitty. His fists flexed at his sides. He didn't know her as Kitty, but the world did—Kitty Wilde, Hollywood A-list and idol to millions. Would there be any of Catherine left in the movie star she was now?

And why did he even care?

He shouldn't. Just as he shouldn't have agreed. He clenched his jaw, fighting back the chaos rising within. He'd made his bed so to speak…the time to turn her away was long gone. And he could hardly leave the island himself. Where would he go? Where would he *want* to go?

Nowhere. That was the cold hard truth. His island was more than just his home; it was his sanctuary, his protection from the past, his haven for the future.

But thanks to his sister, he now had a guest, and one he wasn't ready to face, no matter what good manners dictated. He watched as she walked down the jetty, every step bringing her that bit closer, her walk so elegant even as she lugged what had to be a heavily laden suitcase…

He dragged in a breath, battling the sudden light-headedness. No, he'd wait for nightfall, for the harsh light of day to be gone. In the darkness he could find some protection, something to obscure his scars when she set her infamous blue eyes on him and that picture-perfect smile that had captured the hearts of millions, if not billions.

If she would muster up a smile at all when she saw what he had become…

She glanced up at that precise moment, her eyes behind her shades colliding with his and the world stilled, his heart the only thing capable of movement as it leapt, strong and wild. The most he'd felt in years.

He choked on his own folly as he spun away and broke into a pace that was all the more fierce for the feelings he was trying to outrun. He pounded the trail, through the trees, the landscaped gardens, the burn in his lungs nothing to do with exertion and everything to do with her. He startled Andreas, who was tending to the flowers beside the front door, and almost took out a bustling Dorothea when he burst into the hallway.

'Kyrios de Vere!' She clutched a hand to her chest, her

brown eyes wide, wisps of grey hair escaping her bun as she rushed about getting everything perfect for their guest. 'You startled me!'

He came to an abrupt halt, sucked in a breath. 'Marsel will be here shortly. Can you show Catherine around and I'll join her this evening?'

'But don't you—'

'I'm busy.' He was already moving off, heading for the stairs, and he sensed her frown follow him.

'But—'

'No buts, Dorothea. See it done.'

Yes, he was being discourteous, his manners tossed to the wayside in his desire to avoid facing her, but what did they know of it, what did any of them know of it... This was his house, his domain, and he could act however he damn well chose.

He only wished he could dismiss the nagging guilt as easily.

CHAPTER TWO

RIGHT, SO SHE was here, and he wasn't.

Unease rippled through her as she followed Marsel's directions to the kitchen, grocery bags wrapped in her arms. She felt like she shouldn't be here, that she was invading Alaric's home. A man she no longer knew.

All she had to go on was second-hand. Not the hyped-up, titillated news the world's media reported, but the heartfelt version from his sister. And not just the horrific details of the accident three years ago that had taken the life of his best friend, but the mark it had left. How it changed him both inside and out. How he'd cut himself off so completely.

Would he let her in? Would he talk to her? Would he even make himself known or was she going to spend a month alone?

She tightened her hold on the grocery bags as the hollow ache inside resonated out, her own loss compounded by her fear that whatever bond they'd once shared was over. And in that moment, she didn't know who needed it more…her or Alaric.

'Aah, Miss Wilde, it is so good to meet you!' A woman bustled towards her as she entered the kitchen, her brown eyes sparkling with warmth, her flour-dusted cheeks giving off a glow. 'I'm Dorothea, Kyrios de Vere's housekeeper, and you really shouldn't be carrying those—that is a job for my son!'

Catherine laughed at the woman's flurried greeting. 'It's so good to meet you too, and it's fine. I insisted on helping. Where shall I put them?'

Dorothea hurried across the stone-walled kitchen to the centre island, shoving various ingredients and cooking utensils aside to clear some space on the worn wooden surface. 'Thank you, Miss Wilde.'

'You're welcome.' She placed the bags down and eyed the concrete countertop behind her, its glazed surface covered in flour with a fresh mound of dough at its heart.

'I'm so sorry, Kyrios de Vere's not here.' Dorothea wrung her hands in her apron. 'You see, he is—well, he is rather busy with his work, and—and he did say he was sorry and that he will join you this evening.'

She nodded, though Dorothea's obvious discomfort failed to reassure her and, seeking a distraction, she gestured to the dough. 'What are you making?'

'Fresh pitta to go with souvlaki tonight. It is Kyrios de Vere's favourite.'

Catherine smiled. 'Soon to be mine, I'm sure.'

Fresh baked bread—her weakness. But it was okay, she had a month without a camera on her. She could afford to eat a little luxury so early on in her break.

'Excellent!' Dorothea's cheeks rounded with her smile as she paused before the Belfast sink to wash her hands and Catherine glanced around the room.

It was a rustic delight, all wood and concrete with a splash of colour from the copper handles and pans, and the herbs that hung along one wall creating a pleasing, natural scent. It was a proper kitchen. Well-used, homely and tasteful.

She couldn't stop her thoughts going back to her host…

had he designed this space? Did he cook here too? Or was it all Dorothea and the skill of a talented interior designer?

'Now you should get yourself settled and relaxed.' Dorothea gently shooed her to the door. 'I'll show you to your bedroom.'

'No—no, it's fine. I'll help unload the jeep first.'

'You will not.' The commanding way she said it had Catherine grinning. Not only was she unaccustomed to being bossed about when she wasn't on set, she actually found the older woman's manner quite endearing. 'My son is more than capable, as is his father. You are a guest.'

'Nonsense.' As endearing as it was, Catherine wasn't backing down. 'It's the least I can do for hijacking Marsel's trip to the mainland, and I won't be waited on hand and foot while I'm here.'

'There's no talking her down, Mama.' Marsel bustled into the kitchen before they could make it to the door, his arms laden with bags as he shook his head and gave his mum a sheepish smile. 'I've already tried several times over.'

'It's true, I insisted.' Catherine rested her hand on Dorothea's shoulder. '*Please.* I want to help.'

'You might as well agree, *agápi mou.*' In came Andreas, Marsel's father, his eyes crinkling at the corners with his grin. 'I've already had the same argument with Miss Wilde outside. She's as stubborn as you!'

That earned a huff out of Dorothea and a laugh from the rest, including Catherine, her nerves readily disappearing in the company of their easy banter.

She followed Marsel back out to the jeep and this time he didn't quibble as he handed her a brown paper bag filled with groceries and took one up for himself. 'That's the last of the food.'

As they headed back inside, she surveyed the grounds

once more, this time taking in its beauty rather than try-ing to spy her elusive host. The house flowed over several storeys built into the hillside, its stone walls blending into the surroundings and giving the impression of a century-old farmhouse rather than the luxury villa she'd been ex-pecting. There were pale blue shutters at every window, terracotta pots with flowers flourishing and well-tended rock gardens with a variety of plants and olive trees offer-ing up some verdant relief to the dry terrain.

The sound of running water came from the lowest tier and she could just make out the edge of an infinity pool that dropped off into the ocean, and rattan-covered seat-ing areas positioned to make the most of the far-reach-ing view with distant boats and islands appearing as tiny specks on the horizon.

'Stand there much longer and the food will cook itself.'

She spun to face Marsel waiting in the doorway and grimaced. 'Sorry, it really is quite captivating.'

He grinned as he carried on his way and she followed him inside, the cool air of the house an instant relief to the oppressive heat of the day. It wasn't just the soothing temperature either, it was the earthy tones of the décor, the exposed stone and mortar in the walls, the interesting theme of forged cement, wood and rattan flowing both inside and out.

It was calming, Zen-like, and as she breathed it all in, she realised she could be quite happy here. That if any place could teach her to relax, it was this one. So long as her and Alaric were okay...

She wriggled the bag higher up her chest, righted her shoulders and bolstered her resolve. They *would* be okay.

Helping him wasn't negotiable, helping herself on the other hand...well, she was trying.

She walked into the kitchen and straight into the back of a stock-still Marsel.

'Mama! Papa!'

She peeked around him, her frown of confusion lifting as she took in the scene before her—a blushing Dorothea batting away a now flour-covered Andreas. Catherine didn't need to guess at what Marsel had walked in on.

'It's amazing anything gets done here,' their son admonished, shaking his head and dumping the bags on the island.

Andreas pounded his son's back. 'Says you.'

She laughed at their teasing, the speed with which they succeeded in lifting her from her worries such light relief.

She placed her bag down beside Marsel's and brushed off her hands. 'Is there anything else I can help with?'

She eyed the dough and Dorothea hurried over to her. 'Not today. You should get yourself unpacked and settled in.'

'I really don't mind.' Especially when she felt in desperate need of a distraction to fill the hours between now and dinner when she would finally get to see him. Sticking around the family and their pleasantries definitely appealed more than being left to her thoughts.

'But I do.' Dorothea started to shoo her to the door again. 'Now come, I'll show you to your room.'

'Okay. Okay.' She gave a soft sigh and followed her, pausing briefly to speak to Marsel. 'Thanks again for the lift, I really appreciate it.'

'Yes, Marsel.' The very air seemed to still as all eyes swung to the open doorway and the man now filling it. 'Thank you for bringing Catherine here.'

Alaric!

At least…it had to be…but ten years…the accident and the scar it had left. Her gaze caught on it, the way his bronzed skin pulled together along his cheek, tugging at the corner of his eye and mouth, creating a jagged line in the dark layer of stubble.

Her heart twisted. The sight of the scar in the flesh bringing with it the pain he'd endured, the agony, the loss. It felt like minutes passed when it could only have been seconds, her pulse kick-starting, her eyes blinking away the tears that would have formed as she stepped forward and stalled. He'd said nothing more. Hadn't even moved. No welcome, nothing.

And he was so very different. Taller, broader, the hard cut to his jaw more pronounced as he clenched it tight, his mouth full even in its grim line. His dark hair, neither short nor long, dripped water onto his white T-shirt, the fabric fitting snug to his chest and biceps before gathering at the hips, his loose linen trousers and bare feet far more relaxed than his posture.

Had he been in the shower—is that why he hadn't come to greet her?

It was a nice thought, a relief, but somehow she doubted it, and as she forced her eyes back to his, her thoughts emptied out. It was his eyes that spoke to her the most, those breathtaking blues that conjured up so many memories and seemed to suck the very oxygen from the room. There was no denying who those eyes belonged to. Even devoid of the light, the humour, the love, they were undeniably his, and undeniably cold.

She lifted her chin a fraction and swallowed, her smile so very forced. 'Alaric?'

'Catherine.'

He dipped his head, the movement stilted as his body tightened against the chill spreading within, rapidly taking over the warmth that had assaulted him the second he'd entered the doorway and set eyes on her up close.

She'd twisted her hair up into a knot high on her head since he'd seen her on the jetty, her sunglasses nestled in the golden tresses and unveiling her startling blue eyes that he didn't want to appreciate up close. They made his heart race, his body warm with too many memories, too many feelings. Even when they were filled with the wide-eyed horror they possessed now, her glossy mouth parted, her cheeks flushed pink.

He tried to swallow, tried to regain control, but everything about her made it impossible. Even the simple hairstyle provoked him, the way it exposed the arch of her neck, her delicate collarbone, escaped tendrils teasing at the skin there. Skin that he'd once admired, tickled, caressed even…only not in the way he'd craved.

And now she was here with far too much of that skin on show. Her vest top hanging from two of the skinniest straps, her animal print shorts lightweight and short. Much too short as they exposed her long legs all glossy and bronzed, and…and he really needed to keep his eyes up.

But then he was looking straight into her wide-eyed gaze, her abject horror freezing over his veins once more. And in a way that was better, far safer. It kept him at a distance, reminded him of how times had changed, how they'd both changed.

'Or is it Kitty now?' He couldn't prevent the bitter edge to his voice, didn't want to, and Dorothea's narrowed gaze told him she'd caught it. Caught it and was warning him to behave. To do better.

'I'll answer to either.' Her smile wavered about her lips, a fresh bloom of colour rising from her chest to her face, highlighting her angled cheekbones and the button-like tip to her upturned nose. Features he remembered all too well and bringing the strangest sense of relief that she hadn't succumbed to the surgeon's knife in her quest to achieve Hollywood perfection.

And why would she change when she's perfect enough already?

His jaw pulsed as he buried the unwelcome thought. 'Catherine, it is.'

'It's good to see you.'

Was it? Or was she just being polite. He hadn't mistaken the horror he'd glimpsed, he was sure, so was it regret he could see now? Regret and...curiosity?

Did she want to see for herself the man he had become? The beast even...

The tabloids were rarely kind, and his sister alone knew enough to condemn him.

Dorothea's brows were wagging on his periphery, telling him to respond appropriately, and he cleared his throat, gave a curt nod. 'I trust you had a good journey?'

There. That was polite. That was thoughtful.

'I did...thank you.' She stepped towards him and he fought the urge to back up, fought even harder as her hands lifted— *God*, was she going to embrace him? Hell, no. He spun away. 'I'll show you around.'

He strode down the hall, not daring to wait, not able to breathe until there was enough distance between them. He had no interest in being all touchy-feely. He didn't want her to see him up close. In the face of her perfection, he felt ever more scarred, ever more damaged.

'Hey, Alaric, slow down.'

He didn't. He raked his fingers through his hair and continued on, hearing the soft pad of her footfall behind him. Even the American twang she'd gained over the years riled his blood. Hollywood may not have forced her under

the knife, but ten years of living and breathing that world…
was she even recognisable underneath?

Unlikely.

Did he want to find out?

No.

Did he care?

Did *he*?

He couldn't even mentally deny it. Truth was he
shouldn't care. Caring led to feelings that he'd long ago
denied himself. He didn't deserve to care for another, just
as he didn't deserve another's care.

Further reason he should have refused this crazy visit.
Refused Flo and not risen to her emotional blackmail.

Flo. His meddling little sister. She'd known what strings
to pull, she'd known how to crack his trusty composure—
Catherine. She'd been his Achilles heel back then, and no
matter how he tried to convince himself that was in the
past, that she wasn't his to care for, he hadn't been able
to say no.

And what exactly had Flo told Catherine over the years?
He knew full well his sister's thoughts on how he lived
but just how much of a beast did she think he was? He
certainly looked it and Flo herself had tossed the abusive
label at him in this very space two years ago when he'd
refused to return home to visit their mother after her diag-
nosis. Called him worse last Christmas when he continued
to refuse. But to have those looks of pity, of sadness, from
those he loved, those who'd once seen him as strong, successful, invincible…no, he couldn't stomach it.

But then last month, when she'd begged him to take
Catherine in, he'd cracked. *'Please, Alaric, she needs to
hide away from the media storm brewing before it breaks
her.'*

A media storm triggered by Kitty Wilde's high-profile breakup with her co-star and fellow A-lister, Luke Walker. A man who was everything Alaric wasn't and never could be...

He raised a hand to the right. 'The dining room is here.'

He was surprised he didn't choke on the words as he fought a misplaced surge of jealousy and didn't turn as he sensed her pause to look inside the doorway.

'It's nice.'

'It opens onto the veranda and makes the most of the view. I often eat here but you can choose to eat wherever you like.'

He moved off, making sure his point hit home—that he wasn't expecting her to dine with him; in fact, he'd prefer it if she didn't—and he could practically sense Dorothea's disapproving look should she overhear.

'Alaric?'

She was hurrying after him again, but he refused to pause.

'To the left is my study which you won't need. The next door takes you to the gym. It's fully equipped with a treadmill, bike, cross trainer, rowing machine, weights... If you need any help getting to grips with anything let Marsel or Andreas know.'

'Not you? Can't you...'

He gave her a quick look over his shoulder, careful to give his unscarred side. 'I'd prefer it if they helped you.'

'Oh...'

It was soft, filled with disappointment, and the pang in his chest of undeniable guilt almost had him taking it back.

'There's also a steam room, sauna, jacuzzi and outdoor shower.' He was already moving again. 'There are steps down to the pool too.'

He gestured to the right, to the last door. 'The rest of the floor is made up of the library which you can access here. The bookcases are well stocked, so you should find something to interest you. If not, let Dorothea or Andreas know and they will see it sourced.'

'I'm sure that won't be necessary.'

He waited as she peeked inside, her smile lighting up her face. She'd always loved books. It was an interest they'd once shared and the vision of them together on the U-shaped sofa, book in hand, the glass wall before them with the backdrop of the Aegean Sea, was too quick to form. Clear in its imagery, strong in the alien sense of longing it dredged up.

'It's so tranquil.'

He grunted, *actually grunted*, and continued on his way, heading down the stone steps to the mid-level as she hurried to keep up with him. He really was being a jerk. He knew it. Knew it but couldn't stop. Because stopping meant looking at her again. Looking at her and recalling that fleeting imagery and knowing it may be clear, it may be strong, but it was wrong. Because in it, he too was perfect. Unscarred. Happy.

And it made him angry. He could feel it bubbling in the pit of his gut. There was a time he'd dreamed of them being together. Believed it possible even. That one day he'd walk into her world of glitz and glamor and sweep her off her feet. That he'd be good enough. Successful enough.

But the accident had destroyed that dream...not just destroyed it but taken away his ability to want it. Thoughts of his best friend and the wife and child he'd left behind. The guilt of it cutting as deep now as it had the day he'd learned of Fred's death, and he clenched his fists as his fingers shook.

'Wow!'

The exclamation came from Catherine as she entered the living room behind him and he turned to see her all aglow, her eyes taking in the room, her sigh all breathy and alluring as she walked into the middle and twirled on the spot. 'This is something else.'

He cleared his throat to say something, but all he wanted to admit was that it wasn't the only thing that was. And he wasn't about to let out the obvious. She knew how attractive she was; she courted the cameras day in, day out. Knew how to pose, how best to angle her features…but he found himself lured in by her genuine delight. She had to be accustomed to the best the world had to offer, so why did his home impress her so much.

Unless it was an act?

She did it for a living after all…

'Did you design this space?' Before her eyes could reach him, he headed to the bar at the opposite end of the room.

'Yes.' He took two glasses out from the cupboard beneath the wooden countertop. 'Can I get you a drink?'

'Water would be lovely.'

'Sparkling, still?'

'Sparkling, thank you.' She continued to stroll through the room, her fingers brushing over the furnishings, the neutral-coloured recliners, the distressed wooden sideboard, her eyes lifting to the brightly coloured paintings above. 'I like it.'

Did she like the pictures too? Did she know—

'Did you paint these?'

She turned to look at him and he lowered his gaze, bent to pull a chilled bottle of sparkling water from the undercounter fridge. 'Yes.'

'Recently?'

'No.' It came out gruff. Too gruff. He hadn't painted anything of substance in years. He still didn't have the fine motor skill required in his left hand to do anything close to something he could be satisfied with, let alone hang.

He placed her drink on the side and carried his own to the glass door, sliding it open enough for him to walk out. The instant hit of the midday sun battled with the cool air-conditioned room and he sucked in a deep breath.

He wanted to be able to hold her eye. To hold a conversation. More than anything, he realised, he was at war with himself, because he *wanted* to enjoy her company. All things he would have done—could have done once.

But now, now he felt inadequate, unworthy, broken. Living the life of a hermit with a body that didn't feel like his any more.

He heard her come up behind him and kept his eyes on the ocean, the ripple of the waves, the sailboats all peaceful and serene. 'It was a derelict farmhouse when I bought the island. I had it renovated and extended.'

She walked ahead of him, out to the edge of the balcony, and he followed, comfortable that her eyes were on the view. He paused beside her, keeping his good side facing her.

'I can see why you bought it. I love that you left the stone exposed. It gives the place a soul even as it blends into the land.'

He gave a soft huff, both surprised and pleased that she could see his reasoning so well. 'Part of this floor and the ground floor have been carved out of the cliff. It stops it dominating the landscape and also means the bedrooms on the ground floor tend to stay cool even when the air conditioning is off.'

'You have an upside-down house?'

His lips quirked as a surprising laugh flickered to life. 'I guess it is. And having the pool outside the bedroom is convenient when you like to swim before the day kicks off in earnest.'

'Is that what you do?' She turned to look up at him.

'Yes.'

'Every morning?'

'Yes.'

Her eyes were still on him and he breathed in through his nose, trying to ease the anxiety her continued attention triggered, but it brought with it her scent. Floral and vanilla. Subtly sweet and tempting. He could feel it swirl within his bloodstream, a teasing warmth that he hadn't felt in so long.

It was debilitating to feel such a powerful attraction, unsettling in its gravity, and he reached out for the stone balustrade, gripped it tight. But then he wasn't accustomed to social interaction, social interaction of any sort. He saw Dorothea, Andreas and Marsel. That was it. He hadn't seen another soul in a year, and even then, it had been a visit from his sister that he hadn't even agreed to.

And now here he was, with Catherine. Temptation in its truest form, and it hit him full force once more—his sister had known exactly what she was doing and he'd played straight into her hand.

He was a damn fool.

She turned beside him, resting her elbows on the balustrade and angling her face to the sun, her eyes closed. 'I can see why you moved here.'

She sounded content. Happy. So very different to the chaos raging inside him and he risked a look. He shouldn't have. Ensnared, that was the word for it. Ensnared by the sight of her up close and so at ease.

There was no horror now and he was starting to question whether it had been there in the first place. He couldn't even recall the look as he took her in anew. Her hair shone in varying shades of gold, her thick lashes forming dark crescents over blushing pink cheeks, her lips parted as she breathed out, the hint of tongue glistening between perfect white teeth.

It wasn't *au naturel* though. Her make-up had been expertly applied, the hint of eyeliner following the curve of her lashes, the mascara thickening their lengths, the shimmer across her skin creating what appeared to be a natural flush. Her lips were pink and glossy, as though she had just wet them, when in reality she'd coated them in some expensive product.

She epitomised Hollywood.

And he wanted to hate it. He wanted to use it to keep his distance. To beat back the feelings of old that were threatening to surface and had no place in the now.

'So, the bedrooms, then?' She shifted so quick, her eyes landing on him and narrowing so quickly, he knew she'd witnessed too much.

He cleared his throat, held her eye with more strength than he felt. 'We can get to them this way, or head back inside and go down.'

'I'm easy.'

His pulse spiked, blasted innuendo, and he headed back through the open door, welcoming the chill of the air con that he desperately needed now. He placed his drink on the bar and continued to the stairs.

Was this how it was going to be for the next—how long did he say she could stay? A month? He could hardly think straight and the sooner he got this tour over with the better. His duty as host would be done and he could find some space, some equilibrium, again.

Until dinner at least…

CHAPTER THREE

CATHERINE FOLLOWED IN his wake, an awareness thrumming through her entire body. She wasn't an innocent, she knew desire when it hit her, but this…it had her skin alight, goosebumps prickling in spite of the heat, in spite of his obvious displeasure at her being here too.

And what the hell was that about?

Desiring someone who could barely bring themselves to look at you…

Was it teenage lust coming back to the fore? Was it old feelings trying to find a place in this new arrangement where she couldn't even call herself a friend any more?

A friend would have been able to gain access to the island by now. A friend would have eased him back into the land of the living and not lost the rapport of old. Not that any of his friends, his family even, had succeeded to date.

Was Flo mad to think she could?

'They miss you, you know.'

His shoulders flinched and she paused, her breath catching as she waited for something, anything, but…nothing.

He continued on his way and she knew she'd overstepped already. It was day one of thirty. Waiting at least a week before going in with the whole guilt trip might have been better. Or maybe, not at all?! She wanted to clamp her hand over her mouth, and blamed her emotions that were running high, not to mention the fact that his presence made any coherent thought virtually impossible.

The change in him was so marked. Not just his appearance, but in the way he behaved. He couldn't bring himself to look at her when they were alone and averted his gaze as soon as he spied her looking. He created distance between them at every opportunity.

He was either insecure, or he truly hated having her here, and she didn't want to believe the latter.

But Alaric—insecure, shy, nervous. He'd always been sexy, confident, fun. He was the man that had produced the wild splashes of colour on the paintings adorning the walls in the living room. The man who had once made her laugh so hard she'd almost been sick. The man that had stood up at her sixteenth birthday party and sung her a song full of wicked innuendo and tease.

They'd always had that kind of relationship. That unspoken bond. One that they'd been comfortable enough to joke about but never once risked crossing that line. And then life had intervened, her career taking her to LA, his own across Europe. And after the accident…well, no one had been welcome.

She frowned at his back, the obvious tension still pulling at his shoulders. Her chest ached as she considered the man he was now, and the man he'd once been, even as she took in his visual strength. His shoulders that were so broad, his muscles rippling beneath the light fabric of his T-shirt. He'd always been trim and toned. Now he boasted the kind of muscle you'd find in a heavyweight boxing ring, his frame speaking of a strength that would send her mouth dry, if not for the pain she glimpsed too.

She sipped at her drink, needing it to cool and soothe as she watched him turn on the bottom step and point out the first door on their left.

'This is your room.'

He didn't turn his head; instead he pushed open the door and gestured for her to walk around him.

She eyed him, frustrated, demanding his attention—did he really not want to look at her? Or was he so afraid of her looking at him?

She opened her mouth to say something, but what could she say? She was still Catherine, the same Catherine she had always been.

She caved and walked on in, trying to think up her next move, a way to change the dynamic, but the room took over. *This* was her room?

She eyed him, eyed it. Torn between the impressive vista beyond the glass wall and the room itself. It was stunning. Luxury-spa stunning. From the huge bed that seemed to float on air with its fluffy pillows and crisp white linen, the stone walls and earthen floor, set off perfectly by the infinity pool beyond the glass, the thatched cabana and the turquoise sea.

She was accustomed to presidential suites, penthouses, the best accommodation a hotel could offer, but this was his home and all that paled in comparison.

'You approve?' He came up behind her, his close proximity making her back prickle to life, wishing him closer still.

'It's incredible…'

She spun to face him and instantly regretted it as he moved off, pointing to a display panel beside the door.

'You can adjust the temperature here should you need to. Each room has its own thermostatic control. And if you'd rather have breakfast delivered to your room, a quick buzz to Dorothea with the phone beside your bed and she will see it arranged.'

He strode off to the left, through a stone archway, and the lights beyond came on automatically, illuminating what she assumed were wardrobes. 'Your dressing room leads to your private bathroom.'

She followed him, unsure what captivated her more, him, the room or the amazing ocean view that greeted them in every room, the bathroom no exception.

'The glass allows you to see out, but no one can see in.'

She nodded, silent as she took in the freestanding slipper bath positioned to make the most of the view, the double walk-in shower that seemed to be carved out of the rock with its copper dials and oversized rainwater heads, the twin copper sinks that sat like bowls atop a glossed concrete vanity unit.

'There are facecloths, towels, toiletries, everything you should need. The controls for the shower are self-explanatory, but if you need any help, call—'

'Call Dorothea, Andreas or Marsel.' She quipped, rounding on him. 'I've got the message.'

He didn't look at her. Not that she was surprised, and she opted for another approach. 'If this is the guest bedroom, I'd *love* to see what the master suite looks like.'

It was part tease, part vent, and his eyes flicked to her, so very briefly, and then he was striding back into the bedroom and she was hot on his tail, ready to press further until her eyes met with the painting straight ahead. She was held captive by it. The figures entwined, the vibrant colours, the ardent mood, the artistic flick of the brush that she recognised like a signature...

'This is your room, isn't it?'

He didn't respond as he headed to the glass and flipped a switch on the wall beside it. 'You can use this to draw the blinds and slide the doors open, and the controller slotted beside the bed does the same.'

Tentatively, she closed the distance between them, half scared he'd spook again as he re-flicked the switch to stop the blinds that had started to lower.

'I get it, Alaric.' She was referring to the controls, but as she said it, she felt it run far deeper. To him. To what had happened. To how he felt having her here.

He gave a curt nod and moved to go around her, but she reached out to touch his arm. 'Alaric?' She felt the hard heat of muscle flex beneath her fingers, the zip of electricity that ran through her as she wet her lips. 'Stop a second and just look at me…please.'

He eyed her on his periphery but didn't turn.

'This is your room, isn't it?'

'Does it matter?'

'I don't want to come here and kick you out of your space.' *Especially when I know I'm not welcome*, came the unhelpful inner voice.

'You're not.'

'I am.' She wet her lips again, edgy and unsure. 'I don't want that.'

'Believe me, Catherine, the guest room is perfectly adequate for me, and I don't make use of the dressing room as it is. Judging by your luggage, you will…' He gestured to her bags that were piled up beside the entrance, breaking their eye contact as he hastened in their direction, taking away whatever hope she had of getting through to him. 'I believe Marsel has brought everything down but if you are missing anything or you require anything else, just call.'

'Call anyone but you…' She folded her arms across her chest, fought down the rising sadness.

'I have work I need to get on with, Catherine.'

She nodded, knowing full well it wasn't work that was taking him away.

Or maybe it was, and she was being unfair?

'I'll see you at dinner.' He was already out the door. 'We eat at seven.'

We eat at seven. No, *Is that good for you? Would you prefer to eat earlier?* He seemed to give with one hand and take with the other. She opened her mouth to say something but, too late, he was gone. Not even a *Goodbye, enjoy your afternoon*—nothing.

And now she just felt weirdly…discombobulated. A word she couldn't remember ever using, let alone feeling.

The vibration of her phone coming from her handbag proved a grateful distraction and she dipped to pick it up. It was another message from Flo.

Have you seen him now?

Yes—

She stopped typing and bit into her lip. What else could she say? What else *should* she say? Her friend was already worrying enough…

He was here when I got to the house.

How is he?

She swallowed, she couldn't lie to Flo, especially when she was put on the spot.

Different. Distant.

Did you coax out a smile at least?

Had she? No. There'd been the glimmer of one when she'd referred to his house as upside down, but that was it. The rest of the time…

Not quite.

Was he rude? If he was rude, I want to know. I didn't send you there to be mistreated.

'Mistreated?' she blurted out loud, surprised at her friend's dramatic choice of words.

Don't be silly, Flo. It's a huge adjustment for him. You know that. Isn't that why you sent me?

True. I just hoped, with you being you, he'd at least pretend to play nice.

He's playing just fine. Now cut him some slack and leave him to me. Xx

She hoped her confidence would reassure her heavily pregnant friend, who was under strict doctor's orders to rest, and was relieved when Flo's reply finally came in.

Sorry, honey. I know he's in the best hands. If anyone can help him, it's you, Cath. Thank you. X

She smiled. Now all she needed was to have the same faith in herself.

She turned to the glass, took in the pool and the inviting little ripples in its surface…it looked so calm, so appealing.

Yes, a swim, some sun and some time to lose herself in her script before dinner…

Anything to stop her thinking on Alaric and the tricky path that lay ahead.

Alaric couldn't get away fast enough. Being in his bedroom, having her demand his attention, it had been too much. Too tempting to forget how he looked, too easy to succumb to the feelings that should be ancient history and to allow that connection back in.

He headed back upstairs to his study, collecting his drink on the way and contemplating something stronger. Even though he had hours to go before he'd have to face her again, it wasn't enough.

Flo and her blasted interfering ways. This was all her fault.

His phone chimed with an incoming text. He pulled it out of his back pocket and checked the screen. His mouth twitched. Flo.

Did she have some weird telepathic connection going on?

Her message was short but effective.

Play nice. Please!

He grimaced—had Catherine already reported back?

He dragged a hand down his face and blew out a breath. 'You don't ask for much, little sis,' he murmured, typing his reply: I'm trying.

And swiftly put his phone on Do Not Disturb.

It was enough that he had said yes to inviting her. His sister should just be happy and back off. Did she have no idea how hard this was for him?

He shoved open his study door, took one look at the multitude of displays all curved around his desk and changed his mind. There was only one way to rid himself of the tension—the gym. Gym, then work.

Hours later, he'd succeeded in physically avoiding her, but mentally his head had been filled with her. Her smile, her voice, her eyes as they tried to probe, her lips as she'd wet them with unease. An unease that he'd put there, the gesture upping his guilt every time he recalled it.

Because she wasn't Kitty Wilde the movie star when he glimpsed those weaknesses. She wasn't the woman projected on the big screen, in a magazine, on the internet, all confident and untouchable and unaffected by him. She was Catherine, his childhood friend, a girl he'd once have done anything for and a woman so very real and nervous enough to show it.

And that didn't just make her vulnerable, it made him vulnerable too.

He'd spent hours working out, pounding the treadmill, rowing, weight training, cycling...nothing worked. Nothing could shift her from his mind.

By dinner time, he was no better off—his stomach starving through exertion, yet sick with her unavoidable presence.

Play nice, Flo had said.

Did he know how to play nice?

He hadn't always been a social pariah. But then it wasn't the world that had done the casting out, he'd done it all by himself.

Could he at least *pretend* to be comfortable in company again?

For Flo? For Catherine? For the friendship they'd once shared...?

It was temporary after all, a few weeks, and then he could go back to his carefully controlled existence with a sister who owed him rather than berated him.

The peace alone had to be worth it...

CHAPTER FOUR

Two things struck Catherine at once.

She didn't know what to wear to dinner.

And no mirror existed in Alaric's master suite for her to evaluate her outfits in.

What was a dressing room without mirrors?

Flawed.

She scanned every wall like one would miraculously appear, checked inside the wardrobes, everywhere, and was forced to accept that she wasn't imagining it. There was no mirror. Unless you counted the one above the double vanity unit in the bathroom and there was no way she could check her length in that.

It was all she had though.

Gripping a fluffy white towel around her, she strode up to it and puffed her damp fringe out of her face. She was glowing like a beacon. It didn't matter that the air con was cranked up, and she'd chilled herself off in the shower not ten minutes ago. She could still feel the burn of her run which she'd been forced to do outdoors.

Forced by a sweat-slickened rowing machine, also known as Alaric.

A fresh wave of heat assaulted her as she remembered the view that had greeted her upon opening the gym door. Him, half naked, and rowing as though his life depended on it. His skin glistening with exertion, his muscles flex-ing with such power. He'd been so far in the zone he hadn't spied her gawping—thank heaven!

She'd done a sharp U-turn and hit the trails that weaved through the olive groves surrounding the house. The heat had been unbearable, but it had beat the thoughts of Alaric that every other activity had let in, her script writing in-cluded.

And at least the extra calorie burn would keep the guilt at bay as she enjoyed Dorothea's pitta bread that evening... if only she had a decent mirror to get ready in.

Who didn't have an abundance of mirrors in this day and age? She'd been so caught up in him and the beauty of the house she hadn't picked up on it earlier. But now that she thought about it, she'd seen none. Not even in the gym and all gyms had mirrors to check your form...

She puffed at her fringe once more, eyeing her reflec-tion. She was already running late and the flush to her skin wasn't going to miraculously disappear.

She reached for her make-up bag and froze. No mir-rors. No reflection.

Never mind others seeing him, *he* couldn't bear to see himself.

The realisation worked like ice over her skin, dousing the heat as tears pricked. He wasn't just hiding from the world, he was hiding from himself.

She inhaled through her nose, breathed through the chill and the sadness as she bolstered her resolve.

'You don't need to hide, Alaric,' she whispered. 'Not from me, not from you, not from anyone... I'll show you.'

Alaric checked his watch and adjusted the collar of his shirt.

Why he'd even donned a shirt was beyond him. He was

in his home, he could wear what he liked, but he had a ridiculous desire not to feel any less than he already did in
her presence. Against her notoriety, he didn't just feel ordinary, he felt every one of his scars and more.

Which made him feel even more foolish now as he
waited and waited…it was half seven. How was it possible
to be half an hour late for dinner when all you had to do
was climb two sets of stairs and walk out onto the terrace?

Maybe she too was struggling over what to wear.

Unlikely, but…

He waved Dorothea over as she hovered in the wings.
'Do you want to go and see—'

His question trailed off as he caught sight of movement
behind her and his jaw dropped. She hadn't struggled over
what to wear, that kind of outfit one didn't struggle over…

Where the devil did she think she was? Some presti-
gious awards ceremony being broadcast to the masses? A
fancy soirée?

Her hair was once again twisted high on her head, only
this time the tendrils that fell were purposefully there,
smooth and sleek as they framed her face and brushed
against the bare skin of her shoulders. The dress was a
daring red, its V neckline dipping low between her breasts
and unveiling the curve to each before skimming over her
waist and stopping mid-thigh.

She was all confidence and poise, and he was undone.

He could swear his heart had stopped beating, the ability to swallow, to speak, to move from his semi-twisted
position, evading him as his head remained angled up at
Dorothea, his eyes resting on Kitty—Catherine.

'Ti?' Dorothea pressed, turning to see what had caught
his eye and giving a breathless, 'Ah! Miss Wilde!'

She was already hurrying towards her and Catherine

smiled, her eyes flitting between them both as she stood in the open doorway, the sunset bathing her in gold.

'I worried you'd flushed yourself down the toilet.' Dorothea was all laughs and smiles, her tease bringing out a chuckle from Catherine herself as she raised a hand to her glossy red lips. Sinfully stunning.

'I'm so sorry I'm late, I—'

'Better late than never.' With some effort he forced himself to stand and ignored the look Dorothea sent him, Catherine's less so. Her eyes flicked to him, her lashes lowering, her fingers fluttering to her updo like it needed any more teasing to stay in place.

'Sorry.' It was quiet, demure, her grimace guilt-filled, and so he felt it too—guilt. Guilt at making her feel bad when it was more directed at himself for not being able to control his reaction to her than it was to do with her tardiness.

He looked away and rounded the table, pulling out her chair before gracing her with a smile that felt as alien as it did awkward.

'Would you like to take a seat?'

The nip she gave her plump red lip was swift and disconcerting. Did she truly feel guilty? Surely she was well accustomed to leaving people waiting—wasn't it just the way of things in the world she dominated?

'I will go and bake those pittas.' Dorothea's declaration broke the heavy silence and, thankfully, Catherine came alive. Less of the cute and demure, and more the composed movie star as she walked towards him, her high heels clipping the stone floor, their beat as pronounced as the uptick in his heart rate.

He clenched his jaw shut, dropped his gaze to the chair as he gripped its back and steeled himself for her arrival. He could feel her watching him, her eyes far too curious.

Did she know how much she got to him? After all these years, he should be well versed in dealing with his feelings, especially those sparked by her.

But then he'd spent the last three suppressing any kind of emotion and cutting himself off from the world had made that so much easier. Now he was no longer alone, and he was being tested by the one person he'd never been able to refuse.

'What's the matter, Alaric? You look like you did that day you rescued me from your pool.'

She laughed, the sound and the memory she evoked coaxing out a laugh from so deep within it shook him to the core. As though it were a release, a vent for the choked-up feelings in his chest, in his heart.

Life had been so different back then. *They'd* been different.

She'd been a vibrant wannabe, carefree but innocent too, and deserving of so much. And he'd been a boarding school tearaway with a chip on his shoulder, angry and frustrated by the constant pressure to succeed.

Was it any wonder he'd been so hooked on her?

'You scared the life out of me that day.' He waited as she lowered herself into the chair, her perfume reaching him and making his eyes close for the briefest moment.

'Well, lucky for me, you were there to be my knight in shining armour.'

She looked up at him and he moved before she could read it all in his face. He dragged in a silent breath and navigated the gap between her chair and his, careful not to brush against her. It was madness. Fourteen years ago, when he'd rescued her from the family pool, he wouldn't have thought twice about the contact. She'd been four years younger than him, sweet sixteen, and the way she'd clung to his neck and looked up at him like he was her true saviour…he'd wanted her to be his. He'd wanted to keep her safe, protected, adored. Before she had become a star, before the accident that had left him scarred inside and out.

But now she was here, on his island, seeking protection from the outside world, and that feeling, the sense of being her saviour, flooded his veins with meaning, with warmth, and he knew the danger of letting it in.

The danger of dreaming again for a future he could no longer have.

He sunk down into his seat, took up the bottle of chilled white from its bed of ice and filled both their glasses. It didn't matter what risk it posed to him; she needed this time. Or at least Flo had convinced him that she did, but looking at her so composed, so perfect before him, he found it hard to believe.

Was she really on the run or had his sister exaggerated the situation to give him no choice but to accept her presence here and to socialise once more?

'Why are you truly here, Catherine?'

Her smile flickered on her lips. 'You know why.'

'Because you want to avoid the press?'

She took the drink he'd poured, fingered the condensation forming on the glass and savoured a drawn-out sip. Was it so hard to think up an answer?

He studied her face, trying to read her; instead he was held captive by the way she pressed her glossy red lips together, her hum of appreciation for the wine teasing at his senses, the way her throat bobbed as she swallowed.

'There's a little bit more to it…' he lifted his eyes to hers, a sense that little was an understatement '…but essentially, yes.'

'More to it?' He didn't release her from his gaze and he saw how her lashes fluttered, a flash of pain that he couldn't miss.

She lowered her hand to her stomach, her eyes too, and he wanted to press further, he wanted answers, but he was also scared she'd break, and seeing her break would in turn break him.

He cleared his throat. 'Flo mentioned that you have a script you're writing?'

'Yes.' Slowly her eyes came back to his, her smile small. 'It's something I've wanted to do for a while.'

'And you're here to get it done?'

'That's the plan.'

'So why can't you do that at home?'

She flinched as he brought the conversation back to the heart of the matter.

'Because home is too distracting.' Her fingers trembled as she reached for her wine glass, provoking his concern, his need to know the truth too. 'I'm sure Flo explained.'

'She explained that the press are hounding you over your breakup with…with what's his name…?' He waved a nonchalant hand through the air.

'Luke.' Her eyes narrowed on him. 'As I'm sure you know.'

His smile lifted to one side. 'Guilty as charged.'

Did she also know he couldn't bring himself to say the guy's name without letting the jealousy take hold? Without pondering exactly what went wrong in their relationship and whether there was some truth to what the tabloids were saying? Flo had suggested it was a load of rubbish, and he didn't want to believe it, but… 'Is it true?'

'Is what true?'

'What the press are saying?'

'Is it ever?' She threw back a larger swig of wine. 'Though some of it is, I guess.'

'So, you did have an affair and call off the engagement?'

She choked on her drink as her eyes shot to his. 'No! No, I didn't have an affair. *Damn it*, Alaric.'

'I'm only repeating what the media are saying.'

'And you should know me better than that.'

'I don't know you at all, Catherine, not any more. That's why I'm asking.' Even as he said it, it didn't feel strictly true. And he'd hurt her in saying it, but he needed those walls in place, he needed to keep that distance between them as he pressed on. 'And, regardless of whether you did or not, wasn't it Oscar Wilde who said that it's better to be talked about, than not at all? Surely that applies ever more so in Hollywood. I'm sure your PR people are working it to their advantage right now, using it to build up the hype before your film launches. You are co-stars with an on-screen relationship after all…'

She cocked her head slightly, curiosity sparking in her eyes. 'You seem to know a lot about my work *and* my dating life?'

He ignored her astute observation and directed her back to his remark. 'So, it's a good thing, is it not?'

She pursed her lips and was quiet for so long he wondered whether she'd refuse to comment.

'I'd rather they didn't…'

'Because you don't like the picture they paint?'

She laughed harshly. 'No, Alaric, of course I don't, would you?'

No, and that's why he was quite happy to hide away. Not that he'd admit it.

She blew out a breath. 'At the end of the day they can do and say what they like. The reasons for our breakup are personal to me and Luke. We understand what—what really happened, and that's all that matters.'

He didn't miss the way her voice faltered. 'Even when the suggestion is that you were unfaithful, that the engagement was his way to stamp out the talk and you left anyway.'

She shrugged. 'It's what the press do. It's the nature of the beast and I'm past caring about the media.'

'Why, Catherine? When we were younger you dreamed of fame, you wanted this, you craved it...in fact, I'm rather surprised you didn't keep the relationship with Luke going purely for publicity's sake.'

Her eyes flared, her cheeks flushing beneath the make-up. 'Do you really think so little of me, Alaric?'

He reached for his wine, burying the stab of guilt as he let the chilled liquid soothe the heat that had formed around his words and contemplated his answer—what he wanted to say versus what he thought she wanted to hear.

'Look, let's not pretend...' The words flowed from him with more assurance than he felt. 'You have a successful career that demands you spend your time in the sun so to speak. You want to tell me now that you wish it all away, that you're tired of it?'

Her frown was more of a scowl. 'Is that so hard to believe?'

'But why? You worked so hard to be a media star, to look the part, to act the part, and it comes with the territory.'

'And don't you think a person has a right to some degree of privacy, regardless?'

'You chose this life, Catherine, you chose to step into your mother's shoes and then some. What did you think would happen? That you would miraculously escape the constant attention she revelled in. Strikes me that you're being all woe is me when you only have yourself to blame.'

She bristled, her shoulders rippling as she shifted position. 'If you think so low of me, why let me come and stay?'

'Because the woman I once knew wouldn't need the sanctity of this place unless it was absolutely necessary.'

'And because Flo asked, you couldn't say no?'

He shrugged. 'That too.'

'Seriously, Alaric, if I thought my presence was as unwelcome as this I wouldn't have come.'

Something jarred him deep inside, his eyes snapping to hers. 'You're not unwelcome.'

Liar.

Or was it the truth?

Underneath it all, was he blaming his sister, blaming Catherine, when really what unsettled him the most was the fact that he *did* want her here. That he wanted that glimpse of life off the island. That, above all, he *wanted* to see her again. Regardless of the fact they belonged in separate worlds. Hers was lit up Hollywood style, constantly in the limelight whether she wanted to be or not. And he wanted to stay in the shadows—he worked hard to stay there.

He'd lowered his guard once and a photo of him had appeared everywhere. The pity, the horror, the open commentary on how the heir to the De Vere empire must feel to have not only lost his best friend, but his famed good looks too.

He clenched his fist, his gut rolling with the memory, the image front-page news…and for Cherie, his late friend's wife, to see him still walking the earth when Fred wasn't able.

'Not unwelcome?' she repeated, dragging him out of his pit of despair. 'You could have fooled me.'

Her eyes burned into his, misreading his reaction so entirely, and a small smile touched his lips as a single thought succeeded in breaking through the pain—she would have come anyway. Welcome or not.

He was sure of it.

She frowned. 'What?'

He gave a small shake of the head.

'What, Alaric? Why are you looking at me like that?'

'Because something tells me that even had I said you weren't welcome, you still would have come…eventually.'

Her carefully styled brows drew together. 'What makes you say that?'

'Because, like me, you can't say no to Flo either.'

Her frown eased into a smile and he chuckled because he liked that he knew that about her. He liked her for being so susceptible to Flo and just as weak to her whims as he was. He liked that it exposed the old Catherine beneath the carefully crafted Kitty Wilde shell.

'My sister is the master of getting what she wants.'

Her smile was full now, her blue eyes softening with affection. 'She is…and she wasn't the only one. You once were too.'

A silence descended, their gazes locked as memories rose to the fore, of good times, bad times and everything in between. The air filled with the sound of insects, the rush of waves, and he wished time away. He wished to be back at that pool rescuing her from her tumble and the torrent of abuse from her mother for being so clumsy, to have her look up at him with the same adoration she had then.

'But I won't lie to you, Alaric. I wanted to see you.' She wet her lips, her eyes alive with her honesty, her…concern? 'I wanted to see where you lived. I wanted to understand why you've cut yourself off from the rest of the world, your family. I wanted to see for myself if—' she sucked in a breath '—if you were okay.'

He was drowning in her gaze, trapped within it, her concern teasing at the very heart of him and tightening up his throat, his chest. 'I'm fine.'

'Are you though?'

He clenched his jaw, dragged his eyes from hers to the sun disappearing behind the sea. The glow casting everything it touched in shades of orange and pink. A small sail-boat bobbed in the distance, alone, solitary, and he wished himself upon it. Anywhere but here.

She always saw far too much. She'd always been able to get to him. And wasn't that the true reason Flo had sent her…?

'They *do* miss you, Alaric. We all do.'

He swallowed, his locked jaw aching with the effort to keep it all trapped inside.

'*We?* That's pushing it a bit, don't you think?' Now he looked at her, his derision giving him the confidence to face her off. 'You had no time for us after you made a name for yourself, so forgive me if "we" doesn't ring quite true.'

She visibly flinched, her hand reaching across the table. 'Alaric, you know that's not how it was. You can't mean—'

'Can't I? How many celebrations did you miss over the years? Celebrations that Flo invited you to, only to find you couldn't make it?'

'I was busy—my schedule was full on for a long time and I couldn't just bail on it, but Flo understood. We always made up for it after.'

He nodded, taking in her words but remaining silent. He wasn't about to point out that *he* didn't see her though, that her claim to have missed him was nonsense.

'Just because I was busy, it doesn't mean I didn't miss her, that I didn't miss you. All of you.'

'No? And yet it's been ten years since I saw you last.'

'I tried to come and see you…after the accident.'

His chest spasmed and he fought back the memories trying to invade, the pain as raw as yesterday.

'But you refused to see me. You refused to see anyone.'

'You soon gave up trying.'

'What choice did I have?'

He gripped the table edge, pushed back from it as he

tried to beat it all back. And he knew he was being unfair. He'd been just as busy in the years before the accident, travelling the world with work, rarely in one place for long.

'I'm here now, Alaric,' she said softly, her eyes not releasing him. 'And I want to be here.'

He searched her dizzying blues, seeking a lie, seeing the truth and needing to deflect. 'Was it worth all the sacrifices you made?'

'What do you mean?'

'To be crowned queen of Hollywood—was it worth cutting yourself off from all those who cared about you?'

'Me, cutting myself off? That's a bit rich coming from you.'

He didn't even flinch as he ignored her gibe, accurate though it was.

'There's nothing wrong with prioritising things in your life,' she blustered.

'No? Even when your mother behaved in the exact same way?'

'Alaric, don't…please don't compare me to her.'

'Why, Catherine? She was the one who told you, day in, day out, to put your career first, don't let anything get in the way—your relationships, your friends, your family.'

'Alaric, please…'

She avoided his eye, but he was too riled to back down.

'Do you remember how it was back then? Why you were always at our house when we were younger? Do you remember the reasons that were given, all variations on the same?'

'You've made your point, Alaric. You can drop it.'

No, he felt too close to something, a realisation, not so much for him, but for her…

'Is that the real reason you turned Luke down?' He could almost feel sorry for the guy now. 'Was he another sacrifice that needed to be made in order for you to remain focused on your dream?'

Her eyes flashed. 'You know, it pays for the press to think and print the worst of me, Alaric. What's your excuse?'

He started, surprised at her direct hit, surprised even more by the strength of his answer that he couldn't admit aloud. It paid for him to think the worst because it protected him, stopped him from falling in deep with the girl he'd once cared for deeply and now could never have.

He wanted to dislike her. He wanted to dislike every perfect inch of her that lived and breathed the superficial world of Hollywood. But he couldn't.

'Tell me what really happened between you both—give me your truth.'

She paled beneath her make-up. 'Do you want to talk about what happened three years ago?'

'No.' It was abrupt, immediate, forced out on impulse. Could she honestly think that whatever had gone on between her and Luke came close to what he'd been through? Had she loved the guy so very much that it was equal to the grief of losing someone? 'I can't see what that has to do with you and Luke. It has no relevance, no...'

His words trailed off as he watched her throat bob, her chin nudging upwards. She was in pain. She was suffering. But she'd ended it, hadn't she, so why the pain? 'What really happened?'

She shook her head, wet her lips. 'It doesn't matter. What matters is that I'm not all that different to the girl I was ten years ago...' Her anguish was there in her voice, tangled up in a softly spoken plea for him to see her as she was. 'We were friends then. Can't we be friends still?'

'Friends?' It was so gruff, so messed up with the warning siren in his brain, in his heart. 'A lot has happened since then, Catherine.'

'And?'

'Dinner is served!' Dorothea's voice carried across the terrace, saving him from himself and the answer he didn't want to give.

Catherine spun to face her, her eyes like saucers as she took in the heavily laden tray of food. 'Are you expecting more guests, Alaric?'

Dorothea gave a hearty chuckle as she approached and lowered the tray to the table. 'I believe the key to happiness is a pleasantly full stomach.'

Catherine didn't look capable of arguing as she continued to stare at the dishes Dorothea placed on the table, reeling off a description of each. 'Pork souvlaki. Fresh pitta. Tzatziki. Greek salad with kalamata olives, feta, red onion, cucumber, tomatoes, an ample sprinkling of fresh oregano and, of course, a healthy drizzle of olive oil.'

He'd forgotten how hungry he was, but Catherine looked positively panicked and old memories flickered to life, of her eating like a bird beneath the watchful eye of her mother and him sneaking her extra when the dragon wasn't looking...until she'd stopped taking them.

'I should have warned you—' his voice was colder than he intended, the memory making him suspicious of her slender figure now '—Dorothea will see it her mission to feed you up while you're here.'

She looked from him to Dorothea, a smile forming that he couldn't gauge. 'Thank you, Dorothea. This really does look lovely.'

'And it will taste even better, I promise!' She spun away, the empty tray to her chest. 'Make sure she eats, Kyrios de Vere. It won't hurt to add a little meat to those bones. Now enjoy!'

Catherine's smile faltered as she watched her go and he tried to dampen the age-old concern, the anger at her mother and the mark she'd left on her daughter.

'She treats everyone this way,' he assured her while telling himself he was overreacting. 'Don't take it personally.'

But as she turned back to him, her eyes were alive with laughter. 'It's fine. I think she's wonderful!'

He relaxed back into his seat. 'That's one word for it.'

She laughed. 'You love her really… I can tell.'

She unfolded her napkin and placed it over her lap, unaware of how captivated he was by her. Her pleasure bringing her to life and flooding him with a warmth he couldn't contain.

'She certainly has a way with people.'

'She does. It's refreshing to be around someone who says exactly what they think and doesn't try to dress it up for me.'

'Unless it's me doing the talking.'

She gave him a warning glare but her eyes still danced, her lips twitching with continued laughter, and he picked up the basket of bread between them, a peace offering of sorts. 'Pitta?'

'Please.'

He felt himself smile as she took a piece and watched as she lowered her gaze to the dishes spread out between them.

'As much as this looks lovely, Alaric, you'll need to help me. There's no way I can eat anywhere near half of this.'

His smile grew, he knew better. Dorothea's food had a habit of making you come back for more. 'We'll see, you haven't tasted it yet.'

CHAPTER FIVE

'I'M SO FULL!' Catherine groaned, gripping her hips as she leaned back and took in the food still on her plate. She couldn't eat another bite. She seriously regretted that last mouthful as it was, but she'd been unable to resist its mouth-watering goodness. Dorothea truly was an exceptional cook.

Alaric's soft laugh reached her across the table, its husky edge making her very full stomach quiver as she met his gaze.

'Something funny?'

'You, groaning. It doesn't quite fit the perfect princess you project.'

'The princess?' She arched a brow at him.

'That's what I said.' His hand was resting on the table between them and he turned it over, raised it. 'What can I say, it's how I've always seen you.'

Her temper spiked—a *spoilt* princess?! She rose to the taunt, her lips parting to give him what for, but she stopped. There was something else at play in his eyes, in the smile that touched his lips. Something that looked a lot like *affection*…had he had too much wine along with the food?

'Is that so?' She sounded breathless, she felt breathless, which was utterly ridiculous. She didn't get breathless—

unless she was working up a sweat the good old-fashioned way. And by that she meant in the gym, on the trails, so why was her mind now conjuring up images of her and Alaric, entangled in the sheets, legs akimbo. No. No. *No.*

She was the queen of composure. But as his gaze fell to her lips, projecting the same heated rush she felt inside, that crown was rapidly slipping. Hell, who was she kidding—it had hit the ground the second she'd stepped foot on his island.

'You were always destined for great things, Catherine.' He relaxed back into his seat, and when his eyes lifted to hers, the heat had gone, replaced by…not quite the cool detachment of that day, but something else. A defeatism, a resignation, and it left her as speechless as the swift heat that had preceded it.

Their pre-dinner talk may have taken a difficult turn. The questionable light he threw over the way she lived her life, her priorities these past ten years stirring up a cocktail of guilt, anger and confusion. The way he'd probed into her recent past, Luke and the—the baby she'd lost. She pressed a hand to her lips, the sudden swell of nausea making her truly wish she hadn't eaten so much.

Not that Alaric knew. No one knew but Flo and Luke.

'Are you okay?' He frowned not missing a beat and she nodded swiftly.

'I really shouldn't have eaten so much.'

She took up her glass of water, praying he'd let it go as he glanced at her plate.

'It's hardly much.'

'It is for me.'

His eyes hardened. 'Is that Hollywood talking, or your mother?'

She took a slow sip from her glass, used it to calm the current within. 'It's me talking.'

He nodded, but his expression didn't ease.

Let it go, Alaric.

Her mother may have instigated her carefully controlled diet, but she was the one who had chosen to continue it. A strict diet and exercise regime were hardly rare in her line of work and she wasn't prepared to battle it out with him.

Especially when it hadn't been the true cause of her discomfort.

She shifted her gaze to the horizon as her hands fell to her stomach, pressing into the tender flesh as she tried to push away the pain and focus on her breathing.

She craved the ease they'd gained through dinner. The smiles, even the laughter they'd managed to share as they'd stuck to safer topics. Like his island, her new movie, her script, Flo…

But they'd just been skirting around the past, his and hers, and she knew there was more he'd wanted to say, more he'd wanted to confront her on when he'd pressed: *'Do you remember how it was back then?'*

Of course she remembered.

How could she forget when she'd been made to feel like the unwanted hanger-on by her own parents? Her mother spending more time away than at home, filming, partying, living the life of a singleton when she wasn't one. And how the De Veres would welcome her in, filling her time with playdates, as her father would take to the bottle, the gambling tables, anything to fill his time until her mother returned. Then the almighty arguments would kick off, after her father had got over his joy at having her mother back, and she would escape once more to the house of De Vere, Anastasia de Vere treating her like one of her own.

'Do you ever wonder how our mothers became friends?' She looked back at him with her question, and he shrugged.

'They grew up together.'

'I know. But when you think back, they never really did anything together? It wasn't like they confided in one another, and when they were together, I don't know... I always got the impression Mum was trying to benefit from your mother's contacts as opposed to...'

'Actually caring?'

She nodded, biting her lip as she saw the relationship for what it was and felt the guilt of it.

'Isn't it obvious? Mum did it for you. She knew how your life was. She wanted to keep you close and that meant keeping your mother close too.'

She felt the invisible warmth of Anastasia wrap around her, so many memories coming forth. 'She stayed friends to protect me...'

'We were all protecting you, Catherine.'

Her heart fluttered with his soft-spoken confession, with the way his blue eyes warmed with the compassion and the affection he'd once had for her.

'Be it Flo with her urgent home study requests; my father when he insisted on yours joining him on some social affair just so you could come and stay; me when I came between you and your mother when she was berating you, sneaking you cake when she wouldn't let you have any, making you laugh when she'd have you cry.'

She shook her head, her eyes welling with the depth of feeling in his voice, the memories he recalled. She knew it all, and yet hearing it from his lips now and wishing things were the same, that he could still look at her like that, that he could still feel for her like that...

'I'm sorry,' she managed eventually.

'Why are you sorry?'

'For being such a burden.'

He scowled. 'You were never a burden, Catherine. We

all cared about you. If anyone should be sorry, it's your own damn parents for how they treated you.'

Her throat closed over. He sounded so angry, so vehement on her behalf, so protective. She wanted to reach for him, she wanted to wrap her arms around him, thank him for it all, but she knew he wouldn't welcome it. That for all the progress they were making, they weren't in that place.

She had ten years to make up for—the accident, a bridge to still cross... As for her own truth...once he knew that, he wouldn't want to know her at all.

'How about a walk?'

She started at his sudden suggestion, the surprising normality of it. 'A walk?'

'Yes.' He raked his fingers through his hair, looked out to the ocean glinting in the moonlight. 'It'll help the food go down.'

'Isn't it a bit—' she eyed the start of the trail that weaved through the olive grove '—dark?'

He took in her apprehension with a small smile. 'There are lights that follow the path. I just need to turn them on. I'm sure without the heat of the day, you'll find a tour of the island quite...pleasurable.'

She was surprised to feel her pulse skitter, surprised even more by her own hesitation. What was it about the way he said *pleasurable* that made her blood fire? And why did the idea of going off with him alone feel more intimate than the dinner they'd just shared?

And if it was intimate, why did it bother her so much?

Because your feelings for him are already running away with you...feelings that you can't afford to let in.

This past year had brought with it enough pain, and this could only lead to more. Her aim was to help him return home, clean and simple.

Anything more…she wasn't in the right place for it. Mentally or physically.

'I've already seen it all.' She took up her wine glass, hiding behind it as he raised his brows at her. She took a sip and smiled to offset the pitch to her voice. 'I took a tour this afternoon.'

'You did? With Marsel? Andreas?'

'No. On my own.' She took another sip of the chilled liquid. 'I went for a run.'

'But it must have been thirty degrees.'

'Thirty-one, not that I'm counting.'

He shook his head. 'Do you often run in hot climates?'

'It's not a favourite pastime of mine, no. But then…'

She stopped as the memory of why she had came back to her, in all its muscular, blazing hot glory. She sipped more wine, praying her pulse would calm, the nervous flutter to her stomach would ease and the heat…she really needed that long gone.

'But then?'

She hummed into her glass.

'You said it wasn't what you wanted to do, but then…?'

Oh, dear…

'When I went to use the gym, you were already in there…' She forced herself to hold his eye, even as her cheeks burned with the admission, and it wasn't the only part of her continuing to warm. 'I got the impression you didn't want to be disturbed.'

His eyes raked over her and she was convinced he could read it all. Where were her acting skills when she really needed them?

'So, you took to the trails?'

'I did.'

'I hope you wore sunscreen.'

She wriggled in her seat. 'If you're referring to the fact

that I'm looking a little pink, my skin…it just does that.' It wasn't the fact that the heat of desire currently had her entire insides aflame.

'You should be more careful.'

The severity of his tone jarred her and she frowned. 'Okay, Mum.'

'I'm serious, Catherine. The sun isn't safe, and with your skin tone—'

'I know that, Alaric, I'm not a child.'

He fisted his hand upon the table, his tension palpable. What on earth…?

Anastasia. His mum. The cancer. Oh, God, she was an insensitive idiot. She reached across the table, her hand covering his before she could stop it. 'I'm sorry… I'll be more careful, okay?'

Slowly, he unravelled his fist and, for the briefest of moments, their palms touched. She wanted to keep him there, hold his hand in hers as she addressed the real cause of his concern.

'Anastasia…' She cleared her throat, settling back into her seat as he did the same. 'Flo tells me she's doing okay now.'

'She is.' His eyes glinted back at her, the lines bracketing his mouth cutting deep. 'But cancer's cancer. You live in fear that it'll return.'

'I know.' She chewed the corner of her lip, a second's hesitation as she debated whether to say more and knowing she had to. 'Which is why your refusal to go home is all the more concerning, don't you see?'

'Clever, Catherine. Very clever.'

'What is?'

'Turning this around on me.'

'I wasn't, I was just—' He started to rise and she frowned up at him, her stomach plummeting. 'I thought we were going for a walk.'

'I'm not so sure it's a good idea after all.'

'Seriously, Alaric.' She stood to face him. 'I'm sorry I brought it up but…'

'You promised Flo?'

'Even if I hadn't—' she held his eye, determined '—I would still be asking you the same.'

They stared at one another, locked in a battle of wills. She wasn't ready to call it a night now. She didn't want it to end with him running from her.

'Here's the deal—you keep those thoughts to yourself and we can have our walk.'

She managed the smallest of smiles. 'Or we can run if you like?'

He rewarded her tease with a soft laugh. 'After all that food?'

'Good point.'

But neither of them moved.

An invisible cord seemed to wrap itself around them, urging their bodies closer and closer. Her breaths shortened as his smile evaporated, his eyes falling to her lips that she had unconsciously wet, their depths darkening and full of…want.

He wanted her. Alaric de Vere wanted her.

He wasn't keeping his distance now. He wasn't pushing her away. And then his eyes flickered with some silent thought.

'Though I suggest you change your shoes.'

She swallowed the remnants of lust choking up her throat. 'My shoes?'

'Yes, your shoes.' He pocketed his hands, his mouth a tight line as he looked away. Had she misread the desire there, had it all been in her own head? 'If you've been for a run, you know how rocky the terrain is.'

She glanced down at her impractical heals. 'Of course.'

'And perhaps a jacket? The sea breeze can make it quite chilly at night.'

'Jacket. Shoes. Sure.'

She wanted to cringe. What did she sound like? But then his eyes returned to her, trailing over her front, taking in her exposed skin and the goosebumps now rife, and she forgot her shame. How could a simple look feel like a caress? And why was she craving it so badly?

'Alaric...'

'Yes?'

What would he say, what would he *do*, if he knew the goosebumps had nothing to do with the chill in the air, and everything to do with her body responding to him?

A dangerous question to ponder, Catherine.

She sucked in a breath and forced her legs to move. 'I'll be right back.'

This trip wasn't about reigniting old feelings, it was about the future, his with his family, hers with her work...

And here she was letting her teenage fantasies run away with her as though he was an everyday hot-blooded male and not Alaric. A man who'd been through hell, a man who she wanted to help, not confuse further by...by...

It was selfish, inconsiderate...not happening.

She blew out another breath, trying to let out the pent-up desire with it. She'd barely kept a lid on her feelings for him in her teens. Now she was older, wiser and a world-renowned actor, she should be able to do better.

But saying it and doing it were two different things and the one thing this trip had already proved—her acting skills were non-existent when he was around.

Alaric focused on clearing the table, ignoring Dorothea's protests that she would do it and the probing stare that followed. She was far too attuned to him and his ways and she knew Catherine had some hold over him. A hold he wasn't willing to succumb to.

'She is even more beautiful in person, I think.'

He grunted his response as he helped her load the dishwasher and cringed as she gave a little chuckle.

'I don't need you to say it's so, I see it in your face.'

'Dorothea, may I remind you I pay you to look after this house and my needs and not—'

She fisted her hands on her hips and stared up at him, the action enough to shut him up as quickly as his own mother would. 'Yes, you do, but I know you, and I think she is good for you. It's about time you brought somebody here.'

'I didn't bring her here, my sister did.'

She smiled at him, her eyes welling up—*oh, God.*

'And your sister knows you even better. You mark my words—this is a turning point for you.'

'There is no turning point for me. Catherine is here to write, and in a month, she'll be gone.'

Dorothea gave a little hum, waving off his severity. 'If you say so, *kyrios*. Now go, I have this in hand.'

He hesitated, needing to convince her he was right. Not that he could. Dorothea would maintain her own counsel regardless, but still it nagged at him.

Or was it more that he needed to convince himself?

Convince himself and delay his return to Catherine because he wasn't ready to face her yet. And it was madness.

He'd cut himself off from the world because he couldn't stand to be in the presence of others, of people who saw his scars and pitied him. Felt sorry for him. Or worse, resented him for surviving the plane crash when Fred hadn't been so lucky. He gulped down the surge of emotion—no, he resented himself enough for that.

But Catherine didn't look at him in any of those ways.

That wasn't what he'd witnessed across the table, or when she'd stood before him and looked up into his eyes…

And he'd come so close to succumbing, so close to pulling her into him and kissing those lips that she'd softly parted, subtly wet…

It was the force of that need that had scared the hell out of him.

'Go, *kyrios*!' Dorothea woke him from his stupor, shooing him to the door, her cheeks aglow, her eyes alive. 'Now enjoy your walk.'

She was off her dear sweet mind if she thought he'd let something happen between him and Catherine. Yes, they had a past. Yes, he had feelings for her. But she was a movie star with a life that demanded attention. He, on the other hand, belonged in the shadows and the sooner those around him realised it the better.

Those around you? He could hear the inner voice laughing at him. *You mean you. You're the one getting carried away under her attention, you're the one who wanted to kiss her and forget all else, you're the one losing sight of reality.*

He thrust his fingers through his hair. To even think someone as beautiful and as perfect as Catherine would want him was foolish. To want to act on that thought, foolish still. So why couldn't he shoot it down?

Perhaps because here, on his island, there were no observers, no one to judge a moment's happiness and provoke the survivor's guilt that kept him here.

You don't need others to judge you, you judge yourself enough.

He strode back out onto the terrace far sooner than was wise. He wasn't ready to see her, and yet there she was, a small shawl over her shoulders, the red dress that he'd been unable to take his eyes off and—his lips twitched—

white trainers on her feet. To his mind she'd never looked more beautiful and more endearing to his disobeying heart.

She wasn't his. She would never be his. So why was his heart beating to a different tune entirely?

'I thought you'd got lost.'

His smile spread. 'In my own home?'

'Crazy, I know. But the thought was there.' She smiled up at him as he joined her, her arm slipping through his like it was the most natural thing in the world. 'So, lead the way…'

He reached into his pocket for his phone, accessed the app that controlled the lighting for the entire island and lit the trail.

She clutched him closer with an excited gasp. 'Oh, Alaric, it's stunning!'

Ahead uplighters in the path glowed soft white, complemented by the fairy lights that weaved through the trees in the olive grove.

'When you said it was lit, I wasn't expecting this…since when did you become an old romantic.'

'Romantic?' He gave a choked laugh. 'It has nothing to do with me, I can assure you.'

'No?' She was looking up at him and he kept his eyes on the trail, one foot moving in front of the other. She was too close like this, too comforting, too easy to relax into and forget every worry.

'It's all down to Andreas and Dorothea.'

'Do they live on the island with you?'

'Yes, but Marsel lives back on the mainland. It's far too quiet here to keep him happy.'

'I can believe it. Whereabouts do they live?'

'They have a small house set back from the trail on the other side of the island. You won't have seen it on your run. It's hidden away and gives them privacy from me and vice versa.'

'Sounds perfect.'

They walked in silence a few steps, her gaze taking it all in, and then she said quietly, 'It makes me feel better knowing that you're not alone, alone.'

He scoffed. 'I'm thirty-four, Catherine. I'm quite capable of living alone.'

She opened her mouth to say more and he got there first, taking the conversation back to where it was safe. 'They started small the first Christmas I moved in.'

'Started small?'

'The lights,' he clarified. 'I wasn't interested but Christmas is a big deal here in Greece and it didn't seem fair to let them miss out, so when Dorothea asked...' He shrugged.

'You gave in.' Her voice was as soft as her smile.

'Pretty much. I gave them a budget and have done every year. As the land has matured, the number of adorned trees has grown and, to be honest, taking them down only to put them back up each year feels like more trouble than it's worth.'

'Plus, it's beautiful and you love it really.' She squeezed his arm and he couldn't stop the smile that touched his lips.

'It certainly makes the landscape more interesting at night.'

'Admit it.' She nudged him with her hip. 'It's beautiful...and romantic...'

He felt his lips flicker, felt the warmth creeping through his middle.

'It's okay to appreciate them,' she murmured, her eyes back on the track as they weaved deeper through the olive grove, the sound of the insects increasing around them. 'I promise it won't ruin the cold-hearted hermit you've worked so hard to project the past few years.'

'The what?' He froze, frowning down at her.

But she's not wrong, so why are you so upset?

'You heard me...' She slipped her arm from his. 'Or do you deny that you've been hiding here ever since the accident?'

He stared at her, his teeth grinding. She was the master of switching topics to cause the most effect.

'You don't socialise, you don't see the family. As for friends...when was the last time you saw one?'

His brows drew together as he refused to answer.

'You were the life and soul of the party once, Alaric. And now what? You don't want to be around people? You're happy in your own company, is that what this is? You, happy?'

His teeth continued to grind, his hands forming fists at his sides. 'We agreed to let this go. *You* agreed.'

Her eyes glimmered with something, some emotion he couldn't identify, but he didn't like it. It had his gut twisting, his heart pounding too loud in his ears. 'I did, and I'm sorry.'

He tried to take a steadying breath, but it was filled with her perfume, caught up in the scent of the earth as the sprinklers came alive at ground level, dousing the sun-burned earth.

She reached out, both palms soft on his chest as she nipped her bottom lip in her teeth and gazed up at him, the fairy lights twinkling in her darkened blues and he couldn't look away, couldn't step back.

'I'm sorry to press you, Alaric, I really am. But I'm doing it because people out there...they care about you... *I* care about you.'

His heart squeezed in his chest, his eyes falling to her lips. He only had to bow his head and he could taste them, taste her. How many times had he dreamt of it? Of kissing her, of forking his hands through her golden hair and holding her to him. And now she was pressing closer, or was he moving in?

'Alaric?'

He swallowed past the wedge in his throat. What was he doing? What were they doing? She smoothed her hands up his chest and he knew he should stop her, but he couldn't make his body obey as it thrived on the human contact, not just anyone's but hers.

'Is this what keeps you away?' She cupped his cheek, her thumb not quite sweeping over the scar tissue there—was she afraid of hurting him?

His heart pulsed. 'Leave it alone, Catherine.' It was a growl, a plea. He gripped her wrist and still he couldn't pull her away. It felt too good be touched, to be caught up in her spell.

'I don't want to leave it alone.'

'I'm perfectly happy here.' His voice shook, his body ached. The years of abstinence, the years of not being around people, and now he had her, hypnotising him with her touch, the look of want in her eyes. But she can't want him. Not now. No one could.

'Are you though?' She raised her other hand, cupped his other cheek. 'Truthfully?'

'What are you doing, Catherine?' He tightened his hold on her wrist, brought his hand up to grip her other, her eyes teasing at him, her lips so close, her scent…

'Kiss me, Alaric.'

Kiss me, Alaric…

His ears burned with her breathy request, need sparking so fierce inside, and he needed to quash it. He needed this under control, he needed her to know this couldn't happen. It would never happen. He didn't deserve the happiness she could so readily bring.

But one taste, just one fleeting moment…to know how her lips felt, to know how she tasted…

'What is it you're so afraid of?'

He didn't answer. He couldn't. And so he did the one thing guaranteed to silence her. He kissed her and lost sight of everything—the accident, the past, the reasons this shouldn't happen—all in the brush of her lips against his, the warm sanctity of her mouth, her whimper…oh, that whimper. It was like heaven to his tortured soul, balm to a wound he never thought he'd see gone.

'Catherine…' It was pained, desperate.

'Yes, Alaric,' she moaned against his mouth, her teeth nipping at his bottom lip, her body curving into him. 'I want you.'

I want you.

Only it wasn't Catherine he heard, it was Kitty Wilde. Those same words to her on-screen lover in a recent movie—yes, he'd watched them all, like some twisted fool who wished to taunt himself with her presence when he knew they could never be. Only…

He opened his eyes, saw *her*, and felt everything he knew to be real shatter.

He shook his head, trying to clear the lustful fog, to separate reality from fantasy. 'We can't do this. It's wrong.'

She stepped toward him and he backed away.

'Why? I know you wanted that kiss as much as I did.'

He couldn't look at her. He wanted it more. He was certain of it. And he didn't deserve to get what he wanted. He didn't. Especially with her.

'It's late, we should get back.'

'We've barely stepped out.'

'It's enough.'

He started back towards the house. He needed space

between them. Air to breathe that wasn't filled with her perfume, her temptation.

'Alaric.' She raced up behind him, touched a hand to his shoulder. 'Please!'

He stopped, unable to deny the plea in her voice. 'What?'

'I don't know what's going on here, what's happening between us, but I didn't imagine the way you kissed me back.'

His head dropped forward. He was a selfish fool, an idiot. He hated himself for it. A moment's weakness, a lifetime of guilt—is that how this would go?

'Why are you running away from me?'

'I'm not running away, I'm…'

He was what? She was right. He was running, as far away from the messy feelings she had stirred back to life and the guilt that was swallowing him whole.

'What is it you're so afraid of?'

He spun to face her, uncaring that she was so very close and that the light of the house illuminated every ugly inch of his facial deformity as he used it as a weapon now. A weapon and a defence.

'Look at me, Catherine.' He gripped her arms to hold her close. '*Look* at me!'

'I am looking!' She was just as ferocious, just as angry. 'I still don't see your point.'

He felt her tremble in his hands and released her, sucking in a breath. It wasn't her that trembled, it was him. His entire body quaked. He'd suppressed it for so long, the resentment, the guilt, the anger, and here he was letting it out on her, and she didn't deserve it.

'I'm sorry, Catherine.'

'I don't need you to be sorry. I want you to explain what's going on with you. I want you to stop pushing me away.'

'Just because we were friends once, Catherine—' he recalled her question from earlier, using it to inflict the most damage '—it doesn't mean we can be again.'

Her eyes widened into his, the pain he'd wreaked obvious in their swimming depths, and he reeled away, picking up the pace.

'What the hell happened to you, Alaric? Stop running away and just talk to me!'

'*This* happened, Catherine!' He spun on his heel, flung a hand at his face. 'This!'

Her eyes glistened up at him. 'Is that truly a reason to push us away? You're hurting and we want—we want to help you. Please let us help you.'

He stared at her, struggling to find the words. 'I'm fine, Catherine,' he forced out eventually. 'Why can't you just accept that?'

'Because you're not. The man I knew would never be happy like this.'

'The man you knew doesn't exist any more.'

'Maybe he doesn't…' She wet her lips. 'You can't go through what you have and remain unchanged, but you can embrace the man you are now and accept it.'

'What?' he scoffed. 'Broken, damaged?'

'No.' She shook her head vehemently. 'That's just it— you're choosing to be those things, you're choosing to let your scars define you, to cut yourself off when all we want is for you to come back.'

'I don't belong out there any more.'

'Of course you do and, deep down, you know it too. You *want* it too. I see it when I look into your eyes, I see it when you talk about Flo, I saw it when you kissed me just now…the longing.'

She was stepping towards him again, her hand reaching up to lightly touch his cheek once more. 'We don't see this, Alaric.'

He swallowed, trying to quash the rising tide within.

'We see *you*.'

'But I don't—not any more.'

He pulled away, thrust his hands through his hair as he made for the house—he had to get the hell away from her.

'You can blame the accident and your scars all you like.' She hurried after him, desperation clear in her voice. 'I know Flo does. But you want to know what I think? I think you're scared to live again.'

He shoved open the front door, praying Dorothea and Andreas had called it a night already as she entered hot on his tail.

'I think you're scared of enjoying life and having the rug pulled out from under you again.'

He clenched his fists, kept on going as he hit the stairs at a pace.

'I won't stand for it, Alaric,' she called after him. 'You need to stop feeling so goddamned sorry for yourself and get out there and live.'

He stilled on the next set of stairs, her words striking through the very heart of him as he turned to stare up at her. 'You think this is about me feeling sorry for myself and fearing what life wants to throw at me next?' He shook his head, his smile cold. 'Fred doesn't get to worry about any of that. He doesn't get to wake up next to his wife each morning and watch his own child grow up. He had so much to lose and I... I had nothing. Yet, I'm the one that survived, not him.'

She pressed a hand to her throat, her mouth parting but no words emerging, and he was glad of it...he'd heard enough.

'Goodnight, Catherine.'

He turned away, leaving her stood there as he raced down the remaining steps.

'You had your family, Alaric.' Her soft murmur reached him over the blood pounding in his ears. 'You had us.'

Pain ripped through him and he shook his head, refusing to acknowledge that she was right, relieved at the silence that swiftly followed—no footfall, no more incriminating words...he was free to be alone.

Just the way he wanted to be.

So why did it leave him so very cold?

CHAPTER SIX

THREE DAYS LATER, Catherine was staring at her laptop screen having tried and failed to concentrate on her script. She'd managed it for two days, ploughing her restless energy into the words flowing on the page, telling herself it was best to give Alaric some space after all that had happened, all that had been said...

But she couldn't shake it now. The haunted look in his face when he'd spoken of Fred, of his guilt at living when his best friend didn't. Worse still, that he saw Fred's wife and child as a reason to feel unworthy of living. Did he really wish it had been him?

She'd spent the night after their showdown searching up survivor's guilt, trying to understand as much as she could. The various symptoms that were so very similar to PTSD—flashbacks, anger, irritability, feelings of helplessness, disconnection, fear of the world, sleeping difficulties, headaches, social isolation, thoughts of suicide...

Just how many did he suffer?

The list felt endless and she, helpless. How could she begin to understand how he suffered, how could she begin to help him, if he wouldn't talk to her? Wouldn't even be in the same room as her any more?

At first, she'd wondered if the impossible had happened and he'd left the island but one look at Dorothea's flushed cheeks when she'd enquired as to his whereabouts and she'd known he was very much here and very much avoiding her.

Guilt had been her initial response. Guilt that she'd gone too far in her quest to get through to him and had succeeded in hurting him.

She'd been far too quick to spout off and gone in all guns blazing.

But he'd got to her, angered her hot off the back of their kiss that had stirred up so much inside. And yes, she shouldn't have done it, pleaded with him to kiss her, but then she hadn't been able to stop herself. Not when they'd been so close and that look in his eyes had seared the very heart of her. Even now it coaxed her body to life, the persistent restless energy rushing through her veins and leaving the words on her screen an indistinct blur.

She closed the lid of her laptop and swung her feet from the bed. It was time to confront him, and if she had to play on his good manners that had been instilled in him from birth, she would do. She wasn't expecting him to spend all day, every day, with her, but they could at least eat together.

She knocked on his bedroom door—not that she expected him to be there, but it was the closest place to look first.

No answer. She pressed her ear to the door. No sound.

She headed up a floor—the living area was deserted—up another and checked the gym. No sign. In fact, she hadn't caught him in there since that first day either. Was he working out at night just to avoid the possibility of running into her?

Of all the ridiculous, desperate...

She was just about to barge into his study when Dorothea appeared from the kitchen ahead.

'Miss Wilde!'

She smiled at her as she took hold of the door handle. 'Afternoon, Dorothea.'

The woman hurried forward, her eyes widening. 'What are you—?'

'I'm just going to see what's keeping Alaric so busy he can't see fit to dine with me.'

'But I—'

Catherine pushed open the door before Dorothea could stop her, strode in and halted, her mouth falling open.

She hadn't known what she expected, but it wasn't this...this *tech den*?

Huge flat-screen TVs descended from the ceiling, at least ten, fifteen even, forming a curve before a sunken platform with a desk at its heart, and there he was.

'Catherine! What in the name of—?' Alaric thrust his headset off and tossed it to the desk as he stood, the speed of the move sending his plush leather chair spinning.

She stepped closer, her eyes scanning the huge screens and the moving lines, the constant flicker of numbers...

Dorothea hurried in behind her. 'I'm ever so sorry, *kyrios*. I couldn't— I—'

'What she means is I wasn't stopping for anyone.' She gave him a small smile—*my bad*. She hadn't even considered knocking. It wasn't like his bedroom where he may have been naked after all. She swallowed, forcing out that particular image as she swiftly went back to the screens. They were the focal point of the entire room, the rest of it taken up by his desk, a water cooler, a fridge, a glass wall that led off into what looked like a meeting room with another flat-screen TV and enough seating for ten.

The entire space was white, clinical, businesslike. There was none of the exposed stone and mortar here, the rugged warmth, the relaxed lines of the beautiful building, and she shivered, wishing for the sun again.

That's when it struck her. There was no daylight either. Outside the sky was blue, the sun was bright, it was glorious. But you'd never know it in here. Not a single window existed. Or if they did, they were hidden by cleverly concealed blinds.

Wishing she was dressed in more layers, she wrapped the flimsy fabric of her kimono closer to her bikini-clad body and folded her arms to keep it there.

'It's okay, Dorothea,' Alaric assured the woman who was now wringing the tea towel in her hands. 'You can go back to whatever it was you were doing.'

'I was prepping dinner.'

'Oh, lovely.' Catherine turned to beam at her, hoping the kind woman would see her apology in her face and not the anxious churn in her gut. She hadn't wanted to upset her by barging in here, but her host had hardly given her a choice. 'Your food is always heavenly. What is it tonight?'

Dorothea smiled, her brown eyes softening but not enough to hide her continued concern. 'Lamb kleftiko, another of Kyrios de Vere's favourites.'

'Even better...' she drawled, turning to eye him. 'I assume that means we will finally be dining together again?'

She pinned him with her overbright smile and sensed Dorothea do the same. Two women staring down the giant of a man before them who looked like he'd been caught in a trap. She watched the little pulse working in his jaw and smiled wider. She liked putting him on edge...she liked it a little too much. But it brought out his character. It made him less robotic and more like the Alaric of their youth.

'Yes.' He didn't look at her as he said it. He was rigid, his back so straight she wondered if he might do himself an injury and how amusing would that be? Okay, not amusing, but it did distract her from dwelling on how incredible he looked. What was it with tall, broad men, with dark hair, a tan to envy and muscles that strained the arms of their tee? Especially when the said tee was white with a V neck that gifted a hint of dark hair and was worn with stonewashed jeans slung low at the hips. He was downright edible and—

And you're supposed to be focusing on dragging him out of his cave, not eating him with your eyes!

'Ah, that is wonderful to hear. Company for Miss Wilde at last!' Dorothea clasped her hands together.

Yes, company at last. At least she wasn't alone in thinking his behaviour rude.

Says you, who just barged into his office...

'Indeed,' she spoke over the inner gibe, her voice saccharine sweet, 'it will be lovely to have a dinner companion again.'

His eyes flickered in her direction, his smile more of a grimace.

'Of course it will,' Dorothea spoke up, 'and as it's especially hot today, I will aim for eight-thirty, time for it to cool off a little more.'

'Great.' He sounded like it was anything but great, and it only made Catherine want to laugh. His eyes darted in her direction again and she wondered if the teeniest hint of her laugh had erupted. But at least he looked alive and vibrant in his anger. It beat haunted and lost and...

She tore her eyes from his. 'I'm really looking forward to it, Dorothea.'

'Well, with that agreed, I will leave you both to it.'

And off she went, light on her feet now. Happy.

As the door closed, Catherine turned back to Alaric, trying and failing to prepare herself for how it felt to be around him again. Alone.

'Anyone ever teach you to knock?' He returned to his desk, his eyes scanning the screens.

'Anyone ever teach you how to look after a guest?'

'Thought we'd already been through this. You're Flo's guest, not mine.'

'This isn't Flo's house—island even.' She kept her voice level, refusing to rise to his dig as she sought to play on the goodness within him. 'It's yours and, as such, you are the host.'

'Lucky me.'

She wanted to laugh. She really did. No one spoke to her in this way, not any more. Since she'd hit it big, people fell over themselves to please her, to pander to her...it didn't matter that she didn't want them to, they did it anyway.

Not Alaric though.

He was giving her zero attention as he hunched over his desk, his fingers making light work of the keyboard as he studied the screens. She wanted to ask what he was doing, she wanted to ask what the screens were showing, she wanted to know it all. But while he was distracted, she was free to study him. To watch his muscles flex as he moved, the scarring to the underside of his left arm catching the light.

She wondered how many more scars his body bore and wished she could trace them with her fingers, reassure him as she did that he deserved to live, that he should let her in, let her help him...

The cool air of the room fluttered past her lips as she inhaled softly, her gaze lifting to his eyes that were narrowed in concentration, the grooves either side of his mouth deep as he pressed his lips together.

Sexy didn't even cut it.

'You just going to stand there and stare, or are you going to tell me what it is you want?'

He didn't look at her as he asked and she didn't answer, unless you counted the teasing murmur of a hum that escaped. It was pleasing enough to know that part of him was still so attuned to her, convincing her all the more that she wasn't alone in feeling the way she did.

She descended the steps into his pit, pausing alongside him and mimicking his stance over the desk.

'So this is where you've been hiding?' she said softly, careful to keep the emotional undercurrent out of her voice. The mix of concern, need and pain. It hurt that he'd been avoiding her, it hurt that he'd dismissed their friendship too.

'Just because we were friends once, Catherine, it doesn't mean we can be again.'

Even now those words echoed around her mind and jabbed at her heart.

'I've not been doing anything of the sort.' He flicked her a look and she caught his eyes dip over her length, the move swift but not swift enough. She had her favourite bikini on, a vibrant rainforest scene across the teeny triangles of fabric, set off perfectly by her sunny kimono. The fire was undeniably there, as was the anger at himself for feeling it. She could read it in every taut muscle, the twitch to his jaw, the way he looked away so quick.

'You could have fooled me…' She let her eyes drift back to the screens. 'What is all this?'

'Work.'

'What kind of work?'

'The kind of work that keeps my father happy and my life free of interference.'

'Are you trading?'

He dropped his head forward. 'Are we really doing this?'

'What?'

'Talking about my work.'

'Why not?'

'Because it's work and it's complicated.'

'Too complicated for me, you mean?' Now she really was affronted, and she knew her eyes were shooting daggers as she stared at his bowed head.

'No—though, yes—kind of.'

'Because I'm just a pretty face, right? Incapable of more than just repeating the words fed to me and adding a little Kitty Wilde pizzazz?'

He turned his head, a frown forming. 'Are you serious?'

She wished she'd stayed up on the platform now, missing the height advantage as he glimpsed the vulnerability she worked so hard to hide.

'Maybe.' She made it sound light and breezy, like it didn't bother her in the slightest. Yet the script on her laptop downstairs said otherwise. She was determined to change the world's opinion of her and show them she was more than just looks and make pretend.

He straightened, folding his arms across his chest as he continued to frown at her. 'I don't think you're stupid, Catherine, if that's what you're thinking.'

'You don't?' She gave a short laugh. 'You could have fooled me.'

'I didn't mean it like that.'

'Hey, don't trouble yourself over it, I'm fine. You wouldn't be the first man to treat me like a bimbo.'

'I'm not—' his frown deepened '—is that really what you think I'm doing?'

'You're the one who won't even try to explain this to me.' She gestured to the screens and he surprised her with a real laugh.

'Believe me, that has nothing to do with you! I don't understand the half of it. I can spot an anomaly, something amiss, an opportunity perhaps, but as far as the day-to-day trading goes, I have programs that do it for me.

Genius programmers who work for me and write those genius programs.'

She tilted her head, her shoulders easing just a little. 'So, you're like a glorified facilitator?'

His face softened into something of a smile. 'You could say that. And lucky for me, I'm good at it. It keeps my father happy and off my back.'

'Flo told me you head up the investment side of the business.'

'Exactly. It means aside from the odd conference call, I can keep myself to myself, just the way I like it.'

Her shoulders were hunched once more. 'Is that why you're avoiding me? You're keeping yourself to yourself.'

'I wasn't avoiding—'

Her raised brow cut him off and he tried again, 'Look, I think it's for the best if we keep some distance between us.'

She held his eye as she turned and rested her behind on the edge of his desk. 'Why?'

'I explained that perfectly well the other night.' His eyes dipped to her lips, the roughness to his voice and the vague flush of heat in his cheeks mirroring the rising warmth she felt in the pit of her stomach.

'No, you tried to thrust your viewpoint on me. But newsflash, Alaric, I have my own mind. I make my own decisions.'

He shook his head. 'Don't I know it.'

'What's that supposed to mean?'

His eyes creased a little at the corners, their depths turning wistful with his smile. 'You always did, even when we were young. Once you set your mind to something, you were going to do it regardless.'

She smiled, nostalgia adding to the budding warmth, the growing connection, between them. 'No wonder you saw me as a princess...a spoilt one at that.'

'Spoilt. No. I admired you for it. Envied you even.'

'You *envied* me?'

'Yes, I envied you. I envied you your freedom. My parents were always on at me, checking on my grades, pushing me to do better, to quit messing around with my paintings, to quit the partying, the fun.'

'Ha! You did go and get yourself suspended from boarding school on at least two occasions.'

'For the record—' he cracked a grin and it surprised her with both its sincerity and the chaotic flutters it set off deep inside '—neither of those occasions were my fault.'

There was no angling of his face away, no hiding the scars as he continued to grin at her, and she craved more of him like this, the need like a desperate ache inside.

'No—' her grin was just as wide '—of course they weren't.'

'They *weren't*. One was a science experiment gone wrong—'

'The fire in the boys' changing room?' she proposed, remembering that story very well.

'Yes! And the other...' His smile lifted to one side, transporting them back almost two decades as she remembered the exact same look often appearing with a glint of mischief in his eyes. 'Well, I can't be blamed for that one either.'

'Sneaking into the girls' school after hours—yeah, I'm sure that had nothing to do with you.'

Her laugh was soft, shadowed with pain. That one had stung back then, discovering he'd been caught with a girl and wishing it had been her.

But not now. Now, she'd give anything to see that spark back in his eye, to get a hint of the fun-loving guy that didn't take himself—take life—so seriously.

No wonder Flo had been so desperate to get her to come.

Though what Flo hoped she would achieve and what Catherine's own imagination was proposing were two very different things. Because when Alaric eyed her like he had not one minute ago, want as obvious in his eye as it was in her bloodstream, he was closer to the man he'd once been and she was fully prepared to tease out more of that, if it brought him back to the land of the living.

'It was more of a combined effort—Fred was forever leading me astray.'

His smile turned weak, the haunted look creeping back into his eyes. Fred and Alaric had been thick as thieves, Catherine knew that. Right up until the accident that had taken his friend's life and almost killed him too.

She swallowed down the lump in her throat as she straightened and reached out, her hand gentle on his arm. 'You must miss him.'

He pulled away from her, his hands shoved deep inside his pockets.

'I...' He cleared his throat, the thickness to his voice clawing at her heart. 'He was a big part of my life. But Cherie, she was his wife, and his little girl...to see me return and not him... It had been my idea to go on that lads' weekend. He wouldn't have been on the private jet if not for me.'

He shook his head, unable to continue, and she forced herself to hold still, to give him physical space.

'It wasn't your fault, Alaric. It was an accident. It could have happened to—.'

'To anyone!' he threw at her. 'I've heard it all, Catherine. Nothing you say can make it any better. Every night, I go to bed and see Cherie—Cherie and his daughter stood at his graveside, their lives ruined, and mine—mine—'

He stalked away and she watched him, his pain so palpable she could feel it tearing through her.

'How is Cherie?'

'I don't know.' His voice choked. Guilt. Pain. His shoulders shuddering with it all. 'I haven't spoken to her, not since the funeral.'

'But it was an accident, Alaric,' she tried again, softer. 'There was nothing you could have done.'

He angled his face towards her. 'I should never have suggested the trip.'

'But you did, and it's done, and nothing can change that it happened.'

He scoffed and she could taste the bitterness, the resentment, in him. 'Life goes on regardless.'

She nodded, hearing his words, understanding what he meant, but at the same time…

'Your life needs to go on too, Alaric.'

'That's what I just said.'

'No, you said life goes on regardless…you mean around you. Not for you.'

He shook his head. 'Same difference.'

'No. It's not.'

'Don't stand there and tell me I owe it to him to live my life, Catherine.' He spun to face her. 'I've heard it all, from my mother, my father, Flo, my bleeding counsellor. It's not that simple.'

'I didn't say it was simple, it could never be simple, but have you tried speaking to Cherie, talking to her about how you feel?'

'And put her through that? Put that on her? How selfish do you think I am?'

'You're not selfish, Alaric, you're in pain and until you face it and move on you will always suffer.'

He stared at her, long and hard, but she wanted to show him she wasn't going anywhere, and she wasn't backing down from this.

'It's been three years, Alaric. You can't hide here for ever. Your family miss you. Flo misses you. She's—she's *pregnant*, for heaven's sake.' Her voice quavered, her hand clutching her abdomen in an impulsive gesture as it brought with it the reminder of her own loss. 'Are you really going to miss out on meeting your niece or nephew, spending time with them?'

'Why do you even care so much?' he lashed out. 'You've been so busy the last ten years, pursuing your career, why come back now and interfere? Why pretend you give a damn?'

Her eyes stung, her chest ached, but she refused to let the hurtful words he threw at her in his desperation deter her from pushing further. 'What did your family do to you that was so bad you'd rather hide out here?'

His laugh was harsh. 'Aside from my parents trying to control my every move.'

'Now you're just being melodramatic.'

'*I'm* the dramatic one. Kitty Wilde is stood in my study telling me *I'm* over dramatic.'

She ignored the jibe. 'This isn't a joke, Alaric.'

'I didn't say it was.'

'Then tell me what they did that was so awful for you to turn your back on them, because the way I see it, you survived the crash, but they lost you anyway.'

Alaric stared at her, tormented by the truth of her words.

'What I would have given—' she continued so very quiet, and he wanted to cover his ears like a child as he feared what was coming '—to have a smidgen of the care and attention your parents bestowed on you growing up.'

He felt her pain spear him, his hand reaching out on autopilot, reaching for the vulnerable girl she'd once been and the woman she was now. Neither having had the option of returning to a loving family, and as she backed away, he wanted to howl at the world for its cruelty, its unfairness…

'No!' She held her palm out to ward him off. 'Don't you go softening now because you feel sorry for me. That freedom you envied, I got because my father was too distracted by my mother's absence to care what I was up to. I could have flunked every subject and I don't think they would have noticed. Run away even. But you…you had parents that cared, a sister too…you still have them.'

He folded his arms, hardening himself to her words as he acknowledged her clever orchestration of the entire conversation. Well, no more.

'And after all your family did to you, you still followed in your mother's footsteps. Of all the paths to take, Catherine, I'd hoped you'd do better.'

'I am *better*.'

'Are you?' He felt sick saying it, challenging her when he knew it was deflection, but…

'Just because I became an actor, it doesn't mean—it doesn't mean…' She broke off, her eyes glistening anew as she clutched her abdomen tighter, and he frowned over the move. Her reaction so much stronger than he could have predicted.

She'd been so fierce, so unbreakable, seconds before.

'My mother and I are nothing alike,' she whispered, broken, distraught, and any attempt to deny it died on his lips. 'For one, I don't have a family to let down. There's just me and my career. No competition. No one to neglect.'

'No one to care for?'

She stared at him.

'That's what you mean, isn't it?' he probed, a light-bulb moment leaving him feeling oddly bereft. 'Is that why you broke it off with Luke? He was getting too close and you didn't want to risk him becoming a distraction or some-one you could let down?'

'Don't presume to understand what happened between me and Luke. You don't get to pass judgement on some-thing you know nothing about.'

'I can read between the lines well enough.' He felt ener-gised by the realisation, his defensive walls rebuilding as he realised that whatever existed between him and Cath-erine, whatever the connection, there was no future.

And it wasn't because of how messed up he was. No, it was because Kitty Wilde would never have room in her life for another.

'You may not have had an affair, Catherine, but I can easily imagine that Luke got too serious, and you ran. My guess is you were scared of becoming your mother, scared of having your priorities skewed, scared of abandoning—'

'Stop it, Alaric. Just stop it!' Her entire body trembled, a tear rolling down one cheek and torturing him with its journey. Had her breakup hurt her so very much? Had she loved Luke *that* much and still loved her job more?

He shook his head, shock stealing the breath from his lungs as his jealousy of the man was obliterated with pity.

'Tell me something?' he breathed. 'Is it really worth it?'

'What?'

'Your career, your fame?'

She frowned, swiping the tear away with the back of her hand. 'You don't know what you're talking about.'

'I know that you're alone, that for all you dig at me for living here alone, you're as bad. In fact, for you, it must be worse. Surrounded by people day in, day out, and stand-ing alone…'

'And I repeat, you don't know what you're talking about.'

'No? Tell me, then, do you ever get lonely?'

'Asks the man who lives on his own bleeding island!'

'And I'm happy that way. You're not. You're stood there crying over a man that you chose to leave.'

Her breath shuddered out of her. 'You don't understand.'

'Then explain it to me, make me understand.'

She shook her head. 'I can't.'

'Why?'

'Because—just because.' She wrapped her arms tight around her middle.

'Then let's agree to leave each other's lives alone. You don't want to speak about Luke and what went wrong. And I sure as hell don't want to talk about my reasons for being here.'

'But, Alaric—'

'But nothing, Catherine, you keep your nose out of my business and I'll do the same in return. Now I have work to be getting on with.'

She stared at him, quiet for a moment, and he felt a sickening thud in the pit of his stomach. Had he gone too far? Would she bail on dinner? Would she pack up and leave entirely?

She wet her lips, sucked in a breath through her nose.

'I'll leave you to it.'

She started to walk away, and he called out. 'I'll see you at dinner?'

It was definitely more of a question and she stilled, looked over her shoulder, a second's hesitation and then the smallest of nods.

'Good.' His shoulders eased, his breath leaving him as he watched her go. Taking all the warmth, all the light, with her.

He looked back to the screens and saw nothing but the pain in her eyes, the tears, the sorrow…all over a man she had chosen to leave. A man who had at least managed to earn a place in her heart, and still it hadn't been enough for her to put him first.

Goosebumps spread across his skin, a chill shocking him to the core. This wasn't jealousy, or anger, or guilt, this was fear. Fear of how he felt towards her…how he could feel if he let himself get caught up in her again.

Had that been his sister's plan? Throw temptation in his face and use it to lure him out?

Had his cunning little sister been aware of his feelings towards her friend all along and never let on?

And if that was the case, how would she feel to learn that no matter how he felt, or how much Catherine may feel for him in return, she would always put her career first? That, ultimately, she'd break his heart if he let her…

All good reason to maintain his distance…instead they were having dinner together that evening.

And he shouldn't be looking forward to it.

But this was Catherine, and his heart was overriding his head.

'We care… We don't see this… We see you.'

He ran a hand over his scarred cheek as her words chipped away at his defences.

Not once had she intentionally made him self-conscious. No, he'd been the one seeking to hide it, to not let her see him in all his ugly glory, fearing her pity, her repulsion even. And instead she'd given him her warmth, her attention, her kiss. And that kiss… *Wow*, that kiss. A moment of madness, of weakness, that had left him feeling starved and desperate. He couldn't stop reliving it, over and over.

And in the face of such temptation, such acceptance, he wasn't sure how long he could play dumb to the attraction, especially now he was done hiding from her, physically at least.

CHAPTER SEVEN

CATHERINE WAS PLAYING with fire, but she was angry.

Angry at the way he'd thrown her mother at her, angry at the way life had construed to ruin his and stopped for her the second her baby had been taken from her.

She didn't know how dinner was going to play out, but she'd sure as hell made sure she felt invincible. Flawless make-up, glossy skin and a dress to die for. She wasn't going to let Alaric break her again.

If he didn't want to talk about the past, then fine, she'd let it go. On the proviso that he let hers go too.

She couldn't bear thinking on it, let alone talk of it. The pain, the guilt, the shared suffering with Luke over a baby…a baby they hadn't—*she* hadn't wanted, hadn't planned and miscarried mere weeks after the test result.

But in those weeks so much had changed. She had swung from panic, from fear, from wishing it away to feeling a new life growing inside her, of feeling its importance, its unparalleled importance. Her vision for the future changing so completely because she wouldn't be her mother, she wouldn't…

And just when all had felt good again, better even, it had been snatched away.

The ultimate punishment for her selfishness.

Her hand went to her stomach as she froze on the stairs,

her other hand clutching at the handrail to fend off the fresh wave of grief, of remorse.

She wasn't her mother. She *wasn't*.

Yet she'd failed her child before they'd even been born.

She sucked in a breath and let it out slow. Not even Flo knew the whole truth. The fact she refused to believe it at first, then the resentment...

How could she even begin to tell Alaric that when he already had such a twisted view of who she was?

No, putting words to it would only confirm what he already suspected.

What he already suspected and what she feared.

That she was as bad, if not worse, than her mother ever was.

No. She wanted to forget and she owed him the same consideration over his past too. No matter what Flo had asked of her, what she had set out to achieve in coming here, she needed to respect his decision.

Taking another breath, she combed her fingers through her hair and shook out the waves she had carefully crafted as she'd opted to leave it down, free of restraint as she wished to be free of the past.

Tonight at least...

He was already on the terrace when she got there, a drink in hand, his eyes on the view. She came up behind him, surprised when he didn't detect her approach, and she cleared her throat. 'It's a beautiful evening.'

And it was—the sun casting its soft glow as it sunk into the sea, the heat of the day leaving a subtle warmth in the air—but it wasn't the reason she'd said it. She'd sensed his thoughts were as preoccupied as her own had been and she wanted him to relax, just as she was determined to do so. She wanted him to know that she'd put their impassioned talk behind her and hoped that he could too.

'It is.' He pushed up out of his seat, his eyes raking over her, and the appreciation she spied lit her up inside.

She did love this dress. How the slinky fabric caught the light and gave the appearance of liquid gold. The slender shoestring straps and wrap style creating a low V neckline and allowing the floor-length skirt to part as she walked, revealing her leg from the thigh all the way down to her heels.

She felt sexy. She looked sexy. And that was the confidence she needed to get through the evening.

'You look—' he cleared his throat, stepped out from the table to greet her '—like you're missing a red carpet.'

Her smile faltered before she could stop it. She was too damned sensitive to his opinion, anyone else and she wouldn't care. 'Too much?'

'No.' The smallest of lines appeared between his brows, and his voice was gruff as he pocketed his hands. 'Not at all.'

'Good.' Her smile relaxed with her returning confidence. 'I have to say you look red-carpet worthy yourself.'

He wore dark trousers and a navy shirt unbuttoned at the collar, the fit emphasising his muscular build and trim waist, the colour setting off his tan and the blue of his eyes. He'd combed some product through his hair, taming the wild strands so that they were clear of his face. He'd shaved too, exposing his scar so completely and making something within her pulse. He wasn't hiding it from her, not any more.

She wet her suddenly dry lips and paused before him, pressing her palms into his chest before she could lose her nerve. His body contracted beneath her touch, his lips parting with obvious surprise as she lifted up on tiptoes to press a kiss to his cheek. It was how she would have greeted any man in her acquaintance, but the simple contact thrilled her to the core.

She paused—a second to appreciate his scent, another his warmth—and then she dropped back, moving away as his arm locked around her, keeping her close.

She looked up at him in question.

'You like playing with fire, don't you?'

Her own words came back to her, her make-up, her outfit, a confidence booster as she admitted, 'Only when it's fun.'

'Fun for who? You?'

'For the both of us.'

His eyes glittered, the pulse in his jaw twitched, and she pulled away before she could succumb to the urge burning through her very veins, because all she wanted to do was kiss him. Kiss him and forget everything.

One step free, two, and suddenly she was crushed up against hot, hard muscle, a frisson of excitement rushing south.

'Is this just some game to you, Catherine?'

'If it's a game where we both come away satisfied—' her voice was all breathy with lust '—I'm all for it.'

He growled low in his chest, the rumble filtering through to her. 'What do you want from me?'

'Right this second…you're a clever man, I'll let you work it out.'

His eyes darkened above her, his head drew closer, his voice gruffer still. 'What if I need you to spell it out?'

Her lips curved into a smile, power rushing her veins as she reached closer, the tips of her toes pressing into the ground, her palms smoothing over his shoulders and relishing the strength beneath, the hard muscle she so desperately wanted to explore…

She brushed her lips against his, a little flick of the tip of her tongue against his mouth, and her eyes connected with his. *What are you doing?* came the mental warning, but what left her lips was a simple, 'Enough?'

He lifted his hand, forking it through her hair. 'With you, I don't think it can ever be enough.'

And before she could overthink his words, he was kissing her, kissing her so deep and so thoroughly she was consumed by it. The carnal heat coursing through her as she savoured the taste of his mouth, the pressure of his lips, his tongue as it grazed against hers.

She moaned with the heady rush, her desperation, her frustration…it was everything and not enough at once. She raised her hands to his hair and tugged him closer, pressed her entirety against him. She could feel his heart pounding into her, or was it her heart pounding into him? She didn't know where he ended, and she began, and if they could just stay like this for longer, for ever…

A startled gasp filled the air and they froze, their heads snapping to the left, to a startled Dorothea, who looked about to flee.

'I'll come back!'

'No, no, it's fine.' His broken voice rasped along Catherine's spine and the world seemed to spin. Lack of oxygen through kissing was a real thing. Who knew!

She took a steadying breath, stepped away from him. She could feel her cheeks burning with it all—lustful heat, bashfulness and something that ran deeper…much, much deeper…and she wasn't about to examine it too closely. Not right now.

She smoothed her hands down her dress, making sure it was back in place and gave Dorothea an apologetic grimace. 'So sorry, Dorothea.'

'Don't you go apologising, that's the most exciting thing to happen on this island in for ever!'

Alaric snorted and Catherine's eyes shot to him—had

he really just snorted? She laughed, the sound giddy and happy and so very easy. He looked young again, less tense, the brightness to his eyes, the colour in his cheeks…the warmth deep inside her spread, her feelings with it.

Feelings she really needed to get a handle on. But how could she when she was barely accustomed to feeling this way. Not even with Luke.

This was new. Intense. And for all she'd assumed it was the old merging with the new, she wasn't so sure. Something about Alaric now got to her, dug beneath her skin, had her losing her trusty control…

'Let me help you with that…' She hurried forward to aid Dorothea and quit the panicked direction of her thoughts.

Alaric filled her glass with the red wine he'd been enjoying on her arrival.

Catherine set the side dishes down as Dorothea lifted the main dish from the tray and rested it in the middle of the table, opening up the parchment paper and scrunching it around the dish. Steam rose up, filling the air with the most delicious scent, and Catherine hummed her approval, her eyes closing as she truly appreciated it.

When she opened them again, she caught Alaric watching her, his eyes soft, his expression unguarded, and she saw the same confusing fear that she was starting to feel deep inside. This connection between them had the power to break them if they let it…

She gave him a tentative smile and he followed her lead; the two of them stood there, smiling. An all-knowing Dorothea between them.

'I'll leave you both to enjoy your meal. There are more vegetables in the kitchen should you want any.'

'I think we'll be okay,' he murmured, his eyes not leaving Catherine's. 'You get yourself home.'

'I'll clean up after you finish, and then—'

'No, I'll take care of it…' He turned to Dorothea 'You take the leftover veg and kleftiko to enjoy with Andreas. Have an early night.'

'Well, you don't have to tell me twice!' She grinned as she nodded to them both. *'Kalispera.'*

'Kalispera—and take a bottle from the cellar with you too.'

'Oh, you really are spoiling us! Something tells me I have you to thank, Miss Wilde.' She gave Catherine a wink that had her blushing all over again.

'Kalispera, Dorothea.'

She watched the woman go, the air thickening the further away she walked and the closer they came to being alone again. She looked back at Alaric to find him watching her, the look in his eye making her stomach spin.

'What?'

'I'm just wrestling with reality.'

'Wrestling with reality?' She took up her wine glass and sampled it. Rich, dry and satisfying. Good choice. Though nothing beat the appeal of the man opposite her, looking at her in a way that made her pulse race. 'That sounds quite serious.'

'Oh, it is.'

'Tell me, which bit are you struggling with the most?'

'That you're really here, the great Kitty Wilde—'

'Don't call me that.' It blurted out of her, surprising herself as much as him, and she added softly, 'Please.'

'Okay. As I was saying, it's hard to believe that you're really here, and that we're really doing this.'

'Eating lamb kleftiko and drinking a very expensive—' she squinted at the bottle and smiled '—red Bordeaux?'

He laughed softly as he shook his head. 'Never mind the food and the drink. Do you have any idea how famous you are? How many men would do anything to be in my position?'

She shifted in her seat. 'Don't say that.'

'Why?'

'Because… Because you're not any man, and it makes me uncomfortable.'

'Uncomfortable to own your fame?'

'No. Not really. I just… I'm me when I'm with you. There's no pretence, no act, just me.'

He leaned forward on his elbows. 'Well, just you, how about we eat this and enjoy one another's company?'

She nodded, pleasure sweeping through her as she felt a common ground form for the first time since she'd arrived.

Food was finished. Dorothea's kleftiko was divine as always. His dinner companion…well, she was something else. Always had been, always would be.

And Alaric wasn't naïve. Out of practice, yes. But not naïve.

He knew where things were heading. He also knew it was a bad, bad idea.

He hadn't been with a woman in over three years. The idea of breaking that celibacy with Catherine was insane, foolish, asking for trouble. How could he ever hope to go back to his life as it was after she left?

And yet, every time she looked at him, as a man, a man she desired in spite of his scars, he lost sight of the bad and remembered the good. The connection they had when they were younger, the connection so ready to surface now.

'There's a little left, do you want it?'

He shook his head. 'You?'

She shook her head.

'Another drink?'

'What are you offering?'

'What do you fancy?'

With each question their smiles grew. 'I have champagne, dessert wine, ouzo, a raki?'

She pulled a face. 'Isn't that the drink that strips your liver?'

He laughed. 'I wasn't suggesting more than a shot.'

She grinned and his breath caught. She really was beautiful and not what he expected. Not that he'd known what to expect. Her mother, he supposed. A woman so focused on her career that everything else—*everyone* else—blurred into the background. But she wasn't any of that, despite what he'd told her. He knew she wasn't.

He also knew that her pushing him to discuss the past, to face it and change his outlook for the future, stemmed from a good place. She cared.

And he loved that she cared. He loved it too much. It's that which told him to keep his guard in place. The guard that was swiftly crumbling with the lateness of the hour and the growing sparkle in her eye.

'How about champagne?'

'Sounds perfect.'

He stood and started gathering up the plates. She made to help and he took her hand, gave it a soft squeeze. 'I've got this. I don't want to risk you getting anything on that dress of yours.'

'What, this old thing?' She winked. 'Why don't you let me worry about that?'

He didn't even fight her on it, knowing full well that if she wanted to help she would, and the thought made him smile all the more.

They cleared the table and tidied the kitchen, making sure Dorothea didn't have much to do when she returned in the morning. It felt natural, *too* natural, to be doing such domesticated tasks beside her, but as they worked, she asked him about the origins of the house, and he stopped worrying about how it felt and concentrated on the details she wanted to know. The kind of farm it had once been, who had once lived here, how he'd discovered it...

But with every brush of her body against his, her perfume on the air, the sweet sound of her voice, it became harder and harder to resist pulling her to him.

'I take it you don't often clear up after dinner?'

He was reaching up into the cupboard for two champagne flutes when she asked, and he turned to look at her. 'Are you saying I don't look at home in my own kitchen?'

She pressed her lips together as her eyes danced. 'Something like that.'

'I'll have you know I do chip in on occasion, but I don't like to tread on Dorothea's toes. That woman has a scowl that'll send a grown man running.'

Her eyes continued to dance. 'I can believe it, only...'

He folded his arms. 'Only?'

She nipped her bottom lip, a tea towel in hand as she dried off the casserole dish he had just washed, and the comforting sight coupled with the fire in his veins made his heart pulse.

'Domestic duties carried out by a man...' Her eyes trailed over him. Hunger. Desire. It was all there in the flush to her skin as she stopped drying the dish and took him in. 'A man as well built and rugged as you, I don't know whether to laugh at the strangeness of it or declare it the sexiest sight I've ever seen.'

He was upon her in two strides. 'Let me help you with that.'

He tugged the dish from her, the towel too, dumping them on the side with a clatter. 'That's not help—'

'I wasn't talking about the dish.' He wrapped an arm around her and bit back a groan as she came willingly, pressing her body up against his heightened state. 'I'm talking about the doubts you raise over my masculinity.'

Her lips parted with a soft 'Oh…' that he swallowed with his kiss. A deep, thorough, knee-buckling kiss that had him spinning her into the countertop as she clung to his shoulders, her nails biting through his shirt.

Her frustrated whimpers resonated off the stone walls, his desperate groans too. She curved her leg around him, urging him closer and closer still, but it wasn't enough. He needed more. He needed her all.

She tore her mouth away, her breath coming in pants, his shoulders heaving in tune.

'Is this what you do when a woman emasculates you?'

'If it's you, yes.'

She stared up at him, her cheeks flushed, her eyes hooded, and it was the sexiest sight *he* had ever seen.

'Alaric?'

'Yes?'

'Take me to bed.'

The blood rushed his ears, his core, his ability to breathe lost as she offered him everything he could want. Everything he'd always wanted. 'But—'

She pressed a finger to his lips. 'No buts… I'm not asking for more after tonight. I'm asking to satisfy this need between us before it gets out of our control.'

Out of our control…

He already feared they were long past that point but he couldn't stop it. Not now.

And he didn't want to.

CHAPTER EIGHT

CATHERINE FOLLOWED HIM down the stairs, scarce able to believe this was happening.

The small voice at the back of her mind persisted with its warning. Be careful. That the implications for him, for her, for their futures that were worlds apart, were huge and so she'd made it clear—she wasn't asking for more, this was about one night.

But to be his first…after three long years…it wasn't like he'd had anyone else come here…

Could it really be as simple as walking away after?

Her heart fluttered up into her throat, nerves getting the better of her, and as Alaric pushed open the bedroom door, she tugged him back to her. Kissed him until her head was dizzy with it and she could no longer think, she could no longer worry.

'I've forgotten the champagne,' he said against her lips. 'You get yourself comfy and I'll go.'

She shook her head, pulling him into the room with her, needing his thought-obliterating presence, his warmth, to keep out the warning, the reservation. 'No, I don't need champagne. I just need you.'

And she did need him, more than she'd ever needed anyone, and it scared her as much as it reinforced her belief that this was meant to be.

'I like the way that sounds.' He lifted her up and she hooked her legs around his waist, their lips melding back together as though they'd never get enough. He backed her up against the bed, knelt on it as he lowered her down. 'Especially from you.'

And if he liked it, maybe he wouldn't object to her saying it more. Like every day for the rest of her stay and beyond. Could they continue this when her stay was over? Would it help him return to his family and the land of the living if she were to stay by his side for however long he needed? Could she do that? Would he want her to?

Her thoughts were as frenzied as the heat licking through her.

Stop thinking, she mentally berated herself, surrendering to his kiss, his touch, his body on hers. She kissed him harder, kissed him to mute her thoughts, kissed him to remind herself of what mattered right now…this.

He tore his mouth from hers, dragged kisses from her jaw to her ear and just beneath, where the sensitised pulse point made her whimper and writhe.

'This dress…it's killing me.' He caressed her through the fabric, his touch setting her skin alight. 'The way it looks against your skin, the way it feels…'

'It's a favourite.'

He murmured his agreement into the curve of her neck, his teeth nipping, his lips soft. He hooked his finger beneath one strap and teased it down.

'No bra too…'

Her insides quivered at the lustful heat in his voice, the thrill of what was to come.

'You really are killing me, Catherine.'

'If this is how dying feels—' she forked her fingers through his hair, watched him as he continued to unveil her '—I'd do it a thousand times over with you.'

It came out without thought, without reservation, and his eyes flicked to hers, passion blazing in their depths. She wondered if she'd said too much, overstepped an invisible line…panic pulsed through her, her fingers tightening in his hair.

'You and me both.' It was barely audible, a second's relief before the heat took over, warmth rushing through her core as he exposed one taut and needy peak to the cool air of the room.

She watched enraptured as he wet his bottom lip, the glimpse of tongue making her stomach clench, and he bowed his head, his breath sweeping over the sensitised nipple, his tongue following…

She gripped his shoulders, her nails clawing into his shirt as she arched into the caress, his name a moan on her lips. He cupped her breast, held her steady to his attention, his teeth grazing, his tongue flicking, his mouth sucking her in deep.

Pleasure surged fast and furious within her, her toes curling into the bed sheets as she grasped him like some form of anchor, fearing its intensity and revelling in it all the same. She pressed her head back into the pillow, clamped her eyes shut as she panted for air, cried out for more…

His hand fell to the tie at her waist, a bow the only thing holding her dress in place, and one sharp tug saw it undone.

'On second thoughts,' he murmured over her sensitised skin, 'this dress wouldn't be safe for the red carpet.'

'No?'

'No.' He rose up onto his knees, hemming her in with his thighs—it had never felt so good to be trapped. 'One wrong move and it's…'

He parted the fabric, uncovering her body to demonstrate his point, her small gold thong shimmering in the light as he hungrily took her all in.

'True.' Brazenly she lay there, goosebumps prickling over her skin, her nipples tightening further against the coolness of the room. 'But it does have its benefits for the after party...'

His eyes flashed to hers. 'This is the only after party I want to think about.'

She gave a soft laugh. 'Good. Now get back here.'

His grin was devilish as he dropped forward and she pressed her palms into his chest, preventing him from getting any closer. 'Not so fast.'

She reached for the buttons of his shirt, undid one and felt the tension in his body swell exponentially, saw his jaw tighten, his mouth too. There was a sudden hesitancy in his gaze, a battle between desire and something else.

She wet her lips. 'What is it?'

'I'm not—it's not...' His head dropped forward and his eyes squeezed shut. 'It's not pretty, Catherine.'

'Pretty?' she teased softly, stroking her hand beneath his chin to bring his head back up. 'And you accused me of emasculating you?'

He opened his eyes and she smiled up into his gaze. 'I want you, Alaric.'

She saw his throat bob and his eyes shimmer.

'I want all of you...' Slowly she unbuttoned another, and another, all the while holding his eye. 'I want every scar that makes you who you are now... I want you.'

His breath shuddered out of him, his eyes blazing into hers as he kissed her deeply. 'You have me.'

Her heart pulsed, her fingers unsteady as she stroked the shirt from his shoulders, down his back, savouring the heat of his bare skin, the strength rippling beneath her touch. He rose up when she couldn't reach any further, tugging the rest of it away, and she couldn't breathe for the sight of him. He was everything. He *made* 'pretty' masculine. He was beautiful, sexy, magnificent, and *God*, how she wanted him.

He came back to her, his hands planting into the mattress either side of her, and she shook her head. 'Time to even out the power dynamic.'

He frowned and she shoved him, forcing him onto his back, and he laughed, the sound deep and husky and provoking the fire within.

'I should have known you'd want your way in the bedroom too.' He stroked at her bare thighs as she climbed over him, pulling her arms free of her dress and tossing it aside.

'Complaining?'

He stared up at her, his eyes so intense, so piercing. 'Not at all, princess.'

Princess. It didn't trigger a second's hesitation now. She loved that he had a name for her, loved that this was what he wanted too.

She lowered her hands to his bronzed chest, marvelling at the sheer strength beneath her touch, the trail of dark hair, the journey of scars that travelled down his side...

She leaned forward, her hair brushing against his skin. 'Do they hurt?'

His fingers flexed on her thighs. 'Not so much now, they're mostly numb.'

'Do you mind if I touch them?'

His throat bobbed, his laugh tight. 'You can do anything you like. I've told you I'm yours...'

For tonight, she silently reminded herself, pressing a light kiss to his cheek, tracing the silvery line. 'You're one hell of a specimen, Alaric, I'll give you that.'

Another tight laugh. 'I'm one scarred specimen.'

'So?' She met his gaze. 'They tell a story of your journey, your life...you shouldn't dismiss them, or hide them. Especially from me...'

She pressed a kiss to his collarbone, let her tongue caress the dip in this flesh—another scar, another piece of him. 'You are incredible.'

His nose flared with his breath, and his hands were so large as they lifted to hold her hips, but she wriggled free, dipping to take her desired tour of his body. She kissed every scar, caressed the silver lines with her tongue, her fingertips, showed him how beautiful he was, how strong, and sexy, and relished every groan he gave, every flex of his fingers, his body, as he succumbed to the pleasure she gave.

She reached the waistband to his trousers and rose, her fingers making light work of the button there, the zip too. She shimmied them away, his socks too, their shoes long gone in the journey from the kitchen to bedroom.

She stepped from the bed and his eyes followed her, her smile small. 'You lose yours and I'll lose mine.'

His eyes were dark, hungry, his smile carnal, and she didn't wait, she was too eager to please, too eager to watch his face change as she slid the flimsy fabric down her hips.

She straightened up and he shook his head. 'Catherine. You are...you really are going to be the death of me.'

'I hope not, because I really want this to last the whole night.'

His laugh was gruff.

'Never mind me.' She eyed his briefs. 'I'm waiting.'

He shucked them, the move so quick she squealed when he came at her, his hands on her waist as he pulled her back to the bed with him. He bowed his head to kiss her, her lashes fluttering closed as she wrapped her legs around

his hips and positioned him just where she wanted him
and—froze.

'Protection!' She bit her lip hard, pushing back the
thought that swiftly came next, the memory, the pain…
'Do you have any?'

He cursed and dragged in a breath. 'Not here.'

She sagged beneath him.

'But somewhere?' she said with hope.

He rolled onto his back, his palm pressing into his forehead. 'I'm such a fool. I have some but they pre-date my
move here.'

She wrapped her leg around him, rested her head on
his shoulder as her fingers trailed the curves and planes
of his torso, her heart and breaths still racing with her
need for him.

'Are you on the pill?'

'No. It doesn't agree with me.'

She moved against him, her disobedient body unwill-
ing to stop, though her heart and head told her they must.
'Go and check them anyway. They might still be good.'

'Or we could just…satisfy ourselves in other ways…'
He stroked his hand down her side, cupped her breast
as his thumb rolled over her nipple, and she bit back a
whimper.

'We could, only—' she kissed him, brushing the words
against his lips '—I want to explore so many avenues with
you that it would be nice not to worry about restrictions.'

He laughed as he pulled away and she watched him go,
a smile playing about her lips, her heart light and free as
she refused to let anything spoil this night—not the past,
not the future, nothing.

Alaric opened the bathroom cabinet and took out the
packet he knew he had. After all, he'd only relocated it very

recently to make room for Catherine in the master suite. He hadn't expected to be getting it out again. In fact, he'd almost thrown them away, but the act had felt too final.

Too final? He wanted to laugh as he scanned the packet for a date, struggling to read as his hand shook with the realisation that they were really doing this…and then what?

How could they possibly return to how things were come morning?

Would she expect more? Would he?

Didn't this change everything?

It's one night of passion, came the voice of reason, no more, no less. The future didn't come into it.

But what of Fred? Did one night of bliss make him a traitor to his guilt?

Though surely he would suffer more for having known her, and let her go.

His gut rolled with the emptiness of it, his heart too quick to follow, and he pushed it all from his mind, projecting her instead—Catherine, in his bed, naked and waiting.

He closed the cabinet and caught his reflection in the mirror, the flush to his skin making his scars more garish. Was she crazy? How could she want this? Him?

The contrast between them couldn't be more profound and yet…she *did* want him.

He felt it in every caress of her fingers, her lips, saw it in her eyes and heard it in her voice as she'd made him feel worshipped…*him*.

And shouldn't he be the one doing the worshipping when he had her in his bed?

He strode back into the master bedroom to find her just as he left her. Naked, smiling, wanton.

'I was about to come and look for you.'

'Like that?'

She pushed herself up onto one elbow and gave a nod.

'Now I wish you had...'

He threw the packet down on the bedside table and joined her, his hand reaching out to cup her hip, to stroke at her skin that was so impossibly soft beneath his touch.

How long had it been since he'd touched a woman? His fingers trembled with the truth—too many years to count.

'Miss me that much?'

She leaned into him, her eyes worshipping him all over again. 'Too much.'

She hooked her leg over him, forcing him onto his back as she planted her palms into his chest and let her hair tickle at his skin.

'How long has it been for you?'

He frowned. Was she in his mind? 'A while.'

'Am I the first since you've lived here?'

He chuckled quietly. 'Do you see me hiding any other women here?'

Her eyes sparkled with his tease. 'You want to take it slow?'

He scoffed as he fought the urge to roll her back under him and demonstrate his answer. 'You know that conversation about emasculating me...'

Now she smiled. 'I don't want to be too much for you.'

'Right, that does it.' He rolled her under him, relishing her squeal of delight as he covered her body with his. 'I'm taking the lead.'

He rolled his hips, her moan his reward. As was the surge of colour in her cheeks, her heavy-lidded gaze.

'I want you, Catherine. I don't need to go slow, I don't need your softness. I want this.'

'Then take me.'

He reached out for the packet and rose up, his eyes on hers as he sheathed himself and gritted his teeth against the rush within. Slowly he lowered himself over her, careful to keep his weight on his elbows as he kissed her, loving how she matched him move for move, her legs hooking around his hips, moving him against her.

'Are you sure, Catherine?' He had to ask. It would kill him to stop, but he would...

'I've never been more sure about anything. I want this. I want you, for however long I can have you.'

However long I can have you...

The words echoed through his mind as he took all that she was offering, all that made him feel so complete.

'Alaric!' She clung to his back, her eyes all vivid and blue.

'*You* are incredible.' He returned her compliment as he moved slowly, drawing out the sensation, controlling his need as he sought to build hers. 'You are beautiful... Caring... Kind.'

'Quit it, Alaric!' She clutched him tighter. 'You're filling my head with nonsense.'

'No.' He frowned, her reaction making him still. 'I'm filling it with the truth.'

She shook her head and squeezed her eyes shut.

'Look at me, Catherine.'

She refused and he stroked her hair back from her face.

'Look at me.' He cupped her face, held still until she opened her eyes, and when she did, he couldn't breathe. Her eyes were damp, wet with tears. His throat closed over, his voice hoarse as he assured her, 'You are all of those things and more, never believe otherwise.'

'More action, less words.' She tugged his mouth to hers, kissed him. 'I don't need the platitudes.'

'They're not—'

'Please, no more.'

What was this? His head told him to leave well alone, that whatever it was would only draw them closer together, but he couldn't. He wanted to understand. He *needed* to.

'Catherine, don't shut—'

She shoved him, forcing him onto his back as she tried to take control of the pace.

'Catherine?'

'Please, Alaric. I want this, I want you, no more, no less.'

'Talk to me.'

'No.' Her eyes pleaded with him. 'We're having sex. Fun. That doesn't need words.'

And yet she'd given him plenty. Made him feel desired, wanted, appreciated. Why wouldn't she let him do the same in return? Why did she look...*fearful*?

'What are you afraid of?'

It was his turn to ask the question.

'Nothing.' Though it caught in her throat and he held her hips steady, even as the demands of his body tried to override his heart and the need to hear the truth from her.

'Don't lie to me.'

'Please, Alaric, please.' She trembled in his hold. 'Let us have this.'

She fell forward, kissed him, her hands reaching for his and taking them above his head. He looked up into her eyes that were ablaze with so much and surrendered, giving himself over to her completely, letting her take her pleasure and deliver his own.

Tomorrow, they would walk away from this. They had to because the one thing he knew for sure—this couldn't happen again. He was drowning in her. Not steadily and slowly, not carefully or within his control, he was losing it.

He *was* lost. To her.

And that terrified him enough to keep his mouth shut and abide her demands, to let the thrill of what they were sharing in the now take over.

Because sex was finite.

It had an end.

And with it, this between them would cease to exist and life would be as it was. Safe. Steady. And wholly within his control.

No surprises. No fear. No guilt. No pain.

CHAPTER NINE

CATHERINE WOKE TO the smell of fresh coffee, the caress of the sea breeze across her naked skin and the sound of the waves rolling in the distance…bliss.

Her body ached in the most satisfying of ways and a smile was already on her lips as she untangled herself from the sheets and her lashes fluttered open. Sure enough, the glass door was ajar, a coffee pot was on the bedside table with two mugs, a jug of orange juice, glasses and glazed pastries. Oh, yum.

'Morning, sleepyhead.'

She rolled over to see Alaric stood at the foot of the bed, a towel slung around his hips, another hooked around his bare shoulders. His hair was damp, and his body still glistened from a very recent shower. If only she'd woken up a few minutes earlier, she thought, envying every small rivulet of water as it ran down his torso.

She took a second to catch her breath, another to try and moisten her very dry mouth. How could she want him so much already? They'd slept a few hours at most, the rest of the time they'd been hell-bent on sating this never-ending hunger.

'I was beginning to think I'd have to rouse you.' He lifted the towel from around his neck to dry his hair, an innocent enough move, save for the fact that she was left watching his pecs and abs ripple, his arm muscles bulge… Definitely yum!

She swallowed, lifted her eyes to his that were so blue against his tan and the brightness of the room, and stretched out, aware of how naked she was. His eyes raked over her, projecting every salacious thought that mirrored her own.

He still wanted her.

But they were in unknown territory now…the morning after the most amazing night before.

Were they done? Or did the fact that she was still naked with his eyes feasting over her mean that they could pursue this a little longer because, seriously, if this was how good it felt the morning after, how good would it feel after a few days, a week, two…

She gave him a cat-like smile. 'And how, pray tell, were you hoping to do that?'

His eyes flashed, his lopsided grin hot. 'That would be telling.'

He rounded the bed to come up alongside her and stopped short, some unknown emotion flickering across his face as an invisible wall seemed to erect itself between them.

She opened her mouth to suggest her own possibilities fearing what was coming, but he got there first. 'We should talk.'

She felt her lips pout and she really wasn't the pouty kind. 'After coffee, yeah?' She pushed herself up to sitting. 'I'm no use to anyone without my morning hit.'

And she really wanted to live in the moment just a little longer…

He nodded, his smile small as he started to move away, and she reached out, hooked her fingers in the towel around his waist. 'I wasn't just referring to the caffeine hit…'

One sharp tug and he was on the bed with her, the towel in a heap on the floor, his naked body up against hers. And before she could declare herself triumphant, he was kissing her. She had known from the ease with which he'd landed beside her that he'd wanted it as much as her but to feel his mouth on hers sent her head spinning, her heart too.

'I knew I should have dressed before you woke up.' He brushed the words against her lips, his hands roaming over her as she raked her nails down his back.

'And spoil my fun?' She nipped his lip, playful punishment for the suggestion.

He hissed in a breath, taking up her hands, and threading his fingers through hers, he pinned them above her head. 'It's a good job I told Dorothea to take the day off, you're insatiable.'

'Funny, I was thinking the same about you.'

And then he was kissing her, so thoroughly that had there been any doubt remaining about what breakfast had entailed for him, it was obliterated now.

This was definitely her kind of wake-up call.

Almost an hour later, showered and dressed in a black bikini, she joined Alaric at the table outside her bedroom— or rather, *his* bedroom.

He'd made fresh coffee and whipped up some eggs, ham and slices of bread. The pastries had disappeared with their bedroom escapades and even the memory alone set off the heated flutters deep inside her.

'Wow, you really do know how to spoil a lady.'

He gave her the glimmer of a smile, his eyes not quite lifting to hers. 'If Dorothea found out I served just pastries for breakfast, she'd be beyond mad. Especially as she baked the bread fresh this morning and dropped it off on her way to the cove with Andreas.'

She smiled, her affection for the couple growing with

each passing day. 'Sounds like they have the perfect day planned.'

She only wished theirs could be just as perfect.

Pulling out the chair across from him, she sat and took up her coffee, using its familiar aroma to try and soothe her churning stomach. The elephant in the room was about to make itself known and she really didn't want it to spoil the day. Not when it had been so very perfect from the off.

She planted her elbows on the table and hid behind her cup, sneaking a peek at him beneath her lashes as he squinted out over the pool to the sea beyond. She sensed that his furrowed brow wasn't entirely down to the brightness of the sun and she didn't want to prompt him into revealing his thoughts.

He flicked her a quick look, and another. She lowered her cup to the table and touched a hand to her damp hair, suddenly self-conscious in her unmade state. For the first time she could remember, she'd skipped her morning hair and make-up routine. Not only had she been too eager to be back with him, but he'd succeeded in making her feel comfortable, beautiful, desired just the way she was, and she hadn't felt the need for her protective shield…though now she was reconsidering it as he sent her another look, his eyes narrowing.

'What is it?'

'You're not wearing any make-up.'

A blush crept into her cheeks and she tried for a nonchalant shrug. 'I thought I'd go without. You know, for a change.'

His eyes trailed over her, their depths warming with his smile. 'You don't need it.'

She gave a flustered laugh, filled with a contradictory mix of both relief and anxiety. 'You had me worried for a second.'

She was still worried…

'I mean it, Catherine, you're beautiful without all that.'

Emotion clogged up her throat, his kind words merging with those spoken during the night and making her wish this meant more, that it wasn't just a brief fling but a real, bona fide—

No, don't go there.

She picked up her fork. 'We should eat before these eggs go cold.'

'In this heat?' he murmured, knowing full well she was changing the subject.

'Humour me.'

He did but his eyes were still on her and she wet her lips, scooped up a healthy dollop of scrambled egg and popped it in her mouth. It was delicious—creamy and buttery, and *almost* the perfect distraction.

'This is tasty.' She covered her mouth as she complimented his culinary skills. Though to be fair she hadn't met a man yet who wasn't a pro when it came to scrambled, fried or omelette-style eggs. In nearly all pieces of romantic fiction, be it a book or a play or a movie, the man could always whip up a decent plate of eggs. The thought had a smile teasing at the corners of her mouth.

He eyed her suspiciously. 'What's so funny?'

'You don't want to know.'

Because she was pretty sure that if she told him what was really going through her mind, the unintended suggestion that they were living out their own romantic fairy tale right now, he'd baulk. Not that she wanted a relationship out of this. She *knew* she wouldn't get a relationship out of this. So why couldn't she let them tackle the elephant and be done with it?

Maybe because you're lying to yourself…?

He took up his coffee, sipped at it, his eyes not once releasing her from their spell. 'Try me.'

She shook her head. 'Men and eggs. It's a bit of cliché.'

'I'm a cliché?'

'Not you, per se.' She laughed at his mock wounded expression. 'But you and the cooking up of eggs—yup!'

She was pleased to see the flicker of a smile even though she knew she was about to ruin it. She couldn't eat another bite without getting the impending conversation over.

'So… I've had my coffee, we've had our fun, let's talk.'

He struggled over the mouthful of food he had just taken, and she cursed her timing. Maybe he wasn't about to destroy everything after all. Maybe if she'd just kept her mouth shut, he wouldn't have raised it at all.

'Last night was…' He leaned back in his seat, his frown deepening as he held her gaze.

'Fun?' she suggested with an easy smile—she was supposed to be an actor after all.

'That.'

'But?'

He continued to watch her, his mouth lifting to one side and creasing at the scar tissue there. She had the overwhelming urge to ask if he'd applied sunscreen. Not that he'd appreciate the mollycoddling any more than she had when he'd asked her the same.

He swallowed and looked out to sea, his fingers raking through his hair that had dried wild thanks to the rough attention of her fingers not so long ago.

'You can just come out and say it, Alaric. It was a one night only deal, it was our moment to indulge, and now we're back to…what are we exactly?'

A silent pause and then he looked at her. 'Friends?'

Her mouth parted, her body fit to burst with the overwhelming rush of warmth—Friends.

After all he'd said they couldn't be again…

Now her smile was genuine, because for all she wanted more, more of him, more of this, just more, at least he wasn't rejecting her friendship any more.

And that had to be a good thing.

A very good thing.

'Friends?' Catherine's eyes shone back at him in the late-morning sun, her smile breathtaking. 'Now there's a turn up for the books.'

Her voice was a teasing murmur and he had the over-whelming urge to take her hand and drag her back to bed. He wanted her and would go on wanting her long after she left his island. He knew it, just as well as he knew this thirst would never be quenched.

Clenching his jaw, he looked back to the ocean. Barely a ripple broke the crystal blue surface and he tried to in-stil the same sense of calm within.

'Wouldn't you say?'

And of course she would press him on it. She was the most confident, most tempting woman he had ever known.

'Yes, Catherine. I know what I said the other day. But I'm hardly the sort of man to share the last twelve hours in bed with you and declare you no one to me.'

'Lucky me.'

He gave a soft scoff. 'I'm not sure lucky is the word I would use.'

'Well, lucky for you, I'm the one using it.'

And God he was smiling, a laugh brewing as he took in her bright smile, her eyes that he'd drowned in over and over during the night…this morning too.

He'd been a fool to cross that line with her and think he could come back from it unchanged. An absolute fool.

But given his time again, would he go back and do it differently?

Hell, no. Which likely made him an even bigger fool.

He started to dig into his food, a way to keep his hands busy and her at a distance. Because he was just as hooked, just as in deep, even more so now he'd tasted her, felt that connection, felt how good they were together…how good it could be.

But they were friends, *just* friends, and he needed to get some distance between them again if he hoped to keep his heart safe and keep it that way.

CHAPTER TEN

As far as mornings-after went, Catherine deemed theirs as being rather pleasant overall. Civilised conversation, compliments exchanged, even some laughter along with an agreement that it had been fun but it wouldn't be repeated.

And the best bit—he'd declared them friends once more. A bonus.

But five days later, she was forced to accept he'd only been saying what he thought she wanted to hear because Mr Elusive was back.

Each day he appeared less and less, in the gym, at the pool, for meals… He was ghosting her all over again and it was driving her to distraction. All the more so, because he'd *said* they were friends and she'd believed him.

She was annoyed but not so annoyed as to storm his study again. She didn't want to have to go to him. She shouldn't have to. And she refused to act needy for any man, particularly one that blew hot and cold and then ignored her so completely.

So she'd taken herself off to the trail for another run in the sun. Using the exertion and the oppressive heat to burn him out of her body and mind, not that it was working.

Thirty minutes in and she was *still* thinking about him.

Him and his smile. Him and his eyes. Him and his body and the amazing things he could do with it. More than that, she remembered the look on his face when he'd whispered all those sweet nothings to her and made love to her with— No, not made love...*had sex.*

Because making love...well, that was a different thing entirely, and she wasn't going there.

She swiped her sweat-banded wrist over her brow and turned the volume up on her earphones, using the music to drown out his voice and the images persisting in her head. She took in the beauty of her surroundings—the olive grove, the vibrant blue sea, the clear skies and the rocky path...

She was navigating a particularly uneven patch when the music cut out, replaced by her ring tone. She glanced at her watch. Kelsey. Her agent.

She slowed her pace and answered the call.

'Kelsey, what's up?'

'Are you...*exercising*? Please tell me you are, because with the way you're panting...'

She laughed and drew to a stop, hands on her hips as she sucked in a breath. 'I'm running and it's hot out here.'

'I make it four in the afternoon and you're running outdoors, in Greece, in the height of summer—are you crazy?!'

'A little.' She swiped her forehead once more, squinted against the sun as she watched a distant yacht on the water. 'What is it?'

'I've sent you an email about your press appearances prior to the launch.'

She frowned. 'And you needed to ring me because...'

'Because I need to make sure you look at it.'

'I always keep on top of my email, you know that.'

'True, but...well...'

'Spit it out, Kelsey, it's not like you to beat around the bush.'

'It's Luke.'

'What about him?'

'Well, he'll obviously be there.'

'Ye-e-es,' she drawled, her frown deepening. 'He is my co-star, so I kind of know that already.'

'I know, but—well, I—I just wanted to make sure you're going to be okay.'

'Of course I'm going to be okay, when am I not?'

'It's just with all the press reports lately, what with your mother's opinion being splashed about, coupled with—'

'Wait, back up a step. What exactly has my mother been saying?'

'You haven't seen?'

'No.'

'But it's all over social media.'

'Charlie deals with all that. I've muted my notifications.' Charlie was her PA and a great one at that. She only bothered her when she felt it strictly necessary. And anything her mother was or wasn't doing was of no interest to her.

'Right, of course she does.'

'Do I really need to know?'

'It's just your mother being your mother. She loves the attention and siding with Luke over the suggested affair brings her a *lot* of attention.'

'She's done *what*?'

She could sense Kelsey's grimace at her outburst, but it stung. And she shouldn't be surprised, she shouldn't be hurt, but she was all that and more. Her own bleeding mother!

She took a stabilising breath and another.

'Kitty?' came her agent's soft prompt.

'Luke and I are fine, Kelsey.' She softened her voice. 'It doesn't matter what my mother has said, everyone knows we don't get along and anyone that matters will take her words with a pinch of salt.'

It was the truth. The entire world knew of her estranged relationship with her parents, her mother in particular, and no one knew of the baby she'd lost. No one save for Flo and Luke, and that was the only news she couldn't bear to be made public.

'Good. That's good. It will certainly make things run smoother in front of the camera if you're both on speaking terms still.'

'We're good. We're more than good.' Luke had been incredible, trying to reassure her, trying to help her, not once blaming her for the miscarriage…but she blamed herself enough for the two of them. 'Was there anything else?'

'The red carpet launch LA—who are you taking?'

She frowned again. 'I think the plan is for Luke and I to go together?'

'Really? You want to provoke *that* discussion when the focus of the press should be on the movie and not the status of your on-off relationship.'

She thought of what Alaric had said on the very same subject. 'Any press is good press, right?'

'And what if he wants to attend with someone else?'

'Then I'll go alone.' She was frustrated now, and she knew it was coming through in her voice, her elevated heart rate not helping matters. Thoughts of Alaric helping even less.

'Why don't I ask around, see who—'

'Good God, Kelsey, I don't need a date. I'm quite capable of standing there alone.'

'But so soon after—'

'Leave it, Kelsey. Please.'

'Very well.'

'Is that everything?'

'Yes—oh, no, wait! How is the script coming along? Do you think you'll be in a position for me to start pitching it soon?'

'Hopefully.' That was the one thing going to plan this holiday. Her frustration over Alaric had given her the impetus to lose herself in the pages and the characters she'd been burning to write about for years.

'Excellent. I'll let you get back to your run, then. Just be careful in that heat, yeah? We don't need you suffering heatstroke, or worse, coming back all lobster-like and peeling…there's only so much make-up can do.'

She rolled her eyes. Heaven forbid she did something that stupid for aesthetics' sake. Never mind the cancer risks…

She could just imagine how Alaric would react if he'd overheard Kelsey…if he even came close enough to overhear a conversation again. God, he was frustrating. Caring so much in one moment and pulling a disappearing act the next.

'See ya, Kels.'

'Bye, sweetie.'

She shoved her phone back into the side pocket of her running shorts and took off at speed now. Her frustration over Alaric mounting with frustration over Hollywood and its obsession with perfection, with appearances. She wanted to scream into the wind, keep going until all she could hear was the pounding of her heart in her ears, the music and—

The ground shifted beneath her, a rock coming loose as a jarring pain shot through her ankle. 'Argh!'

She flung her hands out to soften her fall, but she was already tumbling, stone and dirt breaking the skin as she left the path and sunk into the prickly dried-out undergrowth.

Her music went dead, the squawk of the birds she'd disturbed and the trill of the insects the only answer to her cry as she squeezed her eyes shut and hissed through the pain.

Great. Just great!

Alaric stared at the screens in his study but his ability to concentrate was waning.

Waning? Who was he trying to kid…? It had been virtually non-existent since Catherine's arrival. All the more absent since their one night together… The memory alone was enough to send his body into overdrive, the ache in his chest all the more pronounced.

The ache of *guilt* he assured himself because he knew it couldn't be anything else, he wouldn't allow it to be anything else. And he was being a jerk—*again*—so he deserved all the guilt he could throw at himself.

But then he'd tried to be normal, to be a friend. He'd tried to go about his daily routine with her in sight, but every glimpse and his pulse would leap, his body would warm, and he'd smile that ridiculous impulsive smile…and he'd known he was in trouble. So much trouble.

Because he wasn't pretending to be comfortable around her, he *was* comfortable. She made him feel accepted in his own skin, his new skin, and she slotted in here.

She fitted into his life in the most perfect of ways, and the desire to keep her, to want her to stay, was getting harder to resist. She made him forget his guilt, she made him forget everything but the way she made him feel, and he knew that was wrong, so very wrong.

And so he'd avoided temptation altogether. In all likelihood she would detest him by the time this trip was over and then—

'Kyrios de Vere!' The door to his study burst open and

a flushed Dorothea appeared, her hands gesturing frantically. 'Come quick.'

He frowned, launching himself out of his seat and striding towards her. 'What is it?'

'It's Miss Wilde. She's had a fall, a nasty one.'

He cursed under his breath, his pulse spiking as he followed her out. 'Where is she?'

'Andreas is helping her back. He phoned ahead asking me to get you.'

'*Back?* Where's she been?'

'Running.'

He cursed again, felt the heat of the late-afternoon sun beat down on him as they emerged from the house and took a right, to the start of the trail, and… His chest contracted. There she was, hobbling, her arm hooked around Andreas' shoulders for support, her entire body covered in dirt, her running bra and shorts offering no protection at all. She was cut, grazed, her face, her knee, her ankle…

Another stifled curse and he was racing forward, the emotions he'd been working so hard to suppress rising with such force they were choking up his chest.

'What am I going to do with you?' He loomed over her and she glared at him, at least that's what he thought it was meant to be, but the small cut to her lip made it more of a pout and the hiss she gave told him the effort had cost her.

'I'm fine, thanks for asking.' She stared straight ahead. 'You can go back to your work.'

Andreas gave him a look and he stepped in. 'I'll take her.'

'You. Will. *Not.*' She hobbled back, her eyes glistening as she spoke, her rejection cutting deep, but he had to help her. He *had* to.

Closing the distance she'd created, he swept her up in his arms.

'Alaric!' She shoved against him. 'Put me down this second!'

'Quit it, princess.'

It was hurting her to speak. It was hurting him to see her in pain. Why did he feel like even this fall was his fault?

She harrumphed, folding her arms, her body tense in his hold, but at least she wasn't pushing him away now. He snuck a peek. She looked mutinous. Her eyes shooting darts in the direction of an innocent Dorothea as she hurried towards them.

'She's sprained her ankle, I think,' Andreas said to Dorothea. 'She'll need to get it raised and get some ice on it too.'

She nodded as she fell into step beside them, tutting away. 'I knew all this running out here was a bad thing.'

You and me both.

He gritted his teeth, his jaw pulsing with the effort not to say it as Andreas ran ahead to hold open the front door. He strode on in and headed for the stairs.

'I'll take her down to the bedroom. She'll need cleaning up. Can you bring the first aid kit, Dorothea? The ice pack and a glass of water too.' He looked down at her sweat-and dirt-stained face, feeling her pain like a crushing force within. 'Did you not even take a drink with you?'

She flicked him a look that quite accurately depicted the middle finger gesture and he bit back a relieved laugh. Feisty as ever.

'You can hate me all you like, but I'm not leaving you until I know you're okay.'

She mumbled something incoherent under her breath, but before he could ask, she started to tremble in his hold— shock. He held her tighter, wishing he could do more.

'Bring me a whisky too, Andreas.'

The man's brows hit the ceiling.

'It's not for me,' he explained, though he had a feeling he'd be wanting one too, very soon.

Andreas nodded and raced ahead as Dorothea branched off to the kitchen.

'This really isn't necessary,' Catherine grumbled through her teeth that were now chattering incessantly.

'I'll be the judge of that.'

'Dorothea and Andreas are more than capable of taking care of me.'

'You're my guest, you've got hurt on my watch. I'll be the one taking care of you.'

'So now I'm your guest.' She shook her head, grunted. 'You're the most confusing, contradictory man I've ever met!'

'And you're the most frustrating and stubborn woman, so I reckon we're even.'

She glared up at him. 'If you weren't carrying me down concrete steps right now, I'd... I'd...'

'What? Slap me?' He gave her an amused look that only riled her further. 'It's a good job I'm carrying you, then.'

Another emphatic harrumph and then she rested her head against his shoulder, and he forgot the reason she was in his arms, he forgot the reason he'd been hiding out, he forgot everything but the feel of her. The sense that she felt so right there, curled up against him, his arms around her, protecting her...

'I have it all,' Dorothea called down the stairs, her footsteps quick to follow as she hurried after them.

'And I have the whisky, two glasses too, just in case,' Andreas said, joining them.

'Thank you.' Alaric strode into the bedroom, making for the bed.

'You can't put me on there like this.' She started to wriggle against him. 'I'll ruin the sheets.'

He ignored her, placing her down as gently as he could. 'Dorothea, fetch a bowl with fresh water and ice please.'

'Of course.' She placed the items she'd brought down on the side table and left to get the rest.

'Do you want me to pour?' Andreas held up the whisky and glasses.

'No, it's fine. I can take it from here.'

He placed them on the side table. 'Is there anything else I can get?'

'Not right now. I'll call if we need anything.'

He nodded and looked back at Catherine, his face creased up with concern. 'You're in good hands, Miss Wilde.'

She gripped her arms around her middle and gave him a watery smile. 'Thank you, Andreas. For everything.'

Dorothea came bustling in with a bowl, cloths and a towel, placing them down on the foot of the bed. 'Right, let's get you cleaned up.'

Alaric touched a hand to hers. 'It's okay, I've got this.'

'Well, I'm not sure if…' She looked at Catherine and back at him, her hesitation obvious, and he gave her a smile.

'I'm quite capable, I promise.'

'Well, okay, if Miss Wilde is happy.'

Catherine didn't look happy, folded up like she was, knees bent, her head dropped forward, but as she looked up at Dorothea, she gave her a nod and managed another smile.

'Very well, call if you need anything else.'

'We will.' He watched her leave with Andreas, waiting for the door to close before looking back to Catherine and then the whisky. He uncorked the bottle and poured a small measure in both. 'Here, take a sip—it'll help with the shock.'

'I'm not—'

He stared her refusal down, shoving the drink into her hand and grasping her other to place both around the glass. 'You are. You're shaking.'

Dubiously, she eyed both him and the drink but took a disgruntled sip, wincing as the alcohol caught the cut in her lip.

'Is this you making up for the fact you've barely been near me since the other night?'

He reached over her and took up the spare pillows, careful not to knock her as he did so and planting them midway down the bed.

He took the glass from her hands. 'Lay back.'

She didn't move, just looked at him expectant. Waiting for the answer he wasn't going to give.

'Come on, Catherine, you need to get that ankle elevated and iced… Unless you want to find yourself immobile for even longer.'

Her lashes fluttered, the internal debate clear in her glistening blues but eventually, she lay back and gingerly lifted her leg into his awaiting hands. He looked at her ankle, the swelling already apparent near the bone, and fought to keep his expression blank.

'I'm just going to take your trainers off. Let me know if I hurt you.'

She scoffed and he flicked her a quick look. She wasn't scoffing about the potential pain from the sprain, she was scoffing about the pain he'd already inflicted.

'I'm sorry I've not—' carefully he unthreaded the lace on her trainer, loosening off the straps '—been around much.'

'Avoiding me, more like.'

He lifted the heel of her trainer, his other hand holding her calf steady and taking the weight. 'I guess.'

'You avoiding me warrants an *"I guess,"* not a denial, an extra apology.' She cursed.

He knew she was lashing out and why. She had good reason. He was the one in the wrong and she deserved an answer, an explanation. 'If I said I needed some distance between us, would it make you feel any better?'

She frowned. At least she'd stopped shivering but the way she was looking at him now was worse. Like she could see him for what he was—a fool, a man who knew she was too good for him, would always be too good for him, and yet cared for her anyway.

He focused on her foot instead, slowly easing the trainer away and lowering her leg to the pillows. He checked to make sure her ankle was higher than her heart and then removed her other trainer and sock. All the while he could feel her watching him, her curiosity mounting.

'You know, it's just a sprain. I can take it from here.'

'Not until I have you cleaned up. Your cuts need tending to.'

He took up the ice pack Dorothea had brought and curved it around her injury, trying not to wince when she did but feeling it all the same.

'Sorry,' he murmured when she gave a sharp gasp.

'*That's* not your fault.'

No, she was right there too.

'You can go now, Alaric, please.' Her eyes glistened with fresh tears—tears he knew she was refusing to let fall. 'I'm not some child who needs looking after. I can clean myself up.'

He wasn't leaving. If he had his way, free of the accident, free of the guilt, he'd never leave her. Ignoring her protests, he wrung the cloth in the bowl of clean water and brought it to the knee closest to him.

She hissed, her eyes watering all the more, her glare evident behind the tears. 'Please, Alaric, you're going to ruin the bedding too.'

'Do you think I care a damn about the bedding, Catherine?!' He shot her a fierce stare, knowing his inner torment was written in his face, in the thickness to his voice. 'Just lie still.'

He turned and picked up the whisky. 'Here, have some more. It'll help.'

She didn't move, her eyes mistrustful and tearing him apart.

'Please, Catherine, let me take care of you.'

She took a shaky breath, her lashes lowering as she reached out for the glass.

'Thank you.'

It came out so quiet and the tension between his shoulder blades eased. The relief in his heart so very evident.

He rinsed the cloth as she took a sip and gave another wince.

She touched a finger to the cut and cringed. 'I must look a sight.'

He looked at her, really looked, and he couldn't say what he truly thought. That even with a fat lip on the rise, bloody and wounded, she still looked beautiful. Beautiful and vulnerable, and it was a lethal mix to his defences.

He took her hand from her face, touched the cloth to her lip and tried to ignore the way it made him feel, the way she watched him beneath lashes that clung together with her tears and tried to understand him.

'It's a clean cut at least...' His voice was thick, raw, as raw as his heart felt. 'But I think you'll have a lump there for a few days.'

He reached for an ice cube from the tray Dorothea had

brought and wrapped it in a small cloth. 'Here, hold this over it.'

She didn't baulk, just placed her glass down and lay back into the pillows, her eyes to the ceiling as she held the wrapped ice to her lip, her other hand resting on her bare torso. Carefully, he tended to every cut, every graze, the tension in her entire body giving away her continued pain and discomfort.

By the time he'd finished, she looked ready to sleep, and as he brushed her hair back from her eyes, he gave her a small smile.

'I'll send for Dorothea and she can help you change. You look like you could do with some sleep.'

Her brows drew together, her blue eyes swirling with so many questions, so much emotion, he could feel her reaching inside him, silencing his voice, immobilising his body…

And then she blinked and looked away. 'Thank you for taking care of me.'

It was a whisper, so sad and defeated, and he wanted to reach for her, to say anything, do anything, to make it all better. But where did he even begin?

The problems were his, not hers.

'Just go, Alaric. Please.'

Fresh tears welled in the corners of her eyes and he fought the urge to wipe them away. He wanted to climb on the bed, pull her to him, whisper all the sweet nothings raging in his head, his heart, and hold her safe.

And it was that deep-rooted need that had him clearing up the debris and striding for the door. 'Call if you need anything. Dorothea will be straight down.'

'Not you. Got it.'

He could just make out the words said under her breath and forced himself to keep moving and not look back because he knew if he did he would cave. And he'd only end up confusing their relationship more, hurting her even more in the process.

And above all, he wanted to protect her, even if that meant protecting her from his messed-up self.

She gave Dorothea a reluctant smile to placate her.

Wait, Dorothea's eyes took on a look that, if she'd been paying attention to her guest before, you know it's not come to stop a murder.'. The hat, the stilt, the precaution, the non-swim, and a caution would feel like overkill here.

Until then she'd been at the same time shudder by the go about her day as normal, and even time she'd turned herself a year. Of the sun. Don't Dorothea or Arabic or would be enjoying...

CHAPTER ELEVEN

CATHERINE LIFTED HER gaze from her laptop to see Dorothea crossing the poolside, straight for her. *Uh-oh, here we go.*

She lifted the brim of her straw hat and lowered the lid of her laptop to smile at the woman in the hope of softening whatever admonishment was coming and wondered what it was this time. She wasn't putting weight on her three-day-old injury and she was lathered in sunblock. She was being a good patient and she was getting some actual writing done. All was good with the world...well, almost.

'Your shoulder, Miss Wilde, it is in the sun!'

She looked to the left, to the right. Sure enough the sun had moved just enough to expose the tip of her shoulder, but she'd been so engrossed in her script she hadn't noticed.

'Oops, I'll just...' She shifted the laptop, made to rise, and Dorothea practically squeaked.

'You stay right there!'

The woman was already at her side, tilting the parasol to cover all of her once more.

'Maybe it is time you came inside?'

'I like it out here—the view is inspiring and it helps me to focus.' She'd been out there most of the day, the pool taunting her just a bit as she craved a decent swim, but three days into her injury, it was still too tender.

'Is there anything I can get for you?'

She gave Dorothea a smile. 'A new ankle?'

'Aah.' Dorothea's eyes softened, her smile full of sympathy. 'It'll be as good as new before you know it…so long as you continue to rest it properly.' The last she added in that matronly manner of hers and Catherine could feel her cheeks blaze.

Guilty as charged…

She'd been caught at least a dozen times already, trying to go about her day as normal, and each time she'd earned herself a stern ticking off from Dorothea or Andreas, even the distant glare from Alaric the one time he'd caught her trying some very early morning yoga. Very early because she'd hoped to avoid being caught. Yoga because there was nothing much else she could put her body through, and she was an exercise addict. She had to be. Her metabolism alone didn't keep her this trim.

'I'm trying, I just hate being so idle.'

'Me too, so I understand, but still, rest—*nai*?'

'*Nai.*'

'Now, lunch—what can I get you?'

'I'm fine. I'm still full from breakfast.'

She eyed her sceptically. 'Fruit and yogurt is not enough for the whole day.'

'I'll get something later if I'm hungry.'

'You said the same yesterday.'

'I wasn't hungry.'

'And the day before.'

She frowned up at her. 'I wasn't then either.'

Dorothea tutted under her breath. 'You'll waste away.'

Hardly. Though she kept the thought to herself. No exercise meant no calorie burn, which in turn meant weight gain. She'd already gained enough during her time on the island thanks to Dorothea's fabulous cooking and she couldn't risk any more. She had a red carpet movie premiere just around the corner and a dress that was made to fit like a glove. She absolutely could *not* put more weight on.

'I'm fine, honestly.'

Dorothea nodded but the severity in her expression didn't lift. 'You call if you need something bringing out. You're not to climb those stairs, understood?'

Her heart warmed in her chest as she stared up at the woman who treated her more like a caring mother than her own ever had and a genuine smile touched her lips, along with the surprising prick of tears.

Perhaps the emotional turmoil of the past year was catching up with her—*and perhaps you're more hurt by Alaric's avoidance of you than you care to admit?*

'Understood, Miss Wilde?'

She swallowed, refocusing on Dorothea. 'Perfectly... Thank you.'

'You're welcome.'

She watched her go, her mind awash with all that had happened since her arrival. She could see why Alaric chose to stay here. He wasn't as alone as she'd first feared, as alone as his sister and family believed him to be. Dorothea, Andreas, even Marsel, were more like family than staff. Aside from their respectful forms of address, they cared for him and vice versa.

They cared for her too. It was obvious in their warm brown eyes that lit up with their laughter, softened with their compassion and narrowed when they were cross with her for pushing her body too far too quickly. Yes, even when they were giving her a ticking off, she knew it came from a good place.

She shook her head and opened her laptop fully again, ready to get stuck into the adventures of her heroine, Maisy, once more. At least the script was going well. Having bed rest forced upon her meant there wasn't much else she could do to fill her time. And now she had a thorny plot issue to fix. How to get Maisy from the—

'Catherine! What the hell is wrong with you?'

Her eyes snapped up, the man striding towards her immediately dominating her vision and setting her pulse racing. Did he *have* to be so goddamn sexy *all* the time?

'Good afternoon to you too, Alaric.'

He shook his head, pausing at the foot of her sunbed, his hands fisted on his hips, his white tee straining across his chest...did he own T-shirts in any other colour because she'd yet to see him in one. Black would look good, maybe a soft grey...

'I'm kind of busy working so if you have something to say, just come out and say it and then we can both go back to our jobs.' She smiled sweetly. He was, after all, the one who was always too busy to spend any real time with her. The least she could do was return the favour.

'Dorothea says you're not eating properly.'

'Dorothea is worrying unnecessarily.'

He crossed his arms. 'So, you haven't been skipping lunch and surviving on fruit and yogurt all day.'

'No, I've eaten dinner too.'

'According to Dorothea you're only eating a fraction of what she serves up.'

Heat started to unfurl deep within her gut, and it wasn't the good kind. 'Alaric, you're not my moth—' She stalled. Her mother wouldn't care, her mother would be pleased that she was starving herself because she couldn't exercise it off. 'You're not the boss of me, you don't get to come out here and give me a ticking off.'

'I'm not giving you a ticking off.'

Her brows nudged the rim of her straw hat.

'Okay, I am. I'm just... I'm concerned, Catherine.'

'Well, don't be. Now if you don't mind…' Pointedly, she went back to her screen, though tuning him out was nowhere near as easy. Even his cologne reached her now, its rich woody scent teasing at the fire inside that was supposed to be all anger. Only it wasn't. And hell, that served to frustrate her more.

'Where would you like me to put it?'

Dorothea? She peered around him to see the woman returning with a tray of…

'Alaric!' She glared up at him. 'I said I was fine.'

'Tough, we're having a late lunch together.'

'We are not.'

'We *are*—' He broke off, looked away as he raked his fingers through his hair and took a breath before coming back to her, the effort to compose himself obvious. 'Sorry. Please, will you come and have some food with me?'

'Why?'

'Because I'd like to spend time with you.'

She laughed, the sound practically delirious. Did he really think she would cave that easily? That she would believe him even?

'Please, Catherine. I've been an arse, but I'm worried about you. I'm not going to force you to eat if you don't want to, but I would like to spend a little time together.'

'You would?' It sounded as dubious as she felt.

'Yes.'

'So, it's not because you want to make sure I eat something.'

'Can't it be both?'

She studied him intently, feeling her heart flutter in her chest as she saw how much he cared and remembered that he didn't, because he couldn't get away from her fast enough most days.

'I've missed your company.'

It was a raw confession, honest even to her dubious ears, and it cost him to admit it, but it cost her heart more. 'Okay.'

The beginnings of a smile flickered around his mouth, the sexy fullness to that lower lip, the dip in the middle of the top...if she closed her eyes, she'd remember how it felt to kiss them too. She'd also remember how he'd looked at her, with passion and something so much deeper blazing in those blue eyes, something that they hinted at right now.

'Thank you.' His smile widened and he turned to Dorothea. 'The table outside the bedroom is perfect. It's in the shade.'

She closed her laptop and set it down, swinging her legs over the edge of the bed. She shouldn't have agreed, she should have made him suffer like she had, but having him concerned for her made her feel...it made her feel too much.

She pushed herself up and limped forward.

'Oh, no, you don't.' He was by her side in an instant.

'I can walk! Granted, it's awkward but I can manage.'

'What's the point when I'm here to carry you?'

'Whoa, whoa, whoa...' She shook her head, waved him down. 'Help is one thing. Carrying me is—'

Too late, she was already up against his chest and it shouldn't feel good. It really, really shouldn't. But there was something about his strength surrounding her, the warmth of his body against hers...she gave an involuntary little shiver as she revelled in it.

'Are you—*cold*?' He eyed her incredulously.

'Don't be ridiculous.'

Her cheeks flamed and she pinned her hat in place as she hid behind its brim, her inability to act around him making them burn ever deeper. She was Kitty Wilde, an award-winning performer, but with Alaric she was Catherine. There was no facade, no act, just her…exposed, raw and utterly susceptible to him.

Maybe that was the problem.

She was herself…she couldn't hide.

No matter how much he pushed her away.

Alaric only had himself to blame. He was the one that had insisted on picking Catherine up, holding her to him, feeling the connection between them pulse and grow.

He'd been the one determined to step in as one look at Dorothea's face when she'd returned from the poolside to report the exact same news—Catherine isn't eating properly—had urged him to his feet, ready to do battle. Ready to throttle her mother too, but that was an age-old anger, an age-old fight he'd never been able to have outright.

But this, he could.

He glanced down to see her still tucked behind the brim of her straw hat and his frown deepened. Already she'd lost weight, and that wasn't healthy. You didn't lose weight that quickly unless you were sick or on some unsustainable diet. And it was most definitely the latter.

He lowered her onto a seat at the table. 'Are you comfortable? Do you want me to get another chair to raise your ankle?'

She shook her head without looking up. 'No, I'll be fine. It's been elevated plenty this morning.'

'When did you last ice it?'

'About an hour ago.'

'Would you like me to get—'

'Enough, Alaric!' Her eyes shot to his. 'Please sit down and stop fussing.'

He did as she bade, his frown unmoving though.

'So, this is what it takes to get some attention from you? A fall and a busted ankle?'

He set a plate before her and started dishing up the Greek salad Dorothea had prepared and gave her a smile full of forced tease. 'A bit extreme, wouldn't you say?'

'Don't flatter yourself. I certainly didn't do this on purpose.'

'No? I'm not so sure.' He continued with the teasing, desperate to lighten the mood and not get caught up in the look in her eye, the proximity of her bikini-clad body, the kimono she favoured doing nothing to conceal every inch of her appealing body.

'Funny, Alaric, very funny.'

He started slicing off a piece of fresh baked bread.

'No bread for me,' she rushed out.

'But it's still warm from the oven, you'll love it.'

'I'll love it too much, that's the problem.'

He shook his head at her. 'That makes no sense.'

He cut it anyway and placed it on a plate beside her salad. 'In case you change your mind.'

He served himself too, discreetly watching as she took a bite of salad and chewed it over, her eyes on the ocean. How did he broach it with her? It wasn't healthy not to eat, but at the same time, who was he to judge her, to criticise. She was right to say it wasn't his place and yet...

'Stop it.' Her eyes were still on the view.

'Stop what?'

'Stop looking at me like that.'

'I'm not looking at you like anything.'

'Right?' Now she turned to him, her brows drawn together. 'So, you're not judging me, then?'

'If you think I'm judging you, then it suggests you believe I have cause to.'

She shook her head, her lips twitching as she forked up more salad.

'I get that it's hard for you right now,' he tried softly, 'not being able to stick to your workout regime and—'

'What would you know of it?'

'I know you spend almost as many hours keeping active in some way as you do not.'

'And how would you know that when I hardly see you around?'

'I know, Catherine.'

'What?' Her laugh was harsh. 'Do you have cameras dotted about, keeping an eye on me? Is this actually a heavily guarded fortress and you use those computer screens of yours to watch the island's movements?'

'Stop trying to deflect.'

'I'm not.' She dropped her fork. 'Okay, I am. But I don't want to talk about my exercise and eating habits. What I want to talk about is you. I want to talk about Flo and the fact you're going to be an uncle. I want to talk about you coming back to the UK for a visit.'

His blood ran cold, her quick-fire change in focus making his stomach roll. 'We agreed not to talk about it.'

'We agreed not to talk about a lot of things, and I consider my diet very much out of bounds.'

'Your *diet* isn't sensible.'

Her cheeks flared, her lack of make-up making every flush far more evident, every expression far more pure and real, reaching under his skin, right to the very heart of him. He fisted his hand on the table, urging it all away.

'My *diet* is logical. If I'm not exercising, I'm cutting the calories I take in.'

'There's cutting what you consume and then there's not eating. You're inching towards the latter.'

'I'm eating now.'

'Only because I made you.'

'You *encouraged* me. You can't make me do anything I wouldn't do of my own accord.'

His chest eased a little. 'Good...but you can't deny that you love Dorothea's bread, and one slice isn't going to hurt you.'

'A moment on the lips, a lifetime on the hips,' she sing-songed.

'And now you sound like your mother.'

She paled in an instant.

'Hey.' He frowned. 'I was joking.'

'No, you weren't.'

'Well, can you blame me?' There was no use denying it—he'd been joking to an extent but what he'd said was true. 'She used to say it to you all the time. Family barbecues, weddings, birthday parties... If she even caught you looking at dessert, out it came.'

'Yeah, well, she was right to an extent.'

'Why was she right? Why do you have to worry about it so much?'

'Are you really asking me that when you know what I do for a living?'

'And what about body positivity? I thought that was all the rage now.'

'It's Hollywood, Alaric, it'll never change.'

'It will if the people within it change.'

She stared at him for a long moment and he started to think he was getting through to her, making a difference. 'Be that as it may, I still have to get into my designer dress for a movie premiere in a month's time. If I put on even the slightest bit of weight it won't fit.'

'So, get a new dress, you can afford it.'

'It's not that simple,' she choked out with a laugh. 'Do you know how in demand fashion designers are? We're booked in months in advance for the perfect outfit. It doesn't get thrown on last minute.'

He shrugged. 'Your fans, the press, they want to see you, the person in the dress. What does it matter what designer you're wearing, other than the fact you're putting money in their pockets by promoting their wares? Now there's an idea—you could go to an unknown for an outfit, elevate them to your level, rather than throwing money into the same few pockets.'

She tilted her head to the side. 'That's an idea I actually like, but still…even an unknown doesn't pull something off last minute.'

'Then you wear something off the hanger.'

Another choked laugh. 'Absolutely not.'

'Why?'

'Because it's not the done thing.'

'So what?'

'You really don't get it, do you?'

'Oh, I get it. But what it tells me is that all that talk about you not seeing me for this—' he ran the back of his fingers down his scarred cheek '—but who I am inside is bull.'

She frowned at him, her head shaking, her hand reaching out. 'That's totally different and you know it.'

'Do I, Catherine? Because if I listen to you right now, if I look at your actions over the last few days, the eating like a bird, testing your foot long before it's healed, your desperation to keep up appearances, it all becomes a lie. Ultimately, *you* care. Ultimately, it's all about how one looks.'

'In Hollywood, yes. But it's not me.'

'Right, Hollywood.' His laugh was harsh. 'And you and Hollywood are two separate entities.'

'Yes.' She shook her head. 'No. You're twisting my words.'

'You're beautiful, Catherine.'

'See!' She thrust a hand at him. 'Now you're just proving my point!'

'No, I'm not.'

'You are! Telling me I'm beautiful. It doesn't come easy. I work hard to keep myself looking like this. I deprive myself of the foods I like, I work out, I... I...'

She stopped as he shook his head. 'You're beautiful on the inside, Catherine.'

Her laugh was more a scoff. 'That old cliché.'

'Cliché?' He frowned at her, knowing full well he had her. 'But isn't that what you were trying to tell me the other day? That you, my family, they don't see me for my scars, they see who I am underneath?'

Her lips parted but no words emerged.

'Or did I misunderstand?'

'Of course you didn't,' she said softly, folding her hands in her lap. 'I meant everything I said.'

'Just like I meant everything I said in bed the other night, when I told you what I thought of you.'

She opened her mouth, closed it again, pursed it off to the side as she looked to the ocean once more, but he could sense the cogs were turning, that she was processing all he had said. That he had effectively used her own words against her. And it was risky to bring that night up again, the connection they'd shared coming to the surface, but this was more important than the protective wall around his heart.

'Okay. Okay. You win. I get what you're saying. My problem is that Hollywood is my home, not literally but in terms of my career it is.'

'And look what it did to your mother?'

She flicked him a look and he was surprised to see the hint of tears welling, her mother evoking such a deep reaction once more.

'You know how hard I've tried not to become her? That every day it's there as a mantra and still...' She shook her head. 'She creeps in, you know. But I wanted to be an actor. I wanted... I thought I could do it and avoid her mistakes...'

'You were always one for the stage. I don't think you would have been happy doing anything else.'

'Maybe.'

She looked so lost in her own world that he started to regret even pushing her as far as he had, but he wanted her to see it, needed her to see it. 'Honestly, Catherine. So what if you gain a few pounds? So what if you wear a dress off the hanger, or something from an unknown? You're still you. You're still the person who brings characters to life on the big screen, brings joy to people's lives—tears, sadness, happiness.'

The flicker of a smile crossed her lips. 'I'd like to be seen as more than that though, more than beauty over brains. I want to be the creator behind the scenes, I want to write the words that inspire such passion, I want to do more.'

He smiled in the face of her strength, her dream. 'And you will. I meant it when I said you put your mind to something, it happens.'

'I wish I could bottle you.'

He chuckled, feeling the tension in the air lift. 'I'm not sure I'd like that.'

'I would, then I could uncork you every time I doubted myself.'

She smiled at him, and for a second, time stood still, the world fell away. If only things were different, if only the accident hadn't happened, if only their worlds were compatible...

And then she lowered her gaze to the plate with the

slither of bread he had cut and took it up. 'It does look lovely.'

'You don't have to eat it,' he assured her. 'I just didn't want you to deprive yourself because you think it will in some way go against you.'

She laughed softly. 'It is just a piece of bread after all.'

'Hey, not just any bread. Dorothea will be down here with the rolling pin if she hears you say that.'

He offered her the small bowl of olive oil and balsamic vinegar to dip it in and watched as she scooped it to her mouth, her hum of appreciation making him want to groan too.

She chewed it over, catching a little drop from her chin with her finger and licking it clean. 'You know what this means though?'

He was so caught in the movement of her finger, her lips, it took a second for him to register what she had said.

'What's that?'

'You owe me a talk about home.'

Silently, he cursed. He'd walked straight into it, but...

'Lucky we have plenty of days left for that.'

'Is this you saying you're done hiding away?'

He gave her a tight smile. 'I don't really have a choice if I'm to make sure you rest that ankle properly and eat sensibly.'

'Ah...' She tore a piece of bread off and popped it into her mouth, her twinkling blues giving the impression of a gleeful child. 'So true.'

Tiny flutters erupted deep within his gut. 'I'm beginning to think you really did do this on purpose.'

'You'll never know, Alaric... I am an exceptional actor after all.'

He almost glanced at her ankle to double-check it was most definitely bruised and stopped himself. It was enough to still see the cut healing on her bottom lip…another part of her anatomy he really shouldn't look at but for a very different reason.

'Very funny, princess.'

CHAPTER TWELVE

CATHERINE SQUINTED OVER at Alaric sitting at the table outside her room, a book in hand, while she lounged under the parasol with her laptop. As promised, he'd spent nearly every waking hour within viewing distance, rarely getting close enough to provoke the persistent chemistry between them, but close enough to keep his eye on her.

And her, him.

She loved watching him unawares, free to look her fill without him knowing, free to take in the unguarded expression on his face. Over the past few days, she'd found herself doing it more and more, as though she was trying to imprint the memory in her brain so that when she left this place, she'd remember this moment and all the others.

And she hadn't given up hope yet of coaxing him off the island. Flo had messaged that morning to ask how it was going and she'd given her an honest answer—things were improving.

Because they were.

She hadn't told her that the reason was down to an injury she'd sustained, and it had forced him out of hiding. Flo didn't need to know that. And with her friend's pregnancy hormones she'd only go into over-protective mode and hop on a plane herself, a luxury she could readily afford, especially as she'd taken early maternity leave due to the concerns over her blood pressure. And she didn't want to be aggravating that either. So no, she told her everything was in hand and that she was slowly working her magic.

Magic which she really needed to be getting on with. She caught her lower lip in her teeth as she pondered her opening line…she didn't want to spoil the common ground they had found. A way to co-exist without him fleeing.

But she had less than a fortnight to change his mind.

'Out with it.'

She jumped at his low command, issued into the pages of his book.

'Beg your pardon.'

She felt her cheeks flush as he lifted his head, her breath catching as his piercing blue eyes met with hers, heating her from across the distance. 'I reckon you've been watching me for at least a chapter.'

'I have n—' His brows nudged up, a small smile playing about his lips, and she quit her denial, closing her laptop with aplomb. 'I fancy a swim.'

'You sure that's wise?'

'I won't know until I try.' She swung her feet to the ground and sat up. 'Could you help me to the pool, please?'

He watched her slip the kimono from her shoulders and she made sure to draw out the move as she spied the pulse working in his jaw. No, they definitely hadn't lost the spark. If anything, it had intensified with each passing day as they remained in one another's company and tried to fight it, to deny it.

'Of course.'

Closing the book, a thriller judging by the cover, he got to his feet and averted his gaze as he approached. She wondered if his heart was now racing in tune with hers, anticipation of their closing proximity making it hard to think straight.

She stood before he reached her, testing her weight on her ankle and finding it wasn't so painful if she was careful.

'It's not too—*oh*!' He'd wrapped an arm around her bare waist, taking her weight and making her insides thrum in one.

'You were saying?'

She wet her lips and looked up at him. If she was honest, she wasn't quite sure any more. His touch had done its usual task of clearing her head of all thought. And she should be used to it with him helping her everywhere and no longer avoiding her. But there was no getting used to the force of their attraction, or the way his eyes seemed to penetrate her very soul when he looked at her like he was now.

'I was saying…' She looked down and eased her foot forward, using him for support as they made their way to the pool edge. 'It's not too bad today.'

'Good.'

A breeze caught the brim of her hat, blowing it free, and her hand shot up, but he beat her to it, grabbing it and bringing his body around, his front facing hers as he caught both her and her hat and…*oh, my*.

She was pressed right up against his chest, his hand clutching the hat to her back, his other arm locked around her waist.

'Perhaps it's best we leave the hat here.' His voice was thick, low, and he made no attempt to move, no attempt to ease the closeness, to lift the moment.

She nodded, not wanting to risk anything else. Was he going to kiss her? He *looked* like he was going to kiss her…especially as his gaze fell to her mouth, the blue of his eyes drowned out by the lascivious dark and sending an excited jolt straight through her core. 'How's your lip?'

'It's—it's feeling much better,' she breathed, her tongue sweeping briefly across the said body part, easing its sudden dryness while teasing him too.

'Good…' It vibrated through him, his arms flexing around her.

'Alaric?'

He shook his head. 'Don't.'

A frown touched her brow. 'You don't know what I was going to say.'

'I can see it in your face.'

'And I can see it in yours.'

He shook his head. 'You're impossible.'

She gave the smallest of laughs, making her body vibrate against his. '*I'm* the impossible one.'

She could tell he was fighting a grin, could tell he was fighting the pull between them too, but he twisted to toss her hat onto the bed and tugged her towel over it to stop it blowing away. 'Come on, you said you wanted a dip.'

She wanted so many things in that moment and a dip definitely wasn't one of them.

It didn't matter if it was wise, or sensible, she wanted him. And the more time they spent together, the more the connection between them swelled and the more she felt his barriers fall.

She let him lower her to the edge of the pool and she did the rest, enjoying the cool water on her flushed skin as she looked up at him. 'You going to join me?'

'Are you going to behave?'

'Hardly.'

And then he laughed, the sound so glorious, so easy, so different to how he'd been when she'd first arrived, and hope bloomed warm inside her chest. Hope that she could convince him there was more to life than just his island, that he did deserve to live, really live…

She watched as he stripped his T-shirt and tossed it aside, dropping into the water beside her, his eyes finding hers both wary and warm. She reached for his hand and pulled him towards her, saying nothing as she closed the distance between them.

If she didn't try, she wouldn't get...

His eyes fell to her mouth and she did the same, her intent clear, hope soaring as he didn't pull away, hope soaring even more as she reached up, a hand sliding into his hair, her mouth sweeping against his...

'Catherine, this isn't a good idea.'

'It feels like a very good idea.' She dragged the words against his lips, felt his breath shudder through him, heard the groan deep within his chest, and then he was lifting her against him. Hard muscle against pliant flesh. He forked his hand through her hair, tugging her head back to deepen the kiss, his tongue delving and tangling with hers. It was explosive. Like a switch had gone off inside him, inside her...

The water sloshed around them as he backed her up to the wall of the pool, her legs wrapped around his hips, the heat within enough to contend with the sun blazing down.

He tore his mouth away, sucked in a breath as he pressed his forehead to hers, his hands deep within her hair. 'I've wanted to do that for days.'

'You *should* have done.'

He shook his head, his eyes searing hers. 'This can only get messy, Catherine. I don't want to hurt you. I don't.'

'Who's getting hurt? Not me? I'm not asking for a future. I'm not asking for more than my stay here. And I'd much rather spend it like this than constantly fighting it.'

She kissed him to add to her point, kissed him deeper to convince him, kissed him until he was kissing her back harder and more fiercely than she…then she tore her mouth away. 'Now tell me you want to fight this.'

'Hell, no, we're going to bed.'

What is the definition of insanity?

His mind pushed the question as they lay on the bed, naked. A white sheet drawn to the waist, his arm wrapped around her as she lay her head on his shoulder, her leg entwined with his.

The perfect moment.

Aside from the uneven beat to his heart as he considered the answer, knowing full well he was the very epitome of it.

Doing the same thing over and over again and expecting a different result…

In his case, succumbing to the chemistry between them again and not expecting the mark she left on him to grow.

Though maybe it wasn't insanity at all, maybe it was stupidity, because he knew where this would lead. He knew he was falling in deeper and deeper with her. He knew he'd have to fight harder to fend off the belief that this was possible, real, a relationship with a future.

'What are you thinking about?' She snuggled in closer, her head tilting up as her eyes searched out his.

He met her gaze with a smile that not even his worries could quash. 'I'm wondering how soon we can go again.'

'Liar.' She nudged him softly with her hip. 'Though I do approve of your answer.'

He chuckled, his fingers caressing her side as he looked back to the ceiling. He could quite happily lie there for the rest of the day, the week even—work, food, be damned.

'Can I ask you something?'

The loaded question pulled his body taut…so much for being content. 'Of course.'

'Why don't you paint any more?'

She shifted her head to eye the brightly coloured canvas above the bed. 'You're so talented.'

'Was. I *was* talented.'

She frowned at him. 'And you can't paint now?'

'I can't paint, I can't draw, I can't sketch.' He flexed his fingers on her hip, felt the constant tightness there. 'Not like I used to.'

She lowered her gaze to his hand, turned it over. Her fingers delicate as she traced the scar there. 'Have you tried recently?'

'No.' It came out gruff, partly with the pain she'd stirred up, and partly with the shiver her caress triggered.

'From where I'm lying, they still feel pretty talented to me.' She lifted his hand to her lips, kissed his palm softly. 'You should try again.'

He was about to refuse when she looked up at him. 'What does it matter if the work you produce has changed, it doesn't make it any less. You enjoyed it because it felt good for you to create, you enjoyed that time with just you and your canvas. The number of times I would visit when we were kids and you would be in a flurry of creativity, with that wild look in your eye. Almost like a mad professor.'

'A mad what?' He was laughing but this was news to him.

'You know, the nutty professor look—crazy hair, even crazier eyes?'

'Oh, cheers. Very attractive.'

She gave a dainty shrug, her smile small. 'I quite liked the look on you.'

He shook his head, pulled her in closer.

'You shouldn't stop creating just because your work is different now.'

'You'll have a hard time convincing the artist in me of that.'

'But it was therapy for you, creating back then. It would serve the same purpose now....and so what if it's different. Doesn't it make it special in its own way?'

He gave a soft scoff. 'To be reminded that I can no longer do something as well as I used to.'

She lowered her gaze to where her fingers played with the hairs on his chest. 'It's all subjective. There's no such thing as a perfect piece of art, just as there's no perfect book or movie or performance. Who cares if it's not as good in your eyes, if you come to get the same enjoyment out of creating it?'

He stared down at her, heard her words so perfect, so right. No perfect performance...he'd take his hat off to her now, throw her roses on the stage, because what she'd said made *perfect* sense. Sense he hadn't seen before. And he couldn't speak, only hold her closer as the emotion inside swelled.

Fear of not being good enough had stopped him from creating. Fear of the man he was now had stopped him leaving the island. Fear of being resented by his late friend's wife had stopped him from talking to her and dealing with his guilt...but now, with Catherine wrapped up in his arms, he didn't feel afraid any more, he felt capable of anything.

Ready to take out his sketchpad, ready to return home, ready to speak to Cherie...

Through her wholehearted acceptance of him, she'd crept beneath his barriers. Teaching him to embrace the man he was now, not fear it, or loathe it.

'Is this what you had in mind when you agreed to come here, to my island?'

'What?' She pushed up on his chest. 'Seducing you?'

'Luring me into your bed to fill my head with possibility.'

She laughed softly. 'The truth?'

He nodded, loving how her eyes sparkled down at him.

'I wanted to see you. Absolutely, I did. It's been so long…' Her lashes lowered, a second's avoidance as she seemed to withdraw into herself and then she looked at him again. 'I wanted to see how you were for myself and, of course, I wanted to convince you to come home once in a while. I also needed to escape my life…' She closed her eyes, her body trembling against him and exposing that pain again. Pain that revolved around Luke and it was like a knife twisting deep inside him.

'As for getting you into bed *per se*—' her eyes opened, locked with his, and her sudden smile almost had him forgetting the hurt that preceded it '—the second I saw you again I will admit to wanting all of the above.'

'You're totally serious, aren't you.' It was a statement, not a question. He was long past doubting her attraction.

'Err, yeah! All those feelings I had for you when we were kids, teens, imagine that and then being confronted by you now…your bad-boy vibe has a whole lot going for it.'

'My bad-boy vibe?' He choked on a laugh, grabbing her hand to press it to his scarred cheek and hold it there. '*This* gives me a bad-boy vibe?'

Her eyes shimmered into his. 'Hell, yeah.'

She eased her hand from beneath his, to trail it along the scar, her eyes alive with the heated direction of her thoughts, and he flipped her under him, so fast she cried out.

He started to roll back. 'Your ankle! I'm s—'

She cut him off with a kiss. 'My ankle is fine!'

And just like that he was perfecting insanity again.

CHAPTER THIRTEEN

A KNOCK AT the door woke Catherine in an instant and she shot upright, the bed sheet clutched to her chest, eyes wide.

"Alaric!' she whisper-shouted. 'Alaric!'

She shoved him and he grunted, wrapping his arms around her waist. 'What's the emergency?'

'There's someone at the door.'

He squinted up at her, raising his hand to ward off the light from the bedside lamp as she thrust it on. 'What time is it?'

'I've no idea. Late.' Very late, judging by the pitch-black outdoors and the very vocal sounds of the nightlife coming through the small gap they'd left in the sliding door.

The knock came again, followed by Dorothea's voice. 'Miss Wilde... Kyrios de Vere?'

She swallowed. Okay, so that cat was out of the bag... not that it had ever really been in considering her and Alaric had been inseparable for the past week, working together, eating together, sleeping together...ever since their silent understanding to enjoy this time while they could. Not that much sleeping had gone on which explained why they'd fallen asleep in the afternoon and the day had disappeared on them.

'I've brought food,' Dorothea called through the door. 'I thought you may be hungry?'

Alaric chuckled into her hip and she shoved him again.

'Well, she's not wrong.'

'It's not funny.'

'It is a little funny. And she's right, we could do with some food.'

She started to move off the bed—

'You can come in, Dorothea.'

And flung herself back, the sheets clutched to her chest again, as she threw him a mutinous glare.

He chuckled all the more, pushing himself up to sitting and settling back against the headboard, pulling her in closer as the door opened. A blushing Dorothea strode in, eyes averted, her tray out in front of her and loaded with a variety of food.

'I brought a selection as I wasn't sure what you would prefer.' She slid the tray onto the bedside table. 'Now what can I get you to drink?'

'Water would be lovely,' Catherine replied, surprised her voice sounded far more composed than she felt.

'And some…champagne?' Alaric looked at her for approval and she felt her cheeks burn further, her 'yes' more of a squeak as she thanked Dorothea.

'You're most welcome.' Off she went, happy to be on another errand, happier still to see them in bed together, Catherine was sure.

'I can't believe you did that.' She gave him another playful shove and he pulled her back against him, his grin heart-melting, his eyes alive with mischief, and then he kissed her. A long, deep kiss that had her limbs softening, a fresh wave of heat consuming her as her head emptied out.

'She knew anyway,' he murmured against her lips.

'So? We could have at least put some clothes on.'

'Are you kidding? That's not going to bother her. She's

just happy to see me acting like a normal, healthy man again.'

'You mean *virile*?' she teased, the sexual undercurrent building with ease.

He laughed. 'That too.'

She shook her head, her smile uncontainable. It was so easy to lose herself in him, in these days where the outside world couldn't intervene and everything felt so...perfect.

He leaned away to reach for a plate. 'You'll love these.'

She took in the neat pile of glistening vine-covered rolls he offered out to her. 'Ah, dolmades.'

His eyes widened in surprise.

'Hey, I am well-travelled, you know!'

'Clearly.'

She leaned forward, took one up and cupped her hand beneath as she bit into it and licked her lips to scoop up the remnants.

'Nice?'

She chewed it over, the taste explosion divine. Rice, dill, lemon, mint—yum!

She swallowed it down with a nod and a hum.

'Tell me how you're not the size of a house when you eat like this every day,' she teased, offering him a bite.

He laughed before taking it from her fingers with his mouth, chewing it over as his eyes danced. 'Like you, I train hard to balance it out.'

'That makes me feel better. It would suck if you were this trim and got to eat all you wanted without having to put in any effort.'

'Would it now?'

'Yup. Take it from a woman who knows the pain of exercise.'

He smiled at her. 'Ready for another?'

She nodded and he picked one up, pulling it away from her lips at the last second.

'But don't expect me to let you hop on the treadmill tomorrow—that ankle still has to heal.'

'Duh.' She stared into his eyes as she quickly pinched a bite. 'I'm not that stupid.'

His brows nudged upwards.

'I'm not!' She devoured the rest of it before adding, 'Or at least I was, but not now—not any more.'

'Because?'

'Because I'm beautiful on the inside.' She rolled her eyes and gave a laugh, but it caught in her throat. His eyes were on fire, stubborn, insistent, as he forced her to be serious.

'I mean it, Catherine.'

'I know you mean it.' She reassured him softly and he took up her hand, kissed it as his eyes lifted to hers.

'Just remember it…'

He held her eye as he pressed another kiss to her hand and she mentally added for him, *When we're no longer together.*

'Remember it?' he urged, the unsaid words hanging in the air between them, and she nodded.

'You know…' she whispered, her voice trapped in her chest as her heart beat wild with her feelings for him, feelings that were way out of her control, regardless of the untold pact that this would be over when she left. 'You could come visit and remind me as often as you liked…'

'Is this you trying to convince me to leave my island again?'

'Maybe…is it working?'

He shook his head but there was a smile in his eyes. 'You have shown me there's more to life than hiding out here, I'll concede that.'

She leaned back, surprise making her drop the sheet that was covering her modesty, and as his eyes dipped, their naughty gleam threatened to distract her.

'Behave!' She palmed his chest. 'Are you serious?'

He tugged his eyes from her nakedness, and it wasn't salacious heat burning into her now, it was his sincerity. 'Yes, you've shown me to accept the man I am now, to live and laugh again. You've given me hope that I can go home to my family, that I can contact Cherie and try to put it behind me, to move on in some way.'

'You don't deserve the guilt, Alaric.' Her voice was soft but no less vehement. 'You've suffered enough.'

'Perhaps.'

'Are you serious, or are you just humouring me?'

His smile lifted to one side. 'No, I'm not just humouring you. And yes, I'm serious. I'm not looking forward to it. I'm apprehensive about how Cherie will be, I'm apprehensive about how my family will receive me, hell, I'm apprehensive about being out in public at all, but…'

'Those you don't know don't matter, and those that do will love you all the more for coming back to them.'

His eyes softened, his smile too.

'And you're going to be an uncle, Alaric, that's exciting, special. Flo's been going out of her mind worrying about you.'

'I know.'

'But do you know her blood pressure is already through the roof, that she's been forced to take early maternity leave?'

He frowned. 'No. She never said…she…' He looked away, raked his hand through his hair with a curse. 'Why didn't she say anything?'

'I don't know. I guess because you've had so much going on it didn't seem fair. Or maybe she thought you'd see it as her way of guilt-tripping you into coming home again and didn't think that fair either.'

'I knew she'd been out of the office more, I just hadn't… I didn't…' He leaned forward, his knees coming up to rest his arms on them, his head hanging forward. He cursed again. 'I've been so wrapped up in my own world… How could I have been so selfish?'

'You weren't selfish.'

'No?' He rolled his head to look at her.

'No.' She placed a gentle hand on his back. 'You were suffering. And they understand why you left, granted they don't understand why you've stayed away, but when you explain, they'll get it. They'll just be happy to see you again.'

'I see my father regularly.'

'On a screen, Alaric, that's hardly seeing him. And even then, it's all business, isn't it?'

'What more would we talk about?'

She gave a soft scoff. 'Feelings! We all have them unless you're a robot and I *know* you're not. You care, you just like to pretend you don't.'

He said nothing and she stroked his back that was so tense beneath her touch. 'It's not too late, you know. The most important thing is that you're going to go back. They love you and they'll be ready to welcome you home, when you're ready to go there.'

She snuggled into him, forgetting all about the food as she lost herself in their conversation and the milestone they'd hit. 'It'll all work out, I just know it.'

He turned, pressed his lips to her hair. 'I like your optimism.'

'And I like you.'

It came out easily. Honest. And it hit home once more, just how much she liked him and just how much this had to be temporary because for all she denied being like her mother, her actions over the years had told a different story...her actions had told her just how selfish and messed up she was, and she would never expose Alaric to that side of her.

Never.

But what if she could do better? What if she could learn from the past and pave the way to a better future? One that allowed her to love, to be loved, to have it all?

But Alaric didn't know what she had done.

Alaric didn't know what had truly gone down with Luke.

Alaric didn't know just what a screw-up she was deep down and the idea of telling him, of cracking herself open and confessing...

And didn't that make her a nasty piece of work, when he was opening himself up to her, his insecurities, his worries, and still she hadn't told him the truth.

It crushed her inside, crushed her all the more as she accepted that she didn't just like him, she loved him. That she was *in* love with him, and she had to tell him the whole ugly truth. She owed him that at the very least.

She straightened up, drawing her knees to her chest, the sheet too. 'There's something I need to tell you, something that very few people know.'

His head snapped up. 'Are you okay?'

She couldn't answer.

'Are you sick?'

She shook her head. 'No. Not in the way you're thinking.'

He leaned forward, seeking to hold her eye, but she couldn't look at him. 'Flo knows and Luke... I haven't told anyone else.'

He reached out for her, but she leaned away. 'No. Just let

me… I need to get this off my chest, and if you hug me, I'll lose the ability to speak…' Her throat was already clamping closed, the well of emotion rising so sharply she couldn't draw a full breath.

He sat back against the headboard and she didn't need to look to know how wary his gaze had become. 'You know you can tell me anything, Catherine.'

She nodded. She did. But first, she needed to get it straight in her head. And she needed Dorothea to come and go again so that she could be sure there would be no interruptions because, once she started, it would all come spilling out, and then, who knew where they would be…

She was quiet for so long that he wondered if she would say anything at all and then Dorothea returned with the drinks and he realised she'd been waiting for them to be alone. Properly alone.

He poured a drink, one of each, and offered her them both.

She took the water while he favoured the champagne. Not that he felt ready to celebrate anything, it was more to ease his nerves that were fraught with whatever was coming.

'You understand my relationship with my mother better than most. My relationship with my father too. What there is of it.'

'Back then, yes. Not so much now.'

She nodded but said nothing more and he pressed, 'Do you see them much?'

'No. Not particularly. Mum never got over me hitting A-list status. Once she realised my growing fame didn't help her with the roles she was being offered, things turned nasty pretty quickly, and to be honest, I think she'd had enough of playing at family. They divorced soon after and Mum left to be with her latest toy boy and Dad...well, he fell into his own pit of despair and no matter what I did, what I said, he just...'

She gave the smallest of shrugs and his heart ached for her. There he was avoiding his own family who'd always been there for him, when she couldn't even hold the attention of hers.

'He just didn't care. Worse still, I look like her, so seeing me is just a constant reminder of his loss.'

A fire burned in Alaric's gut, his hands fisting as his dislike for the man took hold. He was her father, for Christ's sake, and instead of focusing on what he did have—the love of his daughter—he was so wrapped up in the callous wife he'd lost.

'Anyway, when Luke and I got together it was a whirlwind. It happens like that on set, you know. You're so wrapped up in the characters you're playing that the boundaries blur and before you know it, you're an item. And it's easier that way, dating on set. It's virtually impossible to find time to date outside of it, and we were happy, in our own way...'

She gave him a sad smile and looked away, her eyes lost to the outside world, her sadness, her pain, and his heart caught in his chest.

'I never wanted to become my mother, Alaric, I didn't. And so I found it easier not to get caught up in relationships in the first place, not to feel the pressure of dividing my attention between my work and my loved ones. I figured it would all come later, right? That I'd get to a point in my career where I was content and ready to settle down.'

'But then you met Luke?'

She gave a small nod.

'What happened?' he asked even though the question had goosebumps prickling over his skin. He didn't think he could bear it if she confessed her love for another man, her heartache even...

'I got pregnant.'

The blood drained from his face, shock assaulting him like a punch to the gut. 'You were...' He cleared his throat, tried again. 'You were *pregnant*?'

She shuddered as she took a breath, her eyes flitting to him so very briefly, but he couldn't miss the torment, the sadness, the pain.

'Yes. It wasn't planned. It was the last thing I expected—we expected.' Her voice cracked with emotion, her arms wrapped tight around her legs, the knuckles of the hand closest to him glowing white as she gripped her elbow. 'We were always careful, always used protection, but...but it failed.'

She started to rock, and he didn't dare move, not until he felt she was done.

'I took the morning-after pill—we had no choice. But it—it didn't work. A few weeks later I knew I had to take a test. I didn't feel any different, but I was late. Luke was beside himself, excited with it. He was talking of a future, full on, like it was all a done deal, and I...'

She cleared her throat, her voice so quiet when she spoke again. 'I was terrified. I wasn't ready. It wasn't the right time. I cared for Luke, I did, but a baby...' She shook her head, her body rocking all the more, and he could see the tears building, sense the effort it was taking for her to hold them back.

'What did you do?'

'Nothing. I did nothing.'

She turned to him now, her lower lip trembling, the tears in her eyes overflowing as they ran down her cheeks.

'I lost it. I didn't want it, and then it was gone, like it had never been.'

'Oh, Catherine...' He reached for her and she leaned away.

'Don't. I don't deserve sympathy. Don't you see, I was as bad as my mother in the end. I had a life growing inside me, I was a mother and I—I wished it away.'

'There's lots of reasons to lose a baby, but it never comes down to someone wishing it away, Catherine. You know that.'

She shook her head, stared at him. 'Do I?'

'Of course you do.'

'Luke said the same. He was so good to me, so sweet, but I didn't deserve his kindness... I didn't.'

'Of course you did, you were hurting and—'

'But he knew I wasn't ready. He knew I didn't want... I didn't want...' She couldn't finish and he couldn't stop himself reaching for her. He pulled her to him and this time she came, curling up against him as he rocked her, soothing every sob that wracked her body.

'It wasn't your fault.' He kissed her hair. 'It wasn't.'

'I couldn't marry him. I said yes because of the baby, because I thought it was the right thing to do. And when I lost the baby, I just... I couldn't go through with it.''

'I'm sure Luke would have understood, Catherine. He would have been hurting, just as you are now.'

She sniffed, swiped her palm across her cheeks as she leant back to look up at him. 'I wasn't ready.'

He cupped her jaw, his thumb sweeping over her damp cheek. 'I know, princess.'

'But I—when I lost it, I broke down. I would have given anything to have that time again, to have nurtured it, treasured it. I wanted to be a mother. I wanted to wish away my career and have my baby back.'

Have her baby back *and* Luke? Was this more than just agony over a miscarriage? Was it agony over the only real relationship she'd ever had?

'I'm sure if you went to Luke and spoke to him, he would understand...' He forced himself to say, 'You could still have a future together?'

She frowned through the tears, her head shaking. 'I don't want Luke, I never *loved* Luke.'

His heart pulsed in his chest as her eyes widened into his, so much on show if he was willing to see it. 'What I felt for him is a fraction of what I feel for you, what I've always felt for you, Alaric.'

He clutched her tighter, pulled her up to his chest and sucked in a breath. 'You've got me, right now, you've got me.'

She shuddered against him. 'But don't you see, I'm just as bad as my mother.'

His laugh was tight, incredulous. 'I don't know how you can think that.'

'I wished away my own child.'

'You were blindsided by a pregnancy, that's very different to abandoning your own flesh and blood, Catherine.'

He continued to rock her, stroke her hair, kiss her head, wishing life could be different, that they could somehow merge the two worlds in which they lived to make them compatible.

'I'm ready now, Alaric. It's the reason this script is so important. It's not just about proving I'm more than just Kitty Wilde, the actor. I want my life back. I don't want to be a prisoner to twenty-four-seven filming schedules, PR appearances, interviews... I love film, I always want to be in film, but on my own terms and on the other side of the lens.'

'It sounds like you have it all planned out.'

He could feel the resolve building within her, the strength seeping into her limbs as she pushed up off his chest. 'I'm thirty now, it's time I took control of my life and made room for the people that I love.'

'Flo will certainly be happy to see more of you.'

'And you?' Excitement thrived behind the tears still glistening in her vivid blues. 'Could we see each other more?'

His chest contracted, his body icing over with the impossibility of it. 'I'm not… I know I've said I'll visit home, that I'll speak to Cherie too, but you…me and you—' he couldn't look at her as he finished '—we just don't work outside of this island.'

'You don't know that.' She reached out to touch her palm to his cheek, urging him back to her. 'I've never met anyone that makes me feel the way that you do, Alaric. It's always been there between us, but these past few weeks… it's changed everything. And I know you feel it too.' She lowered her hand to his heart. 'I *know* you do.'

'It doesn't matter what I feel, Catherine.'

He clutched her fingers, his intention to remove her touch, but he couldn't drag them away. He was lost in her gaze swimming with such passion, such confusion, and the contact, no matter what had driven him to stop it, felt unbreakable.

'Why?'

'You and I can't have a relationship.'

'And I repeat…' She sniffed, using the back of her free hand to swipe away more tears as she raised her chin to him. 'Why?'

He couldn't respond. His head was a mess of words, of sentences that didn't make sense, feelings that he couldn't identify, string together, make coherent.

'This feels different to me, this feels special,' she pressed.

'I haven't felt this way about anyone, and… I don't want to make another mistake. I don't want to be my mother. And you tell me that I'm not, so let me prove it, with you.'

'I'm not the man to prove it with, can't you see that? I don't belong in your world.'

'What world?'

'Show business. Hollywood. Being in the public eye. I can't do it, Catherine. Look at me. Can you imagine the tabloids, the cover stories that would appear?'

'Yes…' It came out as a whisper. 'And I wish I could protect you from it. I wish I could say it won't happen, but you and I both know it will. It doesn't mean we have to live in fear of it, that we should give them the power to keep us apart. I don't care what they say, I only—'

'You *should* care.'

'My mother would care, Alaric, and that's not me…or is this *you* proving you don't mean what you say?'

'Don't question my honesty, Catherine. I have never lied to you, and I have let you in. But I can't give you what you deserve.'

'And what is it you think I deserve?'

'The dreams you speak of…the award winning actor-cum-screenwriter. It doesn't matter that you'll be on the other side of the screen. If you go after your dream, you will still be on the red carpet, you will still be in the public eye, you will still be famous. As you deserve. But not with a broken man by your side.'

'You're not broken, Alaric.'

'I'm damaged goods to them.'

She might not find him so horrific, his family might not either. As the queen of appearances, she'd convinced him that he could return to his family and be seen once more, for who he was beyond the scars. And yes, he had the strength, the confidence, to accept who he was now.

But to stand alongside her in the very public eye, the difference so very marked. It would be the subject of every tabloid, the cover story of every gossip rag, the very epitome of Beauty and the Beast, and the press would go wild for it.

It didn't matter that she didn't see him like that, they would.

And to have his happiness splashed across the tabloids, rubbed in the face of Fred's family, Cherie, their child… It was one thing to return, but that…

'So, this really is it?' she said quietly. 'We have this time now and then it's over.'

'It's what has to happen.'

'Not if we don't want it to, not if you feel the same way I do.'

'How can I possibly know how you—'

'I *love* you, Alaric.'

His heart squeezed tight in his chest, warmth exploding out and dousing just as quick.

'I loved you in my teens, I love you all the more now. I know I'm not the best judge of it, not after how my parents were or how they treated me, but I know I don't want this to end, that I want to keep you as part of my life. I want to share the highs and the lows and be there by your side. And I have *never* felt like that about anyone.'

Be there, side by side…

His gut twisted, the pain in his chest like a physical burn, his confession riding his tongue—that he loved her, that he always had, that he always would.

But he couldn't tell her, he couldn't vocalise it and tear them both apart. In a month's time, a year, he would be a blip in her past and she'd move on with her newfound career goals and her dream for a family with someone that deserved her and wasn't so messed up.

'I'm not the right man for you.'

'And shouldn't I be the judge of that?'

He released her hand, threw his feet to the floor and gripped the edge of the bed as he hunched forward. 'Ten years ago, I would have said yes, I would have run with what's in my heart, but not now, Catherine. I'm barely happy in my own company. The idea of being surrounded by the masses on your arm, with you so perfect and me like this…and in the face of Fred's loved ones… I can't do it. I can't.'

'I'm not perfect, Alaric. You of all people know I'm not, and yet, you've shown me to love who I am.' He glanced back at her, unable to resist the lull of her words, their importance. 'To look in the mirror and like what I see, without the make-up. To let my hair dry however it may. To eat what it is I want to eat and not obsess about every calorie, every pound of weight. You've shown me that.'

Her voice shook with her sincerity, her cheeks flushed with the passion he'd instilled in her, and for the briefest of moments, he let it in, all of it. How much he loved her, how much it warmed him to know that he'd made a difference for her too. That she wouldn't leave this island the same person she was when she arrived. That she would be happier, more content, healthier.

'And those people, Fred's loved ones,' she whispered, her hand reaching out to rest on his shoulder. 'They will be happy to see you return to the land of the living, I promise you.'

He stared at her, quiet, contemplative.

'You said you were ready to face your guilt, to talk to Cherie, to move on…'

'Yes. I did. And I meant it.' He closed his eyes, his head filling with an anguished Cherie, their child, the graveside and the rain lashing down. He hung his head forward, shutting Catherine out, quashing the hope she was threatening to bring to life. 'But confronting the past and moving on is one thing, having a fairy-tale ending thrust in Cherie's face, in his family's face, is something else entirely.'

'You have a right to find happiness, Alaric, you have a right to—'

'Stop, Catherine, just stop!' The lull of her words, the picture-perfect future she was trying to paint, was crucifying him. 'I can't do it.'

'Can't or won't?'

He didn't answer. He couldn't. Heart pounding in his ears, he thrust up and strode for the bathroom. Hating himself as he did so, but knowing it was the right thing to do. He slammed the shower on, gripped the back of his head and pressed his forehead into the cold stone wall.

She deserved better, she *would* get better, when she was long gone from this place and the web of seduction he had unintentionally created. He got the beauty of the island, the beauty of escapism, and his presence in the midst of it *made* him the right guy for her.

But he wasn't.

And he couldn't fall into the trap of believing that he was because when it all fell apart, he would be the one unable to come back from it.

He'd be the one trying to claw back what he could of his confidence, of his life, with a heart torn in two.

CHAPTER FOURTEEN

SHE'D PUSHED HIM too far, and all because she'd been swept up in the realisation that she loved him. That she loved him and in three days she would be leaving, and this would be over…unless she could convince him otherwise.

She heard the sound of the shower turning on and fought the urge to follow him.

This wasn't part of the plan, her brain warned. Convincing him to return home to his family, yes, and he'd agreed to it. She could finally give Flo the news she'd been waiting for. Her friend would be ecstatic. *She* should be ecstatic too. Her script was almost done. Her escape had given her space to think, time to relax, time to…fall in love.

And that was the problem.

Falling in love hadn't been part of the plan but now that she felt it, truly felt what it was like to be *in* love with someone, she wasn't ready to walk away.

Not without a fight.

She pushed herself out of bed, taking the sheet with her, and froze. She could just make out the corner of a small book jutting out from beneath his pillow. A book she hadn't seen before. She frowned. What would he keep…?

Her eyes flitted to the bathroom and back again. Tentatively, she leaned over and pulled it out. There were no words, just a plain black cover with a pencil hooked into its spine.

She trailed her fingers over the soft leather. Was it a diary, a notebook, a…*sketchbook*?

Skin abuzz with nerves, with hope—she didn't want to invade his privacy but she had to know—she peeked inside and her stomach came alive. A thousand butterflies desperate to be free as she took in the artist-grade paper, the pencil marks…

Alaric was drawing again; there could be no other explanation for it being under his pillow, in the bed they now shared together.

She opened it fully, her eyes lost in page after page. Various shapes, shading techniques, lines, crosses, smudges… had he been testing himself?

The shapes began to morph into sketches that seemed to be abandoned halfway, of inanimate objects, a glass, a chair…she turned the page again and her hand flew to her mouth.

Oh my God. Was that…?

She dropped onto the bed. Her heart in her throat, her eyes misting over as she saw it for what it was—his first complete picture and it was of *her*.

So obviously her…

She was curled up in the bed sheets on her front, her hair spread out on the pillow, her lips softly parted, her eyes closed. The pencil scratches graduated from light to dark towards the middle, jagged lines, rough, almost wild, but the effect…it was beautiful, impassioned, filled with such feeling.

When had he…?

'You were asleep.'

She jumped, her fingers hovering over the page as her eyes shot to the bathroom doorway. She hadn't heard the shower turn off; she hadn't been aware of anything but the image.

Guilt bloomed in her cheeks, her heart rate wild as she tried to read his expression and failed. How long had he been stood there watching her, a towel around his waist, his body taut with tension?

'You sketched me?' It came out like a whisper.

'It was the only one I didn't bail on…the only one that…' He trailed off, his gaze falling to the drawing as his eyes narrowed. 'I hope you don't mind?'

'Mind?' She wanted to laugh and cry at once, her eyes going back to the breathtaking image. 'Are you crazy? It's incredible.'

She heard his footsteps approach, her heart kicking up in her chest.

'Not as incredible as the real thing.'

If her heart leapt any higher, she'd choke on the damn thing…

'Alaric…' Slowly, she turned to look up at him, wet her lips as she took in the fire now blazing in his blue depths. The question was on her lips again. How can he feel so much and still deny it, deny her? 'I'm not ready for this to be over between us.'

He reached out to cup her jaw, caress her cheek. 'We have three more days.'

'Three more days won't be enough.'

'Stay longer. Your script is going well, you can get it finished…' His fingers and his words were gently teasing her, coaxing her under his spell. 'We could even take a trip to the mainland. I can show you the sights I fell in love with, we can…'

But she was already shaking her head, she had to be real. 'I can't, I have press appearances scheduled, a red carpet launch coming up and a new dress to source in all likelihood.'

'Of course,' he murmured, his other hand reaching out, his fingers combing through her hair as he lowered his mouth to hers. 'Reality beckons.'

'This *is* reality, Alaric. Right now.'

'This is too perfect, to be real.'

And she knew he meant it. She could see it in his gaze, his belief that this only existed on his island, safe from the world outside.

She opened her mouth and he trapped her denial with his kiss. A kiss she let him take because it beat succumbing to the pain of leaving, of this being over.

Because this *was* real. This wasn't here today, gone tomorrow. She'd be feeling it long after she left the island...

Would he? Or would he truly draw a line under it and move on like it hadn't happened?

She couldn't believe it.

She wouldn't.

Three days later, her cases loaded onto Marsel's boat and only Dorothea and Andreas to wave her off, she was forced to accept it had meant more to her than it had to him.

Alaric was as absent as he had been the day she'd arrived.

Looking away from the island as it shrunk in the distance, she rooted in her handbag for her phone. She wanted to update Flo and...she frowned. There was a piece of paper sticking out of her purse, a piece of paper she hadn't put there.

She tugged it out, her fingers trembling as she recognised the artist-grade paper... She unfolded it and the entire world fell away save for the image in her hand. His picture of her.

She gripped the handrail as her knees threatened to buckle, her eyes fixed on the sketch as her vision swam with unshed tears. He'd added a message to her sleeping form.

She dragged in a breath, looked up to the skies that were darkening to a menacing blue, the clouds blowing in thick and fast as she blinked back the tears to enable her to read…

You are you, Catherine.
Only you.
Beautiful inside and out.
Don't ever forget it.
Yours always,
Alaric x

She spun on the spot, gripping the handrail tighter as she stared back at the island, desperate for a glimpse of him. Was he there on the cliff edge, where she thought she'd spied him that first morning?

She leaned closer, her eyes watering against the sea spray and her hair whipping around her face.

'You be careful, Miss Wilde!' Marsel called out. 'The sea's getting choppy with the storm on the rise.'

Slowly, she leaned back in.

'Don't worry, we'll be on land before it's upon us,' he added, misreading her concern.

She gave him a weak smile, her eyes going back to the island, back to him as she willed him to wake up to the possibility of what they could have, if only he'd choose it.

Her. Happiness. And everything in between.

Alaric watched the boat disappear on the horizon, unmoving from his vantage point on the cliff. He hadn't been able to say goodbye, not without caving and promising her the world, promising her the impossible.

He wasn't sure how long he'd remained there for, only that the rain had started to lash with the wind, waking him from the stupor her absence had induced.

He turned away from the ocean that now rolled with the storm and headed back to the house. The scent of food greeted him as he walked in and his empty stomach made itself known. He hadn't eaten since last night, since his last meal with her...

'Well, it's about time you showed your face.' He looked up to see Dorothea in the kitchen doorway, wiping her hands on her apron. She wasn't smiling. 'Your dinner is ready. You can help yourself. Andreas and I are going to head home, unless there's something more you need.'

'No, that's fine. Thank you, Dorothea.'

He rubbed a hand over his rain-soaked face, forked it through his sodden hair. Weary to the bone, more tired and broken than he'd felt in so long. She stepped aside to let him enter the kitchen, but he could feel her eyes still on him as he took in the food on the centre island.

Souvlaki. His favourite. Only now it reminded him of Catherine and her first night on the island. Had it really only been four weeks ago?

'She loves you, Alaric,' came Dorothea's soft assurance. 'And you love her. It's as obvious as the love Andreas and I share.'

He heard her, but said nothing...he couldn't. His chest ached too much to speak, his gut writhed and his eyes pricked. And he didn't cry. He never cried, not even after... after...

'Why did you throw it all away?'

His head snapped around, his eyes spearing hers. But all he saw was his pain reflected back at him, his anguish.

Outside the storm rallied, thunder rattling the windows, rain pelting at the glass; it was nothing compared to the storm within.

'Come on, love.' Andreas appeared at his wife's side, his hand gentle on her shoulder. 'Leave the man be. We should get going before the storm gets any worse.'

She didn't even blink, her eyes on Alaric as she waited for the answer he just couldn't give. 'You should go… Andreas is right.'

She gave a small shake of her head, disappointment shining in her brown eyes as Andreas gave him a grim smile. 'We'll see you in the morning, Kyrios de Vere.'

He gave the faintest of nods and watched them leave, Dorothea's words churning him up inside. She was right, she was so very right. He'd thrown it all away, Catherine's love, and for what? Because he thought he didn't deserve it, that if Fred couldn't have it, he shouldn't. Christ, if Fred were here now, witnessing his pain, he'd kick his ass for being an idiot. He knew it just as well as he knew he was scared.

Scared of not being able to stack up, because he thought he wasn't worthy, and the world would see it, declare it…a real-life Beauty and the Beast.

But, so what?

What did it matter how the world saw them? Not when he had her love. And she had given it to him, over and over, and he'd what? Done exactly what Dorothea accused him of and thrown it all away.

Hadn't he spent his time convincing her that appearances didn't matter, hadn't she changed, learned from it, from him, and then he'd been a hypocrite. Not only throwing her love away, but his words of wisdom too. Because he was the one who'd let appearances get in the way of what truly mattered.

He hunched forward, his hands gripping his thighs. He felt sick, dizzy, the pain too intense to breathe. He needed to get to her, he needed to say he was sorry, but more than that, he needed to tell her that he loved her too.

He ran out into the storm, stared at the tumultuous heavens above and knew he was trapped. His island, his safe haven, was now his prison. He cursed the sky, let the rain beat down on him, punishing the fool in him.

But he was a fool no more. He knew what he had to do, and a plan was already forming. A plan that would prove he could do it, that he had it in him to not just leave the island but step straight into the limelight…for her.

'I'm coming for you, Catherine.'

And she would be worth every excruciating second under the lens because their love was worth it, and he'd rather face his fears by her side than live a life without her.

CHAPTER FIFTEEN

'HEY, KITTY, YOU READY?'

Luke reached across the back seat, took her hand in his and gave it a gentle squeeze.

She nodded, dragging her eyes from the street, the crowds, the flicker of camera flashes and the excited buzz...

'You sure? You've hardly said a word since we left the hotel.'

'I'm fine, honest.' She brushed down the skirt of her shimmering gold gown and remembered the last time she had worn it. The night she had seduced Alaric...or had he seduced her? A sad smile touched her lips.

She'd been right to think her designer dress wouldn't fit, Dorothea's delicious food and her injury had seen to that, but she looked healthy, and the forgiving cut to the wrap dress that Alaric had taken great pleasure in unravelling had been the perfect choice. Even if it did bring with it such poignant memories. From their first time together, to his insistence that she would look perfect in any dress because all the public would care about was seeing her, not the designer label, not the super-skinny frame, or the heavily made-up face, just her.

And she missed him. Missed him more than she'd ever known it possible to miss someone. It was as though she wasn't whole, that a part of her had been left behind with him, on his island. Not that he was there. No, she knew he'd gone back to the UK to visit his family, much to their pleasure, and Flo had been so very grateful to her. The emotion in her friend's voice as she'd told her of his visit to see Cherie and her daughter too, that he'd gained what he so desperately felt he needed, approval to live, some form of closure.

It had made Catherine cry when Flo had told her. Happy tears, bittersweet tears, as she acknowledged that he was free of the guilt, and still, he hadn't been able to come to her. And no matter what she did, she couldn't shift the lonely ache inside.

She gave a snort as she took in the crowds outside and recalled Alaric's words to her on the very same...

'For you, it must be worse. Surrounded by people day in, day out, and standing alone...'

Alone and yet surrounded.

'Are you really sure?' Luke pressed. 'I don't think I've ever heard you snort before a red carpet?'

'Sorry.' She tried for a laugh as she touched a hand to his thigh. 'Lost in my thoughts. Thanks for being my date.'

'Any time.'

She smiled and folded her hands in her lap. Luke had been her rock since her return from Greece. Every press event, every interview, when she lost her trail of thought or lacked the right enthusiasm, he filled the gap.

She couldn't stop herself getting swept away by the memories of the island, of Alaric and the picture he'd drawn, the message he'd written too. It had to mean more. It had to. She'd seen it in his eyes, countless times over— love.

But the more she thought on it, the more she doubted it

all. Had it really been there, or had she just projected her own feelings onto him?

It had been over a week, plenty of time for him to have seen Cherie, his family and reach out. Just a call, a message, anything…

The car came to a stop and she took an unsteady breath, unhooked her seat belt as Luke did the same.

'Time to get this show on the road.' His smile was full of encouragement as his door opened and he stepped out into the raised cheers of the crowd. The shouts for him to look this way as he reached back in to offer her his hand. She took it, stepping out beside him, and then it was her name being shouted along with his.

They smiled under the camera flashes, played their part as they were ushered to the barriers for autographs, handshakes, questions, photos…

'Kitty! Kitty! How does it feel to be back with your ex?'

Luke caught her eye as they exchanged a very slight head shake, a subtle roll of the eyes, their smiles never waning.

'Kitty! Luke! This way, what about a shot of the happy couple?'

'Miss Wilde, give us a smile!'

'Catherine!'

She stumbled in her heels. *Alaric?*

Luke caught her elbow, his brown eyes piercing hers. 'You sure you're okay?'

But she was already scanning the crowd. That voice, her name, it had to be him. But he wouldn't…not with all the press, the cameras, the public…

'Catherine!'

She craned her neck trying to see past the tight frontline, squinting against the camera flashes as she reached up on her tiptoes. She didn't care what she looked like, undignified, desperate…it was him, against all the odds, it was him, she just *knew* it.

'Miss Wilde, Mr Walker, we're ready to take you on through.' The procession organiser was there with security, ushering them on from a respectful distance, but she shook her head. She wasn't going anywhere.

'Catherine!'

She spun in the other direction and the crowd parted, realisation sweeping through the masses that something was amiss. Amiss for them, but not for her. And there he was. Straight down the middle, set back from the red rope barrier, his tall and broad frame dominating those around him, his tux cut to perfection, his face, those eyes, those lips…it really was him.

Her breath rushed from her lungs as she swept forward. 'Alaric!'

'Miss Wilde?' The organiser stepped in front of her as Luke cupped her elbow.

'Kitty? What's going on?'

'There's someone I need to go and see.'

He followed her line of sight before coming back to her. 'Is that him?'

She nodded. She'd told Luke everything, she'd had to after she'd stumbled over one too many interviews and he'd started to worry about her health, her state of mind, after all she'd been through. Some of it by his side…

'Will you be okay?'

She nodded, desperation sending her pulse racing. 'Please.'

His eyes narrowed as he took in the desperate flush to her cheeks, the pleading look in her eyes. 'Go. I've got this.'

'Thank you, Luke.' She rushed to give him a peck on the

cheek, a delight for the eager cameras, and then she was striding for the barrier.

'Miss Wilde, you can't...' Security tried to intercept her, but she wasn't stopping. Alaric was here, at her movie premiere, where there were cameras, there were journalists, the whole world was watching, and still, he was here.

Security stepped into the crowd, following her lead and creating a safe pathway, and as soon as she was free, she was racing towards him.

'Catherine.' It escaped him in a whisper that brought her up short, her eyes desperately searching his for confirmation of what this grand gesture was. 'You look... incredible.'

Warmth flooded her cheeks, her heart fluttering so wildly she thought it might escape. 'What, in this old thing?'

His smile lifted to one side, camera flashes flickering over him, over her, as the crowd shifted their focus from the red carpet, but he didn't seem to notice. Even as security scurried about keeping them at bay and their shouts built:

'Who's this?'

'Is this a new fella?'

'Can we get a name?'

'Wasn't he in that Avenger movie?'

She laughed at that one, tears choking up her throat.

'I'm sorry I let you go without saying goodbye.' He reached out, his hands gentle on her arms, their warmth permeating her skin, her body, her heart.

'Is that why you're here, to say goodbye?'

He laughed softly. 'No. I'm here to say I'm sorry that I let my fear get in the way of telling you how I felt. That even when I let you go, I should have told you still.'

'Told me what, Alaric?' Hope had turned her voice into a whisper.

'That I love you, Catherine. I love you so very much.'

She wet her lips, tears clouding up her vision. She was going to ruin her make-up, but she didn't care, he loved her. *Truly* loved her.

'Why didn't you?'

'Because regardless of my guilt, I still felt you deserved better, that I could never be pictured beside you and seen as equal. Not by the press, the public…'

'And you think I care about all that?'

'No. That's just it. I don't think you do. But I did.'

'And now?'

'Now I'm here, in front of all these cameras that I feared, in front of the world, telling you that I love you, and if you will have me, I'll spend my life making sure I'm worthy of you.'

She pressed a finger to his lips. 'Don't. Don't say that. You are worthy, you always were, because I love you, Alaric, and I always will.'

She combed her fingers through his hair, pulled him down to her lips and sealed her words with a kiss. The camera flashes and the noise from the crowd escalated with the wild fluttering within her heart, the heat of pleasure swirling through her limbs too, until a honk from a car had Alaric breaking away.

'I think we're causing a scene.'

'Wasn't that your intention?'

'Yes and no, but whoever the celeb is in that new car, they're not going to be impressed that the press are now circling us instead of the red carpet.'

'Then come with me?'

'Now?'

'Yes.'

He looked over her head, at the masses and smiled. 'Okay.'

She smiled with him. 'Even if it means getting your picture taken?'

'I think they already have plenty of those.'

'This one we're posing for…' She led him back to the carpet with the aid of the security team, and the procession organiser approached them, her carefully composed smile taking in their new arrival.

'Do we have space for one more?'

'Unlikely, I'm afraid.'

'It's okay,' Alaric said in her ear. 'I have Flo's ticket.'

'You haven't?' Her eyes shot to his. 'How long has she known? She was drilling me only yesterday about her outfit.'

He grimaced. 'Not long enough. I've pledged many hours of free babysitting in exchange.'

She laughed, so very happy that it almost felt like a dream.

'Kitty! Miss Wilde! Who's your friend? Do we get a name?'

She wrapped her arm around him as he did the same and they turned to face the flashes.

'This is Alaric de Vere…' An excited ripple ran through the crowd as recognition of his name spread and she looked up at him as he looked down at her. He didn't care that they knew who he was, that his scars now faced the camera and they'd capture them in their glare, he only cared for her and it was all in his eyes, his smile. 'The love of my life.'

He leaned closer to her. 'This is going to be the longest film in history, isn't it?'

'What makes you say that?'

'Because there are so many ways in which I want to

tell you I love you right now and nearly all of them require us to be alone.'

'Lucky for us I'm wearing the perfect after-party dress.'

He chuckled low in his throat, his mind doing the same journey back in time as her.

'Although…' she murmured, her smile for the crowd, her words for him '…what about a before party?'

He cocked a brow. 'Before?'

'I reckon there's time before the show begins and there's bound to be a quiet corner somewhere…'

His grin turned devilish. 'Are you serious?'

'More than…' She tugged him towards the cinema. 'It's time to live a little.'

'You don't have to tell me twice.'

She was pretty sure she'd told him plenty more times, but she wasn't about to argue the point.

He was here and their life together was truly just beginning.

EPILOGUE

Three years later

'ALARIC, DEAR, THE car is here!'

His mother called up the stairs just as Flo came bustling into the bedroom to help his wife, who was currently enacting some kind of jig in her form-fitting red dress.

'I knew I should have gone for something less…just less…'

Catherine flapped her hands about her, her nerves unusually on show, and he walked up to her, took her hands in his and smiled into her eyes. 'You look spectacular, and Flo has assured me she knows a trick to getting you zipped up.'

She eyed him sceptically as Flo bustled past him and crouched down behind her.

'I sure do, just…give…me…one…*tick*! And *voilà*!' Flo straightened up. 'You're in! This fabric is pure genius.'

'I don't know about genius,' Catherine murmured. 'I'm sure it didn't feel this tight two weeks ago.'

He laughed softly. 'May I remind you that you were only thirty weeks pregnant then? Our little girl has two more weeks on her now.'

She smiled up at him, her blue eyes wide and sparkling. 'True.'

'And the second one always shows more than the first,' Flo added, patting her own tummy that was currently concealing her third.

'You ready?' He smiled down at his radiant wife and gently squeezed her hands.

'I think so.' Her smile wavered and he lifted one of her hands to his lips, kissed it softly. 'You were like this with Max, remember, nine months of hormones and worrying, and out he popped, and you were Kitty Wilde the diva again.'

That earned him a scowl as she withdrew her hands from his and gave him a playful shove. 'Careful, dear husband, or you'll be sleeping in the nursery tonight.'

He chuckled, loving the fire that had crept into her gaze. 'I may need to. I have to be up at the crack of dawn to make sure everything's in place for the charity gala.'

Her smile filled with adoration. 'Have I told you how proud I am of you?'

He reached out and pulled her to him. 'Yes, but you can tell me again if you like. Though the charity venture was your idea.'

'No, my idea was that you joined a support group to talk about what happened, not to finance an entire charity to help others with similar experiences.'

'It was a natural development.'

'And it makes you feel good to know you're helping others. Every time you talk about it, your eyes do that thing.'

'That thing?'

'They sparkle.'

'Sparkle? Are you emasculating me again?'

'Absolutely not. It's *très* sexy…'

He chuckled, his chest rumbling against hers as he bowed his head to kiss her.

'Whoa, whoa, you two—come on! Mum's going to

make the driver a cup of tea if we keep him waiting any longer.'

Catherine gave him a quick peck. 'Flo has a point.'

She took his hand and led the way.

His mother was waiting for them at the bottom of the stairs, Max, their two-year-old son, in her arms and Alaric's father just behind. 'Thanks so much for watching the kids tonight.'

'You're very welcome. We could hardly let Flo miss out on her best friend's premiere. Not to mention her and David haven't had a night out in months.'

'Someone say my name?' His brother-in-law appeared in the hallway, bleary-eyed with his hair and tie askew.

'David!' Flo rushed up to him. 'Have you been asleep?!'

'Guilty as charged.' He grimaced as Flo grasped his tie and wriggled it back into position, attacking his hair next. 'Hey, two kids under three, another on the way, you've got to grab it while you can.'

Catherine laughed. 'You're really selling it.'

'It's a bit late for selling it, my love,' Alaric murmured, kissing Max on the forehead. 'This bun is well and truly cooked. Be good for Nanna and Grampy, okay?'

Max sucked his thumb in response as Nanna gave him a little bob. 'He's always good.'

'As for this one—' he placed his hand on the curve of Catherine's stomach '—not even born yet and she's off to a red carpet premiere.'

Catherine turned to look up at him. 'I'm not sure it's hormones after all, Alaric. This is *my* film, my script brought to life. What if people hate it? What if they don't get it?'

'Shh, my love, you will blow them all away. I promise.'

'You can't—'

He silenced her words with a kiss and earned them a disgusted *'Ew...'* from their two-year-old nephew, who came rushing in and did an about-turn, dashing back out again.

'And I think that's our cue to leave.' Alaric grinned, gesturing for the ladies to go ahead, his brother-in-law too, and then followed, giving his mum a peck to her cheek and his father a hand to the shoulder as he went. 'Thanks again for tonight.'

'You're welcome, son.' His father covered his hand.

'Good luck!' his mother added.

Luck. He didn't need luck. As he watched Catherine step into the car, her cheeks glowing, her stomach blooming with their daughter, he already felt like the luckiest man alive.

* * * * *

COMING SOON!

We really hope you enjoyed reading this book.
If you're looking for more romance, be sure to
head to the shops when new books are
available on

Thursday 6th January

To see which titles are coming soon, please visit

millsandboon.co.uk/nextmonth

MILLS & BOON

THE HEART OF ROMANCE

A ROMANCE FOR EVERY READER

MODERN

Prepare to be swept off your feet by sophisticated, sexy and seductive heroes, in some of the world's most glamourous and romantic locations, where power and passion collide.

HISTORICAL

Escape with historical heroes from time gone by. Whether your passion is for wicked Regency Rakes, muscled Vikings or rugged Highlanders, awaken the romance of the past.

MEDICAL

Set your pulse racing with dedicated, delectable doctors in the high-pressure world of medicine, where emotions run high and passion, comfort and love are the best medicine.

True Love

Celebrate true love with tender stories of heartfelt romance, from the rush of falling in love to the joy a new baby can bring, and a focus on the emotional heart of a relationship.

Desire

Indulge in secrets and scandal, intense drama and plenty of sizzling hot action with powerful and passionate heroes who have it all: wealth, status, good looks…everything but the right woman.

HEROES

Experience all the excitement of a gripping thriller, with an intense romance at its heart. Resourceful, true-to-life women and strong, fearless men face danger and desire - a killer combination!

To see which titles are coming soon, please visit

millsandboon.co.uk/nextmonth

MILLS & BOON

Coming next month

GREEK HEIR TO CLAIM HER HEART
Jennifer Faye

His eyes closed as his lips pressed to hers. He willed her to kiss him back. Surely he hadn't misread things between them. Had he?

And then her hands reached out, cupping his face. Her touch was feathery soft, as though she was afraid he might disappear in a puff of smoke. Her lips slowly moved over his as she took the lead.

Thoughts of his mother's estate slipped from his mind. Worries over selling the island were swept away. In this moment, his thoughts were only of Hermione and how right this kiss felt.

He wanted this moment to go on and on. Because a kiss was normally just a kiss, a prelude to something more. However, with Hermione, it was all by itself an earthmoving event. His lips gently brushed over hers. He didn't want to scare her off. He wanted to hold her in his arms as long as possible.

As he drew her closer, their kiss intensified. His whole body came alive with the rush of adrenaline. He'd never been so consumed with a kiss.

Hermione was unique in so many wonderful and amazing ways. As her lips moved beneath his, he wondered how he'd been so lucky to meet her.

The reality of their circumstances slipped away. The

only thing that mattered right now was him and her. And this kiss that was like a soothing balm on his tattered and torn heart.

He didn't want this moment to end. His hand reached up and gently caressed the smooth skin of her cheek. His fingers slid down to her neck where he felt her rapid pulse. She wanted him as much as she wanted him.

Buzz-buzz.

He didn't want his phone to ruin this moment. He didn't want anything to come between them. It vibrated in his pocket, distracting him from Hermione's tantalizing kiss.

She pulled away. His eyes opened to find her staring at him. He couldn't read her thoughts. Was she happy about the kiss? Or was she angry that he'd overstepped?

She glanced away. "You better answer that. It's probably important. And it's getting late. I'll see you in the morning."

Buzz-buzz.

"But I don't want to answer it. I want us to talk."

She shook her head as she stood. "We've definitely said more than enough for tonight. Good night."

And then she was out the door in a flash. Once more he was left with questions where she was concerned.

Continue reading
GREEK HEIR TO CLAIM HER HEART
Jennifer Faye

Available next month
www.millsandboon.co.uk

MILLS & BOON
MEDICAL
Pulse-Racing Passion

Set your pulse racing with dedicated, delectable doctors in the high-pressure world of medicine, where emotions run high and passion, comfort and love are the best medicine.